Joseph Mengele's Nazi Virus

Millions dead, millions yet to die

By
Philip J. Welch

Table of Contents

Dedication

To the coal miners who provided me good buildings for school.

Acknowledgments

Jack and Mary

About the Author

A historian by degree, a novelist by necessity. He keeps saying he's 'fair to middling, won't bring much at auction.'

I

Moving with the serpentine precision of veterans under a hazy morning sky, the young men came skiing in single file down the last slope leading into their camp. Built of timber found lower down in the mountains, the cluster of raw buildings with tall gables and wood shake roofs looked like civilization to them after three straight weeks higher on the mountain, living on rock and snow.

One after another, they whiffed up small clouds of fresh snow as they slid to a stop in front of their barracks. Racking their skis and poles on the outside wall, they jostled through the narrow door, where they were greeted by warmth and the smell of bee's wax and disinfectant. In anticipation of their arrival, the charge-of-quarters had fired up a cast iron stove at each end of the long open room, driving the chill out of the early autumn air. Their Mausers, beads of moisture erupting on the oiled barrels, were unslung from shoulders and stowed in the gun rack. They quickly shed white field parkas as they headed for their bunks.

<u>Allgemeine</u>, or General Purpose, SS-Man Josef Mengele sat, pulled off his boots, and let out an involuntary sigh of pleasure as his back hit the thin goose-down mattress, a sigh that was echoing throughout the room as men found comfort.

"Listen to you!" sneered the six-foot Wolfgang Hobein, the only one of the dozen men still standing. "I thought you were becoming soldiers, but what do you do at the first opportunity? You wallow in softness like pigs!"

Erik Gunther 'oinked' on the far side of the room, causing snickers, laughs, or groans throughout the barracks.

"Hobein, sit down and relax," Mengele invited. "You will not be so critical of us when you experience something other than rock on your back."

"I wish I could," Hobein admitted, "but you forget, someone has to report to the Commandant."

"Rank does have its responsibilities," Mengele reminded the back of his friend, who was already heading for the door.

The barracks grew quiet. They had traveled since dawn and were soldiers enough to know how to fall asleep quickly, but their eyes behind closed lids stayed bright with the memory of the mountain, of the sun at all angles off of the carpet of snow, and they all drifted to a strange sleep, a shutting down of the senses, but leaving the light on.

They were civilians fulfilling their lawful obligations to complete their basic military training with the <u>Wehrmacht</u>, the regular German Army, on the eleven thousand-foot peaks of the Tyrolean Alps dividing Austria and Italy. It was still uncertain if Mussolini was friend or foe, and this was not considered a friendly border in 1938. The Italians had fought against them in the Great War, and <u>Ill Duce</u> had put fifty thousand troops here just five years ago to stop Hitler on the first attempt to put a Nazi in charge of Austria.

All too soon, it seemed to them, they were aroused by a purposeful Hobein, who came charging back inside the barracks, rattling trash cans as he came and stomping his feet.

"SS men. Fall out! We must leave within the half hour!" Hobein barked.

There were no protests as the men piled willingly out of their bunks. They felt rested and eager to continue the journey. They were excited. Tonight, they were going to hear Der Führer.

Mengele swung his feet to the floor and walked in socks over to his upright locker. He was five feet eight inches tall and weighed one hundred fifty-two pounds. He had broad shoulders and narrow hips. His hair was brown, almost black, and his swarthy complexion darkened further by the sun and the wind. His teeth were in excellent shape, except for the wide gap between the two front ones. He did not like the color of his own brown eyes.

He shed his gray uniform down to his long woolen underwear, put on a brown shirt, black tie–felt good about getting the knot right the first time–and black riding breeches. A nearly new pair of highly polished black leather hobnailed boots were no problem to tug on. He then donned his black tunic, where a black Swastika rolled on a white circle on the left sleeve. He clinched on a black leather Sam Brown belt with the aluminum buckle dominated by the insignia of the German Eagle, its talons rasping a Swastika.

This political insignia, a symbol of good luck to earlier German tribes, was now displayed on the uniforms of all the armed services of the Reich right after Hitler had met the leadership of the army and navy aboard the Battleship <u>Deutschland</u> steaming in the Baltic Sea and agreed to protect them from Roehm and the SA. Now, in Germany, like most civilized nations, the military was firmly under civilian control.

On his head, Mengele squared his black peaked cap with aluminum piping and an eagle in the crown. On the headband just above the polished black visor was the insignia of the SS, the grinning skull in front of the crossed bones.

It felt good to be dressed in the black.

He put a black helmet that he was going to need for tonight's parade, along with a fresh shirt, shaving gear, and toothbrush, into a canvas bag. He turned to Hobein, who was standing ready.

"What did the Commandant have to say?" Mengele asked.

"He did not rant like Sergeant Meier, if that is what you mean," Hobein answered referring to the Wehrmacht non-com who had let all of them know how stupid he thought it was for them to interrupt their training just to attend some political ceremony. The shocked SS men had too much respect for the thick-chested Bavarian to consider reporting the outburst to anyone. He was the man teaching them to position their machine guns and mortars to reach the enemy, to use fulcrums, pulleys, timing and guts to take the high ground.

Mengele was relieved. He did not want to think that the sergeant's attitude was prevalent within the ranks of the professional army.

Hobein consulted his watch. "SS men! Fall out!" he barked.

There was a burst of activity as the men grabbed their rifles and quickly emptied the barracks, forming rank outside. They were all healthy, vigorous-looking young men with strong jaws, clear complexions, and perfect teeth. They had passed numerous physicals and measurements, including an extensive and certified genealogical search back to the year 1750, in proof of non-contamination by Jewish or other Negroid blood.

They were all certified at least one-hundred-seventy-five years pure white.

Hobein brought them to attention, dressed them off, turned them left, and marched them on the muddy track to the motor depot, where one lone canvas back truck was waiting for them, its short bed meaning it was going to be crowded for the men in the back.

The sergeant in charge of the vehicles was surprised when the shorter of the two officers climbed up behind the wheel. The other officer waited until the rest of the men had taken their seats on the wooden benches before joining him in the cab.

Mengele turned the ignition switch on, stepped on the starter, and the engine turned slowly on its six-volt system, caught, and sputtered into life, satisfying the sergeant that he and his men had done their job. Mengele let the engine idle until it smoothed out and the oil pressure stabilized. He pulled the floor shift into grandma gear, let out on the clutch, and as soon as the dual rear wheels gripped the roadway, he shifted smoothly into first gear. The motor depot sergeant was relieved; at least the SS officer knew how to drive, and he watched his truck for a moment as it headed down the mountain and quickly wound from sight.

It turned into an exceptionally mild day. Shafts of sunlight streamed through jagged holes in the thinning cloud cover, teasing them with a glimpse of a dark crystal blue sky. The air lost its cold bite. The men in the bed of the truck rolled up the cover and tied it to the rod framework at the top while Mengele and Hobein slid their windows down into their doors.

The men broke out in song, starting with their national anthem, as the truck growled its way down the mountain track, with miles of valleys, crevices and sharp snow-capped peaks off to their right.

Germany, Germany above all, above all else in the world,

When it steadfastly holds together, offensively and defensively, with brotherhood.

From the Maas to the Memel, from the Etsch to the Belt,

Germany, Germany above all, above all else in the world.

They continued with the "Horst Wessel Song," but lapsed into silence when it was finished as the thin air cut their singing short, everyone content to settle in and watch the most southern part of their Reich in all its glory glide by.

They reached Snalfedon, a small village with one inn and post office, less than a hundred people, all of whom seemed to be out enjoying the mild day, waving at the truck of slow driving soldiers. These Austrians liked the fact that there was a military post nearby; it was good for the local economy. They were in favor of the <u>Anschluss</u> that united them with Germany, in defiance of the Treaty. They were used to being part of an Empire. They trusted the Germans who had followed them into the Great War over Serbia against the English, French, Italians, and later the Americans. Besides, the leader of the Third Reich was actually one of them, an Austrian.

So they enjoyed watching the truck of <u>their</u> soldiers drive with care through their village.

When the truck reached a relatively straight stretch of road, Mengele yelled a warning as he slid his window up and locked it into place, with Hobein mirroring his action. The men in the back quickly unrolled the tarp over their heads and lashed it into place. Mengele went through the gears and soon the truck was barreling along at forty kilometers per hour.

"Hobein," Mengele asked, "have you decided which division you are going to petition?" To placate the Wehrmacht, Der Führer was allowing only three units of SS to be armed with military hardware. The regular army still did not trust the motivations behind the formation of this 'political army.'

"I might not join yet," Hobein answered.

"What!" exclaimed a surprised Mengele. "All you have talked about for two months is about going active. What has changed your mind?"

"It's just that I have another offer to consider."

"Another offer? What kind of offer? And when did all of this take place?"

"From the <u>Reich Security Main Office.</u>" Hobein answered, suppressing the smile that pulled at his lips, "I just talked to my father from the Commandant's office. Heydrich would like to interview me for a position in the <u>Sichierndienst.</u>"

The SD of the SS. The Security Service of the Protective Service. They wore a diamond with an imprint of SD on the sleeve of their tunic just above the cuff.

"Working directly for Heydrich in the Security Service. High intrigue and espionage. Policeman or spy. How splendid for you!" Mengele was happy for his friend. He had never met Heydrich, of course, but his reputation within the Reich, and especially within the SS, was that he was definitely not a man to cross. In fact, he was probably the most feared man in all of the Reich.

"My father thinks it will be a good move for me. I do not know for sure. I like soldiering. I think I would be more effective in the military than in the police."

"I would think it a great opportunity," Mengele said.

"Better than joining <u>Leibstandante Adolf Hitler</u>?"

"If you join a division you are going to be ultimately under the command of the Wehrmacht. If you elect the SD, then you will serve only within the Corps. There has to be some advantage in that. Besides, you will not miss anything. If there is war, we will both end up in the Wehrmacht anyway."

"I see what you mean," Hobein said. "Well, I'll wait and see what they have to offer."

Mengele threw a quick glance at the man sitting beside him in the truck and quickly returned it to the mountain road. "You mean interview with Heydrich and then not take the position if he offers one?"

Hobein frowned. "I had better make up my mind before I see the BrigadeFührer?"

"It appears so, Hobein."

The blond-haired Hobein sat quietly as he looked out of the window. He was trim with a wiry, muscular build, his face long and smooth-skinned, his lips full. It was his light blue eyes under dark brows, however, that enraptured the women. He was from Ulm but had to admit early on to Mengele that his father had been transferred there by the Party from Mecklenburg. Mengele, an anthropologist, was well versed on the physical characteristics of people, and it was rare that such an example of the Nordic ideal as Hobein was indigenous to an area so close to the Swabian Forest.

Hobein loved being a Nazi and a member of the SS. He had just turned twelve when he attended his first Party Rally in Nuremberg with his father, two uncles, and four first cousins.

"He had listened spellbound to Adolf Hitler, who told him why his country was on its knees and in great peril. The Weimar Republic, the parliamentary government formed after the abdication of the Kaiser, was too weak to sustain itself. The Treaty would allow a military force of only 100,000 men, nowhere near the strength required to keep the public order in such tumultuous times of rioting, super inflation, occupation by the Allies, invasion by the Poles, and slugfests in the streets between the National Socialists and the Communists.

To Hobein, it came down to choosing between either National Socialism and the Fatherland or Moscow-dominated Jewish Bolsheviks. That was no choice to Hobein. He threw rocks at Jews even when he had to run from his own German police, who would have locked him up if they could have caught him, although none ever actually chased him.

They reached Innsbruck, and Mengele inched down the narrow streets until they came to a crème colored depot with green trim and an overhang wide enough to cover a platform full of civilians returning from enjoying some of the easiest and the toughest slopes in Europe. He came to a stop, and the men spilled from the back and they all eagerly made their way over to the platform.

Having nothing but the company of other soldiers for over two months, the men could not help but stare at the fraus and frauleins looking stunningly healthy and alluring. The women were enjoying the attention, the civilian men, however, were glaring at the soldiers.

A single electric car with an overhead boom riding the black cable came loaded with new visitors to the slopes. It finally sparked to the top of the long hill and crept to a stop. Departing passengers carrying their skis and poles in the upright position, their boots draped around their necks, luggage under their arms, piled off the car.

The platform became crowded as the two groups of people merged, sorted themselves in their directions, but when those departing reached the now empty car, their way was barred by the meaty palm of a robust conductor who was dressed in an ill-fitting dark blue uniform with straining gold buttons.

"Is this train not going to Munich?" A well-dressed man demanded, as he was pressed forward by other travelers.

"I am sorry, mine Herr," the conductor replied, without a hint of apology, "this is a special train for the SS."

"If that leering ill-mannered group of uniformed young men is all of them, they will not come close to filling the car, Herr Conductor," persisted the man's wife, a tall, rather pretty woman, standing behind her husband, talking to the Conductor, but not taking her eyes off Hobein, who stood just off to the side waiting for the Conductor to call for his men. She would love to ride the train with that one, she thought.

"The SS is not being called to the cities because of von Rath, are they?" the man asked, annoyed at his wife, but for the wrong reason.

"Of course not. They are forming for an annual ceremony," the Conductor explained.

"Ceremony? What happens on November 9th?" The man frowned. He was Austrian and not familiar with all the Nazi holidays, but he was a businessman, and he saw advantages in becoming a Nazi. At the very least, he wanted to appear sympathetic to their cause. Then he remembered.

"Of course. The Beer Hall Putsch! How stupid of me to forget. Please pardon all my silly questions, Herr Conductor. We were just anxious to get home. When can we expect the next train?"

"In less than an hour, Mein Herr." The conductor answered politely. He signaled for the SS to board and was the last one to step inside the car and he slid the doors closed.

The electric motors sparked them into motion, filling the air with a fleeting smell of ozone. They continued their journey north and were soon rolling through a land of deciduous trees, most of the foliage now a euchre carpet on the forest floor, but the oaks were still stubbornly green-leafed while scarlet maples splashed red pennants in protest to the coming winter.

"What was he talking about back there, Herr Conductor?" Mengele asked the big man passing with difficulty down the aisle. "Who is this von Rath?"

"You haven't heard?" The conductor asked incredulously.

"We have had no news for months, Herr Conductor," Hobein reassured him.

"Von Rath is an Undersecretary at the Paris Embassy. A Jew shot him in his office two days ago!" the Conductor announced.

"Incredible," Mengele said. "Why would a Jew be so foolish to shoot a member of our government. Was he insane?"

"Protesting. It seems he was protesting."

"Protesting what?" Hobein asked.

"Why, he was protesting the clever move of Der Führer, who was stopping the Poles from getting rid of fifteen thousand Jews!" The Conductor could see the blank expressions on the men's faces.

"The Poles were going to revoke the citizenship of all Jews holding Polish passports living abroad. That would have made about fifteen thousand of them living in the Reich stateless. We could never make them go home to Poland. The Poles would just say that they weren't <u>their</u> Jews. So Germany would just have to keep them!"

"I would not think the Poles that clever." Mengele mused.

"So what did Der Führer do?" Hobein asked.

"He had all the Jews living in the Reich holding Polish passports hauled out to the Polish border and dumped. Our soldiers prodded them to the East. Der Führer is too smart to allow the Poles to get away with ridding their garbage on us! Grynszpan, the would-be assassin, had parents and family in the deportees."

"And how is von Rath?"

"Hovering over death, I believe."

It wasn't long before the men began singing again, and they were halfway through the official songbook when they crossed into Bavaria, and no matter of the <u>Anschluss</u>, their heart quickened when they passed the boundary into their old country. Their country at least since 1871 when the Second Reich was established under the Hohenzollerns.

It was dark by the time the train reached Rosenheim, where it was switched to a siding, coming to a stop by a well lit platform. A group of Young German Maidens in white dresses covered by blue smocks waited with baskets and kettles of food and drink.

The men could not believe their eyes as the first young woman came bounding up the step into the car. She was an explosion of beauty, smiling broadly with her blond braids falling below and curving around her breasts, light blue eyes shining in the electric lights, creamy smooth skin, and smelling of the potato soup she carried. The men had not eaten since early morning.

All the young women who followed her aboard were between sixteen and nineteen years of age and glowing with the beauty of youth. Having to bring food to hungry young men, the best that Germany had to offer, was the most enjoyable duty they had performed for Der Führer. As the young women passed out the plates and bowls and began to ladle out thick potato soup, they flirted outrageously with the young men. Loaves of fresh bread were passed out. The beverage was water brought from the mountains because the springs in this city were noted for their saltiness.

The men savored the taste of the meal. They savored the smiles, glances, shy nods, and alarmingly blunt eyes of the young women who filled the aisles and filled their cups and were not German; great to have such daughters for her sons.

When everyone was finished eating, the Young Maidens began to gather the soiled plates and cups and stacked them back in the baskets. The men helped them carry it from the train. All of the young women had managed to attract the attention of at least one soldier, and as everyone waited for their departure, they scattered throughout the depot in pairs or in small groups. All along, the platform heads became very close together, the conversations becoming excited whispers as young men and women found someone whom they thought might be special or were worth at least another look, and the ReichsFührer had orchestrated the entire event. This scene was repeated in all the stations on the outskirts of the city, as on any occasion that he could organize. The ReichsFührer's goal was simply to put the very best of the young men of the Reich, with the very best young women of the Reich and let nature take its course.

The Reich needed children of good Aryan blood. Much to the dismay of the churches and to the horror of mothers throughout the Reich, the ReichsFührer-SS, along with the rest of the Party leadership, was encouraging all women to have children, out of wedlock or adultery, if necessary.

It was way after dark when Hobein and Mengele began herding the men back aboard their car, where they all spilled to one side and lowered the windows to hang outside to continue talking to the smiling and waving young women who were left on the platform, a scene that was a couple thousand times old.

They were again rocking in motion, and the men sat quiet; some of them even managed to doze. They thought of their homes, their fathers, mothers, brothers and sisters, and they thought of the young women they knew at home, and they thought of the young women they had just met, and they were so thankful to God that they were born German and they were going to hear Der Führer.

They reached the Viehof, the southern terminus of Munich connecting Innsbruck. They came out as a unit of men in black parade helmets moving together but not marching as they made their way out onto the street that was almost deserted in this part of town at this time of night. They were directed by an SS man wearing a white webbed belt and white gloves to a waiting trolley that was already nearly full of black-suited compatriots. They crowded aboard.

They heard that von Rath had died.

"Now listen!" a SchachFührer yelled from the street, "this car, as marked, will be the one you must look for after the ceremony. Remember where you get off because that is where you will depart from. Heil Hitler!"

The trolley jerked northward along the Isar River, a smooth, murky ribbon dotted with bouncing dirty diamonds of reflected light from across the shore in the night. The street changed names three times before it came to the intersection with Maximillianstrasse, the widest boulevard of the city that ran directly from the river to the square shared by the old Town Hail and the Felderherrnhalle, the Hall of the Generals.

Here the men unloaded and joined maybe two thousand men already formed in rows of twenty abreast. They fell into rank, and more rows formed behind them. These men came from all over Germany, and in uniform, they all looked amazingly alike. They were called to attention, and the order to march sent them down the cobblestone street lit by flickering torchlight between the thirty and forty-meter-high stone buildings, and they set off with the click of the iron in their goosestep the only music that kept them in step.

And they were a precision parade machine.

After almost a kilometer, they were wheeled to the right and marched by the single arch of the east side of the Felderherrnhalle and under a huge Nazi banner that stretched across the street. The square was lit by caldrons of burning oil sitting on top of concrete pillars draped in the Party's red and emblazoned with a gold lame German eagle.

They were ordered into mark time, then ordered to a halt by a voice in the speakers scattered throughout the Plaza. Ten thousand men came together in the square and surrounding streets with one final stomp on the stone; all stood still. Mengele and his file of troops were turned to the left, just off to the side of the huge monument built as an exact replica of Orcagna's Loggiadeilanzi in Florence. Three cavernous arches supported by stone columns rose gracefully into the night, its stone surface shining in the reflections of the fires. The monument had been erected in 1844 to commemorate the deeds of two Austrian Generals, whose statues stood sullen, ignored by the Nazis, who now claimed the monument as their own. The sixteen altars stretched across the back of the edifice were draped in red and full of the bones of the 'old fighters,' men who had died on that day fifteen years ago when Hitler and the Nazis made their first bid for power.

As the Beer Hall Putsch was crumbling, members of the Munich police opened fire on them, killing sixteen and wounding numerous others. Sixteen men died, and Hitler went to Landsberg prison, giving him the opportunity to write Mein Kampf. The dead were not forgotten but martyred, and now their names were stitched in golden thread underneath a gold German eagle along with the inscription, 'On Parade.' On top of each altar was a cauldron of burning oil. From the center arch flanked by two massive stepping-out stone lions in heavy male manes were the steps leading down to the ground two meters away.

All was silent now except for the tolling of the church bells, a slow, measured tolling, a rolling of the heavy brass and iron clapper as the Roman Catholic Churches lent their bell towers to help commemorate a ritual presided over by Himmler, who had a strange view of religion, even encouraging adultery and bigamy if it led to children of good blood for the Reich.

The ReichsFührer-SS Heinrich Himmler strode to the bank of microphones.

"Heil Hitler!" He boomed through the microphones.

"Heil Hitler!" Was an avalanche of response.

"Men of the <u>Schutzstaffle!</u>" the ReichsFührer spoke in his calm, pedantic voice, even now at this, his most favorite ceremony. "It is with great joy that I stand here and look out over this parade of truly magnificent men. Men that I am privileged to present to the greatest man on the face of the earth. The man who has torn up that despicable Treaty and flung it into the faces of those who would keep us weak. The man who has saved us from the mediocrity of being a splintered nation adrift in a world of Jewish confusion!

"We of the Black Corps stand at the threshold of greatness! We who are about to deliver unto our Führer, the oath of total obedience. I am proud to present to Der Führer men of such courage and devotion. Men who will forever battle the enemies of Der Führer and of the Reich!

"Why do we believe in Germany and Der Führer?" He demanded of his men.

The Plaza erupted in a catechistic answer of a strong, clear voice of ten thousand men sharing the same convictions and aspirations.

"Because we believe in God. We believe in the Germany that he created in His world and in Adolf Hitler, whom He sent us!"

The stone buildings glowed with reflected firelight, reminding some of them of the cathedrals they had attended all of their lives. The church bells that had tolled their entry were a familiar form of a call to worship to all of them.

"Mein <u>Schultzstaffle</u>. Der Führer!" Himmler announced, in love with this moment. He turned to the assembled men and raised his arm in a straight-out Fascist parade ground salute. The loudspeakers deployed throughout the square and the adjacent streets blared <u>The Badenweiler March</u>, the lively military tune that always heralded his entrance.

Der Führer, Adolf Hitler, strutted across the marble floor of the Halle to stand just to the left of the microphones. He was dressed in his simple brown tunic pinned with the Iron Cross First Class, Gold Party Badge, and his War Wound Badge. In the Great War, he had fought in over fifty battles, both minor and major. He had risked his life many times for the German people, earning him a right to look into their souls and into history and see the best way to protect the Volk through the millennium.

"Sieg!" The ReichsFührer orchestrate.

"Heil!"

"Sieg!"

"Heil!"

"Sieg!"

"Heil!"

The roar of the men echoed off of the buildings where shadows of gray and black danced. They believed deep in their hearts that the man standing with his hands down at his sides, the man who stood silent and stern and looking out over them with his head slightly cocked upward as the waves of adulation poured over him, was the man who had saved Germany.

The men in the square would have continued in their accolades, but after years of experience, Hitler knew when there was enough. He threw his arms into the air to quiet the crowd, and there was immediate silence.

"My sons of Germany," he began, knowing the assembled would electronically hear every word that he uttered, "this is one of my favorite times of the year. It is when I get to visit with old friends, and together, we retrace our old steps. Together, my old fighters and me. We had great tasks set before us back then, these 'Alte Kampfers' and me.

"And now, year after year, we see the strength of our Fatherland reflected in the steel of the backbone of our young men, who come and proudly join us to pay our respects to our fallen comrades. Our fellow warriors who were the first to give their blood in our struggle for the German people!

"I knew these men. These men who died fifteen years ago to this day. They were a lot like you. They had families and loved ones. They had people dependent upon their earning a daily bread. Most of them had children who ran to greet them when they came home from their labor at the end of a long day.

"That did not stop these men from joining us at the barricades," his voice rose in intensity. "That did not stop these men from joining us in the streets! Our passions ran high because the Fatherland was at stake! The Volk was threatened!

"They knew that the only way to protect their wives and their children was to struggle against those forces that envisioned a Germany forever prostrate!" he clenched his fists and shook them at the heavens. "Forever prostrate with our guts exposed for the hyenas of the East and the hyenas of the West to feast on!

"Kept weak and divided from her own blood!" He pounded a fist into his palm.

He paused, relaxed, and looked down for a moment. Everyone knew that there were no notes in front of Der Führer. As usual, Der Führer spoke only with his heart, and he continued.

"They knew that what was at stake was of so much importance that they kissed their wives and their children good-bye, and they joined in the voice, and in the sweat, and in the struggle, and yes, in the blood!

"And it was their blood in the streets of Munich. That first river of rage that proclaimed to our enemies that we were willing to die! We were willing to die for something that we all hold close in our hearts. It is what we share with our fellow countrymen, our wives, our fathers and mothers, and all the people who have been a part of our <u>Volk</u> from time immortal, and we know that this is our land!

"It does not belong to the Communists!" he raged.

"And it does not belong to the Jew!" he hissed.

His hair fell in front of his eyes, and he impatiently shoved it aside. He was now red in the face, his eyes glazed.

"Because these men understood that the only way to ensure that their wives and children would be safe and that the land, our land, our Germany, our Fatherland, would always belong to their children and their children's children, down through the generations, was only if they did not allow another race to be master over them!"

Der Führer paused. He was fighting his own emotions at this point. His schedule during these three days of celebrations was extremely demanding, but in the past, he seemed to gain strength as the events went on. Now, he felt a strange pang of foreboding, having earlier that day given Goebbels permission to carry out a demonstration against the Jews to punish them for the crime of murdering von Rath. It was time the Jews were sent a serious signal in order to leave no doubt that it would be best for them to get out of Germany, and it should not matter to them that they must leave everything they owned.

The bells began to toll again.

It was time.

It was midnight.

Himmler marched stiffly across the marble floor to take from the color guard, the Blood Flag, the Nazi pennant stained with the blood and gore of the fallen who had marched with Der Führer on that fateful day. Himmler had been with Roehm securing army headquarters when it had happened and was not even arrested when the attempt to take over the government of Bavaria, before marching on Berlin, had been stopped by policemen. He turned and handed the sacred banner to Hitler, who stood out in front of the podium and presented it to the men.

Himmler went to the microphones.

Hitler looked over at his ReichsFührer. Not a very impressive figure to look at, that 'Heine,' Der Führer thought. Even dressed in that magnificent black uniform, he managed to look rumpled and unimportant. Wearing his pince-nez glasses that reflected like two headlights in the torches and looking not at all like Goring, who filled a space with tremendous energy and carried importance like an expression on his face, who, in the early years, had stood broadside and punched more than one Communist to his ass.

But Heine had done all right. The <u>Schutzstaff len</u>, the SS, he had turned over to him in 1929, had been a small group of men, numbering less than three hundred. Lost in the million men of the Brownshirts, the <u>Sturmabteilung</u>, the Stormtroopers, and still under the command of that faggot Chief of Staff, Ernst Roehm, until they killed him in what had come to be called the Night of the Long Knives. The night that Himmler and Goring convinced Hitler to move against the leader of the SA, that para-military organization seeking to continue the revolution and absorb the army, who were a threat to Hitler's power.

"<u>Schutzstafflen</u>! Attention!" Ordered the ReichsFührer.

It was leather, wood, steel and stone coming together and put into motion in a series of sharp explosions as heels clicked in this cathedral in the open night sky.

"Present arms!"

The men snapped their rifles up to parade position. Der Führer stood in front of the steps at the very top, framed by the lions.

"Repeat after me." The ReichsFührer ordered his legions.

"I swear loyalty and courage to you, Adolf Hitler, as Führer and Chancellor of the German Reich.

Loyalty and Bravery.

I vow to thee and to the superiors whom thou shalt appoint, obedience unto the death. So help me God!"

The men repeated the oath, their voices solemn, carrying a tone of finality. There were tears in many eyes of the young men of Germany who stood as a nation in front of their Führer and vowed to kill and to die for him.

"Men of the SS. Remember. 'My Honor is Loyalty.'" The ReichsFührer declared.

Hitler came back over to the microphones, still holding the flag. He snapped his right arm out in a Nazi salute.

"Sieg!" Der Führer bellowed.

"Heil!" Hobein felt a hot glow of rekindled fire in being led in the tribute by Der Führer himself, like at the Party rallies he attended growing up.

"Sieg!"

"Heil!"

"Sieg!"

"Heil!"

Hitler was satisfied. There was no doubt in his mind that these men would die for him, but what was more important was how willing they were going to be to kill for him. He spun on his heel, and there to take the banner was the color guard of chiseled-faced six-footers. He clicked his heels and nodded to his ReichsFührer and then strode down the steps, followed by his personal escort, to walk through the main column of men, and disappeared from view.

The men marched quietly and subdued back the way they had come, feeling the weight of the oath in their hearts. None of them ever doubting for a moment that they would ever fail to live up to their word. They felt like ancient warriors.

Mengele and his troop reached their trolley for the ride back to the rail depot, but before they could board, they heard the sound of many men coming down the street behind them. They heard angry voices and then the unmistakable sounds of shattering glass and violent splintering of wood.

"What is going on?" A white-faced Hans Gunther asked, ready to take some kind of action.

"They are destroying property!" Mengele yelled. "It's a riot. We should do something!"

"Look over there!" Hobein ordered, pointing to a policeman who stood with his hands behind his back on the opposite corner of the street. "That policeman is SS. He is not doing anything. So that is what we will do. Nothing."

The mob came into view, and they would pass a few shops, leaving them unharmed, only (to appear to go berserk in front of others. They attacked the storefronts with stones pried from the streets and long wooden ax handles, having already learned that plate glass has a tendency to shatter in perfect guillotine fashion.

"It must be just the Jew's shops!" said Mengele.

"Then maybe we should help." Hans Gunther suggested.

"No," Hobein stated firmly. "We are still under orders of the Wehrmacht. We do not need to get into any joint operation with this mob, even if they are SA. We will board this train and continue our return unless we are ordered otherwise by a higher authority."

They boarded the trolley, and the driver immediately took them away from the men who were nearing the intersection. Hobein seemed tense as he stared into the night sky, lit by the glow of three fires, as the city passed on their right.

"They must be burning the synagogues," Mengele pointed out, and when he got no response, he looked at his friend. "What is the matter with you, Hobein?"

Hobein turned to look with vacant eyes at Mengele.

"There is nothing the matter, Mengele." Hobein finally replied. "I know what I must do. Most of my life, I have listened to Der Führer tell us that one day we will have to wage war on the Jews, to get them out of our land. It looks like tonight, the very night that I vow my personal obedience to him, he declares open war on them. Then this is where I will join him."

He looked at the glow of the fires over Munich.

"I will join him on the war with the Jew."

II

He had a leisurely dinner with his family in the dining room of the rambling Baroque house. If they were angry with him for not being home over the Christmas holidays, they gave no sign of it. In fact, it had turned into one of the most enjoyable afternoons and evenings he had spent with his parents, who had put aside their low rumble of hostility to each other to focus their attention on him, their eldest son.

As soon as they finished with dessert, a hot apple strudel, they arose from the table and went into the adjacent drawing room, with Josef joining his mother on a dark red velvet cameo sofa. His youngest brother Aloxis, still in awe and open-mouthed admiration of him, sat on the edges of the big, easy chair that Josef had sat in as a child. His father stood as usual.

"How did you find our army, Josef?" Karl Mengele asked, thinking back with a warm feeling to a certain thin Prussian who had kept him alive fighting from the stinking trenches of the last war.

"Our Wehrmacht is the finest army in the world, Father," his son answered, choosing his words carefully and sneaking a wink at his younger brother. He did not want to upset a veteran of the last Imperial Army. "Der Führer would not tolerate anything less. I think they might have been surprised at the enthusiasm of us SS men. We demanded that they teach us everything they could about soldering."

For the first time in his life, Josef did detect a glint of approval in his father's flint gray eyes. Even after all the years it took, it still made him feel good.

Karl Mengele was a stout man with closely cropped, thinning gray hair and of average height who managed to tower over most people. He had built his factory on a flat spot near the confluence of the Donau and Gunzs Rivers, and with a keen sense of salesmanship and a degree in engineering, he soon began to turn out first-class farm implements of his own design. During those early years, he saw little of his wife and sons, spending all his time either at the factory or on the road throughout Germany in his new Benz motor car lining up dealers.

He knew in his heart, however, that it was his wife Walburga who had extended and entrenched their industrial baronage over Gunzsburg, a mid-size hamlet on the western foothills of the Bavarian Mountains. It was when it seemed like all he could do was to keep the mud from his Manlicher, that she had badgered the government,' including the Kaiser himself, until she secured a contract for the manufacture of a wood and iron wagon that hauled many a dead and wounded German soldier from the battlefield.

"I would expect nothing less from you, Josef." - His mother said, patting him on the back of the hand, one of the rare displays of affection she would show anyone, including her husbands and sons. "Herr Hitler is going to need the best of all her people to fight these Bolsheviks."

As a person of substantial wealth, she found the concept of the abolition of private property to be abhorrent and that anyone crazy enough to propagate such ideas should be shot. She worried about the Russians mainly because of their numbers in the East.

She did not worry, however, about the other main problem facing her country, the Jew. After all, her husband and George Diesenhofer, the local Kreisleiter, had managed to beguile and intimidate the three hundred or so Jews who had lived in the area for at least a hundred years, to seek life somewhere else. If those two buffoons could accomplish that much, then the rest of the German people could just do the same. Just drive them from the country.

"Der Führer," Karl Sr. emphasized, raising a bushy gray eyebrow at his wife to admonish her for not using the correct address, "has been warning the German people for almost twenty years. He knows what he will have to do to prepare us for the challenge that lies ahead. He is the leader."

He clasped his hands behind his back and began to pace in front of the blazing fireplace. "I knew years ago that Adolf Hitler was the man who could save Germany! He was the only one who had the strength and the will to defy that despicable document called a treaty. And he had the wisdom to 'see the danger of allowing the Jew to burrow further into the life of the people."

They had all heard it before. It was Karl's early membership in the National Socialists German Workers Party that had boosted Hitler to power and thus had saved Germany. For an Industrialist such as Karl to join a political party with the words Socialist and the words Workers was indeed an event and laid the foundation for these claims.

"When Der Führer came here that second time in 1932, you were away at school, Josef; he promised me that my time spent in the trenches watching my comrades die would not be in vain. That we of the Army were not defeated in the field. Stabbed in the back! That's what happened. We were stabbed in the back by the Jew labor leaders who campaigned for strikes! Stabbed in the back by the Jews who manipulated the collapse of the home front!"

Josef had known of his father's zeal for National Socialism for years but was surprised about how strongly he was really beginning to display it. It seemed that everyone in Germany was beginning to feel very strong, and the movement had made effective orators of quite a cross-section of the population.

All his life, he knew that he and his father had lived in two separate worlds. Roman Catholicism could not unite them. Living in the same house for twenty years had not united them. There had never been any real close interest between them.

Until now.

Now they had Nazism.

"Enough of politics." Walburga interrupted their conversation. "What are the plans for the wedding, Josef!" she demanded to know.

Josef gave an involuntary shake of his head, somewhat irritated at her for interrupting what he thought to be the first conversation he had with his father in years. Then he realized that it wasn't important. He looked at his mother.

How much time his son had spent in front of a mirror measuring down to the millimeter, sizes and distances of his entire face. The diameter of his eyes, the distances between his eyes, from each eye to the edge of the ear, the nose, all of the root diameters, along with some fifty other measurements, just for the face alone. He had taken these measurements on himself along with every other part of his body, knowing that what was in these numbers of distances, cubes, roots, skin tone, and eye color was his genetic make-up. His half of her and his half of him.

All in all, Karl mused, his son was doing quite well. He had really been displeased with him when he could not steer him from the sciences into engineering and manufacturing. Karl Jr., his middle son, also defied him to become a lawyer, but Aloxis, his youngest, did seem to have the correct aptitude for the business. He was satisfied that Josef had learned that efforts without results were useless. His own father, who had been a brickmaker, had instilled that into him, and he was thankful that his oldest evidently understood the vast distance between effort and accomplishment.

"Beppo!" The newly arriving Karl, Jr., the second son, greeted as he came through the doorway, a nickname Josef had earned because of his dark, swarthy complexion. A nickname he hated with a passion but had learned years ago not to flinch. Josef stood as his brother approached, his hand held out for a firm and friendly shake. They smiled at each other. They were genuinely glad to see one another.

"I see that the training did not kill you, Josef," Karl Jr. said. He was an image of his father, and he stepped back to appraise his older brother. "I would say that it streamlined you somewhat. You do look hearty."

"I feel great. It was good to get out of the laboratory."

"And how is Irene?"

"She is doing well. In fact, I have just told Father and Mother that the ceremony will be sometime in July."

"Congratulations, Josef. That indeed is good news," Karl Jr. smiled.

"Junior," Walburga said, "I have no doubt but that you also will be foolish enough to marry a woman from outside the faith and from so far away." She hated the fact that Josef had found a tall, blue-eyed blond woman and a Lutheran at that. She wanted him to marry a short, dark-headed Catholic girl just like she had been. She knew she would never have anything in common with this northerner. This Lutheran.

"Mother, I would marry a Russian peasant girl if she looked like Irene and was half as smart." He replied, winking at his brother. "Why I would even marry her even if she was a Bolshevik."

She had been a stern and cold mother who had held her children at arm's length. The most any of them had elicited from her had been support and respect. Warmth was something that you got from the fire. Or the housekeeper, Maria.

"Do not even make jokes about marrying a Russian.'" His mother ordered.

"Or a Bolshevik!" Karl Sr. said in the factory voice he had developed to get his point across in the noise of his shop floor. He knew he was overreacting, but he had heard talk that his lawyer son had made some inquires on behalf of some Jews! He had not yet had the chance to confront his namesake, wanting to avoid bringing the subject up in front of his wife. He knew she would be upset. Josef's stay was short, and he was not going to let the stupidity of one son interfere with the visit of another.

"Sorry, Mother. Sorry, Father." He atoned. "Josef, you were in Munich on Kristallnacht. Did you see anything?" He asked.

"As a matter of fact, the SA followed us down Maximillionstrasse just after we took Der Führer's oath."

"Did you know what was happening?"

"To tell you the truth, we did not know what to do. Some of the men thought we should stop what looked like a riot, but then we saw that they were hitting only Jewish shops. Then, there was talk of joining them. But a policeman stood by and raised no alarm. So we just kept traveling all night until we were back in the mountains."

"<u>Kristallnacht</u>. Broken glass night. That sounds appropriate. I hope it signals the Jew that he should get out of Germany." Walburga said.

"It was a very expensive signal." Karl Sr. said, remembering a conversation he had with his insurance agent. "The insurance companies threw a fit over the damage. No one bothered to explain to Goebbels that it would be German insurance companies made to pay claims to the Jews, and that was for both the physical damage and reimbursements for what was stolen."

"I can't believe it," Josef said incredulously. "They didn't pay the Jews, did they?"

"Of course they did, Josef. The honor of a German company was at stake." His father explained.

"They paid all the claims to Germans whose property was involved," Karl, Jr. said, "and they paid all the claims of the Jews. Except the Jew's money went into a special fund, and the government confiscated that money."

"Then it turned out all right." Josef was relieved.

"Not really." Karl Sr. explained, "Most of the glass broken was plate glass not manufactured anywhere in Germany. We are going to have to purchase it all from the Belgians, and it will take half their yearly production. It is going to wreak havoc on the foreign currency.

Der Führer was furious when he was told how much this signal to the Jew was going to cost."

"I have heard that Der Führer has forbidden Minister Goebbels from any further activities regarding the Jew. I hear that the responsibility of the Jew has been given solely to the ReichsFührer." Josef said.

They talked and argued into the night. The mother and father were the first to tire, and they both bid their sons good night and goodbye to Josef, who was going to be off so early in the morning. The three boys wandered out into the kitchen, and Maria, the only housekeeper that any of them had ever known, a tiny, thin scarecrow of a woman with the will of iron, fixed them a late snack of cheese and pumpernickel bread. She made them say grace before she allowed them to eat. She knew that the boys would want to talk, so she put out the rest of the strudel and blessed them goodnight.

The boys ate in silent ritual, hungry for the old times when they had snacked late at night, together in this kitchen. Aloxis could not have been five years old when they had begun sharing this the warmest room in the house. The wood cook stove had the cast iron cappers off, and a fire in the box gave off a faint glow.

"Josef," Karl asked, "can you tell me what is going to happen?"

"I have no idea, Karl," Josef answered. "I went back into training. I was released a few days before Christmas. I decided to spend the time with Irene."

"I know. I heard about it from Mother. Three times, I think."

"At least five times with me," Aloxis added.

"Up until now, a Jew could get out of Germany." Karl got back to his subject. "The SS was even helping the Zionist funnel people to Palestine. Now, all of the avenues of exit are being shut down. This is beginning to make a lot of them very nervous.

"I can see that you already know far more about it than I do, Karl. Like I said, I have been out of touch. I do not think any change of our immigration policy regarding Jews is going to be of my concern. I am just going to do my part in making sure that they do not marry Germans."

They talked for over an hour before the oldest brother decided that he had to get some sleep. Josef settled into his own room, his old room, his boyhood bed, and he wallowed in the warm memory of sleeping at home.

It was still dark when he was awakened by the hand of Maria on his shoulder. He had told her earlier when he wanted up and she was there to see that he was awake at his requested time. It had been that way throughout his entire life and he never thought to wonder how Maria was able to be everyone's alarm clock.

He was surprised when Karl Jr. showed up at his door just as he was about to leave to help him with his gear. The early morning air was cold and it was at false dawn when they made their way to the garage, where they both folded back one side of the heavy wooden doors. Karl found the light switch, and the interior of the garage was bathed in a dim light whose bulb soon had fog drifting around it. There was a slight odor of gasoline in the air.

"What a beautiful car, Josef," Karl said, admiring the sleek-looking 1936 Opel Admiral that shone immaculate as it had on the showroom floor. Aloxis had spent the evening helping clean and polish it. The two men rolled the car out onto the driveway. It was a two-passenger coup, sleek with rolling fenders and a paint in bronze except for a cream along the side of the hood that cascaded down the arc of the sloping fenders to finish in a comet cone over the rear fender well. It was a General Motors product with a drophead coupe powered by a 3.6 Liter engine that would allow the car to power along with the best of them.

They loaded his bags in the trunk, except for his medical bag, which he put on the seat beside him. The brothers said goodbye and Josef was soon driving through the countryside blanketed under snow. The sun came out but was lost to the cold fog that hung in the air except in patches where he could see the trees empty of leaves and the branches' thick and thin black veins reaching into the shallow sky. He decided that it was a dismal day and one in which traveling was the only productive thing to do. The car's heater was no more than an icy blast in a thin glove, and only his heavy socks saved his feet.

It was 'the same kind of day fifteen hundred and thirty-two years earlier, in the year 406 A.D., when the Germanic tribes began crossing the frozen Rhine River near Mainz, and the Roman Empire came under immense pressure from these barbarians who managed to even sack Rome itself just three years later.

The Germanic tribes were exploding as they staked their claim to some of the best lands on the earth. Lands of diversity and beauty teeming with wildlife, flat plains suitable for grain farming and mountains and valleys, rivers and streams, and it was theirs.

They just had to have enough children to back up their claim.

Mengele liked the way his life was going. He was achieving some of the scientific recognition he deserved as he had studied under the

Baron. He thought of his first mentor, Professor Mollison, at Munich University. Mollison claimed he could recognize Jewish blood in someone just by looking at their photograph. He had awarded Josef his PhD in Anthropology for his dissertation, 'Racial Morphological Research on the Lower Jaw Section of Four Racial Groups.' Although Josef had yet to complete his medical studies, he had passed the state medical examination and was licensed to practice medicine. His first few months spent in the clinic at Leipzig University made him realize that practicing medicine was not really what he wanted to do. Practicing medicine meant dealing with the people who came to you with their hacking coughs and open sores and expected you to heal them. He wanted to study medicine.

It was after an exceptionally long day at the clinic when he was questioning his own wisdom in taking up medicine instead of manufacturing, when there was a letter waiting for him in the cubicle that served as his room. It was from Professor Baron Otmar Freiherr von Verschuer, Chair of the Institute for Biology and Racial Hygiene in Frankfurt on Maim, and he was inviting him to come to Frankfurt to interview for a position on his staff.

As tired as he was, he wrote a letter of acceptance to Verschurer and a thank you letter to Professor Mollison, knowing that it could have been no one but him who could have secured him an interview with the premier geneticist in Germany, if not the world.

Irene had been disappointed at first. She had thought that they were going to make their lives near her family and friends, but soon dismissed her misgivings as ridiculous because she had studied in three different countries and could converse like a native in four languages, and where they lived was really of no consequence to her.

It was Josef's career, and he thought himself brilliant for choosing. Knife in hand, he could feel the brotherhood of the Corps in its burnished black aluminum handle.

III

The Celts were the first people to use iron to live along the river, but they were driven off by the Chatten just before Christ. The Romans established a thin part of their Empire in this heavily forested area eighty years later, survived the passage of several Alemannic tribes, and stayed until the Franks forded the River Maim around the year 500 A.D. in force enough to establish themselves as the people of these lands.

Charlemagne, the greatest of the Franks, was crowned in Rome as he allied his tribes to the Roman Catholic Church, establishing the Holy Roman Empire, the First Reich. It did last a thousand years, and this city had witnessed fifty of its coronations. Martin Luther battled Rome from here for almost a year. Gustavus Adolphus II brought in his rampaging, raping, plundering Swedes, and they stayed for three years, leaving only to devastate the rest of the country. The French were in and out. A Jewish Ghetto was established in 1521. The Emperor granted the city the right to mint money, and a child of the Ghetto, still living in the Ghetto, Mayer Amschel Rothschild, became the world's first billionaire in 1746 as the first great land deal went down.

Frankfort-on-Maim was built along both sides of the river, and the bridges connecting the urban areas were numerous and varied by almost seven hundred years in age. Except for St. Bartholomew, this city of Goethe, lacked other grand architectural achievements. Unusual for a city that had seen so many coronations.

Mengele connected with the autobahn just south of the city and rode the ring into the Sachsenhausen section without crossing the river. He stopped at the hostelry, where he kept a room. The proprietor, Frau Achen, a sort of dark, dumpy woman who reminded Josef of his mother, welcomed him back. His room was the way that he left it, and it did not take him long to unpack his gear.

He put on a clean shirt and a fresh suit. Shoes, instead of boots, felt funny on his feet. He was close enough to the university that he could walk it, and clutching his top coat tight around the collar against a winter wind, he briskly covered the few blocks.

The Institute was a three-story stone building on one of the wider avenues in the most ornate and fashionable part of the city. It provided office space, lecture rooms, and laboratories for up to a hundred students and a faculty and staff of thirty. The graduate studies taught at the school were biology, medicine, and genetics.

Baron Doctor professor Otmar Freiherr von Verschuer, the Chair of this Institute, was elated as he came out of his last lecture for the day to see Josef Mengele standing in the hall. He immediately thought of the many duties that he could relinquish to his returning student assistant. Josef was in tune with his own beliefs, and was a very promising geneticist indeed, having an eye for detail and was meticulous to a fault, necessary traits for his chosen professions.

The professor was just slightly taller than his assistant, had a slight chest, only a ring of gray hair, and a prominent brow line that dominated his face. His nose was rather long and thin, his ears large, his eyes a light blue. He could never have been considered a handsome man during any of his ages, but he was intent and crisp and quick to grin. He was adored at home by his wife and children, respected by his colleagues, and had the undivided attention of his students. When he was ten years old, he read Darwin's <u>Origin of</u>

<u>Species</u> when it was first published, and from that moment on, he was in pursuit of the nature of things, right down to the core of it all, right down to the genes. Mengele was an important part of his efforts to get to the core of things.

"Heil Hitler!" Mengele greeted his mentor.

"Heil Hitler!. Splendid to see you, Josef. I see that the mountain air has done you good."

"Thank you, professor."

Verschuer and Mengele turned and walked down the hall towards the Doctor's office. Students and faculty nodded respects to the Doctor and greetings to his returning protege, these two men together a familiar sight absent over the past few months. Everyone in the school knew where Mengele had been.

"Josef, you will not believe the amount of work that has piled up around us. I must tell you that I missed your aid in numerous tasks and your presence at my dinner table. By the way, before we get to other things, Frau Verschuer and our daughters demand your appearance at dinner tonight or tomorrow night, whichever is most convenient to you."

"Tonight sounds fine, Herr Doktor." He enjoyed their company tremendously.

"I told her that already." Verschuer smiled. "Dinner will be at eight as usual. Now, there is one thing I want your opinion on immediately."

They entered the Doctor's office. Shelves of leather-bound journals lined one wall, while the other was a display ground for his many degrees and awards. The rest of the room had tall windows. A large, highly lacquered oak desk was full of folders, his intended workload for this evening.

The professor went behind his desk and picked up a heavy accordion manila envelope with circle tabs and a tie string and handed it to Mengele. "Take a look at this, Josef."

Mengele opened it and pulled out the contents. On top was a three-by-five black and white photograph of a young male of twenty. The color swatches attached to a separate sheet indicated that his hair was a blondish brown and his eyes a medium blue with slashes of gray. Mengele envied him his eyes. Next were forms, petitions, and copies of the birth and marriage certificates inclusive of all grandparents. There were numerous police reports and separate affidavits with official seals of the courts.

At the bottom of the stack was an adoption paper, which rendered the testimonials to paternity useless on the mother's side.

"That is Deter Albrin. You see that he was adopted by Hans Albrin when he married the boy's mother, Ethel. Frau Albrin swears that the child was conceived in a rape by a German when she was fourteen years old."

"And the rapist was not identified at the time."

Verschuer nodded. "She can not produce any evidence except from her family, who testify that she indeed was raped, and she has always described the man as tall and blond. All of this unofficially, of course. The family decided not to report the incident to the authorities."

Mengele studied the chart depicting the physical measurements of Deter Albrin and saw no abnormalities. When the offending element was within one generation, it was easy to identify. It was when the genes were dispersed through a few generations that their characteristics became harder to discern.

"What is going on, professor?" Mengele asked, scanning to see if he had missed something. "From what you have told me and from what I see in the files, the original examining physician should have issued the necessary certification."

He referred to the <u>Ehetauglichkeitszeugnisse,</u> the certificate proclaiming a person 'Fit to Marry,' now required by law. It occurred only after a physical examination, blood samples, X-rays, and a genealogical check. Aibrin had passed everything but the genealogical requirements. Now, it was up to a physical examination to determine if he was Aryan or a <u>Mischlinge,</u> half German and Jew, who were, by and large, treated like half people. They were still considered citizens, but their civil rights were severely restricted. For example, they could not marry full-blooded Germans.

"Is the examining physician untrained?"

"I at first thought the same thing. Until I saw that it was Dr. Pfhanmoeller of the Mannheim policlinic for Genetics and Racial Care. An extremely capable man. I wondered myself, why he would send this up to me?"

"And?"

Verschuer grinned ruefully. "It seems we have a political bomb on our hands, Josef. Everyone there now knows of the doubtful paternity. No one has ever before accused Deter of being half-Jew.

But now he wants to marry the same girl that someone in the Party has a keen interest in, and all of a sudden, he is beginning to look a lot like a Jew! It is almost comical, but it is indeed serious. Especially if you consider that if we find him, Aryan, then the rapist was a German and not a Jew."

Mengele smiled sardonically. "Herr Professor. Herr Albrin would never gain entry into the SS. But I can not see any justifiable reason to deny him his certification of German citizenship. He is fit of health. His genetic measurable statistics fall well within the limits of Aryanism. He has no outside appearance or manifestations of Jewishness, especially one generation removed. I would rule this man, Aryan."

These two men found themselves in this position frequently.

Their rulings were set in concrete. They could change lives just by the way someone looked at them. They were functioning under the authority of the Reich Health Office and enforcing the laws passed by the Reichstag and signed by Der Führer.

The Nuremberg Laws of 1935 had codified and directed the route of re-Aryanization of the Reich and ridding it of Jews.

The first one, <u>The Reich Citizenship Law</u>, deprived all non-Aryans of citizenship and continued their removal from civil service jobs, from the universities, from practicing law, and from visiting the German National Forests.

<u>The Law for the Protection of German Blood and German Honor</u> now made it illegal for Jews and Aryans to marry or to have sexual relations. A leer by a Jew at an Aryan woman could be construed as sexual relations, although by this time, it would be closer to insanity.

The Law for the Protection of the Genetic Health of the German People decreed that all prospective marriage-minded people must first undergo physical and genealogical examinations, creating a tremendous amount of work for the medical profession, that was rapidly swelling with new entrants every day. Never before had the ranks of medicine been so open, and never had there been such a cry for people trained to recognize genetic traits.

Verschuer took the file and penned in the finding that Herr Deter Albrin was Germanic and his certification would be issued immediately.

"We just saved Herr Doktor Pfhanmoeller's skin, Josef, but I shudder to think who we just made angry at us." Verschuer closed the file and placed it on top of a stack.

"I feel better about that one, but I could not see any reason to rule otherwise." He picked up a stack of files from the right side of his desk and handed them over to his student.

"Please begin with these. I assure you that the workload will only grow worse." He smiled.

Mengele took the stack of folders through the hall, exchanging greetings with the few students he passed, and entered the lab. Counters and cabinets lined all the walls. A dozen stainless steel sinks were dispersed throughout the room. Shelves were everywhere, supporting large glass jars with grayish organs floating around inside murky fluids. It smelled like a laboratory. It smelled like alcohol, formaldehyde and decaying organic matter, and the radiators hissed this heavy air to warmth.

He took his usual stool down at the far end next to the window, looking out over a side street where, a few blocks away, he could see a gray sliver of the river. Cars were parked along the street below with the snow shoveled ridge along the curb. He raised the window a few inches and lowered his face to feel the shaft of fresh, cold air. He took a deep breath.

He opened the first file and was delighted to see that it contained letters to the editor of Der Erbarzt, a supplement to a weekly medical journal Verschuer had begun editing just after the passage of <u>The Law for the Prevention of Genetically Diseased Offspring</u> (Gesetz zur verbutung erbkranken Nachwuchses) passed in the Reichstag on the same day that they passed the Enabling Act in 1933, which enabled Adolf Hitler to rule through decree, a constitutional prerogative. The Journal had nationwide distribution and was designed by Verschuer to answer questions about the law, and how to turn the law into actuality.

The law stated that people showing certain genetic tendencies should be sterilized so that their seed would end, and future generations would not be burdened with the care of people who could never contribute to the Volk but always subtract from it. These were people with proven genetic deficiencies such as 'feeblemindedness, schizophrenia, manic-depression, insanity, genetic epilepsy, Huntington's chorea, genetic blindness or deafness, and severe alcoholism.'

Most of them were cut and clear cases and there was no hesitancy in issuing the orders for the procedures to take place. It was the one on alcoholism that was the hardest to judge. In Bavaria, the ability to consume huge quantities of beer was deemed a blessing. Everyone in Berlin was familiar with the feel of a stein in their hands. It was where the line between heavy drinking and alcoholism took place, where the genetic worth of an individual could be called into question. He started to rough up an answer.

"The questions seem to have grown in sophistication, Herr Professor. Maybe the German Medical community is finally getting the word on what is expected of them."

"I hope you are right. I still see such a mountain to climb for us, Josef. We are attempting to change the basic way medicine has been practiced, and there are entirely too many doktors out there who will want to continue as they have in the past. National Socialistic medicine requires that we become single-minded." Verschuer leaned back in his chair and grinned. "But that is our struggle."

"Yes, Herr Professor."

Verschuer stood. "I have a surprise for you, Josef. Professor Ernst Rudin will be joining us for lunch."

"Rudin. Here!" Mengele said. "I did not see any notices posted."

"There is none. He will not have time to deliver any of his lectures. He is just stopping off to pick me up as we will be traveling together to meet with the ReichsFührer."

"You and Rudin have an audience with the ReichsFührer!" Mengele was duly impressed.

"Keep that quiet, if you will, Josef." He took his student by the elbow. "Come on. Let's go share a bowl of soup with the Professor."

They left the building by the center doors, stepped out into a cold afternoon and hurried across the wide street to a cafe run by a brother and sister in their sixties who served up an excellent menu. It had a long mahogany bar topped with a dark blue tile. Two barrels of beer sat behind it. The tables were covered by red and white checkered linen. The center one was blocked by a crowd of people from the university.

Herr Doktor Ernst Rudin was a grizzled old man whose eyebrows looked like a wire brush at the end of a long day and whose bushy gray beard made him look more like a sea captain than one of the earliest adherents to the idea of the supremacy of the Nordic race.

To believe in Gobineau's Vision.

Along with Ploetz, Nordenholz, and Thurnwald, he had established the Society for Racial Hygiene. All the geneticists of Germany were to join this organization.

Rudin followed the distracted attention of one of the young men and saw his old friend.

"Herr Professor Verschuer." He greeted. "Heil Hitler!"

"Heil Hitler, Herr Professor." Verschuer answered. The other professors, doctors, and students made way for Verschuer and Mengele, allowing them to sit at the table across from Rudin.

"You remember Josef Mengele, do you not, Professor?" Verschuer asked.

"Of course. I remember that Professor Mollison had many kind words to say about him. It is good to see you again, Josep."

"Thank you, Herr Doktor Professor. Please give my regards to Professor Mollison."

"He will be delighted that you asked to be remembered by him." Rudin looked at Verschuer.

"I was going to tell these bright young men about the <u>Rhinelandbastarde</u>, Herr Doktor."

Verschuer looked at the circle of men. It was not a very well-kept secret anyway. Maybe it should even become published and be damned to public opinion abroad.

"By all means, continue, Herr Professor."

Rudin nodded at his old friend and took a sip of water from the glass in front of him.

"As you know, when the French occupied our Rhineland for fifteen years following the war, they did so with colonial troops from Africa. They put Africans armed with rifles on German soil and made us pay for their upkeep! The German people suffered this indignity for almost a decade before the English and the Americans finally forced the French to withdraw these animals from our soils.

"They left behind five hundred and three half-breed children.

"It sickens me to think of one of our women copulating with apes." One of the student doctors standing around the table complained.

"How could they lower themselves to do it?" asked another.

"There have been many attempts to explain miscegenation," Rudin answered, pulling at his whiskers. "Over the years, I have come to the opinion that if the sexual organs were compatible, some women would copulate with the creatures that you see on the front of those American science-fiction pulp magazines. You know which ones I am speaking of," he winked at Verschuer, "the ones with four eyes, long tendrils, and green shaggy hair."

The men laughed. Verschuer blushed. His big ears turned pink.

"Professor," he protested, "be fair. At the time, the country was in ruins. Hunger was everywhere. We were short almost two million men who had died in the war. That left a lot of women without the prospects of finding a husband. And yet their hormones were raging for conception."

"You are entirely correct, Herr Professor," Rudin cracked, "and those Africans probably looked splendid in their blue uniforms with the red pin-stripping. It did not hurt that they had real money and were well fed while many Germans went hungry."

"I will have to admit," Verschuer said, "that the French were short over two million men, and if they had to import colonial troops to replace the men sent to the Rhineland, then they would have five thousand cases of half-castes in which to contend."

Everyone laughed.

"But Professor," Rudin said, "the French would not know the difference. They have been niggerizing their blood for years."

Everyone laughed again.

"What about these bastards, Professor?" Mengele asked, wanting to hear the end of the story.

"The problem, of course, was what to do with these half-castes," Rudin continued. "Petitions to the Weimar Government were unheeded, indeed, even scoffed at by certain ministers. All we could do for years was just to track these nigger bastards, keeping their files in the basement of the Brown House of the Party in Munich.

"Then, just over a year ago, in a secret operation, ordered by Der Führer, the Gestapo rounded them all up and delivered them to places of surgery. The females had tubal ligations, and the males had vasectomies. Thus, in one week's time, we were able to kill off a genetic bomb that was about to poison our genes for generations upon generations."

The men standing around men who chose to study medicine, men who saw healing as a way of life, who came from all parts of the Reich, some the sons of farmers and some the sons of doctors, cosmopolitan and rural, young and old, men of science, and they all had the slight smile or smug grin of finding out a secret where your side had won a significant victory.

"I have seen a few of them with my own eyes, Herr Professor," Mengele said. "Extremely horrible-looking children. But how did it all take place without any publication of the event?"

"It was true that we had no law that allowed us to accomplish this task. But Der Führer willed it. The Gestapo convinced the mothers of these children that this was the proper thing to do. Since most of these women had since married German men, it turned out to be just as simple as that. The children were still under the age of eighteen, and as long as we had the consent of their mothers, then we were safe from repercussions.

"Herr Professor," Mengele said, "I find it extremely difficult to believe that anyone would protest the sterilization of a nigger."

IV

Verschuer listened in length on the telephone to Gaulieter Klause Funk of Mannheim yell at him for certifying Deter Albrin as Aryan. Once or twice the Professor tried to break into the steady steam of adjectives spewing into his ear from the angry Nazi official on the other end of the line. He even considered hanging up but decided now was not the time to ire even further one of Der Führer's political cronies, especially one who had been just two rows behind the Führer when the Munich police had opened fire.

Funk had taken a ricocheting bullet in the fat of his calf that bled like a stuck pig but never endangered his life. It earned him the coveted blood-red Party Badge and the ear of Der Führer forever.

Besides, he had informed the Professor that he knew to the mark how much money Verschuer had requested in his petition to the German Research Council, all Party money, to fund his projects.

Verschuer began to wonder how the Gauleiter could be so certain that Deter Albrin was indeed a half-Jew, when all the evidence showed otherwise. All matters of race certification are extremely important, but Verschuer constituted one of the supreme judges in the matter and to have his decision challenged by a politician was unprecedented. He also wondered why Funk was so intent on preserving the young woman for his son. Men go to such lengths for themselves in regards to a woman but would tell their sons to just forget her and find another.

Funk had sent the police to stop a wedding that was scheduled immediately after Deter had received his certification. They arrested the bridegroom before the ceremony commenced and put him in jail.

The Albrins, a good, solid German family, with some wealth and influence of their own, had stormed the court for the release of their son and for the officials to stop interfering with a private citizen of the Reich's right to get married.

"Herr Funk, how is your son taking all this?" Verschuer asked, hoping to steer the call into an actual conversation rather than a rant.

"What in God's heaven does that have to do with it!" The high Brown shirt snapped.

"Why-er, Dr. Phanmoeller lead me to believe," Verschuer felt himself on thin ice, "that if it was not for your son's pursuit of the same young woman, Deter Albrin's citizenship would not be in question."

"Herr Doktor," Funk spoke calmly for the first time, "all three of my sons are already married. Besides, the woman is not the issue here. Doktor Phanmoeller has a hand in this somehow. You did not do the physical yourself?"

"Of course not. It was not necessary. We relied on the testimony, photographs, and color swathes. Certification was mandated by this evidence."

"Herr Doktor. Can you not yourself take a look at this man? I am not trained in these matters, but he sure looks like a Jew to me."

Verschuer jumped on the chance. "I would be more than happy to do the examination, Herr Gauleiter. When can you have him here?"

There was a pause.

"That will be a problem, Herr Doktor." The Brownshirt's voice seemed an octave lower.

Verschuer now understood why the Gauleiter had calmed down. "Herr Funk," he said, sitting up straight in his chair. "If you are telling me that, as Gauleiter, you can not have him delivered to me here in Frankfort, then you are not telling me everything. Just who is this Herr Albrin?"

"He is close to Herr Todt." Funk confessed, identifying the clout as coming from Der Führer's master builder, ramrod of the autobahn, bridge maker, and a man who had ready and easy access to Der Führer.

"If you can not get him here to me, Herr Funk, then what do you suggest?"

"That you come here to Mannheim, of course. I am sure that I can get the Gestapo to pick him up and detain him long enough for you to get a good look at him."

The professor thought for a moment. He did not want to make the trip. He also did not like the idea of being in between these two power factions. Der Führer would surely hear of this affair. The decisions from here out had better be ones that Der Führer could at least sanction.

"Herr Funk," Verschuer thought of a safe way out. "Why do I not send my very capable assistant to conduct the physical. He has also reviewed the evidence and judged the young Albrin to be Aryan. I rely on him wholeheartedly. I am sure that if Herr Albrin is half-Jew, then Doktor Mengele will so record."

There was a slight pause. Funk was weighing the alternatives. "That is acceptable. Please send your Doktor, who?"

"Mengele. Josef Mengele."

"Then send your Doktor Josef Mengele, Herr Doktor. The sooner, the better."

Verschuer hung the phone up and thought the situation was becoming very odd. Maybe he should travel with Josef to Mannheim and look at this man himself.

He told Josef later about the entire conversation, including his own misgivings about allowing him to go alone into this den of lions. Mengele had assured his mentor that he would not at all mind the drive south to Mannheim, which was less than fifty miles, to examine this Deter Albrin and rule as he saw him. Let the decision stand on science, not on politics. Instinctively, Verschuer knew that his protege had indeed come to the same correct conclusion.

"How long would the drive take, Josef?"

"Probably an hour and a half."

"We could leave early in the morning, be there by nine, and on our way back by ten. Back here before noon?"

"That is a possibility. Highly unlikely, though, considering the severity of the matter. If Herr Funk is only capable of short-term incarceration, I am afraid that our schedule is at the mercy of too many unforeseen authorities."

"I would be jeopardizing an entire day's schedule?"

"At the least. We could get lucky. But when do you start to reschedule your appointments?" Mengele pointed out.

"Still, I am afraid that if you find this man, Aryan, Gauleiter Funk might try to strangle you. Can you pick me up at my home at seven tomorrow morning?"

"Of course."

"I will make the other arrangements. Let us both go look at this, Deter Albrin." The professor decided. "I would like to see, however," he mused, "the young woman who has inspired such a vicious fight."

Mengele had the Opel serviced the night before and left a tip to the attendant who had the interior polished and gleaming. He was in front of Verschuer's home promptly at seven, and the Professor came immediately out of his house, down his short stone walkway and climbed into the coupe. It made the Professor feel sporty. His wife and daughters came out smiling and waving and thinking their father looked rakish in such a sleek eye-catching auto, and Frau Verschuer yelled cheerfully to Josef to drive carefully.

It was a beautiful late spring early morning countryside alive with farmers working their fields with horses, mules, and an occasional tractor belching plumes of dirty smoke. Mengele proudly pointed out a plow that his father had designed and manufactured.

They arrived in Mannheim and pulled to a stop right on schedule in front of the central police station. Josef lifted a wooden case of instruments from the trunk and followed the older man into the building that was concrete walls with a wainscoting of wood. The room was originally a light beige, but countless smoke and the smell of frightened people had turned it into a lifeless brown. The policeman sitting behind the desk on the slightly raised platform stood to attention. He had been alerted to the expected arrival of two important racial examiners who were to be accorded every respect and cooperation.

He greeted them and showed them down the corridor to the office of the Higher SS Police Official of the Gau, Erich Poltelz, a thin reed of a man with a baritone voice.

They exchanged heils.

"So good of you to come, Herr Professors. I hope this issue gets resolved one way or the other. You can not believe the amount of pressure that this has put on our forces. We try only to carry out the wishes of Der Führer and of the Party, and as directed by the ReichsFührer." The man seemed bent on complaining and explaining. He was a career police officer who suddenly found himself also holding rank in the SS and under their command structure. He suddenly found himself working for Reinhard Heydrich and the experience was still wrecking his health.

"My men have Albrin in custody. I do not know how long we are going to be able to keep him. Can you conduct your examination here in this room?"

"Josef?" Verschuer asked.

"This is fine. There is enough light."

Poltelz just sat there.

"We are ready anytime now, Herr Poltelz."

"Of course, Herr Doktor!" the policeman said, rising to his feet and, in big gangly movements, lurched to the door. "I will send him in immediately. There will be a guard just outside if you require anything."

In less than a minute, there was a knock, and the door was opened and the uniformed officer who had been on the desk stepped inside and motioned for his charge to enter.

Deter Albrin came into the room.

Verschuer and Mengele exchanged knowing looks.

"Would you please be seated," Verschuer requested, indicating the chair closest to the window. "This will not take long, I assure you. We just want to verify some of the information on your file."

The young man strode confidently to take the chair. He stared somewhat defiantly with brooding dark brown eyes under heavy dark brows at his examiners. His hair was blond, thick in texture and combed down. His nose at one time could have been straight but looked to have been broken at least twice. His chin was angular. He was a very handsome youth. His body was lean, and no matter the confident walk and the defiant look, he was nervous. He looked like many German youths, and he could very well be one hundred percent German, but there was one thing that was immediately recognized by both of the examiners. He was not the same man whose photographs they had been sent by Pfhanmoeller.

"Please state your name for our records."

"Deter Albrin."

"Age?"

"Twenty.

The first thing Mengele did was to chart his eyes, finding their color on the same row as his own. His at the beginning of the fifth row, Albrin's at the end of the fifth row, and to think that he had once so admired the color of the eyes that had been indicated on the card.

Albrin's hair was the color of the fiberglass swatch that had been supplied.

He took out his calipers and went to work. Spinning the dials of the micrometers and reading the tiny lines etched into the instruments to the millimeters, he called out the measurements to Verschuer, who penned them down. His concentration on his work soon made the young man relax, and Verschuer had a growing respect for his assistant.

After fifteen minutes, he suddenly stopped. He replaced the instrument he was using back into the case in the spot carved for it, and he went over to where Verschuer handed him the chart he had just completed. They silently came to the same conclusion.

The physical measurements were well within the range of interpretations of the dials of the instruments. What they had so far was physical measurements and hair color reported correctly, and eye color that had definitely been falsified.

Josef picked up a set of shears from his kit and went over to the young man, who sat sullen, shoulders slumped.

"Just for our own records, Herr Albrin," he said, cutting off a lock of hair. He turned to Verschuer, "Do you have any further questions, Herr Doktor?"

"No. That will be all that is necessary. Thank you for coming, Herr Albrin."

The young Albrin stood shakily to his feet and did not look at the two doctors as he put his shirt on and buttoned it up. He did not even bother to ask them what they had found. There was something in their demeanor that he was reading, and he had grown accustomed to not protesting. He knew these men were not fooled for a second. He was afraid for his family, who had helped, and his family doctor, who had helped, and now they were all probably in very grave danger, and he would not be allowed to marry Carola.

Ever since this all began, this challenge to his right to life in the Reich, he could not look into a mirror and not see the Jew rapist looking out of the reflections of his eyes, back into him. No matter which way it turned out, either the Jew or the German, he was still a bastard from the worst of circumstances. He was a bastard of a marauding animal.

But please, God, why can they not rule that it was a marauding German who had forced himself on his mother!

When the door shut behind him, the two doctors sat in silence for a moment, reviewing the evidence. The physical had turned up nothing that would prove or disprove the true parentage. The only thing that bothered the scientists was the deliberate misinformation they had received. If it was not for that then they could probably rule that their first findings were indeed the correct one, but now the flag of suspicion was high flying.

He was Aryan by all dimensions, but there were important forces at work denying him that right.

Mengele took a pair of tweezers from his kit and picked a few strands of the hair he had cut from the subject. He took his magnifying glass and walked over to the window, using the natural light to view the enlarged strands of hair.

"I do not know, Herr Professor. The hair color is correct, but there is something about it that does not seem so natural. It seemed very dry for one thing."

"Like it has been bleached or dyed countless times?"

"Exactly, Herr Professor. Now I wonder why."

"Why all the misrepresentation? I had attributed his numerous fractures of the nose to overzealous sports, but could they have been deliberate to camouflage a definitely appearing Jew nose? Is there something that we are overlooking, Josef? Why did Pfhanmoeller send us the wrong information, or could it have been changed in his office by someone else?"

"Does all that really matter, Herr Doktor?" Mengele asked, closing the sturdy wooden lid and buckling the leather straps of his instrument case. "There is not enough physical evidence to revoke his certification, but for some unexplainable reason, I wish we could."

"You think he is half-Jew, Josef?" Verschuer asked.

Mengele thought for a moment before he answered. "Yes, Herr Professor, I do. I think the man we just looked at is a Mischlinge. I believe his father was indeed a Jew."

"I also think he is Jewish," Verschuer pronounced. "Now, how can we go about proving it, Herr Doktor?"

The policeman Poltelz came back into the room looking hopeful. "Herr Doktors? Please. I have instructions to inform the Gauleiter of your findings."

"Inform Herr Funk that we are not finished with our investigation," Verschuer said, "but tellthe Gauleiter that we understand now why he questioned the genetics of Herr Albrin. Caution him, however, that we have found no conclusive proof to reverse our initial findings. Unless an investigation of the actual occurrence could turn up new evidence."

"All the memories are over twenty years old, Herr Doktors, " the policeman complained. "Besides, our men worked that line of investigation hoping to turn up the identity of the rapist. That would have settled everything. We found nothing new.

"We actually did," Verschuer said. Then he smiled. "Maybe we need to look at a younger Herr Albrin. Take a look at him before his nose was broken."

"Early school photographs," Mengele suggested.

"An excellent idea, Herr Doktor," Verschuer said.

"I can get that for you. The Albrin's children all attended the same school. It will not be hard to obtain those pictures. I will have them to you in Frankfurt by tomorrow morning," the policeman promised.

The two medical men left for Frankfurt, arriving back at the university before lunch. The next morning, Josef was in Verschuer's office when a messenger arrived with the photographs. Albrin was the third from the right, and without the aid of a magnifying glass, the two doctors could see that his nose was broad with a prominent bridge. One thing was certain, he had a Jew nose. The half-Jew had undergone some pain in his attempt to hide his Jewish appearance.

"What do you think, Josef?"

"I think we have a basis for revoking Albrin's <u>Certification of Aryan Descent</u>. In his youth, he certainly displays atypical phenotype.

The Jewish blood admixture is discernible in his genetic characteristics."

"The Gauleiter will be pleased." Verschuer sighed.

V

There was not enough time in the day for Mengele. He had his duties to fulfill to the Professor and the University, his parades with the SS in the evening hours twice a week and alternate weekends, and his own studies and research. Way after midnight, he would fall into bed exhausted and go immediately to sleep, waking early the next morning fully refreshed and excited about his upcoming day. He loved every second of what he was doing.

The latest paper he was working on involved what he hoped to prove was a genetic kinship of the fistulas of the ear and a particularly shaped clef in the chin. He wanted to establish that both characteristics were caused by the same gene. A minute segment of the genetic progeny of a people, but an excellent teaching tool in how to begin to study racial heritage. Verschuer both approved and encouraged this line of research.

Josef missed Irene desperately. He would read and reread her letters. He would create time to dash off short notes to her, telling her how much she meant to him. He would carry her letters around in his pocket, sneaking them out sometime during the day, and it thrilled him just to look at her handwriting. He missed the way she would take his arm in hers when another woman was close and dig her long, sharpened fingernails slightly into his flesh as if to proclaim that this man was hers and that she would fight for him.

He could remember looking into her blue eyes, finding delight in their position on the top row of the chart. And once he had put on a sweater that he had not worn since Christmas, when he had last seen her, and he found a long strand of her honey blond hair, and he wore it curled tight around his finger for the whole day.

She was the only woman that he would ever need in his life. He was fortunate to have found her. She made his life complete. He had his family and his career, and now he had Irene.

She was beautiful, witty, and sexy, and while she had maintained her virginity, she had learned how to please a man with her hands and her lips, and he burned for her in a desire of remembrance. She was also the daughter of a professor who understood the importance of a career. In fact, he knew that she would understand and welcome him home with warm, loving arms after he had spent long hours in the laboratory. He had also found her just in time to comply with the ReichsFührer's decree that in order to remain in the SS, and receive promotions, one must be married and producing children for the Reich.

He was also smug about choosing one of the newest branches of medicine that was rapidly becoming the most important. He was glad that he had not gone into pediatrics, osteology, gynecology, surgery, general practice, or some other specialty. He was thankful that genetics was the only true field of medicine that appealed to him.

Especially with the passage of the Studienordnung, or change in the student curriculum, that was to be implemented on April 1st, 1939. All medical students, doctors, dentists, and midwives in the Reich must now attend mandatory lectures and lab time to study racial genetics. In Germany, a professor was paid a certain percentage of the tuition of every student who opted to sit in the lecture hall, and to have the State decree that your lectures were now mandatory was an asset indeed. The word was passed by the Deputy-Führer Rudolf Hess that one of the facets of National Socialism was to be 'applied biology.' It was formally made a part of the State and the law of the land.

It was also that time of the year when the labs and the libraries were full of students putting in as many hours as humanly possible because both written and oral examinations would be fast approaching. Now, they were going to have to take time out and attend the opening lectures on genetics and racial hygiene conducted by the geneticists in universities throughout the Reich. Established practicing physicians would have to come back to school and learn the discipline of racial judgments.

Verschuer and Mengele had worked on the opening lectures for two weeks, and they were ready. Starting tomorrow, they would begin to train doctors in the difference between good German genetic offspring and genetic traits that, by all means must be prohibited from entering the sperm and egg stream of the <u>Volk</u>.

Ernst Decker caught up with Mengele as he was making his way to the library across the commons of the University, now blazing with tulips and crocus and other early spring flowers, and told him that Professor Verschuer was urgently in need of his presence. Mengele was surprised since he had just spent over an hour with the Professor. He was somewhat apprehensive as he hurried back to the office. Something must be wrong. An undergraduate held the door open for him as he approached the building, and Mengele nodded thanks to the much taller man.

He found Verschuer in his office, putting papers into his brown leather briefcase.

"Josef. Good of you to come so quickly. Something totally unexpected has come up. Rudin and I have been called away to meet with the ReichsFührer. I will not be able to deliver the opening lecture." Verschuer explained.

"Herr Professor, the lectures will have to be rescheduled. I will get to work on that right away." Mengele said, turning to leave.

"No, Josef. We are being disruptive enough. We will stay on schedule."

"Then who will take your place, Herr Professor?"

"Why, you will, of course." Verschuer smiled. "As we speak, the change is being posted."

Mengele was stunned. He had taken on teaching some of the labs, and he had filled in on occasion as a lecturer in an introductory anatomy class, but to address a hall filled with students and doctors, some of them full professors from other disciplines, was at first thought a frightening proposition.

"Do not worry, Josef," Verschuer continued, seeing the concerned look on his student's face, "you will do just fine. You understand how important this is, and you know the subject matter. You must remain empathic. You must see yourself as a harbinger of the new movement. We are revolutionizing the practice of medicine. Thankfully, Der Führer is the first statesman to recognize heredity and race hygiene and make it a leading principle of statesmanship. We must make the most of it. That is my message. You can deliver it."

Mengele now wished he had attended the school at Alte-Reshe, which had been established a few years earlier with the sole purpose of training doctors in the science of judging the genetic worth of an individual, but when he had brought the idea up to Verschuer, he had been told that the only way he should be at the school was as an instructor. Now, he wished he had insisted on going.

Verschuer handed Josef his outline of the opening lecture. "I will leave you to draft your own introduction, Herr Doctor. And good luck."

Mengele spent the next twenty-four hours in a concentrated flurry of writing and polishing and fitful sleep. He was both exalted and apprehensive over the entire affair. He wished that he could be anticipating sitting in the front row and listening to Verschuer instead of standing at the podium delivering the lectures. Then again, this was his first opportunity to address a very important audience, and it would really have an impact on his future. He wrote a letter to Irene telling her what was going on, even hinting about his fears. The next evening he entered the completely full lecture hall precisely fifteen minutes past the hour of four in the afternoon. It was the biggest room in the school, occupying almost half of one side of the building on the second floor. A lectern platform was elevated a step and took up most of the ground floor, leaving a narrow passageway to the elevated seats that rose in tiers. A wired skeleton dangled on a hook set on a tripod on a corner of the platform. On the wall behind Mengele were large colored renditions of all the organs. In the middle of the platform was a long table empty except for a glass and a decanter of water.

Mengele put the stack of papers and five of six books down on the table and turned to face his audience.

"Heil Hitler!" he greeted, a salutation not required by law but good politics.

"Heil Hitler!" The room responded enthusiastically and then settled down to silence. Many of those in attendance were familiar with Mengele and his position with the Herr Doktor. They also knew that Mengele was a member of the SS, an organization that most German citizens respected. Stories were repeated about the Gestapo, this new national police force and all of the Gestapo were SS.

Mengele opened up with a clear strong voice that carried easily to the people who sat in the upper seats.

"Gentlemen. I know how much you are disappointed in not having Professor von Verschuer here. He was called away on matters that required his personal attention. No one is more disappointed than myself.

"I had looked forward to hearing the Professor instill into you, as he has within me, the importance of the task set before the medical profession of the Reich. We are at one of the most important crossroads of medicine, and the road we must take has been mapped out to us by very enlightened men.

"Before I get into the outline of the responsibilities mandated by Der Führer and the National Socialist German Workers Party, I want to relate to you how Herr Professor von Verschuer has influenced me with his insight, his genius, and his teachings. It was the professor, among other voices, who convinced Der Führer that the doctors of Germany understood the challenges that lay before us.

"Put simply. We are to protect the blood of the <u>Volk</u>. And we are to improve the blood of the <u>Volk</u>.

"The Herr Professor joins a chorus of voices proclaiming that every doctor of the Reich must become a 'genetic doctor.' That we must all learn to treat the <u>Volk</u>, and not just the individual, and I quote from his Journal." He opened it to a marked page and continued in a solemn tone.

"Behind the life of every individual, there lies another life-the genetic current, which flows through the generations."

Mengele put the book down and picked up three others. He showed a high-glossed green leather copy to his audience as he came to a stop in front of the center aisle.

"I hope that you can appreciate how close we are in time to the initial discovery that race is of the most prime importance to the state. Arthur Conte de Gobineau, diplomat, philosopher and novelist from 1853 to 1855, published his _Essay on the Inequality_ of the _Human Race_. Gobineau pointed out that race was the prime mover throughout the history of man. That it was a different race of man that learned to fashion weapons from stone, and he eliminated the other upright but smaller race of man who, in their inherent weakness, were more than willing to co-exist. But they were in competition for the bounty of the earth, and they were killed off by the stone-shapers."

He paused, poured himself a glass of water and took a hurried sip. He knew his speech was going well. The men and both women in attendance seemed intent on his words.

"Throughout history," Mengele continued, "this has been demonstrated. It was Alpine Germans who migrated south from the mountains to settle and found Greece, the first great empire of western civilization. And they remained great only until they allowed their blood to be diluted by eastern elements. The Romans maintained their great empire only as long as they kept their bloodlines pure. As soon as they began to assimilate the blood of the conquered peoples of

Africa, they began to decay. While much of his writings have come under attack, they have never been disproved.

"Then came the Englishman Charles Darwin, who opened up the eyes of science with his <u>The Origin of Species,</u> published in 1859. It was natural selection. The traits that assisted survival were transmitted, or the species perished. Man was no different than all the other carbon forms of life on the planet. He adapted to the changing environment, or he perished.

"Genetic indifference could no longer prevail!

"Then there is our Austrian monk, Gregor Johann Mendel. He labored for years among his patch of peas and discovered that the relationship of parentage and offspring was a simple mathematical progression of how traits are blended and passed to future generations.

"So meine Herren," Mengele summed up. "Gobineau told us what was going on. It was a struggle between the races.

"Darwin told us why it was going on. Nature is a survival of the fittest.

"Mendel told us how you had to be to survive as a species, as a race, from generation to generation. Pass the best genes!

"Meine Herren, I hope you realize that genetic scientists had three important pieces of information for the first time in man's history! To not act upon this knowledge would be criminal!

"Alfred Ploetz was one of the first men to see the danger of keeping unfit life alive to reproduce. He was the first to establish a forum for addressing and educating the medical profession that we indeed had the opportunity, and the responsibility, of improving the biology of the human species.' He founded the Journal of Racial and Social Biology in 1904. Along with the psychiatrist Ernst Rudin, a close friend and colleague of our own von Verschuer, the lawyer Anastasius Nordenholz, and the anthropologist Richard Thurnwald, they founded The Society for Racial Hygiene. Today, it is an international organization with thousands of members, and of course, it is listed as one of the suggested societies open to men of good race.

"Professor Ploetz pointed out that there was now a degeneration of the most enlightened of the races because we, as men of medicine, in curing certain conditions visited upon our patients, were circumventing the laws of nature and keeping alive organisms that would have perished, instead of reproducing. An act that flies into the teeth of nature and allows the beginning of a slow degeneration of the germ plasma, that continuous echoing of genetic traits that make a people of kindred blood, and ties them together through the ages, that make a people a Nation.

"He made us realize, even before the astronomical number of fatalities of the last war, that it is the best of the race, the strong young men who die in wars and revolutions, leaving the poorest representatives of the people who then begin to breed a people into mediocrity.

"This knowledge has galvanized our nation into an attack upon these conditions that would reduce us from our present position of being the best example of mankind on the planet."

Mengele paused, taking another drink. The windows were all wide open, bringing in the pleasant spring air.

"Coming with the understanding of the threat to the germ plasma from internal genetic undesirable traits, we come full well into the realization of what the Jews living in our Germany wish to accomplish. They wish nothing more than to breed us with the lower forms of life, debasing our true genetic heritage. We see the evidence of their manipulations throughout the world.

"Thank God that Der Führer recognized in the early twenties the Jewish threat to the <u>Volk</u>. Even without the benefit of the medical profession pointing out to him what was taking place, he made his knowledge of their activities known. And he let the world know that he understood what the Jew was attempting to do."

He reached behind him and picked up a maroon leather-bound book with gold gilt title and edging. It was the professor's copy.

"And I quote from Der Führer's <u>Mein</u> Kampf."

"'The Jewish Doctrine of Marxism rejects the aristocratic principals of Nature and replaces the eternal privilege of power and strength by the mass of numbers and their dead weight. Hence, today, I believe that I am acting in accordance with the will of the Almighty Creator. By defending myself against the Jew, I am fighting for the work of the Lord. With Satanic joy on his face, the black-haired Jewish youth lurks in the wait for the unsuspecting girl, whom he defiles with his blood, thus stealing her from her people. With every means, he tries to destroy the racial foundations of the people he has set out to subjugate. Just so he himself systematically wins women and girls, he does not shrink from pulling down the blood barriers for others, even on a large scale. It was and is Jews who bring Negroes into the Rhineland always with the same secret thought and clear aim of ruining the hated white race.'" Mengele reverently closed the book and put it down.

"So we in the profession of medicine have two enemies that we must combat. The first is our own genetically transmitted diseases. We must enumerate them, isolate them, and then root them out of the germ plasma by sterilization.

"The second enemy is, of course, the Jew. In all walks and endeavors of man, we must rid the Reich of this parasite that has been sucking the substance from our <u>Volk</u>. We must, however, never underestimate our enemy.

"To underline just how cunning and influential our enemy was, and you see that I say 'was' only on the grounds of the strength of Der Führer, I would like to make sure that you are in possession of just how far the Jew had infiltrated.

"In 1934, our capital city, Berlin, with a population of 4,236,400, had a Jew population of 155,000, which is just 3.6 percent. However, of the 3,481 registered doctors, over eighteen hundred of them were Jews! Over half the doctors in our capital city were Jews!

"It was not that the people preferred them. It was their money that allowed them to get control of the State Insurance Company, and they now could determine which doctors could apply for payment. German doctors were slowly being removed from the list to make way for the Jew doctor! The Jew had actually gained control of administering to the medical needs of the <u>Volk</u>!

"Thank God for Der Führer. Without being a geneticist, he could still see into the core of the problem. He could see how the Jew had infested the <u>Volk</u>. He knew what it was going to take to correct the situation, and the Nuremberg Laws were passed. I am sure you are familiar with them. The changes requiring all medical students to participate in this training are really the will of Der Führer. It is also the law of the Reich.

"It should be considered as a sacred duty."

He turned, put the books down, and picked up the papers. He divided the stack and handed them to people on both sides of the aisle and there was the shuffle of paper as everyone took one and passed on the remaining.

"Here is the list of the various publications available and are strongly recommended readings. You see that there are almost two hundred journals that are a ready reference to just where our endeavors should be focused. You will note that our own Professor von Verschuer is the editor of Der Erbarzt, a supplement to the Deutsches Arzteblatt."

Mengele held up a thick green leather-bound book. "The standard text on this subject is by Lentz, Bauer, and Fischer. It is entitled, The Basis of Human Genetic Studies and Racial Hygiene. Three men who are still active in teaching and lighting the way of a science that they helped to discover. I encourage all of you to acquire a copy of their text.

"Under the new directives, you will be required to take classes in genealogy, anthropology, genetics, and forgery. All necessary tools in becoming a genetic doctor. In the laboratory you will stalk the chromosomes of Drosophila Melanogaster, the fruit fly, and watch genetics in action.

"Of course," he explained, "your primary duty will be in examining candidates for marriage and children entering the school system. The earlier that we can detect genetic illness the better."

He walked back to the front of the podium. He thought everything was going well. "I hope that I have adequately outlined the duties you will be expected to fulfill for the Reich. I am sure that most of you are already aware of the monumental changes that will be taking place. I just hope that you look forward to being an instrument of this change as much as I am. Questions, please?"

"Herr Doctor," the first inquiry came from a man sitting in the second tier. He was smoothed-faced with a ruddy complexion, his wide shoulders covered with an English-tailored suit, and Mengele noted that what at first seemed like Italian shoes were actually the first pair of cowboy boots he had ever seen.

"Is it not true," the man asked, "that in his original writings, Professor Ploetz considered the Jew more Aryan than Semitic and the second most advanced race of mankind? That the races had been mixing since 'time immortal,' and he considered miscegenation not of importance?"

Mengele stood stunned. He could see the rest of the room recoil to the statement-question of the stranger. He surely had not anticipated anyone in the audience to be challenging and argumentative. This man did not want a career in medicine in Germany; that much was obvious.

"How is it," the man continued, oblivious to the glares, stares, and shocked expressions of the other men in the room, "that the 'father of German Racial Hygiene' is so far out of step with the National Socialists?"

"I-I do not think that I know you," Mengele said, trying to formulate a response. "Your question, however, shows that you have read the early writings of Professor Ploetz, before certain facts were made known to him. I can assure you that the Professor is now in total agreement with the guidelines as mandated by Der Führer and the National Socialist and demanded by the German medical profession."

"That I am glad to hear," the man chuckled. "By the way, Herr Doctor, I am Robert Joseph Chambers of the great state of Texas, USA," he said, smiling. "Friends call me Bobby Joe."

The room lost the tension. The fact that he was an American explained his lack of fear of speaking out on subjects that by now had been settled as far as the correct position.

"Professor Ploetz sure had the Negro pegged right when he compared their intelligence level to just above the ape," the visitor continued. "Only in Texas, we are not convinced that the monkey might not be just a tad smarter. We know for sure that he is not as lazy. And he smells better."

The room erupted in laughter. A janitor in the hall had never heard such a sound in all the years that he had worked here. No one laughed like that in these hallowed halls.

Mengele relaxed. The man was going to be entertaining, not hostile. No one seemed anxious to leave.

"What brings you to Germany, Herr Chambers?" Mengele asked.

"Why, I am here to see how you are going to handle your Jews." He looked around the room and then addressed everyone.

"In America, we have the same problems that you have. Only ours are a little more complex. You are fortunate just to have the Jews to contend with.”

“Don’t forget we have Gypsies,” a voice sailed from the top. Mengele and the rest of the hall nodded in agreement.

“Okay. You have Jews and Gypsies,” Chambers conceded, “but we have Jews, Niggers, and Greasers. Not to mention a few redskins stinking up the countryside.”

“Greasers?” someone asked.

“Mexicans,” he explained. Then, he grew serious. “We have the same problems, but we do not have the political agenda or party like you have here in Germany. We have managed to effectively keep all the trash in their place except for the Jews. I have been sent here to see how you defend yourself from them.”

“Herr Chambers,” a young overweight undergraduate from Essen spoke up, “how is it that you can keep the Nigger and Mexican in line but have lost control of your Jews.”

“It is far more complicated in America than what you have here under National Socialism and Adolf Hitler. For instance, we have laws against miscegenation in only twenty-four states, but no one is ever prosecuted under them. To do so would be to invite the Feds into your courts, where they would quickly declare the state laws unconstitutional. They can do that because the Jews have entrenched themselves into our legal profession. They have taken over many of the benches of the Federal court system. They are now even on our Supreme Court.”

“Then, Herr Chambers,” Mengele asked, “how is it that you keep your Negroes in line?”

"With the Niggers the KKK, or Klu Klux Klan, has a way of keeping them on the other side of the tracks. That and the fact that even in east Texas, you can find a cottonwood tree."

There was more laughter. Most of the men present had belonged to some type of paramilitary organization, most of them had at least one uniform with insignia and medallions and medals hanging in their closet. One thing that all Germans took seriously was their uniforms, and Germany was a country of uniforms, and the picture of men dressed in white robes with pointed white hats and hooded faces was a hysterical thought to them. To picture these ridiculous outfits instilling fear into big bugged-eyed Niggers was indeed comical.

"I thought that your Klan was only active in the South, Herr Chambers?" another student asked.

"The Klan is active throughout America. In Indiana, for example, there are over three hundred thousand members, something like one out of four belong, and the other three agree with them. That is in the heartland of America. We will have to contend with the Niggers sooner or later because they do one thing extremely well, which is breed, but right now, our main concern is with the same group of people that threaten you, the Jew. I am traveling Germany in hopes of finding ways to keep America WASP."

"WASP?" Mengele asked.

"White Anglo-Saxon Protestant."

"Anglos and Saxons are Germanic tribesmen, Herr Chambers," Mengele said, "but religious inclinations are of really no importance. I have read an article recently," Mengele pointed out, "that in America, the term Caucasian is becoming the accepted terminology when speaking of the white race. The same article pointed out that Jews were no longer counted and identified as a separate people, and the only ones who know how many Jews are actually entering your country are the Jews themselves.”

“White America is not ‘white’ enough to continue to hold onto the Nordic ideal as you have in Germany,” Chambers answered. “The avalanche of Celtics has changed that. And your information is correct. We no longer have control of the number of Jews that are pouring into our land. Only the Jews are privy to such information. Which is why I have been sent here. We must, in America, find ways to stop the Jew from his course of establishing a world order with the ‘chosen people’ in charge.

“He has taken over in New York, and he has taken over in California. Both important cultural centers control the newspapers and the entertainment. You in Germany understand how important it is to control the channels of propaganda. We are losing that in America. Just as the Jew had almost gained control of medicine here in Germany, he has gained control of the information channels reaching the American people.”

“How can America have gotten themselves into such shape?” Mengele continued the exchange.

Chambers had this conversation many times, so he was ready with an explanation. “Because America is becoming a nation of laws, rather than a nation of men. And the Jew is acquiring control of the courts which both interpret and administer the law.”

“Then pass laws like we have. That will solve your problems.” A voice in the back advised.

"I wish it was that easy. Listen. Henry Ford had paid for, and had printed copies of the <u>Protocols</u>. A Federal judge made him destroy them! And that is in the land where freedom of speech and freedom of the press are supposedly held sacrosanct. So you can see that we are already playing catch up with the Jew in America."

"I hope you get the courage to act like we have here in Germany, Herr-or is it, Doctor?"

"Yes, it is, doctor."

"Good. How is America doing, Doctor, in the other realm of hygiene? With dealing with sick genetic people?" Mengele asked, wanting to instill in his audience that the problem was at least as hard to deal with and of the same importance.

"There also we have the legislation on the books. Indiana was the first state to pass a sterilization law. In 1907, it became legal to sterilize the criminally insane and the mentally ill. Only like the other thirty some states to pass comparable legislation, they have been reluctant to exercise these rights in fear of retaliation from the Federal court system. Or they are carrying it out and not publicizing it."

"Herr Doctor," one of the full professors at the university asked, "just how many countries have laws dealing with the rights of a state to terminate undesirable genetic traits?"

Mengele sorted through his notes. "We join a long list including England, the United States, Denmark, Norway, Sweden, Poland, Finland, Switzerland, Lithuania, Latvia, and Japan."

"The Poles would have to sterilize their entire population if they lived up to the letter of the law," someone said, causing everyone to laugh.

Chambers raised his voice high enough to be heard by everyone. "I have traveled in a lot of these countries and none of them come close to implementing the laws then here in Germany.

"You are quite correct, Herr Doctor,' Mengele agreed. "German doctors will not shrink from their duties. Let me again quote from our own Professor Verschuer, from his address to the Kaiser Wilhelm Congress on Racial Hygiene just this past year. He took a sheet of paper from the Professor's book and unfolded it.

"The parallel development of political and scientific ideas is not by chance but rather by internal necessity. We, geneticists and racial hygienists, have been fortunate to have seen our quiet work in the scholar's study and the scientific laboratory find application in the life of the people. Our responsibility has thereby become enormous. We continue quietly with our research, confident that here also, battles will be fought which will be of the greatest consequence for the survival of our people."

"I will be happy to report back home," Chambers drawled, "that you Germans take this racial issue very seriously."

VI

Otmar von Verschuer traveled north by train and reached Paderborn in Westphalia about four hours later that very evening. He was pleased to be met by a RottenFührer, who recognized him from the departing passengers. The man 'heiled,' took his suitcase and showed him the way to a waiting long black sedan. Verschuer got into the back seat.

They were soon speeding away from the village on a hard pan dirt road made devoid of dust and slick in spots by the spring rain. The sun was on the back of Otmar's neck when they entered an expansive valley with the Teutoburger Forest budding alive and looming ever larger through the windshield. After a twenty-minute drive in the growing gloom, the driver pointed to the castle sitting far away on top of a stark, treeless hillside, its form slowly taking shape in the fading light, a three-hundred-year-old man-made symmetry in a silhouette of natural shadows.

"Wewelsburg," the driver simply announced.

The castle had been originally built in the Seventeenth Century as a retreat and safe haven, for the Bishops of Paderborn. These officials of Rome had received their original appointment for these lands from the sacred hand of Charlemagne, the great Frank, the man who founded the Holy Roman Empire. The man who founded the First Reich.

He had united the Germanic people under his banner and championed this new god whose head priest was in Rome. Charlemagne knew that for tribes to become a nation, they must share the same deity.

The pagan Saxons, however, could not see the advantage of giving up their gods merely to adopt the god of a tribe of people called Hebrews. The Hebrew god might be a good enough god for a people living in the desert. People searching for a 'promised land' of 'milk and honey.' If your land was a desert, scrubland, filled with scorpions and serpents, then 'milk and honey' sounded boring but better, but it sounded like a rather bland promised land to a people of the forest and plains of Europe.

People who had learned cultivation of grains, fruits, and vegetables; who had domesticated animals, and had forests ablaze with game and streams teaming with fish; and their gods had given them a land that allowed them to have many children, and while their gods sometimes let bad things happen to them they did not ever remember a great flood that drowned all but one family. They did not ever remember hearing of villages so evil that their god had to destroy them in a ball of fire and shaking of the earth like this Hebrew Sodom and Gomorrah. Or ever turn any of its people into a pillar of salt.

But the Saxons did see, and they did hear, and they did definitely feel, the Norman's ax on the back of their necks.

After close to five thousand Saxon heads rolled in the dirt, Christianity and the God of Abraham, the God of the Hebrews, was delivered to this tribe.

The Bishops of Paderborn were given the power to ensure the Saxons did not go back to their old gods.

The castle was built with traditional turrets anchoring corners, with the two in the rear larger, having housed the stables and livestock. They were open at the top with the battlements still visible. The twin towers in the front were copper topped with spired domes.

Four rectangular wings three stories tall were built between the towers, creating a large courtyard.

The driver stopped the car at a three-hundred-year-old bridge on the Alme River at a guard post. The professor rolled down his window and handed out his identification. A flashlight beamed briefly in his face. His wallet was handed back to him. They were 'heiled' through. They wound their way up the mountain in low gear. The engine whine overcame the sound, but not the feel as the tires thumped over the seams of the newly paved concrete road. They topped over the hill, and they hit a level stretch of road that led around to the front of the castle.

The main entryway was nothing but a gaping hole. The courtyard was lit with strung incandescence under reflective hoods. Piles of sand and stacks of bricks were everywhere.

He was cautioned to be careful by a lanky SS man who took his bag and showed the way around the maze of scaffolds, lights, guards, and workmen. The men carrying the hod and doing the chiseling were dressed in the blue and white stripes of prison garb. Everywhere was the clink of the hammer as rotten mortar was chiseled away deep into the brick, to be blown dry and clean and packed with fresh mortar. In the Teutonburger, there is little stone. Here, you had to build from brick.

Verschuer was directed into what seemed to be the only intact part of the castle and was disappointed to find the main entry hall a shell, its walls stripped. It smelled of mildew and rot. He was shown up three flights of stairs and down a wide, dark hallway. Here, everything was completely restored. The smell of fresh wood and paint was still in the air, the floor freshly lain rough-hewn oak cut from the nearby forest, covered with a thick embroidered dark maroon runner.

"Here you are, GruppenFührer," the SS man said, opening a creaking, hinged, carved wood panel door. "You are to have the Charles Martel Room."

"Charles Martel?" The name was only remotely familiar to the professor.

"The Battle of Tours, GruppenFührer." The SS man answered in explanation. "There is a history in the desk."

The SS man went to the cedar closet, took out the uniform that was hanging in it, and put it over the hook of the dressing stand. "All of the rooms are named after Germanic heroes or kings. Will there be anything else, GruppenFührer?"

"No. Everything is in order."

"Dinner in forty minutes," the SS man announced as he closed the door behind him.

Verschuer was quite pleased. It was a large room with scattered oriental carpets over a stained dark floor. A canopied high poster bed took up the middle of the room. Light came from tapers, but there were oil lamps sitting on top of the mantle above the fireplace where a few small logs were burning out a crackling light and a little heat. The room was comfortable.

Above the mantel was an oil painting in a massive gold frame of the Battle of Tours where the Lord Mayor, "the Hammer Charlemagne's grandfather Charles Martel, had defeated the Moors and put an end to their invasion of Germanic lands. A large picture of

Der Führer shown from the waist up and dressed in his brown uniform, hung on the wall between the two windows.

The Professor dressed with care, having a hard time tugging on the calf-high black leather dress boots. On his collar was the triple oakleaf with one pip at the bottom denoting that he was a GruppenFührer, a major-general. He thought it would be funny if Josef could see him now. No one even knew that Rudin and he even belonged to the SS; their membership was kept secret by the ReichsFührer's orders.

He looked at himself in the full-length mirror and was pleased with his reflection. The uniform made him stand taller and stiffer, and as he peered out from under the visor of the peaked cap, he imagined himself a battle-hardened veteran and a stern, disciplined military man.

A knock on the door startled him.

He stepped away from the mirror, took his hat off, put it under his arm and barked out an invitation to enter. Verschuer did not recognize a clean-shaven Rudin in uniform, until he took off his cap, showing his shock of snow-white hair. Rudin grinned as if embarrassed in playing soldier. His eyes, however, revealed that he was enjoying it. They exchanged 'Heil Hitlers!'

"Can you imagine how much money the ReichsFührer is spending on renovating this castle?" Rudin asked excitedly.

"I am happy to see that the ReichsFührer has such money, Herr Pro–GruppenFührer, and is not afraid to display it. At least he can not cry poor when we ask him for some of it."

Rudin grinned, displaying his obviously false teeth. Then, he grew serious. "Heydrich informs me that we are to have a private audience with the ReichsFührer just after dinner."

"Splendid. Is Whittle here?" Verschuer asked.

"I have not had a chance to see him, but I am told that he's here."

"Then what are you concerned about, Ernst?" Verschuer asked his old friend. "I am sure we will be able to convince the ReichsFührer."

"It's Heydrich. He insisted on showing me around earlier, but he was just being the policeman. He has a way of trying to slice information from you. He gives me the creeps. It upsets him that our membership in the SS is kept secret. He really does not like the fact that he does not know our business with the ReichsFührer."

"Come now, Professor," Verschuer reassured his older compatriot. "The ReichsFührer must have his reasons for keeping GruppenFührer Heydrich out of it. We are safe following Himmler's orders."

He leaned closer and whispered. "Of course, if the rumors are true about Heydrich being half Jewish, it would explain the ReichsFührer's order that we talk to no one but him about this."

"Which means we must be more than careful, Herr Professor," Rudin warned. "There are rumors about Der Führer also."

Both men understood how thin the ice was that they were treading. Verschuer was surprised, however, that Rudin would come to fear Heydrich so completely after just one meeting.

"Then we will do nothing that will make Heydrich an enemy, Herr Professor."

"Having access to the ReichsFührer without his knowing our business makes us an enemy in his eyes. I am sure of that. But there is nothing to be done about it." He shrugged off the bad feelings. "I do think I look the silly old fool," he grinned.

"Nonsense, Herr GruppenFührer." Verschuer replied, "You cut a splendid figure."

"Otmar. The uniforms and the ceremonies are for the young and the military. They do not sit so well with men of science such as us. Give us a laboratory and a line of inquiry. That is where we are at home."

"The times call for some extraordinary behavior from all of us, Herr Professor. The stakes are tremendous." He went to the door and opened it and motioned for the older man to follow.

"Come, Herr Professor, let us find the dining hall. I am hungry, and I am sure that the table will be suitable for kings."

They went down the stairs and were directed to the right by an SS man stationed in the unfinished main entry hall, and from there, it was just a matter of following the smell of food to a large dining room that was lit by a dozen candelabra hanging on chains from the beamed ceiling. A picture of a stern-faced Adolf Hitler clad in armor and astride a white charger dominated one wall. In the middle of the room was a massive round table with intricately carved captain chairs.

The room was full of ranking Allgemeine SS officers. The doctors recognized all of them from their pictures that had appeared in the newspapers over the past five years since the National Socialists had taken power. It made them both realize just how unknown and unimportant they were in comparison with the men who were taking their seats around the table. The two doctors sat down in adjoining chairs and were greeted by the other men. They did not see Whittle.

White-jacketed SS men came from the kitchen pulling a kettle. Metal bowls were dealt out by the staff, and they all soon had bowls of steaming hot stew. The linen and napkins were embroidered with black swastikas. The silverware had been cast with the same emblem on the knife, fork and spoon. The plates in fired porcelain, were also adorned with this, set in motion, Aryan symbol of good luck.

Across from Rudin sat the most recognizable face, Alfred Rosenberg, the Party theologian. Born of German parents in the Baltic State of Latvia, he was attending college in Leningrad when the door of his room was opened just after midnight by a stranger who handed him a printed book, with a preface by a Professor Sergyet Nilus, a priest of the Russian Orthodox Church. Professor Nilus explained that the extraordinary document had been given to him by a friend, who had been given it by a woman, who stole it from a highly newly initiated leader of Freemasonry in France.

It was entitled <u>The Protocols of the Meetings of the Learned Elders of Zion</u>. The printed text was a reproduction of the handwritten notes of the man who had attended a meeting and who was to embark upon a life filled with even more power and even more riches, but for his carelessness in losing his notes, he was soon found floating face down in the Seine.

Rosenberg had fled Russia while the Revolution was still taking place, bringing the document into Germany with him. He wrote his own book, <u>The Myth of the Twentieth Century</u>, and he had preached in his tailored suit and wide-brimmed hat from atop a soap box in the streets of Germany that the Jew was the enemy of the Aryan Race and with his dupes, the Freemasons, the Jew was intent on debasing and enslaving the hated other races of mankind. Adolf Hitler heard him and, of course, agreed with him.

Seated next to Rosenberg was Walter Darre. Born in Argentina, he came back to his Fatherland at an early age, read Gobineau, Chamberlain, and Rosenberg, and then penned his <u>Blood and Soil</u>, in which he expounded on the theory that only people of good Germanic stock should be in possession of the fertile lands of Europe, for only in their hands was the caliber of competency necessary to achieve the true utilization of the earth. He was instrumental in establishing the Artamens, that agriculture society that the young Himmler had joined, attempting to breed a superior chicken. Darre, as head of the <u>Race and Resettlement Office</u>, was responsible for drawing up the guidelines for the examinations of all persons desiring entry into the SS and reviewed all applications of marriage of its membership.

Next was Leonardo Conti, the Reich Health Minister, who had the ear of Der Führer when it came to the health considerations of the Reich. He was intent on putting the bran back into the bread and continuing his campaign to get people to eat less fat and consume more vegetables. Together, with Der Führer, he attacked the use of tobacco and alcohol.

Then came Julius Friedrich Lehmann, a renowned publisher who recognized and nodded at the two professors. Lehmann had taken over the publishing of 'The Journal of Racial and Biological Hygiene' and made it a trumpet of Nordic supremacy. His publications continually denounced the Jews as a cancer, as a cell run amok threatening the life of the Aryan man.

Rheinhard Heydrich was next. Thin faced, tall, angular and muscular with a falsetto voice, he was both a master swordsman and accomplished violinist who had entertained the dinner guests of Admiral Cannaris before he was drummed out of the Kreigsmarine for womanizing. It did not take him long to display his talents to Himmler and then to Hitler, and he was soon in charge of the Sipo, the security police; the Kripo, the criminal police; the Gestapo, the secret state police, and the SD, which included both foreign and domestic intelligence agencies. He kept files on everyone, including all the Party hierarchy. When he addressed a remark to any of the other men around the table, he was sure to get their attention, but Verschuer noticed that some of them showed no fear of him. He realized that Rudin refused to look in his direction and he wondered what Heydrich had said to his mentor and colleague that had instilled so much dread in the usually fearless and outspoken psychiatrist.

Seating next to Heydrich was the diminutive Josef 'Sepp' Dietrich of the <u>Libestandarte</u> <u>Adolf</u> <u>Hitler</u>. Everyone in the Reich was familiar with Sepp. He was the rule that proved the exception in every fashion. He stood just over five feet tall, but when it came time to select the leader of the core of men whose duty it was to protect the life of Adolf Hitler, then there was no other contender to equal the zeal, cunning, and ruthlessness of the man who had fought in the first great tank battle of World War I. His quick wit and outrageous blunt sense of humor made him ideal company with just about everyone in the Party, including Der Führer, who held him in unequaled esteem. He had been a major participant in the 'Night of the Long Knives' with his pistol and steely nerves, as Hitler, Goring, and Himmler silenced once and for all the leadership of the Storm Troopers who wished to continue the revolution, even to absorbing the Wehrmacht.

Sitting next to Sepp was the dour-faced Theodore Eicke, who had set up the strict life of the concentration camps and had instilled within the guards the _esprit_ _de_ _corps_ that only harshness and ruthlessness was the way to maintain order. It was his orders that 'Work Will Set You Free' was to be the motto of the camps, which up until now confined mostly Communists, criminals, and homosexuals. There were a little over thirty thousand Jews imprisoned at the time, but they could gain their immediate release if they pledged to leave Germany but leave all their wealth behind. In the face of protest from other authorities, Eicke would set free men whose work was hard enough to gain their freedom. He was also the man who had walked into the stifling hot, smelly cell and had given Roehm, the Chief of Staff, the opportunity to take his own life, but had to return and pump the entire cylinder of his revolver into the faggot who had control of the three million men of the _Sturmabteilungen,_ of the Storm Troopers, those brown shirt ruffians who had protected and helped propel Adolf Hitler and the Nazis to power. Eicke had effectively held off Heydrich's attempt to gain control of the camps and was busy forming and militarily training his _Totenkopfverbande_ or Death's Head Division.

The men finished their meal and were served brandy and cigars, something that would never have taken place if Der Führer was present, but most of them swirled the amber-colored liquor in the crystal goblets and puffed on tobacco grown and rolled in Cuba. Heydrich and a few of the men left the room. Rudin and Verschuer were standing and talking to Conti and Lehmann when Walter Darre walked over to them.

"Herr Professor Verschuer," he asked, "might I have a word with you?"

"But of course, Herr GruppenFührer," Verschuer replied, surprised that the two men would have any need of privacy but followed Darre over to an unoccupied part of the expansive room.

"Herr Professor, you have one Josef Mengele functioning as your assistant?" Darre asked.

"That is correct, Herr GruppenFührer." Verschuer confirmed, now truly puzzled.

"I wanted as a courtesy to you to tell you that there is a problem with his petition for marriage," Darre said.

"Problem. What kind of problem? I have met his intended, Herr GruppenFührer and she seems the perfect match for Josef."

"It is her paternal grandfather," Darre explained. "On the application he is listed as an American, one Lyons Dumler. But Mister Dumler has refused to acknowledge that he indeed was the sire of Irene Schoenbein's father, even though he agreed to the child support awarded in the courts. The fact that he was already married at the time might be the real reason for his denials. But, under these circumstances, we can not certify her. Of course, Herr Doctor Mengele can still marry the woman under German law, but he will have to leave the ranks of the SS if he does."

"Thank you for telling me, Herr GruppenFührer. I do not know how Josef will react. He is thirty-one years old, and with Der Führer's decree that he must marry under the civil service laws and begin producing children leaves him not much time to find a suitable alternative. If we lose him from the ranks of the SS, it will surely be our loss."

"I can not do anything other than enforce the regulations, Herr Doctor," Darre said defensively.

"I would not want you to, Herr GruppenFührer. I was just stating a fact. It is out of our hands anyway, is it not?"

"You could petition the ReichsFührer, Herr Doctor, but I can tell you from past experience that he is unbending in his enforcement of the regulations. He even finds the time to look at all the photos of the intended brides."

"I am in a position where I do not want to approach the ReichsFührer on such a matter. I will leave it to you and Mengele to come to the right conclusion." He found himself becoming angry with having to deal with this just now as he was seeking funding for a project in which he had hoped to utilize Mengele's talents.

They heard a commotion in the outer hall and a chorus of 'Heil Hitlers,' and they turned to where the ReichsFührer and his aide, GruppenFührer Wolff, and Horrace Whittle came striding through the door.

Verschuer was always amazed when he came into the presence of the ReichsFührer, Heinrich Himmler. With his medium height, thin chest, weak chin, and sparse mustache and the perpetual dark shadows of a beard, gave him the appearance of being soft and indolent. His pince-nez glasses added to the impression of weakness, and Rudin often wondered if the ReichsFührer was one of those men whose successes were a direct cause of his opposition continually underestimating him.

He was ReichsFührer-SS. He was in control of Heydrich, all the police agencies, and the concentration camps. He was responsible only to Der Führer, and he was building a private army that was loyal only to the Party. He had helped bury Strasser, the Berlin National Socialist who could have challenged Hitler for leadership of the Party, had outmaneuvered Goebbels, gaining control of the Jewish question, had taken the Gestapo from Goring, and had led the men who put away the leadership of the SA, the Stormtroopers. It was as if nature had given him the countenance of a teddy bear and the bite of a cobra.

"Heil Hitler!" He greeted his underlings.

"Heil Hitler!" The men responded, in the straight arm stiff outward parade ground salute in the expanse of the room.

The ReichsFührer shook the hands of all the men who stood to greet him, making his way around the table. He took his chair with Wolff standing directly behind him. Whittle sat next to him, nodding at Verschuer and Rudin.

Whittle was the youngest man at the table. He had light blue eyes and a full head of sandy hair. As far as personal wealth, he was also the richest man assembled, having already amassed a small fortune. His membership in the SS was also kept secret. He was English.

The latecomers were served a plate of steaming food, and the ReichsFührer ate with an unusual relish. Men who knew him were surprised when he drank a whole glass of wine and allowed another to be poured for him. He wiped his mouth on the napkin he took from his lap. The table was quickly cleared.

"Meine GruppenFührers," he finally began, "I am sorry that I have acted like a hungry wolf in front of you," he looked at his assistant, who smiled over the joke. "Der Führer has kept us extremely busy for the past weeks, and today was especially demanding.

"Please excuse the dust and the noise as we restore this castle that is to become the spiritual center of our New Order. A new order based on the purity of our bloodlines. It is in this common ancestry that we derive our strength. That we derive our superiority.

"The accomplishments of Der Führer over the past few years have been tremendous. Much of his success lies in his ability to read the character and hearts of the people. Without Der Führer, we would still be paying homage to that despicable Treaty they imposed upon us at Versailles. We were made to pay for the entire cost of the struggle. Our army would be a paltry one hundred thousand men, which would leave our borders and our lands open for any of the enemies that surround us. We would have no Luftwaffe. Our fleet was nothing more than a flotilla of destroyers with a few cruiser-class ships, and we would be denied the right of having U-boats.

"Schleswig-Holstein would be a part of Denmark. Our Germanic people in Austria would still be in the abyss of despair, hunger, and unemployment, exploited by her hostile neighbors. Czechoslovakia would be threatening our Reich on our southern border and still holding dominion over our countrymen in the Sudenland.

"Our people would be full of despair and devoid of pride and subjugated to the onslaught of the Jew who poured into our country from the east under the Communist banner after that traitorous government at Weimar had signed that Jewish-inspired document. At a time when our monetary system was in a shambles brought about by a world banking system dominated by the Jew, previously improvised Jewish peasants showed up in our country with their pockets full of hard money provided by their fellow Jews in the New World, and they bought our factories, our lands, our banks, and even tried to purchase our souls!

"The Jewish population soared to over seven hundred and fifty thousand. They began to take control of our government, our schools and universities, our banks, and our medical profession. They began to gain control of our courts. The fruit of following the guidelines of their Protocols was near fulfillment. The Jew was smiling from New York to Moscow and felt close to his centuries-long quest for complete domination of the Western world."

"Under the leadership of Adolf Hitler, our Führer, we have once again become the strongest nation on the continent of Europe. Of the entire world, all of our people are at work. Everyone is fed. We are eliminating weak genetic lines that do nothing but poison our <u>Volk</u>. We are becoming once again a nation of men!" He took off his glasses, and Verschuer could see that the wine had put some red into the ReichsFührer's eyes.

"There is one other thing I must ask of you before this evening is over." There was a change in his tone of voice. "Of course, we are to all meet in the Supreme Leaders Hall at midnight for a ceremony that will not take long. Afterwards, however, I ask that all of you return immediately to your rooms."

They all looked at one another, puzzled at such a request.

"All of you have passed an exceedingly thorough investigation of your genetic bloodlines." The ReichsFührer explained with a half smile. "You are of pure blood and the best representation of the Aryan stock. I have long thought that men of accomplishment should continue and contribute to the blood of the people with suitable women; women of impeccable genetic characteristics exhibiting beauty and intelligence. I have arranged for such women to visit each of you later in your chambers. Their calendars have been calculated to ensure that each of them are extremely susceptible to conception."

There were shocked looks, nervous laughter, and disbelief on some of the men's faces. Verschuer looked at Rudin, whose crinkled old face broke out in a thin laugh.

"ReichsFührer," Rudin said, "you might send me a young woman who is ready to conceive, but her time might pass before I could seed her!"

Everyone laughed. Verschuer thought of his wife, whom he had remained faithful to all these years. Maybe he could. For the good of the Fatherland. The question was would he tell her afterwards. And if he did, what would that do to their relationship? He would have a few hours to think about this. Maybe he could find a way to avoid it without defying the wishes of the ReichsFührer.

"Gentlemen. This is something that is strictly voluntary," Himmler spoke lightly, "but I promise you these women will never show up at your doorsteps with an infant in her arms demanding that you care for them. These women know they are to enter one of the many houses I have begun to set up throughout Germany. I call these homes <u>Lebensborn.</u>" Meaning 'high born.'

"We can thank the Jews for contributing their proceeds from the insurance companies' settlement for Crystal Night. I managed to obtain all the proceeds just for the broken glass.

The money is going for many causes, but homes to care for newborn pure-blood children are of extreme importance to me. The children will be raised in accordance with my directions. They will be educated and equipped to take over the necessary responsibility of forming the new ruling class of the Third Reich. I just ask that you do your best to contribute your seed for the good of the Volk."

The smile left the men. They understood the seriousness of the ReichsFührer's request, and while some of them thought it outlandish, they now realized that in just a few short hours, they were to be visited by young, beautiful women, and they would have the rest of the night alone with them with the sole purpose of getting them pregnant. They all thought silently that there were far worse things to be called upon to do for the <u>Volk</u>.

"Now, GruppenFührers," the ReichsFührer continued, "please take the time to talk among yourselves and tour the castle. I promise you that in just a few short months, the place will be unique in its restoration to detail and incorporation of facilities that will make all of you do nothing but anticipate your visits here."

Himmler stood, 'heiled,' and left the dining hall, followed by his assistant.

The rest of the officers broke into groups and continued earlier discussions. There were sheepish grins bleating away just underneath tightly drawn lips on many of their faces. They all avoided making any comment that would open up talk about what was expected of them later in their rooms. The thought that a young, supple, beautiful woman would be waiting for them in their rooms added an element of excitement to what they had all assumed would be an evening devoid of women. The thought that now they were now being called upon to father a child for the Fatherland was exciting.

Wolff came back into the room, caught Verschuer's eye, and motioned for him. Verschuer alerted Rudin, who tugged Whittle on his sleeve, and they followed the staff officer back down the hallway and into the next wing. They came to a stop in the darkened hall in front of the private office of the ReichsFührer. A white web belted SS sentry turned to rap loudly on the door and swung it open.

They stepped into an office full of ancient and medieval armaments, the windows draped in heavy green. The ReichsFührer sat at his desk, a gooseneck lamp illuminating the folder in front of him. The doctors knew that it was the outline for their project.

"Please be seated, GruppenFührers," the ReichsFührer greeted, indicating the chairs and sofa on the other side of the desk. The men sat down. Wolff remained standing by the door but picked up a signal from Himmler and excused himself, shutting the door behind him.

"I wish I understood everything in your proposal, Herr Doktors," Himmler began, "but as a layman, I find much of your explanation less decipherable than Latin or Greek, two languages I must confess that I have struggled with since I was a boy."

"ReichsFührer," Verschuer said, "we are on the verge of some startling discoveries in the field of genetics. Experimentation has progressed to such a point that we felt it our duty to inform you of the potential of our line of research."

"I appreciate that Doctors, but I am still in the dark as to where you hope to go with this."

"We know that certain antisocial behaviors could very well be genetically determined," Rudin explained.

Himmler nodded.

"We know that certain physical diseases are also genetically determined. We now know exactly what in the body chemistry constitutes the genes."

"I understand all that, Herr Professors," the ReichsFührer interrupted, "tell me of the chemistry that you talk about in this report."

Rudin took a deep breath. This was the part that was difficult to substantiate.

"In 1869, a brilliant German biochemist, Johann Friedrich Miescher, extracted from the cellular debris of pus, a substance made primarily of nitrogen and phosphorus. Since it came from the nucleus of the cell, he called this material <u>nuclein</u>. Later research that has been kept entirely secret has established that this is the part of human chemistry that determines what an organism actually is, and will become. Herr ReichsFührer, it is the very blueprint for all living organisms!"

"The fruit fly, the simple creature that it is, has only four chromosomes," Verschuer continued, "all humans have forty-eight, ReichsFührer, each of them far more complex simply because they are longer, but chemically they are the same."

The men of science could see the look of bewilderment on Himmler's face.

"ReichsFührer," Verschuer explained, "knowing where the chemistry of inheritance lies and being able to read the genetic map imprinted into the <u>nuclein</u> of any individual, it could be possible to identify their genetic inheritance. We could determine their racial traits by chemistry. We could put a person under the microscope, so to speak, and see if they have Semitic genes."

Now, they were making sense. If there was a way to determine a Jew by his chemistry, then that was indeed a course of study that required funding. It would eliminate subjective judgments.

The ReichsFührer smiled. He could become the teacher instead of the pupil, a position in which he was far more familiar and comfortable. Only Der Führer had the power and the intellect to keep him silent and feeling like a school child.

"You realize that in all new directives and laws, we are to omit any reference to 'Semitic' peoples." He informed the other men. He saw their puzzled glances at one another.

They had not a clue.

"When the American industrialist Henry Ford was visiting Berlin less than a year ago," Himmler explained, "he brought to light some historical facts to Der Führer that I know some German researchers have also sustained. Even the Jewish scholar Ceasar Lombroso, for example, estimated in 1900 that only five percent of the Jews of Europe were actually of Afro-Asiatic descent.

"The 'Semitic Jew' are of a tribe originating in the north Arabian desert, now, as then, part of Egypt. They are the only ones that can claim blood kinship to the Hebrews of Abraham. They came to live in northwestern Mesopotamia around 1800 B.C. They are the people that later followed Moses out of Egypt.

"Herr Ford enlightened Der Führer that practically all the Jews in Europe, and the ones who later emigrated to America, infecting that country, were actually descendants of a people called Chazars. They once occupied thousands of square miles of territory between the Caspian and Black Seas northward almost to Moscow. Roughly the geographic area constituting the just recently abolished Russian Pale. They were a Finno-Turkish people who had wallowed in the worship of phallic symbols to the extent that one of their rulers in the seventh century, King Bulan, was sickened by his peoples' preoccupation with their genitals. He understood that it was destroying the very fabric of their culture, what little of it they had developed. He invited spokesmen of the three major monotheistic religions of the Western and Near Eastern worlds to his court to explain their thinking and their deities.

"After listening to the priests for Christianity, mullahs for Islam, and rabbis for Talmudism, the king elected to take his people into the religion, espousing that they were the 'chosen ones.'

"They invited true genetic Jews from Babylonia to help them in their transition, to teach them to become practitioners of Talmudism. These Chazars are the breed of people that are out to dominate the world. They are the ones who have declared war on the Aryan Race. They are the 'Jews' of Europe. They are the Jews that are our enemies. They are the people who have blueprinted the way they are to achieve world domination in their <u>Protocols!</u>"

Both professors and Whittle sat in considered silence. The historical information they had just been instructed about meant little to them. It did not matter if the Jews that were the cancer to the <u>Volk</u> came from Asia or from another planet. The ReichsFührer was not yet grasping the elements of genetics.

"ReichsFührer," Verschuer broke the silence, "the beautiful thing about science is that we are not dependent upon history in ascertaining who is our enemy. We can identify the Jew no matter if he originates from Palestine, the Arabian desert, or from western Asia."

The hour was growing late. "GruppenFührers, I understand what you are saying. Do not think for one moment that I am being argumentative. If we can identify a Jew by some sort of test that you can develop, then develop it."

Whittle decided that now was the time for the final argument. "ReichsFührer, let me also say this. If we can learn to determine what genetically makes a Jew, we could also learn to develop a disease that kills only Jews."

The ReichsFührer leaned forward over his desk with a look of shock and amazement.

"What do you mean?" He demanded to know.

Rudin wondered if they had gone too far but realized that they were losing him anyway, so they might as well divulge everything.

"ReichsFührer, if we could totally blueprint the human genetic code, we could also design a disease that could attack and kill only a specific targeted group of genetic kindred," Whittle explained.

"This is possible?" Himmler asked, incredulously.

"Yes, ReichsFührer. It is possible," Verschuer answered emphatically. "Let me give you an example of something that we have already discovered of the races and colors only people of light skin produce the enzyme lactase, essential for digesting the lactose sugar in milk. We know that there must be thousands of such variations in the genetic code of the races. It is just a matter of finding them. I have already published a study where I have identified over fifty diseases that are genetically determined. We would just need to focus our research on diseases that afflict only the Jews, and it is immaterial about their historical origins."

The ReichsFührer sat quietly. He had just about been ready to award these men a slight increase in their funding, but now the possibilities of the research were opening up new vistas.

"Do the Jews have a disease that is prevalent only to them?" He asked.

"There is only one that we are aware of at this time. It is a severe xeroderma pigmentosum first isolated and identified by the Jew dermatologist Moritz Kaposi."

"Let me also point out, ReichsFührer," Rudin warned, "that there are many Jews at work in laboratories throughout the world."

The ReichsFührer turned pale, realizing immediately the implication. "Do you think the Jews are aware of all this and are presently working on a disease that will kill only Germans?"

"No, we do not," Verschuer reassured him. "Only we can not be sure. We like to think that all the important work in genetics has been accomplished by German scientists. But an American by the name of Morgan, I believe he is the grandson of a famous Confederate general, working out of a lab in a place called Cold Harbor in Massachusetts, close to the Jewish-controlled city of New York, and could actually be funded by them, pioneered all the information on the genetic make-up of the fruit fly. Consider that and the amount of Jews in the medical profession throughout the world, we can not rule out their having the same information that we have. We do believe, however, that they have not identified <u>nuclein</u> as the actual blueprint for the cells to split and replicate, which gives us quite a head start."

"What makes you so sure of this?"

"Simply because the Jew has not sought some advantage in its discovery. They are not exploiting it."

The ReichsFührer realized that the time of the ceremony was growing near. He looked at the two esteemed professors and the Englishman across the desk and realized that if Der Führer was here, he would go into a rage even thinking about the Jew working to create a disease, a biological weapon, focused on the <u>Volk</u> as its target.

"Gentlemen, I appreciate very much all of the things you have told me. How are you actually pursuing this research? What if you are successful in isolating a gene. How are you going to distribute it?"

"ReichsFührer," Whittle said, "we are following the science discovered by the French Canadian de'Herrelle. We are hopeful in finding a virus suitable for us to 'load' the gene on."

"Where is this 'combining of genes' taking place that you describe in this report, and who is doing it? And where is all this research taking place?" The ReichsFührer wanted to know.

Rudin glanced at Verschuer, who immediately nodded. "The young biochemist who has accomplished this is named Ulrich Richard," Rudin informed him. "He is presently working in our lab at the University in Munich."

Himmler seemed thoughtful; the light glancing off his lenses hid his eyes from the two professors who sat directly across the desk from him.

"Please inform this young man that he is to transfer to this castle. He is to continue his research here, at Wewelsburg. Something this important should take place in the tightest of security."

"ReichsFührer," Rudin was first to object. "There is no laboratory here."

"Then draw up plans for the type of room you need. Make a list of equipment. Return this to me before the end of the week. You will have the finest of labs, and we will not have a security problem. Now, where is this virus research taking place?"

"Right now, we are working in our previous colony, Cameroon, in Africa. There is no way that we can find a suitable organism here in Westphalia," Whittle informed him.

Himmler nodded and sat quietly for a moment. "You realize that until now, we have pursued a policy of forcing the Jews from our lands, even working closely with the Zionists to filter Jews into Palestine over the protests of the British, not to mention the Arabs. But Der Führer has misgivings about allowing their concentration in a land of their own. They will always be our enemies. We have not yet formulated a final solution to the problem, but I see much promise in what you are proposing.

"I will be increasing your funding to sixteen thousand Reichsmarks a month. To each of your universities at Frankfurt, and at Munich. Will that be adequate?" He asked.

"More than generous, ReichsFührer," Rudin answered, knowing that it was not going to be hard to get Richard to move.

"I hope so. That brings your monies to more than the combined budget of the physics and chemistry chairs in both of your respective universities. I do believe that Der Führer would agree with my decision, and I will be informing him of our conversations here tonight. I am sure that you will also receive matching funds from the German Research Council, at least, that is what I will recommend to Der Führer. Just how far away do you think is the successful conclusion of your research?"

Verschuer's first impression was to shorten the estimation considerably but decided now was not the time to make undeliverable promises. He opted to be realistic.

"It could be as much as a decade, ReichsFührer," he finally answered, or as little as a few years."

Rudin was silently relieved at the answer. Whittle would have shortened the estimation.

"Herr professors," Himmler said, "please devote all of your time to supervising this project. Understand the importance that both Der Führer and I will be assigned to your research."

He looked at his wristwatch. "Now, if you will excuse me, I must prepare for this evening's ceremony. I will see you in the Chamber."

Just a short time later, the GruppenFührers fell in line in the hallway leading through the double four-inch thick oak doors hanging on the heavy iron hinges. SS men dressed in shining steel armor and holding halberds crossed in front of the entrance that used to lead to where the bishops had kept their horses but were now the Supreme Chambers of Deputies.

They heard the chime of a deep-throat clock. They stood silently counting until twelve was reached, and the guards snapped to attention and opened the doors. The men marched in a double file, going either to the right or the left as they entered the chamber and circled around the outer perimeter of the red, black, and clay-colored brick dome until they came to a stop in front of one of the eight stone pedestals aligned along the outer wall. The last four men to enter the chamber took to an inner circle and stood directly behind their stone pedestals that formed around a shallow pit directly below the Swastika bricked into the center of the dome. Torches burned, casting the cathedral in an undulating circle of smoky, bouncing light.

When all the men were at their pedestals, and without any order to do so, they all stepped in unison up on the stone platforms that were theirs, and only theirs, for all of eternity, or for at least one thousand years. They had been told earlier that when they died, they would have their coats of arms burned, and the urn containing their ashes would set where they now stood.

Rudin, being the oldest man present, thought that it would not be very long for him, as he almost lost his balance when he stepped up on his stone platform and had the fleeting thought that he might be the only man to fall and kill himself on his own altar, but he regained his balance. He was right all along. Ceremonies and uniforms are for the young.

The ReichsFührer entered the chamber dressed in a full replica of the battle armor and broad sword worn by the Saxon, Henry Fowler, who had stopped the invading Magyar archers and checked their advance into the Germanic lands over a thousand years earlier and had been elected by the German princes to become King Heinrich I. The metal armor clinked as he stepped down into his position in the center of the shallow pit. He pulled his sword, the scrape of steel echoing in the chamber as it cleared its scabbard. With a thunk, he stuck the point of the sword in the mortar between the brick floor and rested both hands enclosed in mailed gloves on top of the golden hilt.

The only sound was the crackling of the torches. Himmler began the ceremony he hoped to turn into a ritual that would be performed by the appointed ReichsFührers down through the ages or for, at the very least, one thousand years.

"We are the Nordic Ring." The ReichsFührer intoned. "We are the Nordic Ring!" The rest of the men responded. "We are the sons of the first man and the first woman."

The ReichsFührer continued. "We are all sons of Mannus, the son of the God Tuisto. We are of the sons of the tribes of the Chatti, Tencteri, Usipetes, Sicambri, Marsi, Bructeri, Frisians, Chauci, Saxons, Cherusci, and the Suevi, who were first among the Semmones. We are the sons of the Longobardi, the Marcomanni, the Ubii, and the Batavians.

"Our tribes have long ago combined into the Visigoths, Ostrogoths, Burgundians, Lombards, Vandals, Franks, Angles, Saxons, and Jutes.

"In their name, I call this <u>Gefolge</u> to order as in ancient times.

"Our blood is of their blood."

"Our blood is of their blood," the men echoed.

"We swear our loyalty to Der Führer, Adolf Hitler. We swear our fidelity to Gobineau's Vision. A vision where the mountains and plains and streams and all of the lands of Europe are all inhabited by people of one blood under the Aryan symbol of the Swastika.

"Whose sons are of Mannus, created by our one God, Tusito.

"The Aryan Man.

"We swear to you our Führer, Adolf Hitler." "We swear to you, Gobineau." The men intoned. And then every man in the chamber spoke their vow. "We pledge our fidelity to the Nordic Race!"

VII

Mengele woke earlier than usual the day that the professor was to return from Wewelsburg. He knew Verschuer would have heard how well the lecture had gone, and he looked forward to getting a compliment from his mentor. The long official envelope from the Reich Central Race and Resettlement Office was in the morning post. He was glad that everything was falling into place. He stepped outside into a beautiful morning under a light blue sky with scattered hazy breezes of white clouds.

He carefully ripped an edge from the envelope protecting the contents, and shook out the folded form. He saw it immediately with his eyes, but his brain was reluctant to register the word 'DENIED' stamped in bold red letters across the face of his application to marry.

There had to be some mistake.

There just had to be.

When he finally came to realize that the letter was actually addressed to him, and that was not a mistake. When he finally came to realize that the details explaining the denial were not a mistake, when he finally admitted to himself that the love of his life was now threatening his very career in the SS, he became livid.

How could this be happening? Why had he not seen it coming? He was a geneticist, for God's sake and an SS man. He would not be so foolish as to fall in love and want to marry a woman who could be a one-eighth Jew! Irene was truly Aryan. There had to be a way to get this American to admit paternity. It was as simple as that. It would have been better if all her grandparents had been born in Germany, but before he had become serious about Irene, he had inquired about her heritage, and while the Dumler connection was not as fortuitous as he would have liked, he had researched them enough to be satisfied that they were of good Anglo-Saxon stock, they were of good Germanic Blood.

His usual brisk step was leaden as he wadded to the University. He felt sick about facing the professor. He wondered if maybe the professor could help him, even though he could not think of a way to ask him. But had not the good Doktor just returned from a meeting with the ReichsFührer himself, and what was the use of having friends in high places if one was afraid to ask them for assistance.

A few moments later, with the envelope still in his hands, he entered the professor's office. Mengele could tell that the older man was aware of what had occurred.

"I am so sorry, Josef," Verschuer consoled, "GruppenFührer Darre told me himself of the difficulties."

"Do you think anything can be done, Herr professor?" Mengele exerted the effort to keep his voice low and strong.

"If Dumler can not be persuaded to own up to his paternity, I do not know that anything can be done. GruppenFührer Darre has already informed me that this has happened quite a few times, but the ReichsFührer has refused to waive any application. Does Irene know of the ruling?"

"I have not spoken with her yet. I plan on calling her this evening. I was hoping to form a plan of protest with the ReichsFührer before I talked to her. I did not want to just drop it on her without any sense of hope."

Verschuer was thoughtful. He knew what would be the easiest solution. "Josef. Have you considered altering your plans?"

Of course, that thought had already crossed Mengele's mind fifty times since he opened the envelope, but hearing it phrased out loud made him realize how much he had wanted to marry this woman, no matter how much he loved being an SS man. He loved the black uniform and the way it made him feel, but Irene was the woman that he loved, and he was not going to give her up. He could well marry her under German law, and he would still be a Doktor, and he would still be a geneticist, and he could still become a professor. He would give up his membership in the <u>Allgemeine</u> <u>Schutzstaffele</u>. He would give up the SS.

"No, professor. It is a matter of honor that I live up to my commitments to her," he said with finality. Honor and commitment were the words men spoke to men; he did not talk of love.

"Then this is what you must do, Josef," Verschuer said, thinking of a way that might make a difference. "We will submit a detailed physical genetic examination of her. She must solicit letters from all of her friends and acquaintances. From her past teachers. From the neighbors. Anyone that she can think of, and it would not hurt if some of them held party office. They must all say the same thing. They must all say that Irene displays nothing but Nordic behavior. That she looks like a Nordic German, and she behaves like a Nordic woman. It is a long shot, but to do nothing seems very wrong."

Mengele felt a surge of hope. Maybe with the influence of the Doktor and testimonials from a few dozen people, the ReichsFührer may allow him to marry Irene and maintain his membership in the Corps.

"Thank you, Herr Professor. I am sure that Irene will be able to generate a sufficient volume of mail that might make a difference."

Verschuer could see that he had instilled more hope than he had actually felt. He knew the depths of Himmler's feelings about keeping the sanctity of his organization. His policies and beliefs had brought much scorn on him by other high-ranking Nazis, but no one, including Goring or Goebbels, had deterred him from his course.

After supper at his rooming house, Mengele excused himself early from the table and went into the sitting room. He closed the sliding wooden pocket doors behind him. He sat in the chair beside the telephone nook, took the receiver from the hook, and dialed the operator, who immediately came on the line. He gave her Irene's phone number in Freiburg.

It was answered by a thankful but apprehensive Frau Schoenbein.

"Oh, Josef. Irene found out this morning. This is terrible. She has been in her room all day. I do hope you can find a way to resolve this," she said, thinking that Mengele could be calling to back out of the wedding plans. She liked Josef; he seemed to be very attentive to her daughter's needs, and Irene was not the easiest girl to get along with, having her outspoken ways. She was almost twenty-two, and a doctor proposing marriage did not come along every day. Even her husband liked Josef, and he had not cared for too many of the young men who had courted his daughter. But she also knew how much being in the SS meant to her prospective son-in-law.

"One moment, Josef and I will get her for you."

It seemed like an eternity before Irene came on the line, but she had actually been standing beside her mother the whole time, not having ventured from the house all day and never far from the phone, afraid that she would miss his call.

"Hello, Josef." Her voice was without its usual buoyancy.

"Hello, Irene." He answered, his voice flat.

There was a long silence.

"Oh, Josef, I am so sorry about all of this! I did everything that you asked of me. We were honest on the questionnaire, as you instructed. I sat for the photographs and submitted them. I even, Josef, had a pelvic examination by a doktor who is also in the SS, and it meant so much to me to learn that I should not have any trouble having babies.

"My father is also heartsick," she continued on. "He feels the shame of a man who is, after all of these years, still denied by his own father. He tried to place a telephone call to Herr Dumler this afternoon to plead with the man on behalf of his granddaughter, but the man refused even to accept his call. My father is so angry that he has left the house. Mother is worried that he will come home drunk, something that you know he never does."

She realized that she was now just rattling on but she could not stop herself. She had cried all day just thinking that she might not be able to marry Josef because she could not prove that her grandfather was not a Jew. It hurt worse knowing that it was that Mongoloid looking man with thin, weak eyes and a weak chin who was determined that she was unfit! She was hurt, but she was also angry. She was trying to hide both of these emotions.

"If you want out of your engagement because of this, I will understand," she finally said, taking the plunge and putting out the only solution she could see, but putting a tremor in her voice that she knew that he would pick up on.

"Irene, please. First of all, we are not going to alter our wedding plans."

"Oh, Josef," she cried, relieved and elated into the telephone, "I do love you so!"

Listening to her say those few words made him know that he had made the right decision. When he thought of her slim, long-legged body and her long, graceful fingers, and the way her lips were hot with love and promise on his and the way she made his stomach feel like an arena where butterflies lifted weights from his groin, he knew that no matter how good it felt to put on that black uniform of the Corps, it was going to feel so much better to be inside the pink flesh of this woman.

"Now listen, Irene, I am going to make you my wife. Even if Der Führer or the Pope said otherwise. Nothing is going to change that. But the Professor has given me a plan that might make a difference to the ReichsFührer." He went on to explain what he wanted her to do.

Irene was relieved and elated that Josef had chosen her over a uniform, although not completely sure why. She would have felt mortified if his decision had gone the other way. She realized that it would have become common knowledge that she had been dumped because her blood was suspected. With his renewed pledge, she was going to be saved from that stigma. She would do everything that he asked. She hoped it would work. If it didn't, if she had to enter the marriage on such a note, well, she did not know if she would ever be able to make up for his having to leave his beloved Corps.

Throughout that spring and early summer the ReichsFührer Heinrich Himmler had never before felt so much pressure. He thought about how rapidly things were taking place. Der Führer had accomplished much since taking over as Chancellor of Germany in 1933. First, the Saarland had elected in their plebiscite to return to Germany, and France's Treaty right to mine German coal for fifteen years had come to an end.

Der Führer reintroduced conscription into the Armed Services in March 1935, in defiance of the Treaty. One year later to the month, he caught the French Cabinet in one of their scandalous political upheavals. He sent the ReichsFührer into the Rhineland to take back Germany's natural defensive border with the French. The English judged them to just be occupying land that was really part of Germany and did nothing to oppose them, which was a good thing. Der Führer had instructed his army to beat a hasty retreat if anyone contested their maneuver, but no one did, and another clause of the Treaty had been abrogated.

Two years later, in March 1938, the Anschluss with Austria was completed in direct violation of the Treaty. In September of that same year, Hitler now had time to listen to the voices of the Germanic people living in the Sudetenland, which was now part of the country of Czechoslovakia, a country created by the Treaty at the end of World War I.

With Austria becoming part of the Reich, Czechoslovakia had no defensive borders against Germany, which could now invade from the south. Hitler demanded self-autonomy for the Germans living in this border area, and at Munich on September 30th, Britain and France allowed him to have this area populated mostly with German people. Six months later, Der Führer sent his troops into Bohemia and

Moravia, declaring them a Projectorite of the Reich, which really pissed Chamberlain off because Hitler had promised not to do that at Munich, and Winston Churchill was screaming I told you so. Der Führer allowed Slovakia to remain independent only as long as they remained allies. Hungary immediately took Ruthenia and Poland grabbed what was left, and Czechoslovakia, a country created by the Treaty that drew political lines leaving over thirty million people occupying positions of being one race under the dominion of another race, was the first of these countries to cease to exist.

A few weeks later, Lithuania was forced to give up Memelland and the city of Memel on the Baltic to Der Führer, areas with heavy German populations, but no one cared because no one had a treaty with the Lithuanians.

Now Der Führer took aim on the territory that most infuriated him, the Polish Corridor, the 'Corridor to the Sea.'

The ReichsFührer knew that the time was fast approaching when he would need all of the men that he could find, and now he was faced with losing another one simply because the woman his SS man wanted to marry could not prove herself pure Aryan.

He studied the photographs of one Irene Schoenbein. There was a frontal shot and one of each of her profiles. There was also one of her in a bathing suit. Her hair was loose and she had the pictures taken without having on any make-up, as per her instructions. In a neat stack were the letters of many people who wrote to the ReichsFührer attesting that Irene was a very excellent example of the Nordic Ideal, in words and deeds as well as appearances.

She was a Nordic beauty, just like he had always and continually encouraged his men to find. He was relieved for a change not having to look at the photographs of dumpy, dark-eyed, dark-haired girls that his tall, young blond men always seemed to prefer to marry. These women seemed to be always able to prove their blood to be pure to the year 1750, and he had no way of preventing these marriages. It just sickened him to do so. Now, as he looked at photos of Irene, he could see the personification of what he wanted all of his men to find. She was a Nordic beauty, but by his own policy, she must be denied as a suitable wife of an SS man.

He found himself longing for those days when he was young and traveling throughout Bavaria astride the thirty cubic-inch Italian motorcycle, carrying out party business for Gregor Strasser and other important party officials. That was in the days when the party was becoming focused, and they had yet to have the firm hand of Adolf Hitler to steer them all together. He had spent many a night in front of a small campfire, first wrestling the tube from the tire to patch a hole and then stuffing it back between the rim and the tire, inflating it with the hand pump that he carried, and then staring into the warm flickering yellows and red flames and dreaming the dreams of men who become men of the ages. He had not realized then that a simple marriage between two Germans could cause him so much consternation.

He looked at the application and noted the colors designated by number and then picked up the Fiberglass swatches from his top desk drawer. Her hair was a white blond, probably two or three shades lighter than his own wife. He checked the color of her eyes and saw that they were on the top row between the third and fourth ideal.

He looked at Mengele's photograph, thinking he looked the typical Swabian, except he was dark enough to pass for a Gypsy, but of course he had already proven his blood pure. He wondered if maybe his original estimates were realistic of one hundred years to breed the Volk back to the Nordic Ideal.

The Nordic Ideal.

Dolichocephalics.

Tall, long-headed, narrow-faced, well-defined chin, narrow nose—in all much like the face on the Renaissance King chess piece—with very high roots; soft hair (golden blond) and receding light (blue or gray) eyes, pink, white skin in color.

This Irene Schoenbein would contribute to that end far more so than his SS man Mengele. Germany would need the blood of such children that would come from their union. Only the SS could not take the chance, yet Verschuer 's argument had a lot of merit.

He decided to change policy. He would allow Josef Mengele to remain in the SS if he married Irene Schoenbein. He would not allow, however, any of their offspring to be listed in the <u>Sippenbuch</u>. The registry that listed the continuation of people of pure blood, breeding with people of pure blood, and the people listed in the <u>Sippenbuch</u> would be assured positions of prestige and power. They would form the basis of the ruling elite down through the ages.

He felt relieved after making his decision, and he penciled his directive in the corner of the application. He would be able to save the enlistment of quite a few good men in the future by treating them the same way. He only hoped that he could educate his Corps that he wanted the best of both worlds; he wanted them to find the tall blond women, and he wanted them to find women who could pass all the requirements.

Irene was relieved when she found out that she was not going to be the cause of Josef having to leave the SS. Verschuer felt honored that the ReichsFührer had followed his suggestion. Josef was elated in being able to remain in the Corps but silently bitter that any of his children by Irene would not receive the birthday gifts of the silver beakers presented on his children's birthday by the ReichsFührer, that they would be omitted from the rolls of the future ruling class. Walburga felt betrayed by the ReichsFührer. She had hoped that Irene's suspected blood would end the wedding and her son would find a good Swabian Catholic to be his bride. She did however, take the pains to have the wedding ceremonies moved to Obertsdorf, just north of Munich. She had emphatically stated that she was not healthy enough to make the trip all the way to Freiburg to wed in the home city of her future daughter-in-law.

Josef Mengele and Irene Schoenbien were married near the first of July in a Catholic ceremony in the large ornate Cathedral near the center of this city. The ReichsFührer demanded that they also carry out the ceremony of the SS where they were joined together, not under the cross, but under the lighting SS runes. Irene felt the strangeness of both ceremonies. She was Lutheran, and she had participated in a Roman Catholic ritual. She was a Christian but later that same day had participated in a private Pagan ritual.

No matter the ritual. She felt married for the first time to Josef that night when he penetrated deep inside her, and when he ejaculated, she wondered idly if they were SS Pagan or Catholic sperm seeking to impregnate her.

VIII

The old <u>babushka</u>, her face as creviced as the earth after a long drought and clothes the color of the earth but clean and rubbed thin by the many washings–but never enough to remove all of the fleas–sat her young grandchildren before her. She told them the tale that her own grandmother had told her when she was no older than five, but she remembered it as if it was just yesterday. She began her story in a thin, crackling voice, speaking with shriveled lips from a mouth that held no teeth. The children sat quietly and attentively.

"There were once three brothers who lived in the rich, fertile northern lands of the Vistula," she began her tale. "The river was very good to them. The river was full of fish, and the forests were full of game. But they soon came to realize that there were becoming too many of them. They were becoming crowded with all of their children, and they were afraid they would wear the land out and fish the rivers out, and then they would all starve.

"But as brothers, they wished nothing more than to settle the issue peacefully. Their names were Rus, Lech, and Czech.

"Then, one day, they decided that something would have to be done, or there would be so many that they would all have to struggle for the fish from the rivers and the game from the forests. The three brothers, Rus, Lech, and Czech, went into the forest. Lech climbed the highest tree that they could find, and from atop his perch swaying in the wind, he looked into the lands around them. He yelled down to his brothers that in the east was a great fertile steppe and rich river valleys and enough land for a family to grow for centuries. His brother Rus said that sounded just fine to him, and he gathered his family and his herds, and they moved off into the east. They are now the great nation of the Russians.

"Lech then looked to the south. He yelled down to his brother Czech that the land there had mountains and valleys and rivers and a much brighter sun that would be warmer than the wind-swept land they were all accustomed to, and the land would allow for a large family to prosper and Czech said that sounded fine to him, and he gathered his family and his herds, and he moved them to the south. They are now the great nation of the Czechs.

"Then Lech looked to the west, and he saw dense forests and a fierce-looking people, and the last thing he could do was turn his family to the west to be devoured by those people.

"To the north was the sea.

"As he pondered his choices while climbing down from the tree, he spied a bird's nest, and everything suddenly became clear to him. Since his brothers Rus and Czech had already left and taken their families with them, then there would be enough land for his family to remain just right where they were. He started a new city in the middle of the forest, and he called it Gniezno, or 'bird's nest,' and it is still a city today, and Lech's family soon grew into the tribe of the Poliane."

She looked at children who were of her blood, and she was delighted that there were so many of them. She sat back in her chair, nodded her head, and just before she took her afternoon nap, she had one more thing to say to her children's children.

"Have many children. Or Rus or Czech will want this land back. Or the Germans will come and take it away from you."

The Poles.

As these Slavic people grew in numbers so did the forest people that Lech had seen in the west.

The Germans.

These men of stout bodies and fierce nature soon began to raid the villages of the Poliane, killing any man who resisted and tying the able-bodied men, women, and children together; they marched them back into their own land, where they ended up on the border with the Romans who desired just two things from the German barbarians, the long golden tresses from the German women to be woven into wigs for their own women, and these docile people from the east. The Romans worked them on heavy projects that just required physical effort and used the whip just enough to get the most out of them, and their name, the Slav, which means 'glorious' in their own language, soon gave the world the name of slave, as the Slav entered one of the most prolonged periods of the condition known as slavery, where one race has complete dominion over another race. The problem of being people of the field meant that they lived in a field and had no natural defensive barriers to the east and west in the North German Plain. The Carpathian Mountains to the south had enough passes to be useless against men on horseback. The Poles were easy prey over thousands of years, and in the thirteenth century when Batu, the grandson of the Great Genghis Khan, led his Mongol horsemen three times through the land with only rape, pillage and murder as their sole reason for being there, the population of the Poliane was devastated to the point that the Polish noblemen realized that only people made princes, earls, and kings. They invited northern Europeans by the enticement of giving them land, an offer taken by Dutch, Czechs, Flemings, Walloons, and a great many Germans, and the lands were repopulated by people carrying white blood capable of working with their hands and their minds.

The Poliane, the field people, could not ever quite stabilize their borders, nor would the aristocracy of their race share the benefits, but only the burdens of being a nation with the peasants, so they always remained weak and over the centuries, everyone took their turn with them. Lithuanians to the north, Prussians to the west, Russians to the east, the Magyars, Czechs, Austrians, and at times, it seemed like every Mongol tribe of the east coming up from the south, and even some Swedes spent some time in the fields killing the men and impregnating their women.

They were an open plain for battle, and this land bore the brunt of the Asiatic men of the East. They had served for a long time under the heavy hand of the Russians, and they had learned from all of their masters how to be a master in your own house. The Treaty resurrected them and gave them a chance to be a nation again, and in two years, they proved they were a Nation. They went to war with Russia over land and won; invaded Germany but was turned back just outside of Berlin by the Friekorps; and seized Vilna from Lithuania, telling the League of Nations to stuff it when it protested.

They were governed by 'colonels' fashioned on the great Pilsudski, who became a virtual dictator as he led the coup d'etat that put the military in complete control. They later took Teschen when Germany moved into Moravia and Bohemia, declaring it a Protectorate, as Czechoslovakia was dissolving from the map. The military aristocracy still knew how to treat their peasants, which was the same way they had been treating them for four hundred years.

All the Poliane really had was their Roman Catholic church.

The Poles hated all the other people who lived within their borders, and for a change, they had control of the police, prisons, and the army.

And the 'Polish Corridor,' that piece of Prussia that had been loped off Germany to punish her for losing the war and to give Poland a chance to survive by providing her access to the sea, had actually sealed her doom as a nation. Knowing that the Germans were not going to allow this piece of land to remain Polish, the 'colonels' were spending over seventy percent of the country's wealth on the military, and every penny they could borrow from the French government, to be taken in credits to purchase French military hardware. They had one of the best armies in the field of Europe in the late 1920s, but it was 1939, and Der Führer turned his entire attention to the 'Polish Question.'

Der Führer told the world that no great Nation can stand by and watch people of their blood being mistreated by other people solely on the basis of their being given this dominion at a table of map drawers in Versailles. Germany was no longer going to sit back and allow the Poles to mistreat the Germans who had lived there for centuries. Hitler handed the Poles a sixteen-point plan that demanded that a plebiscite be taken in Danzig to determine whose flag they would fly. The city was still eighty-five percent German, and a strip of land through the 'Corridor' that was German so they could maintain the tracks instead of the lackadaisical way the Poles maintained the road, causing many derailments and loss of life, and they were sick and tired of having to get off the train at the 'Polish borders' and carry their luggage through customs on their way to East Prussia, still a vibrant part of the Reich.

Instead of considering the proposals, the Polish government relied on the newly signed Mutual Assistance Pact they had just concluded in July 1939 with the French and the English, which gave them the courage to tell Hitler that any questions regarding 'their' territory were falling on death ears. A week later, Der Führer abrogated the five-year-old non-aggression pact he had earlier negotiated with the Poles.

Der Führer had hoped for a better response from the English. The French, he knew, would follow where the English led them. Could they not understand that as fellow Aryans, they must realize that it was going to be a war of Race, and the Germanic Tribes must stick together. He thought that there could be only one reason why the English would go to war over Poland, and Der Führer addressed it in a speech at the Knoll Opera House and later at the Reichstag.

He wished to be a "prophet," he railed, to get their attention, and then continued in his explanatory and promissory tone of voice, which could be written in granite.

"If international finance-Jewry in and outside Europe should succeed once again in plunging the peoples into a world war, then the result would not be the Bolshevisation of the earth and thereby the victory of Jewry, but the annihilation of the Jewish race in Europe."

Stalin had sat back and watched the turn of events on his western borders and wondered if the English and the French would indeed have the backbone to back up their pledges, having lost much faith when Czechoslovakia had disappeared from the map at such rapid pace. He had offered to align his country with Poland, England, and France, but the English refused to consider his claims against the Baltic States, and when the English military entourage that finally reached Moscow three weeks late consisting of minor officials who did not have the power to say what their governments would or would not do in case Germany attacked Poland, Stalin decided that it was the time to talk to the Germans.

On August 23rd, the 'Man of Steel,' who really knew how to treat a peasant, having a body count of five to seven million Ukrainians as they starved to death while he exported the food they had grown, stood beaming behind his foreign minister Molotov as he signed a ten-year non-aggression pact with Ribbentrop after just three hours of talks. The rest of the world was shocked as the Communists and the Fascists shook hands and signed a non-aggression treaty. An inconceivable event had taken place. Nazism and Communism had signed a document promising peace between them.

Der Führer then called his ReichsFührer to issue him his orders for the upcoming invasion. He informed him that he had ordered his generals to prepare to strike Poland no later than September 1st. Since the Poles were unwilling to discuss the deplorable conditions of the Germans living behind the Polish borders, especially in the Corridor, which had filled up with Jews since the Treaty, then all that was left was a military solution, and it was about damn time. Hitler was going to war, and he did not care what the rest of Europe was going to do.

The German General staff was panicked. They screamed their vulnerability. The English and the French would immediately attack from the west while they were still locked in the struggle with the three million men of the Polish Army deployed over thirty thousand square miles. They would once again be in a two-front war that could only lead to their own destruction.

Der Führer had merely scoffed at their fears and ranted against their hesitancy. He had built this army in defiance of the world and yet could still not feel comfortable that his own military was in goose step with his planning. What did they think all of their training for the past twenty years had been about? Even before Hitler had come to power, the German Army had worked on ways of fighting the Poles.

Himmler knew that the actual details of the fighting were completely out of his hands. He did not think in terms of tactics or war strategies. He was proud that the SS was going to be contributing three divisions to the effort; the <u>Leibstandarte</u> <u>Adolf</u> <u>Hitler,</u> <u>Verfugungstruppe</u>, and the <u>Totenkopfverbande</u>, even though they were to be under the command of the Wehrmacht. These men he was sending into war were the genetic best that the Reich had to offer, and he was sure they would represent themselves and the SS extremely well in battle, of which he had no doubt or misgivings.

His problem, as outlined by Der Führer, was to deal with the thirty million people inhabiting Poland, including Poles, White Russians, Gorals, Lemkes, Kashubs, Gypies, Rumenians, and, of course, over three million Jews. Thirty percent of the 'Polish' population were minority ethnic groups. It was his job to deal with all of them, and he thought the job impossible without the help and steel-trap mind of Heydrich, who was with him when Der Führer ordered that "Whatever we can find in the shape of an upper middle class in Poland is to be liquidated; should anything take its place, it will be placed under guard and done away with at an appropriate time."

Heydrich was made responsible for putting together a group of men from the Police and his own SD, men who could follow their orders and eliminate the intelligencia and the professionals, trouble-making priests, and anyone else who could continue to oppose the will of the Reich after the conquest.

In one last effort to give his Aryan brothers a reason not to stab him in the back and to convince his countrymen that he had no choice but to launch an attack, he instructed Himmler and Heydrich to create a series of border incidents with the Poles sufficient enough to cause the appropriate response.

War was inevitable. And it was going to break out over a piece of land that had once been lived in by a lot of Germans but was now mostly full of Jews and Poles, and many people had been telling the world it was going to happen ever since it was created by the pencil drawers on the maps in Versailles in 1919.

ReichsFührer Himmler was surprised but pleased when General Halder, the Chief of the Wehrmacht General Staff, did not ask any questions but delivered the dozen uniforms of the Polish Army, and SS-SturmbannFührer Alfred Naujocks preceded with the 'action' called 'Canned Goods.'

Hobein was in charge of the detachment of SD operatives that brought the dozen prisoners from Oranienburg, the first concentration camp established by the SS, to a wooded area just outside Hochlinde and had them dress in these uniforms. When one of the SD men pointed out that all of the uniforms were of the same size and none of the prisoners were, Hobein began to wonder if it would make any difference that a man's trouser was too short but shrugged it off. He ordered his men to proceed, and the prisoners struggled into their ill-fitting clothes. When they were correctly attired, they were told they were being vaccinated, and the pilocarpin injections soon stopped all of their hearts.

The dead men were loaded onto a Polish Army truck and taken to the outskirts of Gleiwitz, where they were carried inside the radio station and laid about the transmitting room and on the grounds in front of the door.

A Polish-speaking SD man took over the microphone from the usual speaker who had been placed in his position months earlier but who was an SS man and knew to return to Berlin and await further orders. The airways soon came alive with the voice of a raging German yelling in Polish, stating that he was in the vanguard of the Polish invasion force and he was screaming that now was the time for people who were opposed to the Nazis to take to the streets and bring the government down.

As Hobein listened to the man rant and rave, he realized that he was a professional actor, and as the man's face turned red and the spittle flew from his mouth as he got into his role, Hobein had the fleeting thought that the Germans in the vicinity of the broadcast would surely believe it, but he doubted if the English and the French would ever even hear it. He signaled his men and the room was filled with small arms fire, and the now dead prisoners received gunshot wounds to show they were killed trying to defend the station. The incident was over.

Dead German men dressed in ill-fitting Polish Army uniforms were shot by SD men dressed in the uniform of the border police, and all of the pretexts were satisfied.

Der Führer told his people that the Poles had invaded them.

First over the borders were the long-range bombers, the Junkers-88s and the Heinkels, their targets the railroad junctions and all the embarkation and forming spots of the Polish Armies that had yet to mobilize because their allies, the French and the English had urged them to do nothing to antagonize Hitler, so the reserves, the backbone of the army, kept getting bombed and strafed whenever they concentrated. Their planes, mostly outdated and under-armed, fought well over the first week as they were fast enough to take the slow, lumbering bombers, but as soon as the Messerschmitt 109 showed up, they were dead. Germany gained air superiority very quickly and the Polish cities were open for bombing.

The motorized armies crossed the frontier in three different places and headed in seven different directions. The German Army rolled over the resistance but did not challenge the Polish Army, but encircled it and isolated it into pockets of resistance that did not stand long against the German infantry and artillery and the tanks that blasted them into submission.

The Poles had known they were never going to contain the Germans on the plain, and they tried to fall back to defend the east bank of their rivers just as they had planned, but the roads were soon choked with the streaming peasants and people who rushed eastward in an attempt to evade the advancing Germans. The Polish Army could not move along the few roads, and the weather remained 'Hitler weather' because it did not rain when usually the heavens would turn the roads to a quagmire, but remained clear blue sky overhead that only let you spy the Stuka from a long way off before you heard the scream of this devil plane that made many a man shit his pants as the siren made a man feel that the bomb was going to fall right on top of his head.

On September 3rd, after two days of demanding that the Germans stop their assault, the English declared war on Germany which was soon followed later that day by the French.

World War II was underway.

Some of the Polish Army managed to fall back to begin to form a defensive line on the east side of the Bug, Vistula and Narew Rivers, narrow bands of water that just might let them regroup in enough concentrations to stop the Germans. The war was reported in the newspapers around the world as going, if not well for the Poles, was at least becoming a stabilized line that would allow the English and the French enough time to open the other front against the Germans. But the Polish cities were being bombed by the Luftwaffe, and the only Germans to really suffer or take casualties in the fighting were the Germans who had lived in the lands for hundreds of years, and they were felled upon by their Polish neighbors as soon as the Germans had crossed the border. Five thousand of these Germans living under the flag of the Pole, felt the fatal club, pitchfork and rifle of the Pole, as they sought to punish the Germans living under their flag, in the country given to them by the line-drawers in Versailles.

Just when the Poles had managed to get its defensive set behind its rivers, just when the Germans were going to have to start to pay the consequence for their actions, just when the remnants of the Army began to turn its guns to the west, an event in the East erased any chance they had to continue fighting.

Stalin had at first assembled and reinforced his armies on the Polish border, telling the world that he was not going to allow the Germans to attack him like he had attacked the Pole, and when his forces were in position, he launched his attack on Poland on the 17th of September telling the world that he had to in order to protect the White Russian minorities that lived in Poland. The only way to do that was to take the eastern half of Poland while Germany took the western half. Of course, Hitler and Stalin had worked out all the details prior to the fighting, and Winston Churchill vilified the Germans but praised the Russians. He called Hitler a killer and Stalin, a savior, but they were both killing Poles and taking Polish territory.

By the first of October, Poland had ceased to exist, and the Canadians, Australians, New Zealanders, and all the people flying a flag with a part of the Union Jack on it declared war on Germany. Der Führer had hoped that England would have come to her senses and change her centuries-old policy of not allowing any one nation to become dominant in Europe.

Der Führer had guaranteed England her empire. Edward VIII had heard that message and had backed Hitler and was once photographed wearing the Swastika on his sleeve, but Churchill pressured him into abdicating the throne of England on the pretext that he wanted to marry a divorced American woman long after the fact that Henry VIII established that as King of England, he could marry anyone he chose, and divorce them just as easily.

The English Empire.

The largest empire that any Nation had ever acquired or ever hoped to acquire, and it was done by Anglos and Saxons living on an island in the North Atlantic, conquering and putting their flag over thirteen million square miles of territory scattered throughout and covering almost twenty-five percent the globe, with Ben Johnson stating in the late nineteenth century that the 'sun never sat on the British Empire,' and over five hundred million people paid homage to the King or Queen of England.

Der Führer recognized only an Aryan race could achieve such conquests, and he admired the English, that blend of Germanic Anglo-Saxon people. He begrudgingly realized that the French had achieved masterly over four million square miles of the planet and ruled over one hundred million people and they were of the Germanic Franks. Surely, these Aryan brothers should realize that if they warred on one another, then only the Slavs would gain. That only the Communists would eventually prevail. That the Jew would win.

For now, however, the point was mute. His Aryan cousins had declared war on him. He would deal with them in good time. Now, he must endeavor to begin shaping the Germanic Empire in the East. In October, he appointed his ReichsFührer as Reich Commissariat for the Strengthening of German Nationhood after reading Himmler's "Some Thoughts on the Treatment of Foreign Populations in the East."

The first thing was to incorporate into the Reich those areas that had been part of the Reich before the Treaty. What once was Germany was Germany again. The rest of the conquered lands left after Russia took everything east of the Bug, was placed under the control of the politician Hans Frank and was termed the Government General.

The land that had once been populated by Germans was now infested with Jews and Slavic Poles who were rounded up out of their homes and sent to the Government General, which, throughout the winter, had to contend with the migration of almost five hundred and fifty thousand Jews and over three hundred thousand Poles who were living on German land and they were driven from their homes and herded into the central portion of Poland. Many of them were taken in the other direction to form working parties. From the occupied part that was now under the control of Russia, over 134,000 Volksdeutsch, ethnic Germans, were herded westward as Hitler wanted his people, and Stalin was more than willing to rid the Soviets of these Germans. From Lithuania came another 100,000 Germans as the Red Flag flapping there meant that more confused and upset people marched under makeshift signs welcoming them home to the Reich, and they were shown the way to their new homes, for the most part, furnished, or they were interned in camps waiting to be inspected by a racial examiner who could send you on down into the Government General were things were becoming crowded, and they did not give you a farm like they promised.

The 'Corridor' lands were in a state of turmoil. On paper, it was very simple. Germanic people living in parts of Poland and the Baltic States were to be incorporated into the Reich. If they had blond hair and blue eyes, they would be considered Aryan and could be re-'Germanized.' Slavic-looking Poles were to be shoved into the Government-General and reduced to a nation of helots, neither learning to read nor count past five hundred, but merely serve their new Masters by performing the drudgery of tasks. They were to once again pull the plows. They were to continue to be treated like Poliane.

The Jews were to be treated differently. They were to be concentrated in Ghettos with the largest to be in Warsaw. In the memorandum still circulating in the higher offices of the Reich, there was talk of transplanting them to a suitable country, say the island of Madagascar, which the Poles themselves had looked at some years earlier and had come to the conclusion that the island was not large enough to contain the three million Jews that lived under their flag of Poland.

Of course, the SS in the form of the Eisatzgruppe was responsible for rousting the people from their beds and ordering them to begin the march to the south and east, and it did not matter that it was the dead of winter and many of them froze to death as they were thrown out into the elements and ordered to do nothing more than leave and to go in that direction, and if they protested or resisted they were shot. The Germans left no doubt of who was in control.

Josef Mengele sat behind a small wooden desk in an unheated room in an old school house on the outskirts of Possen and tried to put at ease the old couple that sat across from him. They were born not twenty miles east of here, and they had grown up on the fringes of neighboring villages. They spoke nothing but German, and they had refused to leave when the Pole and the Jew moved in to take the land next to you and tried to strangle them off of the ground, but they would not yield and move back into Germany, and now Germany had moved back into their lands. They were proud and sat straight in their chairs, their bodies tightly closed, not in fear but in unity, and they were proud to be German. And Mengele had to agree.

After a few questions, he told them that they were the type of people that the Reich needed, especially after they had told him they had nine children. He stamped their papers and signed his names to the forms they presented him and they were escorted from the building and were free to walk back to their farms. They were proven to be German, and they could remain.

Verschurer had not liked it one bit, but concealed it well and the militia of the <u>Volksdeutsch</u> that Himmler had incorporated under the jurisdiction of the SS. They had told the Polish Army officers in their surrender terms that the populations would be treated fairly, and here, these men were hauling them off by the truckloads and shooting them by firing squads. Blakowitz clamored the High Command with evidence showing that wholesale murder was taking place and it must be stopped at once, and that was the cry of the officers of the Wehrmacht.

Both the Wehrmacht and the SS were relieved when Der Führer ordered the army back into the Reich to prepare for the upcoming showdown with the West, in a war with the West, a war that was being called the 'phoney war' because serious hostilities had yet to take place.

Mengele was getting bored with his duties and was rescued with orders to proceed to Cracow and make up a special assignment requested by the ReichsFührer himself. Mengele was thrilled that his reputation of a certain expertise was the reason for his transfer. He had become nothing more than a rubber stamp as the people he inspected had come with two hundred relatives attesting to their genealogy. To declare one of them suspect was to declare all of them suspect, and the Reich needed people. His instructions were to find the good blood, to recognize it in all the faces of the people who lived on the land.

He was tired of sitting at this small desk on the rapidly growing cold plains and looking at a stock of people who had already weeded out anyone of questionable blood. He was thankful when his orders came.

IX

Mengele had the window down and was resting his elbow on the metal sill of the train as it backed underneath the massive arched steel and glass dome of the Krakow station in the southern end of the Government-General of Poland. Dirty light filtered through the debris and bird nests accumulated atop the wire-reinforced glass canopy. The train came to a full stop in a final snort of steam billowing out of the bowels of the tired six-ton iron engine, and everything was quiet and still for that second or two interval when everyone was trying to figure out if they had stopped or not, and then the doors of the cars slid open. Men in the uniforms of the German Police and the German Army and the German Administrators of the Nazi Party, a sea of brown and gray and black who now ruled here, piled off of the train. They were joined by a few men dressed in business suits, a couple of workmen, but hardly any women or children.

As he made his way down the concrete platform, Mengele could feel in his own heels that special click of manhood, the step of the conqueror. He could see the same stride in the men who joined him as they spilled into the one-hundred-year-old edifice and walked across its marbled floors to come out into the Polish 'swine' sunny winter day.

The city's structures had been untouched by the war. Unlike Warsaw, which nobly defended itself, took a terrible pounding, suffered many dead, only to then surrender. The leadership of Krakow were students of history, and their city had been conquered over the past few hundred years, even when they resisted the Austrians, Mongols, Swedes, Russians, Lithuanians, Hungarians, Bohemians, Turks and Romanians. They had learned not to defend their city. They had raised the white flag of surrender as soon as the Germans showed up, and they felt that they still had their city, and they did not care whose flag it was presently flying.

The people of Krakow had learned that you preserve your city by allowing the conqueror to move in and make himself at home. He would stay at the most for a few hundred years, but usually, it was just for a few years, and other forces would drive them out, and you would still have your city. When you are a city in the middle of a plain, or at the foot of mountains like Krakow, you eventually learn to fly the white flag; or you learn like Warsaw that now the conqueror can even drop bombs on you out of the sky and they can destroy the places that you live and the places where you work and the places were you bought your food, and it does not matter, they end up fucking your wives and daughters anyway, so you might as well preserve your buildings by waving the white flag, because, after all, your grandpas built them.

Krakow had learned how to preserve itself as a city.

Mengele pulled the collar of his overcoat tighter as he felt the cold winter air. He crossed the plaza that had only the ghosts of the food vendors that used to inhabit this pavilion leading to the boulevard that ran into the heart of the city. He stopped at the edge of the sidewalk and looked down the line of awaiting taxis. He started in their direction.

"Heil Hitler! Herr Doktor," Hobein said, coming up behind him.

"Heil Hitler! ObersturmbannFührer Hobein." Mengele greeted, turning to find his old comrade, acknowledging his promotion. He saw that Hobein was wearing the SD on his sleeve. He had joined Heydrich just as he said that he would.

"It is good to see you, Hobein."

"What brings you to the Government-General, Mengele?"

"Is that the policeman in you inquiring?"

Hobein smiled. "I'm not sure. But I do not think so. But come along. I have a car."

He picked up one of Mengele's bags and headed to a Czechoslovakian Tartras sedan that was waiting by the curb. A short almost chubby soft looking sergeant stood beside it.

Mengele loaded his remaining possessions and trailed after Hobein. They sat his bags by the trunk, where they were stowed by the methodically moving sergeant. Mengele followed Hobein into the back seat of the big sedan. It had been a long time since he had been in a car built by the Czechs. He was impressed by the coachwork and the attention to detail as they stitched together the interior. They paid the same attention to detail.

When they were building weapons, and now they were building them for the Reich from their Skoda plant in Bohemia, the second largest heavy steel and munitions facility in Europe, second only to the Krupp works at Essen. The Czechs were craftsmen.

"I'm billeted in the Grand," Mengele said.

"I think you will find the accommodations to your liking, but the atmosphere a little chilly."

"What do you mean?" Mengele asked.

"The hotel is full of Wehrmacht officers. You will not be greeted with any respect from them."

"And why not?"

"Because you are SS," Hobein explained.

"You mean they dislike us as always? I know they tried to have our armed units disbanded because they supposedly took needless causalities. Instead, Der Führer authorized a slight increase in our numbers and an upgrade in our equipment. I hear we are getting panzers."

"No. They like us a lot less. And it is not because SS units showed more spark than the Wehrmacht units." Hobein wished he had been with one of those fighting units of the SS.

"What has been going on, Hobein?" Mengele demanded to know, feeling that Hobein was content to talk around the edges of what was on his mind.

Hobein looked at Mengele. "The order from the ReichsFührer and GruppenFührer Heydrich was they were to go about their duties in complete secrecy, leave their work at work, and not talk about it. Hobein did not want the order to include proven men of National Socialist beliefs like Mengele, not even stopping to think that so far, all Mengele had done was talk about being a National Socialist.

"It was really a work of art, Herr Doktor," he began, speaking quickly. "We followed the infantry. They did not even know we were there. We worked from prepared lists giving us the names, addresses, and members of the household. They were political leaders, troublesome priests, teachers and university professors. I remember one industrialist living in a palace, an architect, and more than a few engineers."

"And?"

"And we found them. And we lined them up. And we shot them." Hobein said calmly, both men hearing the confession in his voice.

"Who did? Who is 'we'?" Mengele wanted complete clarification. He wanted to be able to someday tell Verschuer exactly how it had all taken place in the East.

"The <u>Einsatzgruppe</u>, of course. Policemen and other SS men throughout the branches, assembled together to carry out the orders of Der Führer, as directed by the ReichsFührer and GruppenFührer Heydrich."

"There were <u>Einsatzgruppe</u> in Possen, Ulrich." Mengele said. "I was convinced that they were just shooting partisans."

"That is what we say here in the Government-General. But we are given our orders and our lists, and we go to work daily. The Wehrmacht thinks we are over-zealous in our duties, and now, with the enemy militarily defeated, they have more time to protest and interfere with our carrying out our orders."

"I can tell you that the Wehrmacht, in Possen, was enraged over the way the militia attacked their once Polish neighbors in the new Gaus," Mengele said, referring to the areas once again incorporated into the Reich.

"Believe me. We do not have the luxury of a hostile militia in this area to keep the Wehrmacht busy. The Polish 'swine' of Krakow go out of their way to ingrate themselves with the Wehrmacht."

"How extensive are the actions that you are talking about?"

"I do not know the exact number, but I can tell you that I heard GruppenFührer Heydrich say at a dinner on September 29th, that only three percent of that class of people in Poland remained that could do harm to the Reich."

"And the Jew?" Mengele asked.

"For the most part, herded into the ghettos of the larger cities. But, if we can catch a small enough group of them away from everyone, we treat them like 'Polish intelligentsia.' I would say that would be standard procedure throughout the conquered territories. Of course, they are always proven partisans."

Mengele looked at his friend. There was a glaze over the light blue eyes, but other than that, his face was relaxed and sure of himself as ever. Mengele wondered if Verschuer was aware of the strength of the conviction of Der Führer and the ReichsFührer and of the men in the field who were carrying out their orders to kill people who were not under arms. It was permissible to kill Jews, if it could be done without raising a cry loud enough that the Jews in New York heard it. The Swedes had big ears, and they could not keep their noses out of inquiring about the civilian populations in the conquered lands. The Germans did not want to enrage London, even if they were at war with them, and they did not want to enrage New York and bring them into the war.

The heavy auto turned onto Florianska Street and drove into Market Square, dominated by Cloth Hall, a huge rectangular building constructed in the Thirteenth Century for the purpose of weaving, dyeing, and trading textiles. Soon after its construction, Armenian rug merchants moved in and assured its success. It had originally been built for pure function, but fire and fate had given it the opportunity to be resurrected by an Italian architect, who adored it with the appropriate filigree and gargoyles.

They passed the Church of Panna Marja. The structure sat at a slight angle to everything else in the square, creating pie-shaped yards on each side of the largest cathedral of the city, with two spires of unequal height, topped with different capitals, testifying to the fact that the Poles could not agree on anything amongst themselves, even when they were simply building a church.

The car came to a stop in front of one of the many doorways surrounding the Market. Mengele looked out the window and did not see any hotel.

"That door there," Hobein informed him, pointing to one guarded by SS sentries, "is your new office. Or at least that is the headquarters for the Reich Race and Resettlement Office, which I assume you have been ordered to. Do not worry. We will take your bags on to the hotel."

"You really are the policeman, Hobein," Mengele complimented him. "This simplifies everything for me."

"I will be having dinner at the hotel around seven. It is that building to the right of where we came into the plaza. It is a five-minute walk from here. I hope that you can join me."

"I will try."

They heiled each other.

Mengele got out of the car, which quickly sped off, Sergeant Schultz not one to linger. He turned and crossed the walk to where one cold, bored SS man examined his identification and nodded for the other man to open the door. Everyone heiled each other.

The narrow lobby smelled mostly of old cigar leftovers from when the Austrian General Staff had occupied the building, just over twenty years ago. From the way it was laid out, with a narrow lobby and wide steps along the left wall leading up, made Mengele think that, at one time, it had to have been a residential hotel.

The place was crowded with SS men standing in small groups, whispering to each other as they waited to see the officials who had offices there. Two Gestapo agents positioned themselves in opposite corners, one standing with his hands casually behind his back, the other sitting and reading a newspaper. As if in isolation, in one corner were three women, dressed in brown and looking dark, stern, and foreboding. Everyone else in the room seemed intent on not looking their way, and after just a glance, Mengele's eyes moved on as if eye contact with one of them could turn a man to stone. There were a few Poles, most of them seemingly young married couples, and Mengele was struck by how fair they all seemed as they sat sullen and quietly together in a half dozen chairs.

He went up to the clerk who was sitting with his back to the wall and facing the room. They exchanged the half-salute heils to Der Führer, suitable for use indoors.

"Doktor Josef Mengele reporting to ObersturmbannFührer Ludwig Effenhauser."

"Very good, Doktor," the man said, immediately getting to his feet and motioning for Mengele to follow. They crossed the room and up the stairs. Mengele could feel the softness in the steps as he followed the clerk up the long, straight flight to the second story, passing SS men to the outside on their way down. The upper floor was full of men in uniform who paid him and his guide no attention as they wove their way around them and down a long hall. They came to a stop at a thick wooden door with a top panel of obscure glass.

The clerk knocked loudly and, without waiting for an answer, opened it, stuck his head in and announced that UnterstrumbannFührer Doktor Josef Mengele had arrived and had been shown directly up, just as he had been ordered, as if to remind the StandartenFührer of his own orders.

"Heil Hitler!" Mengele said, stepping into the room with the clerk closing the door behind him.

"Heil Hitler!"

Ludwig Effenhauser seemed a man unfettered by the tidal wave of people that swirled around him. He had a wide forehead and a long, straight jawline that blocked off his face, which gave him the appearance of a man not being easily moved. His eyebrows were very dark over dark brown eyes, almost black eyes, and they held not a hint of apology for their color. He had been born on a farm outside Munich, and he had enlisted in the SS even before Heinrich Himmler, but he proved his blood pure in a genealogical tree that got lost after a few hundred years, attesting that he had nothing but Germanic blood. He had never flinched from any of his duties, nor had he ever failed to live up to the assignments given him. He had many years of practice of not letting his feelings show on his face, but he wondered if maybe being the head man of the Reich Race and Resettlement Office in Krakow was going to be the first position that he had ever failed at and everyone would be able to read it in his eyes. Either the task was too immense, or the leadership was lacking, but for now, he was going nowhere in concluding his objectives. He was not sure that he understood his orders, and he had asked the ReichsFührer for some specialists to implement his new orders, and Mengele was the first of them to arrive.

"Welcome to Krakow, Herr Doktor."

"Thank you, Herr StandartenFührer."

"It is a mad house out there?"

"So it seems, Herr StandartenFührer."

"Just like all of Poland, is it not?" Effenhauser asked, hopefully.

"I have not seen very many calm spots," Mengele reassured him.

"Come on. Let's get some fresh air," the senior man ordered, putting on his coat and peaked cap, picking up a folder and leading the way out the back door of his office and up three flights of narrow dusty steps and crossing the floored attic space to open a narrow set of French doors. They stepped out onto the porch of a dormer built into the high pitch of the gabled roof. The air was chilly and full of the smell of sulfur as coal from upper Silesia heated the city. They were on the backside of the building, and they looked down on the row of wood-fenced bleak gardens that were behind each of the structures that lined the narrow alley. They had to look up to see the Wawel, a sprawling magnificent castle built on a knoll overlooking the strategic point where the Vistula becomes navigable as the waters pour from the Carpathians. It was the home and the burial place of the Polish kings for centuries, and it too was untouched by the bombs of this the latest war that flowed over it and around it, but not directly on top of it.

"What do you think, Herr Doktor?" Effenhauser asked, offering the panorama as if it were a painting in his own private collection.

"Very impressive," Mengele commented.

"The only good thing I can find that I like about Krakow," the older man said sadly, "is this view." He opened the briefcase and handed Mengele a leather folder that was only a few pages thick. It did not take Mengele long to read the contents, and then, with a nod, he handed the papers back to Effenhauser's outstretched hands.

"Do you understand what we are being ordered to do, Herr Doktor?"

"I understand the orders, Herr StandartenFührer," Mengele replied.

"Good!" Effenhauser snapped, in a voice that established whose opinion really was important in this matter. "From what I can fathom from all this, the Polish 'swine' are to be grouped into four major classifications. Racial Germans who have been living in Poland for over a year and who aid us in curtailing any resistance. Meaning that the Germans wanted to pick-ax every person with a Polish name, and they could not care less how long they had lived together as neighbors. They are to be considered German and we do not have to do anything to encourage them to be any more German than they already are, for that I can attest to personally.

"Then there are the passive racial Germans who think they are Poles, but we judge could be easily Germanized, but they have to have a fifty percent working knowledge of our language. Does that mean they can count to ten in twos in German?

"Persons of doubtful German origins,' he continued with disgust, "and believe it when I tell you that this Slavic spittle will lie through their Polish "swine" teeth attesting that they have a lot of German relatives if they think there is something to gain by it, and when we implement these orders we are going to attest that there is something to be gained in being German! And last, and there are quite a few of them, I am ashamed to say, is the German element living in Poland who refuse to accept National Socialism. They are to be treated the same as Polish 'swine,' which is what is left of them after we comb out the good blood. Is that correct?"

"That is how I understand it." Mengele immediately replied.

"Then part of my orders is to find German blood flowing in Polish veins!" He bemoaned.

Mengele was struck silent. He had not expected to be held accountable for the orders of the ReichsFührer or to explain the reasons behind them, especially to his superior officer.

He had some of the answers, though. "StandartenFührer, there are a lot of people who have lived here for centuries who are actually "Polandized" Germans. The orders are simply to find German blood by looking for its outward appearance. For example, in the lobby of this very building, there are six young Poles who seem to have characteristics of a good race.

"You mean they have blond hair and blue eyes?"

Mengele did not hesitate. "That is one of the easier recognizable genetic characteristics that make for a good German," Mengele explained. "Of course, there are the Slavic blue eyes, which means we have to be very careful in our selections."

"Neither you, me, nor the ReichsFührer fit that physical description, Herr Doktor. Neither do most of the men under my command. Nor do the majority of the police, and we in this office, have to rely on the police officials to enforce our decisions. Most of them will not understand that now Polish 'swine' who look like they could be Germans are to be transformed into Germans, in fact, exalted, if the color of their eyes is blue and they have blond hair. Most of the police that I know are not going to readily grasp the concept, Herr Doktor, that you can make Germans out of Poles! I know that I have a problem with it!"

He looked at the paling face of the young doctor and decided to take him off the hook, knowing that the man's workload was going to be tremendous, and he did not need to be hampered about questioning the loyalty of his own commanding officer.

"Relax, Herr Doktor," he ordered. "I voiced the same concerns to the ReichsFührer, and he responded by telling me that he would be sending me professionals who would know how to interpret and implement the orders. He would be sending people who could help me find the German blood flowing in Polish veins."

"I will be able to do that, StandartenFührer," Mengele assured him, relieved about his commander's loyalty.

"Then start by delivering me an outline of how we are to begin," Effenhauser ordered. "I want it on my desk by nine hundred hours. The clerk in charge will find you a desk to work from. You are dismissed."

Effenhauser wanted some time alone on top of his building with his view of the Wawel.

Mengele complied with his orders. An organizational chart and plan for implementation were placed on the desk of StandartenFührer Effenhauser by the clerk before Mengele left the building later that same evening. It was only a short walk to the hotel through the almost empty streets, where he found his room to be spacious and just down the hall from the lavatory.

He entered the dining room just after seven. The place was lit by Italian chandeliers new enough to be electrified porcelain fixtures that brought you light in a wrap of flowers and cherubs, but it did not soften the severity of all the tables being taken by men in uniforms. Polish waiters danced around the tables, serving the Germans a variety of foods wheeled to their tables and under glass.

He finally spied Hobein, sitting with two other SD men against the outside wall. He nodded at a few of the officers as he made his way towards his friend's table only to be, for the most part, ignored. Only other SS men recognized his nods. Mengele stopped behind the one empty chair at the table for four.

"Heil Hitler!"

"Heil Hitler! Mengele. Good to see you that you could join us," Hobein said, indicating that he should sit down.

"You remember Schultz, do you **not?"**

"How are you this evening, UnterscharFührer?" Mengele asked the non-corn, who merely nodded in reply and did not stop picking his duck apart with his fingers and shoving the pieces of dark fowl into his small mouth and munching away. Mengele wondered if there was anything between the ears of the oval-faced Bavarian with the sad dropping eyelids and listless brown eyes, short thick mustache cut off sharp Der Führer style.

Hobein introduced the other man as Erick Aretin, a man newly promoted and put in command of a sonderkommando of his own. He was stationed to the west of here and was glad to be in the city enjoying civilization.

"Herr Doktor. Good to meet you." Aretin acknowledged Mengele in a formal but friendly manner.

A Polish waiter, a Krakow native, appeared immediately by Mengele's side. He sat the knives and forks and spoons in the proper positions, handed Mengele the menu on a large white card, and was surprised when he ordered mineral water. SS men were usually big drinkers.

As the waiter moved off, Mengele felt the presence of someone else. He looked up to see a Wehrmacht Major standing there, holding his gloves before him and looking angrily across the table at Hobein. He was red in the face and still dressed in his field uniform, and the veins in his forehead throbbed out in anger.

"You SS men are not going to get by with it this time!" He spat, shaking his gloves over the table.

Schultz just glanced at the movement and continued to chew. Aretin sat silent and staring, his eyes filled with anger as he glared at the intruder. He did not get into the city very often, and it was a real treat to dine at the Grand and now here was a Wehrmacht officer interrupting dinner, the mark of a truly uncivilized man. Mengele thought that Hobein had been understating how much animosity the Wehrmacht had for the SS. They all waited for Hobein to handle the situation.

"We SS men do not have to 'get by' with anything, ever," Hobein said calmly, his wrists at the edge of the table, his hands holding a knife and a fork pointing at the Major.

"Well, you left some witnesses this time!" The Major gloated.

"Major. We leave witnesses all the time. I do not know, nor do I care to, what particular incident you are referring to. If you think we have left someone alive, or if you know someone that we tried to shoot, and they are out talking about it, then I would like to know their names and their present location. They are an enemy of the Reich and must be dealt with, and that means we need to take another shot at them."

"These were innocent people that you slaughtered today! This is going in the report to General Blaskowitz. He is compiling the charges that are going to be placed against you and your kind!"

Hobein's face remained unchanged. "Please calm down, Herr Major," he soothed, "I can assure you that I was going about my duties for the Reich, and I quote from my orders, suppressing all anti-Reich and anti-German elements in the rear of the fighting troops, in particular counter-espionage, arrest of politically reliable persons, confiscation of weapons, safeguarding important counter-espionage activities...

"I have heard enough of this rubbish. So has the rest of the Army." The Major warned.

"I would hope that the army would learn to do its job and quit interfering with the police who are doing their jobs!" Hobein stormed, his voice rising to the point that now not only the tables closest to them were following the confrontation, but the whole room was alerted to their heated exchange. A Gestapo agent looked on in curiosity. A Major-General of Artillery was halfway through his duck, pulling the pieces of meat from the bones with the tiny forks provided when he turned to see the commotion, and the meaning of the last words he heard sunk in, and he knew what they must be arguing about and he went back to his delicious duck.

The Wehrmacht Major narrowed his eyelids and started to lean over the table and put his face in Hobein's, then thought the better of it. He pointed his finger at Hobein instead. "I promise you that one day you will be held accountable!"

He turned on his heel and marched indignantly through the door and out of sight. The clink of silverware began again.

Mengele snapped his white napkin free and floated it to his lap. "Friend of yours, Hobein?"

Aretin laughed. He liked Mengele already. Schultz even grunted.

"I told you they would not be cordial, Mengele," Hobein said, "but they are not usually as vocal as that."

"We need someone to stand up for us," Aretin complained.

"Those pompous holier-than-thou Wehrmacht officers had better learn that we are doing nothing but carrying out the wishes of Der Führer. They should be smart enough to realize that we are not carrying out these actions on our own," Hobein said.

"Sometimes I think they live in a dream world. Have not any of them read Mein Kampf?" Mengele wondered.

"I hear that the ReichsFührer and GruppenFührer Heydrich are treated coolly by the Wehrmacht high brass anytime they meet. It has become so bad that I understand that the ReichsFührer is going to conduct some high-level meetings with Wehrmacht officers and set them straight on our duties," Aretin added hopefully.

"I wish they would hurry up. Our job is difficult enough without being treated with contempt by our own countrymen." Hobein started to eat again. "Part of the problem could be solved if we knew who was really in charge here in the Government-General."

"What do you mean?" Mengele asked.

"Technically, the Government-General is still under Military Armies East and under the command of Major-General Blaskowitz stationed in Warsaw. It is also under the control of Hans Frank as Governor-General. Frank is already trying to stop the further dumping of Jews here in the Government-General. He argues that they will never be able to stabilize the area and turn it into anything productive for the Reich if it is to nothing but a rubbish heap for the rest of Europe's Jews."

"Where does he expect the Jews to be sent?" Aretin asked.

"To Palestine or Madagascar," Hobein answered.

"They have been talking about that for years," Mengele said. "I think there are too many Jews in Europe for those two areas to absorb. The Governor-General had better get used to the idea of housing the Jews. I do not see any alternatives. They must leave the Reich; that is the only thing that is for certain. They are a diseased organism that must be dissected from the blood of the Volk."

"I love to hear you doktors talk," Aretin said, winking at Hobein.

"We offer another alternative," Hobein said softly, pointing with his index and then flexing it like he was pulling a trigger.

Everyone knew what he was talking about. Aretin was the first to speak.

"There are millions of Jews. We can not carry out a 'special treatment' on all of them, especially if it is to be kept quiet," he argued. He could not help but think back to the first of September when it was still hot in Poland, and they had taken a group of Jews into the woods away from the eyes of witnesses, and they had shot and killed them and thrown them into a ditch. He remembered most of the flies that were thick and noisy as they descended on the dead, and he had wondered if flies could hear gunshots. He had heard that sharks in the ocean knew explosions meant food in the water, and he had wondered if the flies knew that gunshots meant meat for them. He had come into the war as an enlisted man and he had many people in front of his sights during the first month of hostilities. He was glad these killings were coming to a close. He did not mind going out a couple of times a day and ordering a firing squad up where they had ten men to shoot one person. He did not want to go back to where he was the sole gunman responsible for putting a bullet into ten people.

"Well, I can tell you one thing," he stated emphatically, "you can not shoot them all."

X

Sigismund Sosnowski was a wiry, strong little lad with a daredevil attitude. He had just turned six, but when it came to climbing, anything he could get a toe or hand hold on was scaled. Or he would jump up to grab something to seek an advantage, and he thought perpetual motion and being in a deep, restful sleep, dreaming of high adventure and heroic deeds, were the only things in existence. Other than, of course, his mother, who was so beautiful and always smelled so good and always hugged him so tightly. Then there were his grandmas and grandpas that he shared with his cousins, but he still cried when he remembered the tall, thin, jovial man with a large waxed mustache, who would tickle him along his ribs as he twirled him about as they laughed and laughed.

The day had come when his father put on the uniform, like all the other children's fathers did on occasion, and they went off together like they sometimes did, but this time he did not come back. He had heard all the adults say it was war. War was the time when your fathers put on their uniforms, and they went off, and they were killed and buried or marched off to the west or to the east, but they did not ever come back.

Men in other uniforms speaking a strange language moved in, and they were the Germans, the Hitlerites, and everyone was afraid of them. They had already killed thousands, and they would not hesitate to kill you, so you had better stay away from them on the streets, or they just might decide to kill one more, right now.

Now, when he and his mother were out in public, he was always tucked tightly beside her where she demanded that he stay. She had heard rumors that the Hitlerites were stealing children. They had been along the shops of the street in search of food, and immediately after getting enough for the evening meal; bread, turnips, and a tiny piece of sausage, they started home, hugging the edges of the buildings to be out of the way of the chilly spring wind.

He saw her before she saw him, and he managed to squirm almost inside his mother's full pleated skirt. He tried not to peep out at this apparition hovering in the doorway across the street. She was dressed in a brown smock, gray apron and white starched scarf folded in shape on top of her head, and ankle-high heavy laced shoes as if to give her the appearance of being a nun of some unknown order of the Church. Her face was as mean as any hawk that he could imagine, and his eyes were wide open in fear as he had hidden his face. He did not want to take a second look, but he could not help himself, and she spied his bright blue eyes, peering fearfully from behind his mother's skirt as they were scurrying home.

She had just caught a glimpse of the boy, but even with the hat covering all of his head and the ear flaps down and buttoned under his little chin, she had a hunch that he would be fair-headed. The mother and child moved quickly down the street, the mother not yet alerted to being observed. The German woman now could see the youngster's legs, and he was almost running in keeping up with the mother's long stride and she was satisfied that the child was not deformed and in good health.

Gertrude Langefeldt stayed on the opposite side of the street, knowing how to keep them in sight without spooking them as she followed them down the rest of that long block past the doors of the closing shops. They turned at the first intersection, and before long, they came to a row of brick townhouses where the Poles climbed a set of stone steps and disappeared inside. The sidewalks in front of these houses were extra wide, providing a place where children could play right out in front of their homes, and neighbors could stroll in the evenings and exchange greetings and talk about worldly and family events.

She strode by, checking the number on the building, and when she reached the corner, she penciled the address down in her book. She now had over a dozen places listed where she knew a child of good blood resided. She was pleased with her day's work. She knew she had been right in staying in this upper-middle-class section of the city. True, there were fewer children residing here, and the mothers seemed to do a much tighter job of securing them, but she had not seen one Slavic-looking child in the entire neighborhood. All of the children that she had seen had eyes of gray to blue, and hair dark to light blond.

Children to please the heart of the ReichsFührer.

She had been in the city for a little over four months, and it was getting harder all of the time. The order was to procure children of good blood, remove them from the custody of their parents, send them north to Kalisz for further examination, and establish procedures for processing greater numbers of them. At Kalisz, the children would undergo a six-month indoctrination establishing Germanism in them before they were brought into the Reich. Infants and toddlers under five were to be given a complete physical and genetic examination. If they passed, they were to be sent directly to the Lebensborns, where they would be placed for immediate adoption.

During the first few months of the occupation, the entire responsibility was left to the police, which was like sending bombers after mice. The children learned to scamper and scurry to safety anytime they saw men dressed in the other uniforms. As the children disappeared from the view of the police, the demand for children grew inside the Reich by childless couples of means and childless couples of men of high SS rank, who needed a child for all the reasons a man and wife need a child, plus all of the political pressure put on by the ReichsFührer, who was constantly harping that all SS officers should have at least four children. Der Führer was even pinning medals on women who had children, and when they reached six, they were to be accorded the same military salutations as a field-marshal by all Hitler Youth. Motherhood was taken seriously by the Nazis.

The top Nazis who toured the lands and cities of Poland were in amazement at the amount of people of good blood who lived there. Hans Frank, the Governor-General, had even told Borman once, 'When I think that with those blue eyes and fair hair they talk Polish, it seems absolutely incredible.'

It was incredible that the Poles had defended western Europe against the invading hordes of the East for so many centuries, or at least since the Mongols had their way with the populations, when the land was replenished with the people of Germanic blood who proved their superiority by maintaining good genetic traits of Nordic appearance by keeping their wives and daughters from being raped by the men of the East. It was for a reason that the seat of the kings of Poland for so many centuries in Warsaw was called Saxon Palace.

All these 'Germanic' Poles must be identified and indoctrinated to being of good blood, and the ReichsFührer had vowed to take advantage of all people of good blood that he could discover. They were German in their heritage and they must become German again. They must not be left out of the Reich, or they would become the leadership of the rebellion.

Langefeldt had volunteered for duty in the GovernmentGeneral as soon as the notice went up in the rooming house in Essen that was occupied by women of the <u>Nationalsozialistische Volkswohlfahrt</u>, a welfare organization of the Party but now essentially under the 'request' of the ReichsFührer. Although the notice did not outline the details of the duty required, she had a pretty good idea of what was going on. A year earlier, she and a few others were serving coffee and rolls to men of the <u>Deutschland Division</u>, when they were visited and addressed by the ReichsFührer, who at first did not impress her. She was stirred by his words, however, at last coming to a complete understanding of the nature of the struggle.

In his speech the ReichsFührer had said, "All the good blood in the world, all the Germanic blood that is not on the German side, may one day be our ruin. Hence, every male of the best Germanic blood whom we bring to Germany and turn into a Teutonic-minded man means one more combatant on our side and one less on the other. I really intend to take German blood from wherever it is to be found in the world, to rob and steal it wherever I can."

So when the notice had gone up, she knew immediately that in the East, she could wear her uniform all of the time. She did not mind being referred to as a 'little brown sister.' She could have gone to work in one of the Lebensborns, but catering to spoiled pregnant young girls was not in her nature, nor had she ever heard of 'little brown sisters' moving into one of those nice big houses and playing maid and servant to a 'little blonde sister.'

It was growing dark, and the streets were almost empty before she gave up on finding any more children that day. She walked unafraid even though she was off of the thoroughfares and the Market Square, where the German patrols and police squads and teams of Gestapo were visibly present. She did not worry that some Pole would step out of an alley and bash her brains out. If she turned up missing, or if she was found dead, then reprisals would be taken by shooting ten Poles. She felt as safe as if she was in Berlin.

She reached the house on a bluff overlooking the Vistula that she and three other 'little brown sisters' shared. They had started out quartered in the Grand, but after a few weeks, they could no longer tolerate the friction that seemed to charge the air between the Wehrmacht and the SS. They had decided to move, and Sister Carmen lucked into finding this house built by a riverboat captain that was large enough for them not to get into each other's way and yet small enough for them to become a family.

The women had much in common. They were all close to forty, Carmen being the youngest, and none of them had ever been married. All of them had taken the ReichsFührer's and the Party leader's advice over the years by trying to become pregnant by a good German man, but they were all either not given enough opportunities, except for Carmen, to display their fertility, or they were all barren. None of them had ever been pregnant. Gertrude did not miss the sensual side of life, having never experienced it, and she turned a deaf ear to the moans and thrashing coming from Sister Carmen's room as she passed by on her way to her own room. She changed her shoes to house mules, the softness of the warm cotton on her feet feeling luxurious, and then back down the steps to the kitchen where the other two women were preparing dinner.

"Something smells very good," Gertrude said, resisting taking a peak under the sputtering lid of the large enameled cook pot tended by Ingrid. Hilda sat at the large wooden table full of index cards and a couple of sheets of typing paper full of names. Gertrude knew the women were inseparable, even working the streets together searching for children.

"We have a leg of lamb that has been stewing in potatoes and onions for the past two hours."' Ingrid said, lifting the lid with a pot holder and stirring the contents with a wooden ladle to help fill the kitchen with the aroma to heighten the appetite. She was a tall, thin rail of a woman with pronounced limbs and joints that poked out of her aproned brown-clothed bony frame. Her skin, however, was aglow with health. She was not the type of person usually found around food, but she was an excellent cook who loved to see people devour her endeavors. It was the only joy she had ever found in life. She had been the prime mover in getting the women out of the hotel into a house of their own with a kitchen.

"I guess you heard Sister Carmen," Hilda said, casting beady little gray eyes to the ceiling where they could faintly hear a low thumping reverberating through the old timbers. A wicked little grin formed on her fat face.

Gertrude was somewhat embarrassed. She did not want to talk about one sister when she was not there. She really did not want to talk about what Carmen was doing in her own bedroom, but Hilda was fascinated by the mere thought that just through a few walls and a ceiling, there was a man putting his penis into a vagina, and she wondered why she could not have a man inside of her, she wondered why she would never feel life grow inside of her.

Since Hilda had teamed up with the bone pile, Ingrid did nothing but steadily put weight on her already stocky frame, starting with wide shoulders going straight down to wide hips forming a solid block, with a fleshy face sporting a mole on her chin and a permanent scowl on her face all added to the severity of her looks. Her dark brown hair was thinning in the front and Gertrude could see the pink of the scalp from where she stood.

"Sister Hilda. Surely, you do not begrudge Carmen her attempts to mother a child for the Reich. The man with her is of good blood, is he not?" Gertrude asked and then realized that Carmen's appetite for men many times exceeded her judgment. "She is not with a Pole?" She asked, alarmed at the thought.

"It sounds like he has a pole!" Hilda gushed, causing Ingrid to crackle to the ceiling and Gertrude to stand uncertain, and then realized what Hilda was referring to and she still did not quite understand it.

"We have not yet got a look at this one," Ingrid explained, controlling her laughing when she saw that Gertrude was clearly embarrassed.

"I really can not see Carmen as a 'little blond sister,' Hilda continued. "Having to live with just other women would not do for her."

"I hear that when you are pregnant, you lose all your desire for a man." Ingrid mused. She stirred the vegetables around the darkening gray meat, and there was a parade of children in her mind that she never got to cook for.

Gertrude focused on the table in front of Hilda and grew concerned. If these two women had arrived home at least two hours ago, and Carmen had beat them home, then they all had to be in dereliction of their duty. They were not out in the streets long enough looking for that exceptional child, that perfectly formed blue-eyed blond-haired child for the Reich.

This was the time of the evening when the women compared and consolidated their information as to sightings and confirmed addresses and names, if possible, of suitable children for presentation to the RuSHA office on a daily basis. They liked to do it first thing in the morning.

"Here, I have Carmen's," Ingrid said, wiping her hands on her apron and reaching inside to pull out a few pieces of rolled-up papers and hand them over to Gertrude. "She left them on the table for us."

It was worse than Gertrude thought.

"There are only four places on this list." She announced, turning the paper sideways to read Carmen in both directions on the same scrap of paper. These must be her field notes because the ones she turned in were far more organized and much neater.

"How many did you two find today?" Gertrude asked, looking at the long list in front of Hilda, who shot a worried look to Ingrid whose eyes went to the ceiling once again as she turned around to the stove.

"Actually, Carmen did better than us," Hilda confessed.

"How many did you find?" Gertrude demanded, getting excited.

"One apiece. Two total!" Hilda answered in a very low voice.

Gertrude thought of the deriding statements she would be taking from the SS man in the morning. Since she had concentrated on true quality they now would be submitting only eighteen new names to the RuSHA office, when around fifty names was the norm. She was shocked into silence. She had not even realized that the women were disgruntled, and as a leader, she should have been aware that women under her charge were capable of simply not doing their duty that day and then not being remorseful.

"It is just that we see the same children day after day," Hilda complained. "We followed one for over a mile this morning, and when he got home, we realized we had already seen the child last week and had already reported him. What is the use of locating these children if we are going to allow them to remain where they are?"

Gertrude ignored her question and pointed to the list in front of Hilda. "Then what is that?"

Hilda scooped up the lists and handed them to her. "It is a list of children we have already turned in, but who we have seen in the past few days."

"You were planning on turning them in tomorrow?"

"Yes. At least that way, we will know if anyone is even paying any attention to what we are doing."

Gertrude sat down across from the woman, impressed with the maneuver. She was intent and content to pursue her original orders not questioning them, but she had to admit that she had felt the discouragement on tracking and finding one already listed. Maybe it would be to their advantage if they did call to light that the full implementation of the ReichsFührer's wishes were not being carried out. The police, all members of the RuSHA, were not doing their part.

"I have some names I can add to that list." She finally pronounced, causing the other two women to break into ugly smiles of relief.

The next morning, Langefeldt and her three companions marched past the statue of Ladislaus Jagiello, the Lithuanian who led the Poles against the Teutonic Knights and defeated them in 1410, past a white stucco house with triangular window mantels, the house where Goethe wrote that Faust lived, and through the plaza where Copernicus had walked with his teacher Ptolemy.

They swung in step through the doors of the RuSHA office, just like they had every morning for the past few months. They were the first ones to arrive, and the duty clerk, RottenFührer Orbright, stood up when they entered and 'heiled' them. He took their lists and was surprised to see over a couple of hundred addresses, some with names and even a brief genealogy.

"Thank you, Sisters. It seems that you had a good day," he said, reading the list with more attention. "Oh, I see. These children have already been recorded!" He looked up, demanding an answer.

"Yes, they have, RottenFührer," Langefeldt explained, "but all of these children were seen in the past few days. We felt it important to point out that someone is not keeping up with their duties."

"It is not us here at RuSHA, Sister." The RottenFührer countered. "We determine as much about the children you find as we possibly can, and we turn this information over to RuSHA on a daily basis."

"Then it is up to someone to point out to the police that they have to comply with the wishes of the ReichsFührer and bring these children in for evaluation."

The rest of the women stood resolute beside and behind her as they all faced off against the SS man.

"Sisters! Please!" The RottenFührer said, holding up his hand in surrender. "I am not arguing with you that there is not a problem. I am just trying to impress upon you that we are doing our best here at Race to comply with the ReichsFührer's wishes. We have no authority over the police. We can only depend on their cooperation." He wondered if she was allowed to talk to him like this but was stymied by what he could do about it. He wondered what he had done wrong in life that his position put him in a meeting with these ugly women so early in the morning, except the one with the short blond hair who was even quite pretty.

"Then get your men off of their asses and get these children into our hands!" Langefeldt ordered, earning her the immense respect and admiration of Sisters Hilda, Ingrid, and Carmen.

Orbright gulped. His stomach turned over. Come to think of it, he had not had any good duty since crossing the border, unlike most of his comrades who seemed to be thoroughly enjoying themselves in Poland.

"Sisters. Believe me. We will do the best we can." Orbright promised.

"If the best you can is leaving these children where they are, then I am afraid we will have to write the ReichsFührer and report to him our frustrations in not having the cooperation of Race or of the Police in this matter," Langefeldt warned.

"Sister Langefeldt. I think this may be a matter you might want to take up with the duty officer. If you will excuse me one moment I will inform him of your complaints and intentions."

He did not wait for their acknowledged compliance but walked quickly past them, where he turned the corner and down the dark hall to knock on the first door. He knew it soon would become common knowledge that he could not handle four 'little brown sisters.

The women looked questioning at one another. They had not thought they would be forcing the issue so quickly. They were quiet as they took their usual seats in the corner of the large room. On the wall directly across from them was a portrait of Der Führer in a heavy gold gilt frame. All of the women could feel the weight of Der Führer's eyes.

The RottenFührer was gone just a few minutes when he re-entered the room. "If you will kindly wait, Sisters, UntersturmFührer Doktor Mengele would like a word with you."

A short time later, the women's resolve dissolved with the entry of the handsome, self-assured SS Doktor in a tailored black uniform came strutting into the room. His boots were a polished black mirror. He had a Swabian look about him, and even though he was smiling, the women were instinctively on guard. Langefeldt wondered how receptive this Gypsy looking man was going to be toward acquiring children of fair complexions. Carmen thought she would love to have an afternoon with him. She could smell his aftershave talc.

"Sisters. I am Josef Mengele. RottenFührer Orbright has informed me of the problem, and I must tell you that I could not agree with you more." He pulled out a chair from against the wall and sat in it close to and facing the women.

"I have been telling the police for months that they were not getting the job done when it came to acquiring men and women on the lists we have complied for labor and other services. I have not been involved with the children, but I agree with you that it is of prime importance." He assured them.

Langefeldt did not know if the Doktor was sincere or was just defusing their anger. "What are you planning on doing about it, Herr Doktor?"

"I have a friend at RuSHA. I spoke with him just now on the telephone. If you Sisters would be so kind as to take the rest of this day to refine the locations of some of the most promising youngsters and then be here at ten tomorrow morning for a joint operation with the police, he says they can remove quite a number of them tomorrow." Mengele smiled.

The women looked smugly at one another. Sister Langefeldt fixed Mengele with her steely eyes, "I am so thankful that we are at last going to be doing something, Herr Doktor. But may I ask what is going to be expected of us tomorrow?" The rest of the women turned an attentive ear to his explanation.

Mengele could see that Langefeldt was not one to be blindsided. He admired her for it. He decided he would tell her the whole conversation he just had with Hobein.

"My friend at RuSHA tells me the hardest part is in the actual grabbing of the children. Mothers go mad and attack them. The children themselves go berserk, biting and scratching while they scream their lungs out."

The women grew somber. It was becoming clear to them now what they were facing. They had pushed the issue, and now this Doktor and some policeman friend of his were actually putting them on the spot. They could decline and take the heat out of their correspondence with the ReichsFührer. They could go back to doing their ordered daily routine. Or they could accept this challenge and demonstrate just how effective and dedicated they were.

Langefeldt looked at the other women and saw no weakening of their intentions. We will be here, Herr Doktor."

The next morning, they were prompt, and when they reached the front of the RuSHA building, they saw a line of automobiles and three canvas-topped trucks. They were not even allowed to warm themselves from the walk from their house but were met by Mengele and a tall, very handsome policeman, who was all smiles when he greeted Carmen, who had to visibly restrain herself from wrapping her arms and legs around Hobein. Hilda and Ingrid shot each other, knowing the looks of who had been in Carmen's room the other night.

Gertrude climbed into the back seat of a Tartas sedan with Carmen's ObersturmFührer. The doctor stood up at the top of the steps and nodded at them as they pulled out into the plaza.

"Where to?" Hobein asked.

Langefeldt was quick with her response. The sedan sped down the street past the cathedral. One of the lorries lumbered to keep up. They headed to the neighborhood that had the wide sidewalks.

It was going to be a glorious spring day. The sky was a solid sheet of dark blue with a bright yellow sun climbing quickly and warmly but still throwing cool shadows. One of those days when the children would be begging to go outside. Cooped up in fear for the entire bleak winter since the Hitlerites had come here, the children would be breaking hearts and wills to be out on this day. If you can not breathe a fresh breath of spring air as a child, then your future is indeed very bleak. Few of the mothers could deny their children this breath of hope. The English and French were supposed to be at war with the Hitlerites, though there was no news of it on the radio.

The car and truck pulled to a stop at the curb. The street was full of children. They were playing children's games and so far ignored the two vehicles. Some adult women on the street stood stunned as they stared wide-eyed in fear at the Germans. They did not have any idea what they should do or what was going to happen. Better just do nothing a wait a see what the Germans were going to do.

The policeman in the front seat whistled softly. "Now, how are we going to keep this from turning into a riot?" He had been bitten by a kid once and attacked by a mother.

"Sister. If you would be so kind. Pick us out some good ones." Hobein ordered, as he climbed out and stood at the front of the automobile, where he was joined by the other two men.

Langefeldt walked over to the closest children, three little girls playing with their dolls.

"Aren't your dolls just beautiful," she smiled, bending over to get closer to the little girls. She remembered them. She had seen them before. Two of them were sisters one year apart, and the other was a first cousin. They were very promising six and seven-year-olds.

The three little girls looked in wide-eyed wonder at the woman who was staring at them so intently. They all clutched their dolls a little tighter.

"You must all come with me. We are going to take you to a very special place where you will be looked after." She took two of the girls by their hands and led them off with the cousin following, and when they reached the bed of the truck, they were lifted up into it one at a time by one of the policemen and told to move all the way forward and take a seat. They all still clutched their dolls tightly.

Hobein thought that it was too easy, and if reading his mind, the rest of the street erupted as the adults started screaming for the children to get inside. It was a whirl of limbs moving quickly in the directions of their homes. The women were running back and forth across the street, shooing the children towards their own doors. Women inside heard the commotion, and stepping out into the day and seeing the canvas lorries parked just down the street sent them into shrieking voices calling out for their children.

Hobein and the other two SS men stood transfixed as the street emptied out in front of them as if an air raid had taken place. Langefeldt stood at the end of the truck to make sure the three little girls stayed put, but they were immobilized with fear as they felt their isolation. They huddled together, three little blond-headed girls and three rag dolls.

The street was soon empty. Hobein sent Orbright back to take over at the tailgate of the truck. Langefeldt marched to join the men.

"The empathize was to be on male children, Fraulein." Hobein reminded her. Male children were closer to the soldier status all men took in the Reich. Male children were to be the most desirous.

Langefeldt led them across the street to the first address that she took from her book and they rang the bell and knocked loudly. There was no response from inside. Hobein tried the door, and it was locked. He unbuckled his holster and signaled the two Schutzen. With a few well-aimed raps with their rifle butts, the door splintered open.

Hobein followed them in and saw the woman standing in the dining room behind her table with her two children cowering behind her.

"You Polish Swine!" Hobein yelled, "We are the Police! Do you not know to open your door when the Police come knocking!"

The woman could not speak German. She did not know what this Hitlerite was saying. She understood only something about the police. Her father was usually here, but he went to see a sick friend, and it was just as well that he was not home. He would probably do something stupid, and she would have to bury him tomorrow.

Then the 'brown one' stepped around the raging German and reached behind the Polish woman to take the two boys by their skinny arms, pulled them out from behind their mother and yanked them to the door. Hobein stepped in front of the now pleading and crying woman and put his finger in her face.

"You should be thankful to us, you Polish slut! We are going to give your boys a free medical examination. That is all. Just stay inside until we clear the street. It is mandatory that all children be examined by the Reich Health Authorities. Heil Hitler!"

The men spun on their heels and followed Hobein out the door. The two boys were already stowed in the back of the truck. They followed Langefeldt across the street to the next address, and the door was opened without the necessity of battering it open by a middle-aged woman with scared eyes and a timid nature. She did not speak German either, but she had watched as the Crenzy boys had been taken to the truck where the Kronskis girls were already captive. She stood motionless in the front room. Standing beside her was her own son, fully dressed for the outside. She kissed him on the cheek and let him be led off by the woman dressed in brown.

The lorry crept down the street to keep pace with the unit that was growing in confidence as they learned how to take children out of their homes. The only resistance they met came from an eighty-five-year-old man who had protested the removal of his great-grandson, and Hobein pistol-whipped him, and order was immediately restored. The truck filled up rapidly. Then they started finding the children not at home. They were let into three straight houses that had no children present.

"We should have worked from both ends of the street." Langefeldt complained.

"On the contrary, Fraulein," Hobein said, looking into the almost full lorry, "I think we have done extremely well."

"There is one more we should at least try to get," Langefeldt said, looking at her book. "I saw him for the first time yesterday. I think he might be a perfect little boy."

"Then, by all means," Hobein replied, "let us see if he is at home."

The door was not answered, and they followed the procedures they had developed over the morning and the door was hammered open by the two soldiers. The apartment appeared empty. The privates gave it a quick search and reported that they did not see anyone. Hobein walked into the front room and looked around. On the table were photographs of a young, handsome Polish Calvary officer with a big mustache and a beautiful young Polish woman holding a fine young son. They all seemed to look nobly into the camera. He wondered if the man was dead or a prisoner. It did not matter.

Langefeldt stood silently in the hall, listening in the emptiness after the two enlisted men tromped past her out into the street. They both heard the very faint noise and when Hobein turned and looked at her, she could not suppress her triumphant smile.

She followed Hobein into the kitchen, where he surveyed it, and immediately came upon their hiding place. They were crammed into a broom closet. The mother was twisted into an odd angle at the bottom of the narrow closet with her son curled on top of her.

Hobein had liked this woman from her photographs. He could see a lot of Germanic elements in her, and her son was as Nordic as any child he had ever seen. He was glad that she had tried hard to save him. He was surprised at how easily the women were giving up their children. He knew it was because they were giving them to another woman. For some reason, they trusted these German women dressed in brown simply because they were women, and they hoped in their hearts that no woman could let harm come to a child. The men with guns ensured that the children would be taken, but at least the children were going with a woman in charge of their care.

The young Polish woman sat her son off of her onto the kitchen floor but held tightly to his arm as she struggled to uncoil her body from the close confines of the closet. She finally managed to crawl out onto the floor. She stood defiantly, propelling her son behind her.

"It is just for a medical examination, Fraulein," Hobein said, bewildered by his own politeness.

"He is healthy enough for me. He does not need an examination." The young Polish woman spoke German.

Hobein smiled. "It is good to hear the language of the <u>Volk</u> spoken by natives of this city. Or are you German?"

"No. I am Polish. But I will teach my son to speak German if you let him stay with me, Herr German Officer," she pleaded, looking at Hobein with her big blue eyes. Somehow, she understood what it was all about. She was willing to become her son's tutor of Teutonism if only they would allow him to stay with her. There had been complications when he was born, and he was the only child she was ever going to have. He was such a beautiful child, and she loved him so much that she would do anything to keep him with her.

"We will take him now for his examination. We will take into consideration your offer, Fraulein." Hobein lied.

The young mother knew that she was no match for the Germans who stood in her kitchen and were taking away her child. When she realized her hopelessness she felt her heart actually break. She could feel it tear and separate, and she looked at her son with eyes that were numb with desolation. She seemed a stranger to him, and Hobein could see the surrender in her eyes.

The ugly woman in the brown dress took the boy by the hand and led him out into the street, where the truck waited right outside the door. One of the men whisked him off of his feet and almost tossed him inside the back end of the truck. The boy recognized all the children crouching in fear in this canvas cave. The back flap was pulled into place and lashed shut, throwing them into darkness, and all of a sudden, the spring air was replaced by the smell of canvas and urine as some of the children just could not help themselves, and of vomit, as the fear had caused one child to be sick.

It was the first time that he had ridden in the back of a truck, and he held on to the staked sides as they bounced down the cobblestone street and he was amazed at how noisy it was. He could hear other children crying. There was no child older than seven sharing the ride with him, so there was no one to take control or console the younger children, so he concentrated on remembering his mother's whispered instructions just before the Hitlerites had reached their apartment.

The truck finally came to a stop, and within seconds, the back flap was untied and rolled to the top. The ride had been long enough that the sunlight hurt the children's eyes.

"Out!" The Hitlerite shouted, holding both arms up and beckoning to the nearest child to come to him. Sigismund had anticipated this and had managed to squirm to the middle of the truck with some children in front of him. The first child out was Stefan Tachisnsky, and he was lifted to the ground, where the Sister directed him up the steps into the building. The rest of the children crowded closer to the front because they all thought that anything would be better than where they were, and these were adults, and you obeyed adults, and the first children off had not been beaten or anything, so they began to push forward to get off. Sigismund had no choice but to ride the tide, and he did not fight the strong grip of the soldier who grabbed him under his arms and lifted him to the street. He fell in line and had no chance to escape. He had no idea where he was, but he was ushered down a long hallway with another soldier standing halfway to propel them all forward, a long line of children, boys and girls, all blond and blue-eyed.

They came out into a large room that already held close to a hundred children, all sitting and squatting on the cold concrete floor. There were a few little boys and a few little girls scattered about who had the courage to cry, and as the sobs racked their bodies, a steady stream of tears soaked the front of their coats.

The Brown Sister yelled at them to sit down, and when they all just stood looking at her, she grabbed the nearest child and forced her to sit. With a withering look, she buckled the legs of the other children, who obeyed and followed their example to the floor. Sigismund sat in the second row so he would be close enough to see everything that was going on but out of the aisle closest to the Hitlerites.

Brown sisters stood in front of the blocks of children.

Sigismund was the only child who could understand what the Hitlerites were saying. He had recognized Langefeldt as being the witch he had seen in the doorway just the other day, and was surprised that there were women even uglier than her. These women were not like his mother at all. He would hate to have any of them as his mother. Maybe, he thought, all Hitlerite women are like these women, and this is what made you a Hitlerite, having an ugly mother. Then he saw Carmen and decided that could not be the answer.

He watched as a man wearing a white coat entered the room to stand by the door and survey the assembled children. He had dark hair and dark eyes and he stood there with a half smile, and Sigismund automatically dropped his head when he felt the eyes scanning him.

"Sisters," Mengele said, "we want to take the opportunity of making this exercise a learning experience for all of us. We must realize that the more accurate we are at this end of the pipeline, the more we will make efficient utilization of the Reich's resources. We must learn to recognize, at a glance, that general characteristic that makes these children Germanic. Let us see what we have gathered today for the Reich.

Sigismund knew he could easily dart past the ugly woman, but there were only three ways out of the room, and there was an SS man standing by all the exits.

The women got the children to their feet and lined them five deep against the wall. Gertrude's group ended up being closest to the exit, and they were the first to be herded off. Sigismund did not like his positioning but there was nothing he could do about it now. They went down a ramp into the basement, where the floors and walls were concrete, and they entered a shower room that was cool and humid. They were allowed to use the water closets and then made to undress and stack their clothes on a table. The water was lukewarm, and one of the really ugly brown women used her finger to point out where she wanted soap applied. She had a black rubber apron over her gray one, and she continually yelled at them to 'wash,' 'wash,' 'rinse,' rinse,' but he was the only one who understood the ranting woman. He dried himself with a somewhat damp towel, and they were told to dress only to their underwear and to carry the rest of their clothes. They were to put on their shoes but not their socks. It was the first time Sigismund had ever done that, and he did not like the feel of the leather sticking to his cool, still wet skin. The kids did as they were told. It was the first time he had seen naked girls, and they were unlike his mother.

They were taken back by a different route to the same room they had just left. There were children still lined up to leave to go to the showers, and they looked at the damp, partially clad, returning children with disappointment because they were hoping the Hitlerites were taking them off to feed them, and instead, they were just taking them off to the showers.

The activity had put an element of control into the children, and none were crying as they lined back up in the entry hall, now looking like wet, bewildered babies as they queried and were kept in line by SS men.

Sigismund was one of the first five children to be taken into a room directly off of the main one. Here, the ceiling was much lower but the large windows that framed the wall threw the room into a brightness lit by the overhead strong spring sun. The warm air inside this room took the chill from the children's skins. There were a half dozen benches, and the room was full of ugly women dressed in brown and men dressed in black. The white-coated doctor stood in front of them. He beckoned for Langefeldt to send him the first child, and she put her hand between the shoulder blades of Sigismund, and he cursed himself for being stupid enough to be made to go first. His mother had taught him better than that.

He walked up to the doctor, who smiled at him, showing wide gapped teeth giving him a clownish look, a Gypsy look, and Sigismund did not find him a fearful man. The doctor picked him up, sat him on a stool, and tugged his shoes off. He picked him up again and stood him upright, pulled down his underwear and took them off of him so that the boy stood naked at the same height as the doctor and high enough for all of the people of the audience to have an unobstructed look at him. He pretended not to understand, but he listened as the doctor addressed the other Hitlerites.

"What have we here," he said, admiring the perfect little boy standing in front of him. "Excellent. Just excellent. Herr Police and Frauleins, you will have to learn to make judgments with a quick glance, and it is always helpful that you know what you are looking for. This male child standing before us is the perfect example of what we seek in these children. Look at the proportion of his arms to his torso." Mengele took Sigismund's hands and stretched them as far as he could down his leg. "Look that even at such a young age, we can see the outline of lean muscles yet to develop. His testicles and penis are appropriate for his age. Mengele spun him around where his back was to the audience.

"Well-formed buttocks and muscular back legs." Sigismund was spun back around. "Strong chin, long jawline. Wide shoulders. Narrow face. Look at the eyes. Blue. Teutonic blue. The hair is obviously one of the correct shades of blond. Sister Langefeldt, this is one of the children that you brought us?" He asked, knowing that it was.

"Yes, Herr Doktor," she proudly answered.

"You are to be commended." Mengele blew on the metal rim of his stethoscope to take away the chill and listened to the heart and lungs of the child. He was satisfied it was all clear and normal.

"I noticed when I looked over the group that all the ones that you brought us should not have any trouble passing our requirements. I wish that was true of all of the children in the hall, but I am afraid that some of them should have been left on the streets. We will get to them soon enough."

Mengele smiled at Sigismund again and lifted him down. "Put all of your clothes back on and go sit in that corner." He almost whispered. Sigismund did as directed. This still was not the time to escape. Mengele motioned for one of the Kronskis girls, and he put her through the same thing, sat her down and told her to join the boy in the corner. Soon all five children had undergone their examinations, Mengele lecturing throughout the ordeal.

There were three girls and two boys in this first group, and they were all the ideal. When the last of these five had laced his shoes, Gertrude took all of them from the room, with Sigismund in the lead. He was wondering how the turn of events had put him in such a precarious spot of not watching it happen to someone else before it happened to you. They passed five other children coming into the room and Sigismund did not recognize any of them.

They were all really getting hungry now. They had been picked up before lunch, and the sweatmeats and barley cereals were long from their ribs. Without going outdoors they entered another building, this one with a domed roof supported by steel arches. Sigismund knew he could climb these rafters if he had to, and that was a possibility because there were tall metal framed windows with wire-reinforced opaque glass. Some of the panels near the top were open. But that could wait. He could smell potato soup so he obediently walked along with the other four children as they followed the woman to a long table. At one end was a stack of bowls and some spoons.

The soup was warm and good. They had milk to drink and each was cut a healthy size hunk of bread. They were told by a Polish-speaking SS man that if they did not eat all of their bread, then they should put it in their pocket for them to eat later. They hated hearing that. They had hoped to be back home for dinner, even for the miserable rations the Germans let them have.

They were almost at the bottom of their bowls when the doors they had used opened with a bang that echoed off of the roof, and five more children were following another ugly Brown Sister over to the table. Sigismund saw that it was not the group that had followed them to the doctor, and he wondered what happened to them. He had understood what the doctor had said, and he had listened as the other children had been talked about, and he knew that these Hitlerites wanted blond hair and blue eyes above all else. He had noticed that the five that had come into the room when they were leaving it were not here eating soup. He remembered they did not have light hair. He could not recall what color eyes they had.

This was still no time for escape even though within sprinting distance was a long line of doors with wide metal bar openers. He knew that all you had to do was hit them at full speed, and those kinds of doors would pop right open for you. Unless, of course, they were locked, and then he was going to look foolish, and it would alert the Hitlerites that he was intent on escaping and getting back to his mother. He thought if he could do that, escape and get back to his mother, then the Germans would say, 'Well, that Sigismund really did a great job getting away from us and back to his mother. We will just let him stay there.' At least, that is what he hoped. But first, he had to escape, and he had to do it without killing any of them because then they could never forgive him and leave him alone.

The room filled up rapidly. A Brown Sister had taken their bowls and spoons from them and had washed them in a tub of soapy water, rinsed them in another tub and took them back to the head of the table. It was becoming a production line. There was only enough table to seat twenty children and Sigismund and his group were the first to finish and made to stand and walk in single file over to one of the doors. Sigismund was first in line again, and this time he decided that being first was the place to be. He knew he would be running out of chances of escape if everything kept up like it was. He was tired, and he fought to stay alert as the soup and bread was making him sleepy.

He was not tall enough to see anything out the windows that lined the tops of the doors, only the underside of a wide overhang. He could really hear the trains now, and he knew the next place they would be going to be taken was aboard one of them. He did not believe it but she left them there as she walked back over to the table and collected the next five children. Her back was to him long enough for him to step to the door and press silently and slowly down on the bar. He found that it was unlocked, and he stepped back into line with Tachisnsky wide-eyed at his boldness. Sigismund peeped around him to where the ugly Brown Sister was bringing along another five to line up, only this time, she did not catch him looking, or she might have guessed that he was up to something. The room now had maybe fifty children between the ages of five and eight.

There were now fifteen children in single file lined up behind him, and he turned and pointed to the other door. Before he could see Tachisnsky nod in understanding, Sigismund bolted through the door with a loud clang and then froze to check his options. He was on a long loading dock going in both directions. He could see a train backing up on the rails to the stops at the far end of the building. He heard the doors bang open behind him. He heard the Hitlerites yelling. The children were running and screaming as they made for their freedom.

He made up his mind and made the three-foot jump to land between the steel rails. He scrambled up and ran as fast as he could, blood coming from a cut on his hands from the sharp rocks. He could hear yelling now and more doors banging open, and there were fifty kids and twenty doors; none of them were locked, and only four adults to contain them and the children easily overcame the first attempt for the Hitlerites to stop them.

He could hear angry German voices yelling for the children to stop and come back. He could hear threats, and he could hear the yelling in pain of a child who must have been caught by one of the Hitlerites who saw no humor in a half day's work down the drain and having been made a fool of by some Polish 'Swine' kids. Some goddammed Polish babies.

Sigismund slithered under a rail car to find a short open field lined with a tall fence. None of the other kids had made the jump from the dock to follow him but instead went in both directions, screaming and yelling and running and doing everything they could to avoid capture.

He saw that there was no one in pursuit of him, the Hitlerites having their hands full containing the kids on the dock. They did have them hemmed in again, as the two ends of the dock were quickly sealed off by policemen. The herding took place all over again, but now all of the Germans were enraged. Sigismund watched as Langefeldt smacked a young girl, the blow loud enough for him to hear above the din. Then he could see as the doctor in the white coat finally appeared. He could not hear what he was saying, but even from this distance, he could tell that the Doctor was bawling out the Brown Sister.

He kept low and started across the open field to the fence, and without stopping, he began to climb it by poking his toes into the gaps, and he scampered up the barrier and slung himself over the top. He did not want to dangle up here to be seen, so he dropped from the top of the wire, the farthest he had ever done, and he was surprised when the pain shot up both legs when he hit the ground.

His legs still felt numb when he stood and ran down the street to duck into an alley and he did not stop until he was a few blocks away from the rail center. He sat in a doorway to collect his breath and to feel around on his bones. For a few seconds back then he had worried that he might have broken something, but he seemed to be intact. He had made his escape as his mother had told him to do. Now, he must find a way to get back to her. He would stay in the alleys and back streets until it got dark. He would find his mother; he was sure of that.

It took over an hour for the Police to recapture all of the children but one. The mass attempt at escape had delayed the departure of the train already loaded with Poles in their early teens, infuriating the Nazis. The truly blond Polish girls were to be taken to places where they were to begin having children by Germans and then never to see the child after birth, for they were to be raised by someone else. Just produce good blond-haired, blue-eyed children; that was to be their prime endeavor over the next few years. The young men were to be sent to the factories and mines.

It was a long train. It was going to be carrying a lot of contraband back into the Reich. Only this time, it was human cargo. This train had three cars reserved for children, toddlers, and babies. Over the next few years, thousands of Polish children would be taken into Germany.

Sigismund Sosnowski would never be one of them.

<h1 style="text-align: center;">XI</h1>

UntersturmFührer-SS Doctor Josef Mengele sat behind the steering wheel of the two-and-a-half ton Ford dark olive green army truck built in Belgium. It was June 22, 1941, three hours past midnight on the shortest night of the year. He could make out the white cross painted flat on the hood, identifying it as a medical vehicle. They were in a sea of men and equipment, but there were no lights or campfires. Everywhere, it was dark and quiet, except to the East, where the bullfrogs bellowed the night alive along the Bug River.

The infantrymen he had seen had already wrapped their rifles, canteens, and gas masks in their blankets to muffle sounds, and they were as silent as ghosts as they had made their way past the parked trucks. He was with the Fourth Medical Company of the Seventeenth Army in Army Group South, deployed along the Bug River from south of the Pripyat Marshes on a winding front ending at the Black Sea.

The preceding August, he had transferred from the Allgemeine-SS to the Waffen-SS but was refused posting to an SS outfit. That was secondary to him at the moment. He was just happy to be in any part of the German Army at the front.

He had spent his time in Poland functioning as an anthropologist and genealogist for the Reich Central Race and Resettlement Office, and his continuing requests for transfer to the West during the brief fighting had been denied. So he had spent long hours judging people on their racial merits. He was coming to think that he also could smell Jewish blood.

While he believed in the importance of his work, other sons of Germany had swept triumphant throughout Europe, conquering Norway, Denmark, the Netherlands, Belgium, France, Yugoslavia, Greece, and the island of Crete. They did not only not damage their war machine during these conquests, but instilled it with a pride and a swagger that could only be felt by battle-tested victorious veterans.

Mengele, like most young men, yearned to see the elephant, just as he would yearn for a woman. Not having served at the front in a post-war victorious Germany was something that he did not even care to consider.

Private Hans Horn sat like a rumpled bag in the bench seat next to him. His usually handsome, cheerful face was contorted with a dreadful anticipation. He came from a small village in Wurttemburg, situated between the Black and Swabian Forests in the foothills of the Alps. He was wondering why he had the misfortune of being assigned to drive this SS doctor. The army was full of regular doctors, and he would have just as soon spent his time in this invasion with someone who wasn't quite so elated at being here.

They had been directed to their spot and ordered to kill their engines by a snarling and impatient sergeant with the bearing of a field marshal. They were just south of the village of Jaroslav, some three kilometers from the river and the nearest Russian. Of f to the right was a bakery unit, their team of draft horses still harnessed loosely to the wagons that contained their ovens. There were almost seven hundred thousand horses in this invasion force, hauling everything from artillery pieces to the xylophones of the bands of the greatest German army ever assembled.

Mengele knew that they were just behind a motorized sonnderkomando of the SS.

The truck windows were down, letting in the warm summer night air, and they could still feel the heat from the cooling engine. Their blouses were wet and sticking to their skins. They could see artillery pieces taking form in the gathering light, their long barrels erect and pointing to the east.

Adolf Hitler was about to launch the greatest invasion of all time and at last come to grips with the archenemy of the German people, the Jewish Bolsheviks of the Union of the Soviet Socialist Republics.

The German General Staff was left with no choice but to ignore the inner voices warning them that fighting a two-front war was asking for disaster. The English were still undefeated and hunkered down on their island fortress, with their navy sailing supreme in the North Atlantic. Hitler had assured the English of this superiority at sea when he had signed the naval treaty limiting the size of the Kreigsmarine to just thirty-five percent of the tonnage of the Royal Navy.

No one pointed out to the English prior to signing of the treaty, except the French newspapers, that the German shipyards would have to hum at full capacity for years just in order to achieve this parity. The agreement was a German diplomatic coup, getting the cooperation of the English in trashing a clause of the Versailles Treaty, which had limited the Kreigsmarine to just thirty-six surface ships and no U-boats. The fact that they could begin the construction of submarines was the most important part of the pact with the Germans.

Hitler had intended the treaty to assure the British of their right to hold her position in the world and maintain unchallenged control of her overseas empire. He also refrained from crushing the British Expeditionary forces at Dunkirk, which consisted of just nine divisions, hoping the British would come to their senses and not challenge the Reich in their conquest of the East.

In fact, the English, along with their American cousins, would be invited to help settle the vast expanse of land conquered from the Slavs. But the English could not break the centuries-long habit of interfering in the affairs of the continent, always siding with the weaker to prevent any one European nation from becoming dominant. In diplomacy, it was called maintaining the Balance of Power.

The German General Staff was somewhat reassured with their easy string of victories and the construction of the autobahn. This first major public works project of the Nazis was designed to facilitate the movement of armies between two fronts if the need arose. The High Command was beginning to feel that there was a possibility of winning this war.

Hitler assured them that all they would have to do in Russia was to "kick in the door and the whole rotten structure would come tumbling down," and the Führer had been right about so many things.

Hitler had told his Generals that he could not afford to wait for England's surrender when it became obvious that Gorings' Battle of Britain was lost. "England's hope is Russia and America," he explained. "If Russia is lost, America will be also, because the loss of Russia will result in an enormous rise of Japan in East Asia. If Russia is smashed, then England's last hope is extinguished. Then Germany will be the master of Europe and the Balkans."

The High Command of the Wehrmacht did not yet understand that they were in a war of conquest, based on the racism of the Nazis.

They had forgotten the speech that Hitler had made in the Reichstag on January 30, 1939. "In my life, I have often been a prophet, and most of the time, I have been laughed at. During my struggle for power, the Jews laughed at my prophecy that I would someday assume the leadership of the state. I suppose that the laughter of Jewry is now choking in their throats. Today, I will be a prophet again. If international Jewry should succeed once more in plunging the peoples into a world war, the consequence will not be the Boilshevization of the earth and a victory of Jewry, but on the contrary, the destruction of the Jewish race in Europe."

Although the activities of the SS in Poland should have convinced the German General Staff of the seriousness of the Nazi's intent to carry out their racial beliefs, the officers corps of the Wehrmacht took some comfort in that their protests had curtailed somewhat the activities of the <u>Einsatzgruppen</u> in Poland. They were not the defenders of the Jews. However, they just did not want their blood on their hands.

Most of them had not even read <u>Mein Kampf</u>, let alone fathom the beliefs of Hitler and the Nazis. All they knew for sure was that the Nazis had rebuilt their army. While most of them were either Lutheran or Catholic, they were all professional soldiers.

They were the dogs of the war of Germany. Their High Command came from the old Junker class of Prussia that had over a century of following their Kaiser into battle. Eight hundred years earlier, they had followed Frederick I, their red-bearded Barbarossa, the Holy Roman Emperor, into the holy lands on the third crusade to take the birthplace of Christ from the infidels. They were the descendants of the Teutonic Knights.

With von Brauchitsch as Commander-in-Chief of the Army; von Leeb as Commander Army Group North, whose primary objective was Lennigrad, the birthplace of bolshevikism; von Bock as commander of Army Group Center that was aimed at Moscow; and von Rundstedt as Commander of Army Group South, the old traditional Junker class of Prussia, the 'vons' were very much in command of the hierarchy of the German Army they had helped rebuild.

They fought Hitler over tactics and objectives throughout the course of the war, but in the beginning, they secretly loved him for allowing them to wage war. Like all generals, they loved the smell of gunpowder.

On this night, they were very much in agreement with Der Führer. They viewed the army of the Soviet Republic as inferior. Stalin, in order to solidify his position, had removed from the Red Army its leadership. Eighty percent of the colonels, ninety percent of the generals, and all but one of the field marshals had faced either the firing squads or deportation to Siberia in the blood purge of 1937. Stalin rid himself of the Jews in the Army built by the Jew Trotsky.

The impact of this depletion of trained officers was severely felt when the mighty Red Army was fought to a standstill when they invaded Finland. Before it was over, the Soviets had to use over a million men to subdue the Finnish army of just two hundred thousand. The Communists then occupied huge hunks of Finnish territory, including their third-largest city.

Hitler had agreed only for Stalin to 'exert influence' there, not to invade and conquer. Finland was the source of the Reich's nickel and the gateway to Sweden where Germany got her iron ore. The Scandinavians were people of the Aryan Race. Stalin was demanding Scandinavia. He might just as well asked for Berlin. They both knew it was just a matter of time.

Stalin had taken advantage of Hitler's preoccupation in the West in order to advance the Communists' hegemony, annexing the Baltic States of Lithuania, Latvia and Estonia, including a portion of Lithuania settled mostly by Germans, which was to have been reserved for the Reich according to the secret provisions of the German-Russian Non-Aggression Pact of 1939. This was the agreement that divided Poland between them roughly along the borders of the Bug River.

Stalin then occupied Bessarabia in eastern Rumania, also part of the deal, but he then took over Northern Bukovina, which put him in a position to threaten the Ploesti oil fields, which were critical to the Reich and was not part of the deal.

In less than a year, while Germany was conquering Western Europe, Stalin added over 175,000 square miles to the Union of the Soviet Socialist Republic and subjugated over twenty million people to communism.

He knew that Lenin would have approved. World Revolution was off to a good start.

Hitler and the leading National Socialists could not believe that the English and her American cousins did not recognize that Stalin was on a course of destroying Western civilization with their Jewish-inspired Bolshevism. He would never have invaded the West if

England and France had not declared war on Germany. He was forced into securing the west in order for him to subdue the beast of the East.

After winning the West, Hitler had transferred over eighty percent of his army to the eastern borders of the Reich. It had taken over seventeen thousand train loads to amass this force. The drone of engines could be heard for miles into Soviet territory, and Stalin had even been given details of the invasion at least one week in advance by his master spy Richard Sorge, a German journalist in Tokoyo. His generals were warning him that the Germans were going to attack.

He refused to believe them. He did not want to believe them. He had been re-equipping the Soviet Army for the conflict that he knew was coming. He had begun to move his factories east to the Urals. But he was not quite ready. He had wanted to take only a passive tone to Hitler in order to gain time to become strong enough to smash the Reich in one massive invasion. He ordered that no act that could be considered provocation be committed by the Soviet forces. He was dismayed at how easily the Germans had taken France but felt by 1943, the Union would be strong enough to assure the military dominance of communism throughout Europe.

Hitler knew he had to strike first. He had positioned an army of over three million men from the Baltic Sea to the Black Sea. The sole objective was to destroy the Soviet Army of five million men. It was important that the war be over quickly. With the Reich's population at eighty-nine million and the Soviet's population at one hundred and ninety-three million, a war of attrition meant the defeat of Germany and the victory of the Slavic hordes.

Hitler was convinced that Blitzkrieg would work in Russia. He was so confident of this that he left the manufacturing sector on the normal peacetime production schedules. He did not want to deprive the German population of their normal supply of goods and services. Armaments manufactured in the conquered territories, especially Czechoslovakia, helped ease the production requirements and the chronic labor shortage.

The German General Staff would have felt better if their allies of Italy, Romania, Hungary, and Slovakia could be depended on. They knew that the Rumanians and the Hungarians were more prone to shell each other than the Russians and that the Italians were treacherous at best. When Hitler asked one of his generals about Italy joining the war, the general replied that if they came in as a belligerent, then three divisions could hold them south of the Tyrols, but if they came in as an ally, then it would take ten divisions to give them some backbone.

Only the Finns had the respect of the German generals, and they were to enter the war against Russia, reinforced by the Army of Norway, as 'cobelligerents,' not wanting to associate themselves with the radical racial policies of the Nazi party.

But these were questions of politics, national boundaries and economic systems. They did not concern Josef Mengele. He understood that it was a war of race, and the purpose of the fighting men of the Reich was to eliminate the <u>Untermenschen,</u> those people whose bloodlines had been tainted by the Oriental and the African, and to make room for the Aryan Race, the white race. The Superior Race.

Hitler now called on all members of the armed forces, not just of the SS, to wage a "war of extermination." The Soviets had not signed the Hague Convention, where civilized nations laid down rules for killing one another. Nor had they signed the Geneva Convention on the treatment of prisoners. Their captured soldiers were not to be accorded any of the rights granted by this document.

"The war against Russia will be such that it can not be fought in a gentlemanly fashion. This struggle is one of ideologies and racial differences and will have to be conducted with unprecedented, merciless, and unrelenting harshness."

Hitler went further to get his message to his army. He gave any member of the army, right down to the private first class, the right to execute civilians who took up arms or were guilty of plotting against their conquerors, and no member of the Wehrmacht could suffer any legal consequence of any crimes carried out on the Soviet people. The Soviets were animals to be dealt with in any way the soldiers of the Reich saw fit. All members of the Wehrmacht were under strict orders to liquidate all captured political commissars of the Red Army, those Communist party officials assigned to all army units to ensure compliance with Party orders. This would have the same impact as having all members of the Nazi Party executed upon capture, an order quickly issued by Stalin.

The stage was set for the most mechanized bloody conflict of all times.

The National Socialist German Workers Party had battled the Communists in the streets of Berlin, Munich, Leipzig, Dresden, Hanover, and all the other cities of Germany, with fists and clubs and tooth and nail, and above all, brutality, now had the industrial capacity of an entire nation to continue the conflict.

Hans, his stomach tied into acidic knots and the taste in his mouth sour and metallic, started to say something to Mengele, but he could not think of any words. After pondering it for what seemed a long time, he decided he would ask this SS doctor how much longer he thought it would be, when the night sounds suddenly stopped. He could hear no more katydids. He could no more crickets. Everything seemed to go black and silent, but just for a second.

What was left of the dark was erased in the flash of the artillery, which lit up the windshield in front of their faces. The thunder of the guns crashed into Horn's ears, destroying all notions of what he had been preparing himself. He thought that he could be inside the bowels of an erupting volcano. An icy shudder shook him in the warm confines of the cab.

He shut his eyes and wished that he was back in his village fishing with his father and uncles in that small stream that ran cold and clear and always filled their creels with enough trout for a Friday feast.

In just a few seconds he had listened to the guns long enough. He had enough of this war. Anything that could sound so terrifying had to be evil. He was not a coward. He was just a gentle person raised by a jovial father and affectionate mother in a loving family, and he had never thought that he would be placed in a position of taking the life of another, even if they were 'inferior.'

When he was drafted he had opted for the medical corps. If he had to be in this war he did not want to serve his fatherland by killing.

As the guns raged around him, he realized that war was going to be even more horrible than he had anticipated. The weapons he could hear on the giving end, with their roar of the heavens and their flashes of hell, would be tearing flesh and bones apart on the receiving end.

He thought for a second that the Russians would immediately surrender. That no one could survive the barrage of shells that were falling on them. Then he realized how ridiculous he was becoming. He still wished that the guns would stop.

The heavy field pieces were fired as fast as the crews could load them. 88s, 105s and 150s lobbed shells into enemy territory from up to three miles away, and the shorter range canons and howitzers, that the German batteries had managed to inch close enough to the frontier without alerting the Soviets, took direct aim on their targets across the river.

Blitzkrieg in Russia was just beginning. There were over seven thousand pieces of artillery along the fifteen-hundred-mile front, putting shells into the forward defensive position of the Soviet Army.

Hans then miraculously heard above this din the aircraft of the Luftwaffe, the higher pitch whine of the fighters in contrast to the slow rumble of the bombers as they winged their way into Russian territory. He had no way of knowing it, but the German Luftwaffe would catch the Russian Air Force on the ground and destroy over eighteen hundred Soviet aircraft in the first eight hours of the invasion.

One of the Luftwaffe's primary targets were the telephone exchanges that carried the military communications along with the normal civilian transmissions. The switching stations were easily identified, all the telephone lines converged on them, and by ten o'clock that morning, most of them were reduced to smoking rubble. When Moscow tried to contact the front to find out what was going on, they got a busy signal.

By a ruse, dressing German troops in Russian uniforms, and outright frontal assaults, racing motorcycle platoons across bridges into Soviet territory, all the important crossings of the Bug River were captured intact within an hour of beginning the attack.

Then the Panzer Armies rolled into the Soviet Union, blasting anything that looked remotely like resistance. The morning air was full of dew, gunpowder and blue exhaust smoke. It settled on the soldiers' skin like snake oil. The spearhead was motorcycles with M-34 machine guns mounted in sidecars, light tanks, armored cars and half-track infantry carriers, backed by the main battle tanks, the Pzk's III's and IV's.

The Red Army was simply overwhelmed within hours as the German mechanized units sliced their way into Soviet territory at full speed with the immediate support of the infantry. Once the river was breached, the Germans had the two superlatives on their side; surprise and supply.

The Russians outnumbered them by two million men with associated hardware and munitions, but it was spread out over the expanse of the Soviet Union. Even with the assurances of the master spy Richard Sorge in Tokyo that the Japanese were going to attack the United States and were not a threat to Russia on the eastern front, Stalin was reluctant but began to make preparations for pulling his Asian divisions westward to reinforce his already formidable force facing the Germans.

The primary objective of the Wehrmacht was to destroy the Red Army. In simple terms, the armored armies would cut off the Russians from supply and communication with Moscow by rapidly moving pincers of armor. After isolating and containing Red Army units, the

German infantry and artillery would reduce the pockets. Meaning, kill them until they gave up.

The initial surge of the Germans gained them tremendous amounts of territory, but the amount of prisoners taken was far below what they had hoped. They did not want the Communists to withdraw because their troop concentrations would become such that they would be able to simply overwhelm the invading German forces. This was what the Soviet High Command originally envisioned, the sacrifice of the forward units in order for two things to play in their favor; time and distance.

These advanced units, however, were supposed to delay and destroy much of the invading forces. Stalin's orders for counterattacks came far too late and were never really possible. By the second week, huge amounts of equipment and men were being lost to the Germans, despite the bravery of the individual Russian soldier. Prisoners were beginning to number in the hundreds of thousands.

Soviet resistance was strongest in the South. Stalin had guessed correctly that Hitler's prime target would be Ukraine, the 'bread-basket' of Europe; the Donert's basin with its huge coal and iron ore reserves; and the Caucasus with its oil derricks, especially at Baku on the Caspian Sea, rivaling Texas in oil generating capacity.

He stationed his best leadership and newest equipment in this area. Von Rundstedt had to admit early in the campaign that he was engaging a staunch adversary, far more resilient than anything the Reich had ever faced.

Mengele was still behind the wheel when their truck entered the pontoon bridge, a marvel of floating wooden barges, wood decking and huge 'C' clamps holding it all together, spanning the Bug River.

A special bridging company of engineers had erected it to relieve the traffic on the existing concrete and steel bridge that was presently crammed with the artillery pieces pulled by half-tracks, trucks and the heavy draft horses.

Mengele wished that he had allowed Horn to do his job of driving the truck; it was just that he was reluctant to relinquish the wheel. He had always loved driving, even putting it down as one of his favorite sports on his original SS questionnaire forms. He wanted to look at all of the things that were going on around him but knew better than to take his eyes off the truck in front of them.

The convoy was traveling at less than ten kilometers an hour, but steering the truck across the narrow wooden planks was causing him to ache severely between the shoulder blades. His hands were wet and slippery on the steering wheel. He decided that at the first opportunity, he would take his rightful place on the passenger side.

He was thankful when the far bank came under his wheels. He downshifted without too much grind in the gearbox, and the truck growled its way up the slight incline and they were on a flat track on the Russian side of the river, which just a few months shy of two years had also been Poland. A Poland that no longer existed.

"Well, Horn," Mengele said, openly relieved to be across the river without causing any mishap, "we are in Russia!"

"Herr UnterstrumFührer," Horn replied, " I would rather be in Villingen."

Mengele laughed. "Where is your sense of duty, Horn? You must be the only man in this great army who would rather be at home with his sisters and mother."

Just then, they passed the first German casualties they were to see that day. A motorcycle recon unit, made up of eight men whose job it was to find the enemy and assess its strength, had run smack into a well-concealed machine gun that stopped them dead on the road. The machines were twisted, burnt pieces of junk, and the men were covered by ponchos. The flies were thick over the dead Germans, but they were a black swam over the Russians who had been blasted apart by a Panzer and left open flesh for the flies.

"I believe that any of those men there would be more than happy to be traveling home with me," Horn said quietly.

"They are heroes of the Fatherland, Horn."

"I'm sorry UnterstrumFührer. They looked like dead men to me."

Mengele glared at him, but it was lost on Horn because he had to turn his eyes back to the truck in front of them. He realized that the road to Lviv might be open, and the convoy might not stop until it got there. He could be trapped behind the wheel for the next few hours, and then when they got there, he would be worn out. He now knew he loved driving powerful sedans on hard pavement but hated driving big trucks on dirt in convoys at slow speeds.

"Herr Doctor," Horn said, sensing the fatigue setting in on his driver and not relishing being in the close confines of the cab with a cross SS man. "I can take the wheel." He volunteered.

"We can not stop, Horn."

"Just let me in on the other side, Herr Doctor." Horn opened the door and squeezed out onto the running board, shutting the door behind him. He grabbed the canvas covering the bed of the truck, pulled himself up and put his foot on the open window frame. He laid down on top of the cab, swung himself with his feet going over the hood and dropped down on the driver's side running board.

"Put it in neutral and get to the other side, Herr Doctor."

Horn opened the door and pushed on Mengele's shoulder. Mengele kicked it out of gear and slid under the floor shifter to the other side of the cab. Horn settled quickly behind the wheel, stepped the clutch in, and eased the truck into gear.

Mengele stretched aching muscles and felt grateful for being out from behind that monster steering wheel.

He decided that he wouldn't have that talk with the commanding officer about Horn after all. Maybe that was why the Major had assigned Horn to him in the first place, already aware that Horn had a bad attitude but seemingly solid abilities. Mengele decided that he would make a good soldier out of Horn.

They pulled into Lviv just before sunset.

The city had been founded on the Pelteu River in 1250 by a Ruthenian Prince of Galicia. Eleven years later, the first invaders, the Tartars, sacked the city. Poland acquired it in 1340, and it developed into a prosperous hub of southeastern Europe. The city was full of churches, both baroque and Renaissance, reflecting its' important religious ties to three branches of Catholicism; Roman, Greek and Armenian.

The city was inhabited by Poles, Ruthenians, Wallachians, Armenians, Ukrainians, and over one hundred thousand Jews. The Einsatzgruppe that had arrived ahead of the medical units had established their barracks in a dormitory of the university. They would be busy for the next few months in the city and outlying areas.

Their job was going to be more difficult than usual because the city had fallen so rapidly that there were no antitank trenches to serve as ready-made mass graves for the Jews and Gypsies. It took a while to dig graves big enough for the masses.

They identified the hospital by the field ambulances parked in front of the side doors. Horn stopped the truck, snapped it into reverse, and ignoring the horns and hollering behind them, he bulldogged his way backward to the side doors. The street around them was full of men in motion as the mechanized infantry of the First Panzers continued their chase of von Kleist's First Panzer Corps across the flat plains of the Ukraine.

The hospital was a stone and plaster two-story that the army had taken over simply by removing the existing patients to the streets, where they were immediately carried off by anxious relatives. Lviv was just enough inside the front to be an ideal staging area for the wounded to be treated and stabilized before being sent west. Right now, there was only room for one-way traffic across the bridges, and the wounded would have to wait.

Mengele entered the hospital through the main double doors and had to step over men as soon as he entered the lobby. He looked down the dark corridor and saw the bleeding, broken, and brunt soldiers lying without sound on the cold concrete floor. He looked at the man at his feet and could see that the blood seeping through the field bandages made the man look as if he was lying under a red blanket. He started to lift his foot and almost slipped on the blood-slicked floor. The man looked up at him with hollow but accusing eyes.

Mengele realized with horror that he was the first doctor on the scene. Which didn't make sense unless Major Kirst and the rest had either been in one of the burnt-out trucks they had passed or they had gone to the wrong hospital in the city. Mengele knew that he was in the right place, that he was a doctor, and there were men dying all around him. He also knew he was already exhausted.

He stepped over unprotesting men, as if it was their lot to be shot to pieces and blown to bits on the battlefield and brought to this hospital to die from lack of medical care or motherly comfort.

He looked down the hallway to see two ambulance drivers about to wedge another wounded man into the file.

"You there. Stretcher-bearers!" his voice echoed down the hall. He could feel the eyes on him of men alert enough to realize that a doctor had finally arrived. They were surprised to see a doctor with a death's head insignia on his peaked cap but were relieved that someone had finally arrived to take charge.

The two finished removing the man from their blood-stained canvas liter. The taller of the two men folded it and slung it over his shoulder. They tip-toed through the dead and dying and stopped where Mengele stood waiting.

Horn came in. He stared in horror at the scene around him. The smell of urine, vomit, feces, and blood made him gulp sour air as nausea swept the hunger away that he had been feeling for the past few hours. He listened to the coughing and spitting and wondered why they were not yelling and screaming in pain. How could men, with their bodies twisted, bent, broken, burnt, and bleeding, just lie in silence on the cold concrete floor, accepting their fate with dull, expressionless faces. Horn did not understand wound shock.

The two ambulance drivers, both men in their early forties who were assigned their duties because it was felt that they were not capable of the long, grueling demands of the infantry, were glad that someone had finally showed up at this hell hole and maybe some of these men would not die.

"Have you seen anything of the doctors that are supposed to be here?" Mengele demanded.

"No, UnterstrumFührer," Herbert Savel, the tall, lanky one, answered, guessing correctly at Mengele's rank.

"We tried to tell Lieutenant Meyers what was going on here," Max Schultz, an overweight truck driver from Dresden, explained, "but he kept assuring us that the medical staff would show up." He lowered his eyes. "We were ordered to do our assigned duties. Render field care and transport the wounded to this location."

These two men had lingered longer at the hospital this time, the fighting dwindling in the approaching night, giving water to men capable of drinking. They had run out of morphine hours ago and had not had a chance to stop and get some more. They had tried their best, along with the other drivers, to loosen the tourniquets they had applied, knowing that in the chaos, young men were losing lives and limbs.

Mengele turned to Horn, ignoring the sick look on his face. "Tell the ambulance drivers out front not to bring any new wounded here. Find an officer and send them in here." Horn was happy to go to the fresh air.

Mengele turned back to Schultz and Savel, who knew instinctively that they were not going to be getting any rest tonight.

The long day was going to go into a long night.

"Follow me. He ordered, as he stepped over the men and took the steps up to the second floor two at a time. Savel leaned the stretcher against the wall, and he and Schultz followed Mengele.

A quick inspection revealed that the second floor appeared to be empty. There were six wards with twelve heavy-iron hospital beds in each one. They started to go back down the steps when Mengele ordered Schultz to get a quick inventory of a storeroom just at the top of the stairwell.

A Soviet soldier, just two days shy of celebrating his eighteenth birthday, had been hiding there ever since the city had been overrun. His nerves were frayed from listening to the activities of the occupying enemy, and he had considered surrendering at least every other second for the past three hours, but the idea of surrender was worse than the thought of death.

He was hoping to use the dark to escape out of the city. He had come to the hospital earlier in the day to visit a comrade who had been sent by military doctors to this civilian hospital for a serious surgery. When the Germans arrived, he had hidden and listened as they had carried the civilian patients out into the street. He did not know for sure what had become of his friend.

When Schultz suddenly opened the door, the startled young soldier fired, the bullet striking the German in the face. Schultz staggered back to the wall, slid to a sitting position, the surprise on his face masked by the blood oozing from the hole the bullet had made in his cheekbone. He was dead before his body quit moving.

Savel stood stunned, staring at his friend, thinking there was something wrong with his own eyes. Mengele pulled his Waither P-38 from the brown leather holster, stepped in front of the door, firing until he emptied the clip, never really focusing on a target.

The room was dark and full of gun smoke. He stood in the doorway and could not see a thing. He realized he could be a target, but instead of backing away, he removed the empty clip and inserted a loaded one.

Savel looked at his dead friend. He had watched men die all day. He had seen dead men all day. But it was only now that he realized there was a rule in warfare, of all warfare, anytime or anywhere, of the 'suddenly you are dead' syndrome. Schultz was alive, and suddenly, he was dead.

Men in war could actually get used to it.

Savel, after one day of war, was now used to it.

Mengele stood silent as the smoke dissipated. He could see the Soviet sprawled unmoving on the floor. He stepped into the room, his hand finding the switch, flicking on the low-wattage bulb that barely gave off enough light for Mengele to inspect the first man he had ever killed.

He was in his late teens, not much more than a child, but his age was not important. What was important to Mengele was his racial characteristics. After examining the man's facial features, Mengele decided that he had killed a Cossack. It was funny. He had always thought that the first person he would personally kill would be a Jew.

"UnterstrumFührer. Schultz is dead." Savel noticed the slight smile on Mengele's face as he came back out into the hallway.

I am sorry about Schultz, Savel." Mengele said, leaning over the dead German and feeling for a non-existent pulse. Horn was coming back into the hospital just as they reached the bottom of the steps. He had four Wehrmacht soldiers with him.

"A sergeant from a workshop company could spare us just these men for now," he explained, "but he promised to inform his battalion commander of the situation here."

Mengele pointed to the men waiting patiently on the floor. He knew that most required surgery, but he would not have the time to devote time-consuming procedures to any one of them. He decided that he would supervise first aid treatment and hope that the surgical teams would not be long in arriving.

"Get these men into beds. Start with the ward in the northern corner and work your way to the first floor south. Leave the room next to the operating room empty for now."

He pointed to two of the men. "You two make sure that his hospital is secure. We have found one enemy already, and I do not want any more surprises."

The two men immediately unslung their weapons and went off to do the search.

More stretcher-bearers came into the lobby, having arrived after Horn had redirected the ones that were out front. They looked around for an empty spot to unload the man on their stretcher.

"Take him directly upstairs," Mengele ordered, and as the two men walked by, he could see that the man on the canvas was already dead.

"Stop! What is the meaning of this!" Mengele's eyes became slits of anger. "You know this man is dead. Why are you bringing him into a hospital."

"We have our orders, doctor," one of them protested.

"You have new orders. It makes little sense to keep on bringing men here just to die, and it makes no sense in bringing dead men here. Take him out back and start a pool for the graves units." He remembered the flies. "Make sure that you cover them tightly with ponchos. Then you will report back to me." He still was not sure that he had them convinced. "Carry out my orders, or I will make sure you are shot for insubordination."

He turned back to Horn. "Get that truck unloaded. We will be needing everything on it. And find a walking wounded that you can post outside to redirect any new ambulances. If you see any officer out front, send him in here, but I do not want you to wait out there. Get back in here and find me as soon as you can."

The hospital became a blur of movement and activity. The beds upstairs were rapidly filled as the men carried the wounded to the areas directed by Mengele. The men from the workshop units were mechanics. They were trained in all facets of repairing the panzers and trucks of the mechanical German army, but their first aid training was just a couple hours of instruction during basic training.

But they were all good men and they had compassion for their fellow soldiers, and they tried to cheer up the men as they carried them to the wards and rolled them into the beds.

Mengele washed up past his elbows in a porcelain sink, the water running cold, leaving a soapy film on his skin. He pulled on surgical gloves that he had found in a cupboard just outside the doors to the operating room.

He knew the wounds he would face would be mostly burns, penetrations or lacerations, but wound shock would be all they had time to treat. They would be treated for the pain, loss of body heat, bleeding and toxemia. He knew what supplies he had on the truck, and there was not going to be enough tannic acid to treat the burn wounds that he had already seen.

The first dozen men that he treated were all going to have a bout of gas gangrene. The wounds were severe enough for germs to cause a gas that would spread infection throughout the body. He was using a salve form of Urea, a medicine extracted from the maggots of a breed of flies that produced allantoin, the only antibiotic known to fight this type of infection.

He knew that in a lot of the cases, he was already too late, and the high fevers brought on by the spreading infections would kill many.

They worked throughout the night, taking time between patients to give the place some organization. Soon all the beds were taken, including the ones next to the operating room that Mengele had hoped to reserve for post-operative care. The least serious, the walking wounded, were pressed into service carting supplies.

They had stripped the sheets from the beds under Mengele's orders because of the shortage of blankets, and they doubled and tripled them over top of the men. Many of the wounded had reached high states of fevers, sending them into delirium where they no longer cared about their shredded body parts.

Horn had located a field kitchen bivouacked not far from the hospital, and after telling the sergeant in charge about the situation at the hospital, the career man had gathered his grumbling cooks from their sleep, and soon the aroma of coffee and hot potato soup was waking hungry men.

Mengele and Horn, who had assisted him throughout the night, were emerging from the operating room on the first floor, where he had just finished more than a dozen amputations that were both critical and obvious, when the double doors were almost taken off their hinges by a colonel who came charging in, followed by three members of his staff.

The colonel, a well-built, pugnacious-faced man who lived and breathed armor and believed that there was nothing more sacred than the care of his men wounded on the field of battle, except, of course, the mechanical care of his tanks, looked around the hallways of the hospital and flew into a rage. Similar to the one he had just thrown when he found out that he was going to be one tank short because the maintenance crew assigned to repair a cracked distributor was playing nurse.

"Who is in charge of this pigsty!" He demanded in a cannon of a voice.

Mengele looked around him as if seeing the place for the first time. Bloody bandages were piled against the wall, with the flies buzzing them like beehives. Remnants of boxes and crates containing medical supplies remained where they had been opened, their debris scattered across the floor. Discarded equipment and pieces of uniforms littered the place. The smell was even worse than when Mengele had first arrived, but even Horn had gotten used to it. While the men had somewhat been cleaned up on their placement into the beds, Mengele had lacked the manpower to observe even the rudiments of sanitary requirements in the hallways.

"Heil Hitler!" Mengele greeted, clicking his heels together and throwing the colonel a sharp Nazi salute.

The colonel ignored it, the greeting not yet incorporated into the main stream army replacing the traditional military acknowledgment. That mandatory requirement would not take place until after disgruntled army officers had tried to blow Hitler up in the bunker.

He glared at the man in front of him in the filthy surgical gown. The man was a disgrace. Unshaven and covered with blood and gore, down to his boots that had pieces of bones clinging to them. The enlisted man by his side looked and smelled the same.

"I am UnterstrumFührer Josef Mengele, Colonel," he introduced himself. "I apologize for the conditions that you see here. We have been short-handed all night, and I am afraid that the medical care that these men have received has been far inferior to what the general staff had intended and Der Führer has ordered."

"And how many men are on duty here?" Colonel Muller asked, not bringing himself to address this place as a hospital.

"Including myself and Horn here, there are five other ambulance personnel, and four men from a service unit." Mengele was numb from exhaustion. "There was one more driver, Colonel, but he was killed by a Cossack who had been hiding in the store room upstairs."

"How many casualties are in this place?"

Horn handed Mengele a clipboard. He looked at the names and numbers and finally managed to grasp the figure the Colonel was seeking. "At last count, there were one hundred and thirty-five under our care, for what it was." He flipped a page over. "We have another seventy dead out back, that is unless the graves registration people have finally got there."

Muller looked into the eyes of the man in front of him. He recognized the glaze of utter exhaustion. Whatever had taken place here was not the fault of this SS man. He did not have much time for the attack was to continue at the first sign of light. They had been told not to wait on the infantry that had marched almost all night long but were still five kilometers away.

He began his tour of the building on the first floor, visiting the room off of surgery where most of the men were asleep, but those awake were being spooned potato soup by the cooks who had cooked it.

It did not take him but a few minutes to visit every room of the hospital. Mengele was in no condition or mood, to follow the Colonel and his entourage. He took off the soiled smock, wadded it into a ball, and bounced it off the wall, where it disappeared into the debris cluttering the floor.

Colonel Muller was much calmer by the time he got back from his tour of the hospital. He was a veteran of the first great war, where men died in the thousands fighting over the same piece of ground while living in the trenches dug into the French countryside.

He was no stranger to death. He had been wounded twice himself, and he understood what went on in the medical facilities. He began to realize just how well these few men, led by just one doctor, had actually functioned.

When he had first entered the place, he thought he would court-martial and maybe shoot the entire medical staff. He knew that the casualties of the first day of battle were far below what had been anticipated, so there could be no excuse for the conditions that he had seen coming through the door.

When he was upstairs he woke up a private who was asleep on his feet while he wrapped fresh bandages on the burnt hands of a gunner who had crawled out of a burning panzer. Savel had told him what the place had been like all evening, how a Russian had killed his friend and how the SS doctor downstairs had stood boldly in the doorway and had shot the Russian. Then, without pause, had organized the treatment of the men who had lain forgotten for hours.

Colonel Muller walked briskly down the stairs, putting his hand on Mengele's shoulder to prevent him from rising.

"Stay seated, Herr Doctor." His voice was subdued. "I do not know what happened to the rest of your unit, but for their own sake, they better be dead. Nor do I know why you have been left here to fend for yourselves. These are things I will find out about. But for now, Herr Doctor, what can I do to help. What does this hospital need?"

"If there are not at least four surgical teams in here in the next hour, I believe another twenty men will die. There is a desperate need for plasma, morphine, and sulfur. The place needs at least two dozen orderlies to clean up, and if the graves registration people aren't here soon, then the dead will outnumber the wounded on the premises."

Mengele smiled wide enough to expose the gaps in his teeth. "I would take that as a personal insult to my medical skills, Colonel."

Colonel Muller turned to the major on his right. "Get a hold of Leitner at Army Group South. Tell him I want just what UnterstrumFührer Mengele has requested, and tell him I want it done within the next hour. Seventeenth Army is just a few kilometers away, and I know they will be able to supply the necessary men and materials." The major hurried out.

He looked at Mengele. "Can you hold out here for another hour?"

"As long as we don't have to get up from these steps, Colonel," Mengele answered in all seriousness.

"Then stay there, UnterstrumFührer." Colonel Muller quickly left the hospital, hurrying back to the panzers that would soon be off chasing the motorcycles of his recon units.

To Mengele and Horn and the rest of the men who had worked throughout the night trying to stem the onslaught of death from the young men of Germany, it was an eternity before an entire medical company poured through the doors and immediately went to work. They ignored the two men sitting stonily on the steps staring at them.

No one noticed when they stood and staggered out of the building into the street. The fresh air was a knife of pleasure to their nostrils and lungs. The early morning sun felt good on their faces, but it seemed to fill their eyes with sand.

Neither of them could even remember climbing into the back of their now empty truck, and the clamor of an entire infantry army passing by them did not disturb their sleep, if falling into a black oblivion of beautiful unconsciousness was sleep.

From Lviv to the city of Rostov on the Don is almost eight hundred miles of true rolling steppe. Above a bedrock of granite, it is a spread of sandy bess soils that is almost yellow in the north descending through a spectrum of earth colors to the black soils of the south.

It was this dirt that once had grown grains that fed the Greek Empire, that the wheels of the wagons, the treads of the trucks, the cleats of the tracked vehicles and the tanks, the hooves of the horses, and the step of the men now ground into golden clouds of dust and black clouds of dust that made your horses sneeze and snort and stare at you with watery eyes, or your engine to cough and spit and stall as air filters clogged and carburetors ran rich spewing silky smoking oily flags that let the enemy guns find you.

Nothing of value was to be left for the Germans as the Russians implemented the scorched earth policy ordered by the son of peasants, Josef Vissarionovich Djugashvili. The Boss, the man of steel, who renamed himself Josef Stalin. The first Slav to rule over the Russians since the Vikings had rowed up the river and established Moscow by "invitation" from the Slavic tribes living there.

This white domination of the eastern half of Europe would continue until the Communists shot to death in the moist, mildewed, filthy basement of a farmhouse, Tsar Nicholas, his German wife Alexanderia, and their sickly son and four beautiful daughters.

The last Nordic ruler of Russia, first cousin to the King of England, and first cousin to the Kaiser of Germany, Tsar Nicolas I, was dead. A Georgian, maybe part Ossentian, but a true Caucasian, a white-Asian, ruled in the name of the Communist party. He ruled over all the Slavs and all the other peoples that had been conquered by the

Russians for centuries. Between 1923 and 1928, he would kill seventeen million people, the majority of them Ukrainians.

Now, he was ordering the destruction of everything that the invading Germans could use. He called on all brothers and sisters of the Motherland to fight and die over every inch of the sacred soil of Mother Russia and not give the invading Hun anything but death. This was the same man who had just re-conquered the Ukraines from their brief interlude of blissful self-rule, and had stolen their crops and left them to grub grains from lands that were theirs for generations but now belonged to the collectives, and millions starved to death.

Many Ukraines, remembering how the Germans had conducted themselves when they had occupied huge tracts of the territory in the last great war, threw flowers at the advancing armor. Even the Jews ran to the streets to wave and cheer, which made a unit of the Einsatzgruppen look at one another, at first in disbelief, and then they burst out in gut-splitting laughter. These Jews surely had not read Mein Kampf. The Russians did not bother to tell the Jews that the Hitlerites were killing their kind just about anywhere they found them.

The women and young girls of Ukraine freely offered themselves to the handsome lads from the West, wishing to do nothing more than wed these battle-hardened men and to be taken back to the Fatherland, where it was not so cold and not so hot and not so boring. And the young men of the Reich, of the Aryan Race, falling madly in love with these lovely young girls of the steppes, these untermenchen, only to have their requests for marriage turn into hours of excruciating long lectures on the matters of racial purity.

The racial polices, the hangman's knot, and the firing squads of the <u>Einsatzgruppen</u> of the SS would change a lot of attitudes.

But young men do not make good soldiers for very long without the embrace, however fleeting, of willing young women, or protesting young women, or for that matter, willing old women, or protesting old women. Men, especially young men, who through the ages seem to constitute the bulk of all armies, lose their flair for death without at least the hope of having the flesh of a woman wrapped around their manhood.

General Joseph Hooker of the Union Army in the Civil War understood this when he established the camp of women near his army training on the Potomac, thus earning the name of 'hookers' for the second oldest profession, prostitution.

The German General Staff and the hierarchy of the Nazi Party understood fornication as a necessary part of waging war.

It kept your young men free of thoughts of love, which muddled a man's mind and made him a timid target. The Women's Service Corps was established to allow the men to concentrate on lust, which was a more fitting emotion for men on the battlefield.

Made up of volunteers and pros from the conquered territories and the Fatherland, the corps followed the men of the German army and gave them wet willing women from a menu of nationalities, including Czech, Hungarian, Polish, Norwegian, Romanian, French, and even some black-eyed black hair women from Spain.

Hans Horn wasn't sure if he should accept the chit offered by UnterstrumFührer Mengele to the billet of the Women's Service Corps. He had just turned nineteen and had stood over a hundred men and watched them die, their eyes wide and looking at him for an answer that he didn't have; he had worked sixteen and twenty-hour days for the past month; he had been shot at and shelled countless times, and he had even become hardened to kicking amputated limbs out of his way without a second thought.

He had smelled, touched, and tasted the texture of death, but he had never been inside a woman. He was a virgin.

Josepf Mengele fingered the edges of the Iron Cross Second Class he wore on his blouse pocket. He knew he was one of the few doctors in the entire Army Group to wear such a decoration, having been awarded it for heroics in the face of the enemy. Colonel Muller submitted him for the honors because of his taking command of a disastrous situation at the Lviv hospital, but the actual medal was based on his shooting the Russian soldier in the store room. The work at the hospital was just that, work. No one got the Iron Cross for just work.

The medal got stares from his colleagues in the field tents and commandeered buildings, treating the wounded men of the Reich as the army fought the tenacious Soviets, who had begun to believe that there was a Mother Russia even though many were not Russians. There was no place in the war zone where the German soldier could really feel safe.

Except maybe in the billet of the Women's Service Corps. At least for an afternoon.

"Go on, Hans," Mengele urged, "you have earned it. Get away from this for a few hours and I promise you that you will come back a new man with a new attitude." Mengele smiled wide enough to show the wide, gapped front teeth.

"But I do not see you visiting the women, Herr Doctor," Hans protested.

"Hans, I am a married man much older than you. Believe me," he assured him, "if I was you, I would be clamoring for this leave and this opportunity."

Horn reached out reluctantly, took the pink ticket from Mengele and put it in his pocket. He did not want to hear the hoots and whistles of the other men as he made his way out of the school-turned-hospital as the Fourth set up shop to treat the First Panzer and the Seventeenth Infantry in the village of Tarnopol, just a few kilometers from the Stalin line.

They both knew that soon there was not going to be any opportunity for rest and relaxation, as the dwindling summer began to put an urgency into the step of the soldiers of the Reich and a sharper attitude in the already razor-edge command voice of the officers.

Horn climbed into the back of a truck that headed west, a direction that only the driver had traveled since the invasion began. Horn did not know any of the men he was sharing the ride with, but most of them evidently had the opportunity of visiting the women before, their talk graphic about what they were going to do.

They discussed and argued over the merits of what each one of the women had to offer. For twenty kilometers, there was a raging argument over who was the best, the French or the Czech women. Since he didn't have an opinion, Hans just stared out the back of the canvas canopied vehicle at the land that he had passed over for what seemed centuries, and he tried to ignore the hot cinders that were starting to glow in his groin as he listened to the talk of the experienced teenagers around him talk about the women that were coming closer with every bounce and jolt of the roadbed.

The truck finally came into a junction with a few houses and a partially damaged hotel on the main thoroughfare of Zolochev, where Atila had once stopped to water his horses, and the men immediately jumped down from the back of the truck and raced into the lobby where they were met by the proprietor, who as a young boy had carried the hod for his grandfather who had built this hotel.

"Take it easy, young soldiers!" He ordered, causing the young men to pause in their headlong dash. They were not used to taking orders from civilians, and they were definitely not used to taking orders from Ukrainians, but there was a manner about this man that made them slow their assault.

"You have all evening to enjoy yourselves and relax. Please, come to the bar and have a schnapps to calm your nerves and put some steel in your spike before you meet the lovely ladies upstairs," he grinned, displaying huge yellow tobacco-stained teeth.

He had learned long ago that he made more of a profit if the men began their drinking before sex than after sex. If they ran up to the women immediately upon arrival, it did not take them but a few seconds to be heading back down the steps, wondering how it could have happened so quickly, and the quickness of it all would depress them to where they did not even enjoy the drink. So the whores made money, and he did not. But if he could get some schnapps into them before they went upstairs, their attitude was in the right place, and the whores had to work harder for their money, and he made more of it.

Taking the Ukrainian's advice, most of the men went to the bar while a couple ignored him and took the steps three at a time as they bounded for the upstairs, all of them hoping that there was not going to be a line. In times of war, men line up for everything, even for the opportunity of being inside a woman.

The bar was crowded and full of cigarette smoke, and the soldiers were served by a big-boned, beautiful blond girl with radiant creamy white skin, who knew how to flirt and bend over the tables, displaying mounds of breasts and crevices of cleavage that soon erased all thoughts of death from the young German minds. When she poured schnapps into their cups, there was not a man among them who would not give a month's pay to wallow with her and cram her nipples into their hungry mouths.

They laughed and downed their drinks in great gulps and demanded that she pour them another while she politely refused their offer of the pink slips that she could redeem for Deutschmarks.

Horn sipped the bitter ale and wandered from the bar. He just wanted to go upstairs and get it over with. He knew he wanted a woman, but he could hear his mother telling him since the time he had turned a teenager that he should only lie with a woman good enough to marry.

He tried to stop thinking of his mother because he surely wasn't going to find someone good enough to marry in this place. Besides, he had made the trip for the specific purpose of losing his virginity, and if Saint Peter would not let him into heaven because he wanted to know what it was like to be inside a woman before a Russian killed him, then maybe there was something wrong with the whole idea of getting into heaven. And he thought the devil was winning out, and he knew that he should only label lust as lust. He decided that he would just go into the bar and get drunk when he felt a soft touch on his shoulder.

He spun quickly and stopped, shocked as he gazed into the most beautiful, deep, glowing, iridescent blue eyes he had ever seen. She was just about as tall as he, and her eyes looked back into his, and they both felt an embrace, a visual emergence of each other's spirit, of each other's soul.

Her skin was pink from the sun and smooth over small cheekbones. Her lips were full over a soft, rounded chin. A mane of long yellow hair fell to her shoulders. She was dressed in a tight blue dress with a high neckline trimmed in lace. Her breasts were full, with the nipples stretching through the thin cotton fabric. He could see the dress contour over her flat stomach and narrow waist. She looked to be in her early twenties.

Hans was in love. She was so beautiful that his heart ached as he looked at her. The spot on his shoulder where she had touched him was afire. He felt his knees grow weak, and a painfully dry lump formed in his throat.

Carola Maffel liked the quiet, handsome young man in front of her. She had stood in the shadows of a hallway and had watched this group of soldiers pour through the door. She did not know why, but since the moment she had first laid eyes on him she could not take her eyes off of him. He did not seem exceptionally handsome. She had been surprisingly happy when he emerged alone from the bar to stand at the foot of the steps, his face in turmoil. She knew innocence when she saw it but could not understand why she was drawn to him. She hated being where she was and doing what she was doing. Her choice to become a whore had not been simple. Other German women guilty of having sexual relations with a Jew were just publicly humiliated by the brown shirts and sent to classes on racial purity. The charges of miscegenation against her, however, made her the target of a Nazi Gauleiter who persisted in having her.

She loathed the short, fat, evil man from her town who had grabbed and fondled her right after her thirteenth birthday in his own house while her mother was busy helping the man's wife clean the upper rooms. Not having a father, he had died in the trenches with a Frenchman's bullet in his brain. Her mother had remained unmarried by choice, so the incident went unavenged as she was afraid to even tell her mother.

The Gauleiter, a cousin to the all-important Martin Borman, had sent policemen to bring her to his office as soon as he heard that she was home visiting her dying mother. He sat behind his big desk with the red, white, and black Nazi flag draped on the wall behind him, with three different pictures of Hitler on the other three walls, and told her that she was still under the charge of miscegenation from three years ago, and gave her a choice.

She could either become his mistress willingly and live in relative splendor, or he would send her to the nearest concentration camp, where she would become his mistress unwillingly and live in squalor.

She had encouraged him but begged him for just one day to think it over. Sitting there and looking at this toad of a man, made the bile rise in her throat, causing her breath to go rancid. He was beaming when she left, actually rubbing his hands together in anticipation. She knew that she could not escape the clutches of this monster as long as she stayed in Germany.

Her mother died that night with the priest standing by her bedside to give Extreme Unction, and she made her decision. She knew only one way out, and the German Officer who enrolled her into the Service Corps sampled her in the baggage room before she boarded the train east to catch up with Army Group South.

Over the past month, she had collected many of the pink tickets, going numb from the waist down when the soldiers grunted and groaned and ground themselves into relief. During those times her mind would think of Deter and remember how they were as children, and how they were as friends, and how they were as lovers.

As she stood in front of this young German and read his eyes, part of her softened, exposing the young woman desiring the love of the man she loved, shut off when a Nazi doctor had refused their application for marriage and had even sent Deter to the concentration camp where he was to die trying to escape.

She looked at the insignia on his collar. "And what is it that you do?" Her voice was soft, the song of an angel.

"I am a medical orderly and field medic." He was surprised that his voice was light and unquivering.

She studied his face for a moment. It was a gentle face. She liked it very much. She liked his dark brown eyes in contrast to his bright blond hair, almost the same color as hers. She could see that he was a muscular and wiry young man.

"Why are you in the medical corps? Why are you not a tanker or an infantryman?"

He was afraid that she was going to find him a coward and walk away. He could not think of a suitable lie, so he told her the truth. "I don't want to kill anyone."

She smiled. "A German soldier that doesn't want to kill anyone. Do they know about this at headquarters?"

"Even Der Führer knows. He has even threatened to send me to France for punishment."

"A German soldier who does not want to kill anyone and has a sense of humor. Are you some kind of spy?"

"Yes. I am a spy, and I was sent here to keep you in sight at all times," he whispered seriously.

"Do you want to go upstairs now so you will have time to drink with your friends?" She tested.

"I have no friends here. And drinking is not one of my favorite things, but…"

"Yes?"

"I want to love you forever!" he blurted out, his face screwing into intensity.

Her eyes widened, and she threw her head back, startled. She looked into his determined and truthful face and began to laugh, a light laugh that was not at him but at their situation, and he understood immediately what she was laughing at, and a wide grin broke over his face, with the corners of his lips tucked in making it more wolfish than sheepish. She liked the smile he was giving her.

"Come on, let's go somewhere where there can be some privacy."

She pulled him by his hand, and he followed, focusing on the feel of her hand in his, knowing that he would forever feel the warm pressure and the dancing electricity of her skin. For some reason, he did not want her to see his trousers bulging from his erection.

She did not want to take him upstairs to the room that she shared with three other women; one Czech, one Pole, and one Uzbek. They all fought like cats in a wet sack, but now they would have their mouths shut for a change, except for the mandatory moaning. The room would be a forum of fornication without joy and a hub of activity as the men in the bar would begin to make their excursions up the stairs.

She was never interested in the money that she was making. The men got to choose and there were times that she would have a line waiting out in the hall while the other women were idle.

Under other circumstances, her life would be in danger from three jealous whores, which was as dangerous as tight rope walking with one leg above a vat of acid, but she was German, and they were not German. With just a whisper in an ear, she could have them taken to the wall and shot. They knew that. They were cordial to her at all times. They hated her guts with a passion.

They would thank her for taking the afternoon off.

Carola led Hans through the kitchen, where she picked up a loaf of bread, wrapped it in table linen, grabbed a bottle of wine off of the counter, and winked at the cook as they went out the back door that led to the narrow alley that twisted and turned and finally came out into the open on the southern edge of town. They walked hand in hand out into the steppes to the creek in a copse of trees that she had discovered soon after her arrival.

They were both silently elated that the place was empty. The sun was just overhead, and the short walk in the summer of Ukraine sent rivulets of sweat down their cheeks. The shade of the trees was a welcome coolness that they savored as they sat down by the thin, running black water.

She pulled her skirt up past her knees, removed her sandals and soaked her feet. He could not stop his eyes from casting furtive glances at the shadows formed between her thighs. He stepped directly in front of her, now wanting her to see the effect she was having on him. He wanted her to know that he was a man. He forgot about talking. He forgot about listening. He just stood there in a trance, his mouth partially open, taking short breaths. He was on fire, but it was a beautiful burning. He felt an ache in his loins, but it was a pleasant ache. It was the ache of a man. And he now knew for sure that he was a man.

She met his glaze and soaked in the desire that she saw in his eyes. She knew lust, and she knew love, and she knew that right now, right here, no matter what else had happened or would happen, that she and this young, healthy, handsome man in front of her would have the best of both possible worlds. They would have lusty love.

At least for an afternoon.

She stood and pulled her dress over her head and let it fall to the ground, and she stood naked before him. The shock of her beautiful image, of her round arrogant breasts with the engorged nipples, the flat hard muscular stomach, the rounded hips and shapely long legs, burnt its way into an ecstasy of image into his brain. He wished he could freeze time. He wished he could have this moment forever and forever repeating itself time after time as the most wonderful woman in the world was his and standing there for him to feast his eyes on, and he wished that what he was now feeling could echo throughout time.

She stepped forward and put her arms around his neck, and her lips were wet and hot and pressed to the very essence of his soul, his mind searching and mapping every crease of her lips on his. He breathed deep, wanting to rob the odor from her and make it a permanent part of his inhalations. He wanted to taste more of her.

Together they got him out of his uniform, and they fell to the ground on the edge of the water as her nipples seemed to explode in his mouth and when she wrapped her hand around his penis, slowly moving the foreskin over its huge engorged head, he now knew that it only got better.

She grabbed him by the hair and yanked his head up off her nipple. She loved his biting, chewing, hungry, teasing teeth, but she wanted something else now. She spread her legs wide under him, and reaching down, she had to pull his penis where it was straight and flint hard from off of his stomach. When she loaded it into her it was a lightning bolt of pleasure to both of them.

He had never been inside a woman before, and she had not bothered to count the men who had been inside her. But now, there was no one else in the entire world. Nothing else mattered or would ever matter. As he took long, hard strokes pounding her into the loose soft soils of the creek bed, her heels riding his buttocks demanding more and more, she was delirious with delight as she was sure he would have come quickly, but instead bounced hard off of her firm ass but softly off of the lips of her vagina, sending splendid spasm after spasm as her orgasms moved throughout her entire body, causing her toes to curl in painful pleasure.

She was taken beyond this world. She had managed to have orgasms with Deter, but now she understood that she was too young then to fully understand the depths of her sexuality. Now every stroke of the young man above her was exploding novas of primordial pleasure, and she was on the edge of unconsciousness when she felt his penis become even harder as he froze in mid-stroke and gasped as his ejaculations began. He was young and strong and full of semen, and she trembled every time she felt the pumping along the entire length of him. She had been wet from her own juices, but now they were awash in each other's hot fluids as he lay spent, whimpering and unmoving on top of her while her vagina milked him, searching for his very last drop of sperm and sensation.

They fell momentarily asleep with him soft but still deep inside her. They seemed to wake at the same time, and they stared silently into each other eyes. Without talking, they laughed with each other, shared with each other, and put themselves in that place where only a special man for a special woman can find themselves. All of the chemistry was perfect, and she felt him grow rigid and hungry inside her. She did not think she was close to orgasm, but when he started to come, she found herself exploding in spasms of pleasure.

He rolled off and pulled her atop of him, where she buried her face into his neck, and he breathed in the smell and felt the tantalizing tickle of her hair on his face. Neither wanted to move. They lay there a long time, feeling flesh on flesh.

Then, they were pulled out of their heaven by earthly voices that seemed to grow stronger. With a sigh, she rolled off, and with an ease of each other's company, they put their clothes on. They devoured the bread between them, taking turns sipping the wine from the bottles. She had not thought to bring glasses, but it gave them another opportunity of tasting each other as he hoped the wetness on the rim of the bottle was from her own lips.

It was the grandest meal that either of them had ever had. He laid back against the bank and pulled her to him, where she put her head on his chest.

He began to talk about his life and how it was back in his village and about his family and what he wanted out of life. He wanted her to know every detail so she could judge whether or not she wanted to share her life with him. It poured out as a river and she swam sadly in a life she knew would never be hers.

"I love you," he said, squeezing her hard against him.

She raised up and looked at him. "I know you love me," she said softly, "and you know that I love you. And we are both being ridiculous. You will get on the truck that brought you here just a few hours ago, and it will take you back to where it was that you came from and we will never see each other again.

He could see the tears in her eyes, and he kissed them, tasting the saltiness on her eyelashes. He started to protest, but she put her finger on his lips.

"Don't make it hard on us, Hans. We have a few hours left. Let us just enjoy being together."

"I can't let you go now, Carola. I have found you, and I will make you mine forever." He vowed.

"I will always be yours, Hans, but I can never be yours again. She sat up and looked away. "It is wartime, Hans. I am a whore." She could hear him stop breathing beside her. She turned and looked at the hurt in his eyes as he wrestled with the realization that she was a whore and many men had her, and many more would have her.

"That is not important now. That is the past." His voice rose in urgency. "We must get away together. We must go now.

"Go where, Hans. There is no place for us. You can not go anywhere. I will not let you even consider deserting this army. I detest everything that the Nazis are doing, but I will not take any chance for you to be lined against the wall and shot for desertion."

"There has to be hope somehow for us, Carola. It just can not end with me going back to where there is killing and you going back to a whore's bed!" She knew he was not angry with her but at the war. Both of their worlds had changed drastically this afternoon.

She thought carefully about what she was about to say. "Hans, I did not think that it would be possible for me to love anyone ever again. I just know that my life was nothing until I saw you come through that doorway among all those other young men, all dressed like you in your uniforms. Like a thousand other young men, I have seen. But now I know that I must have loved you from the first moment that I saw you."

She took his hands and brought them up to her mouth, where she bit his fingers. "Your loving must have driven me a little crazy. I will not go back to being a whore. I will go back to Germany and try to find work in a factory." He was starting to beam. "And immediately after this war is over, I will come to Villingen, and I will find you."

She kissed him softly on the lips, "And if it is to be, then you will be waiting there for me."

"No. Go to my home now. You will love my parents, and they will love you. I will write them to expect you. I will tell them that we are to be married as soon as I can get leave. You must do this my way!" He begged.

"Hans, I just do not know." She grabbed him on the arm, her nails biting deep into his flesh. "And will you tell your parents that you are sending them a whore that you bedded in Russia?"

"No. I will tell them that I am sending them the woman that I love. That will be enough for them."

"And what if you change your mind about me, Hans. This afternoon will soon fade and tarnish as you remember that all I was, after all, was a whore. Then I will be living in your parents' house, and you will have to think of a way to get rid of me. I promise you that I will find you after this war. Then you can decide if you still want me."

"And if this war never ends?"

"Wars always end, Hans."

It was dark before they got back to the hotel. They had time for one last crushing embrace as Hans had to jump into the back of the already moving truck as it headed east. He soon lost sight of her in the darkness, but he never lost sight of her in his mind.

The next morning, Carola woke up violently nauseous, and as she retched above the chamber pot, she instinctively rejoiced in her morning sickness, not considering for a second that the child created inside her could be from anyone but her Hans.

XII

Mengele immediately noticed the change in Hans. When he had quizzed him about his afternoon off, Horn had just shrugged, smiled, and said it was great. But Mengele could see a drastic difference in his orderly since he had returned from Zolochev. Where before he seemed to be able to anticipate and solve problems, he was now late in performing most of his tasks, and his initiative had become non-existent. He had become preoccupied and quiet. Mengele missed the sardonic wit of the youngster who had become a friend and trusted ally.

Now it seemed like all he did was stare off into the distance with a pained expression on his face.

Hans had requested more trips to the rear, wanting to verify that the afternoon had not been a dream and Carola had indeed given up whoring. The mere thought of her with another man began to tear up his soul, but the battle was furious and producing an increase in wounded as the surge was once again forward.

Kleist of First Panzer and Stuelpnagel of Seventeenth Infantry continued to make excellent advancements per day of operation, but resistance had stiffened since they had crossed the Stalin Line, the Soviet border, prior to the dismemberment of Poland. In their southwesterly direction of attack, von Rundstedt discovered dwindling choices of roads to send his divisions down to arrive at the same point, and heavy woods that offered cover for the resistance. It did not help that in previous situations where the Poles, French, and Greeks had surrendered, and the British escaped, the Russians fought to their last round, and sometimes even beyond.

The Russian army stationed in the south had been preparing for an invasion of Romania, and was too strong to give in easily to the attacking Germans. If Stalin could have launched first, it would have been in this part of eastern Europe, where he could deprive the Germans of their only source of natural oil.

While the chemical expertise of the Germans had allowed them to develop techniques of synthetic fuels and lubricant production, it was still not as fast, or as cheap a process as pumping it out of the ground. The capture of the Ploesti oil fields in Rumania would have been the death knell of the mechanized army of Der Führer.

Stalin would have had Western Europe at his feet. The Communist Party would rule supreme from the Pacific across the expanse of two continents to the Atlantic Ocean, and from the ice lands of the Arctic to the balmy Mediterranean. If this had occurred, Karl Marx, the Jew, would have been proven correct. There indeed was a "specter haunting Europe." It was the specter of Communism.

But Hitler had not waited, and his initial blow devastated the Soviets, who were now reeling, trying to reorganize, and rewarding some of their failing officers with the firing squad. Party cronyism and Stalin's purges had devastated the ability level of the officer corps. It had not, however, interfered with the development of the more modern weapons on the field.

Von Rundstedt had six hundred tanks assigned to him, most of them the updated Pzkw III's and IV's, with a top speed of twenty-four miles per hour and armed with either a 37mm or 75mm short-barreled gun. They faced over twenty-four hundred Soviet tanks, most of them the outdated T-26's and T-28's, and although they were armed with 45mm and 75mm short-barreled guns, their thin skins left them easy prey to the German gunners who turned them first into steel targets and then into steel tombs for Stalin's more experienced tank crews.

But the big difference had been in tactics. Only the Germans had amassed their armor into attack units supported by the infantry and the artillery. The Russians had tried this just once in the Spanish Civil War when D.G. Pavlov led his tanks into the village of Esquirvas, where the close confines of the buildings took away their maneuverability and firepower, and the pedestrian Nationalists destroyed them piece-meal. The Soviets immediately disbanded their concentrated tank mentality and went back to the old way of letting the tanks support the infantry and the artillery. They went back to letting the tail wag the donkey.

Mengele was tired of seeing the poor field treatment of the wounded men as they were pouring into the surgical tent of the Fourth. It was pitched within a couple of kilometers of the heavy exchanges, and the doctors had to yell out their orders to their surgical assistants as the crash of the big guns filled the medical camp. As he amputated the leg of a mortar man who had not had his tourniquet loosened for over two hours, causing the limb to begin to rot for lack of blood and become unredeemable, he decided to do something.

After work that evening, a little past midnight, he found the company commander sitting on a wooden crate, his boots off beside him, and his bloody surgical gown at his feet. Mengele sat down wearily beside him.

"Herr Major," Mengele said, "the men at the front are botching their jobs. The men we have been receiving have not been getting the proper first care in the field."

Major Alford Reim looked at Mengele with empty eyes, trying to understand what he had just been told. Of course, the men at the front were not following procedures, but what did this SS intend for him to do about it. The hospital staff was doing their best as far as the Major was concerned, but he knew he should listen to this SS doctor, even though he thought him to be just a mediocre surgeon. Mengele had proven himself resourceful in other ways in the past. And he was wearing the Iron Cross, even if it was second class.

"I agree with you, Lieutenant. Just what do you have on your mind?"

"It seems to be a matter of inexperience because I know they have had many hours of training. They seem to just be forgetting the basics."

I agree. And so… ?"

"I want to go up tomorrow morning with them. Try to offer some field training, just remind them of some simple things they need to look for."

Damn, the Major thought, it sounded like a good idea, but with his brain and body fogged with fatigue, it was not the best time to think about giving permission to this doctor to go up where the cannon and rifle can really reach you so you can teach school under fire. If he got himself killed, then it would be the Major explaining why one of his surgeons was up in the fighting. No matter what else you had in an army, it seemed like you were always short of doctors, especially when a son or nephew of a gauleiter was shot.

"Mengele, everything you say is true," the Major replied in a voice wedged between war and weariness, "but I would just as soon not have to tell Colonel Petry I was short a doctor because he got his ass shot off being where he wasn't supposed to be."

"I understand, Herr Major. But when we start trying to explain our dismal record here on men dying, after they had reached us, and we try to lay the blame on the medics and ambulance drivers, they are probably going to tell us that we should have taken steps to correct the situation."

"I guess writing a report and submitting it to the division tonight would not suffice?" the Major asked, feeling that he didn't need this after such a bloody day.

"They would probably respond by asking us what we intended to do about it."

Riem thought for a moment. It would make him a surgeon short in the operating room tomorrow, but the bloodied had been arriving in such bad shape lately that a lot of the doctors were becoming extremely vocal about their own ineffectiveness. When they are all dying under your scalpel you begin to shy away from the incision, for no matter how badly mauled the men were when they got to you, it seemed always necessary to cut their flesh even more as you groped inside them to find the pieces of metal, rocks, sticks, and sometimes bones of blown apart buddies that brought them to you in the first place.

"Okay, Mengele. Go on up there and see what you can do, but I hope you have the good sense not to lead the charge."

"I need to take Private Horn with me, if you have no objections."

"Objections? I can't think of any reason why Majors have to explain the singular deaths of privates. Take Private Horn with you."

"Thank you, Sir." Mengele stood up. "We will take an ambulance and drive up tonight."

Horn, at first, was not thrilled about the idea. He did not like being volunteered for anything that was going to bring him any closer to death than he already was. He had known that even being associated with this SS man was not good, but after Lvov, he had begun to like him. All he had seen him do was to work hard keeping men alive, having only heard about his shooting of the Cossack in the closet, and if it hadn't been for his insistence to take that leave day, he would not have had Carola in his life.

But now, just a few days after his life had changed forever, he was beginning to wonder if indeed Mengele had actually done him any favor. What if she were, right now, back in her bed in the hotel with a man on top of her and a line of men waiting out in the hall? He tried to tell himself that it was for real, and she was for real, and she really did love him, and that she hadn't gone back to her room to giggle with the other whores about how much of a fool she had made of a virgin German soldier. He wished he knew what he was really supposed to know.

So, maybe going to the front wasn't such a bad idea. Maybe it would get his mind off Carola. She would either be there for him after the war, or she would not. He would either live through this war, or he wouldn't. But God, she had been so beautiful standing naked by the creek.

Horn practically idled the ambulance the few kilometers to where the leading German units had spent the night. They got there just seconds before a dozen tanks started their engines, fouling the early morning air with the exhaust fumes. A column of IVs headed out at full speed, the recon unit not necessary because they knew exactly what lay across the four hundred meters of slightly rolling terrain to the trees where they had chased the Soviets the night before.

The German tanks were fanned out over the field when, from out of the woods, came churning at thirty-two miles an hour, powered by a 500 horsepower twelve-cylinder diesel engine, a column of Soviet T-34s straight from the factory at Stalingrad. Their long-barreled 76mm guns firing as they came, sending a 6.21kg high-speed shell at a muzzle velocity of 680 meters a second that exploded on target, and a half dozen German tanks and crews were dead just moments after beginning the attack.

The Germans closed the gap and began firing when they got within range, but their shells could not penetrate, merely leaving the outline of dirty snowballs, on the thick steel sides of the Soviet tanks. The superior speed of the Soviet tank enabled them to keep their range while they pounded the Germans.

The Pak's 37mm, the anti-tank gun of the Panzerjaegers, were man-handled forward as they tried to get an angle on the tracks, the seemingly only spot that the lighter guns of the Germans could be effective.

The T-34s mauled them, machine-gunned them, and ran over them, leaving plenty of men with a variety of wounds on the field for Mengele and Horn to begin their instructions, but for now, the battle was going backward for the Germans.

Just when the crews inside the Russian tanks were beginning to feel invulnerable; just when they were beginning to feel that they were going to do nothing that day but kill a lot of Germans; just when they were imagining themselves receiving the Order of Lenin from Stalin himself; the Stuka's showed up screaming from the sky with their one-hundred pound phosphorus bombs, and all of a sudden thirty-two tons of tank was crushed and burning, their crews already dead and the smell of burning flesh sweetening the odor of already burning oil and steel.

The dust from the explosions settled enough for Mengele to see that the other Russian tanks were not running, but headed directly into the German armor. They instinctively knew that they would not have time to make it back to the trees and now sought to close the distance to take the Stukas out of the fight.

That spelled their doom. The sweating Germans brought up their anti-aircraft weapons, the most mobile of their heavy caliber guns in the field, the 88s, and as the T-34s became pinned in by the Germans, the long reach of the 88s sent them into flames. Only two Russian tanks were left, and they were overcome by members of the motorized infantry who succeeded in attaching satchel charges to the trap shots, the area just underneath the back of the turret, and shot their crews when they tried to escape from the hatches on the rear of their demobilized tanks.

It had been over forty minutes of intense rushing by everyone before the Germans could take the initiative, but the Russians were burning in the field, and the panzers were once again rolling southwesterly.

It had taken tanks, aircraft, artillery, and infantry to overcome just a dozen of these, the latest of the Russian tanks, but their destruction left the Russian infantry, now just men on foot, up against men on foot with tanks. When that happened and you were on relatively open ground between hiding places, then you either called on divine intervention, surrendered, or they killed you.

Since God does not make it a habit of showing up on the battlefield, except of course for the Jews in biblical times, then that really just leaves you two choices, and it was just as true in this war as it has been true in every war ever fought. The men of Russia chose to continue fighting, and they fought until there was no fight left. They lay dead and bleeding throughout the field.

In the middle of this melee, Mengele was rushing about, looking over the shoulders of the medics, barking orders and instructions. He refused to become involved with the actual administering to the wounded, and a few men died at his feet as he yelled for someone to come to attend to them.

The ambulance drivers and the medics did not know where he came from, but he was a doctor and he was right here with them, with the bullets and shells flying by their heads and the explosions shaking the ground, and he was yelling at them that this bandage was too tight, or it should be a compression bandage, or just to load this one with morphine because when half your body is blown away then you were not going to make it off the field, so let them at least die without the pain.

The doctors back at the Fourth noticed as soon as the wounded started to arrive that there was a definite improvement in their condition. When one of the doctors commented on this, Major Reim offhandedly remarked that he had sent Mengele to the front to give some field training to the medics.

He smiled to himself. Now, if only Mengele could get back alive.

Mengele and Horn worked in that field for the rest of the day. He changed some of the things the men were used to doing, but for the most part, he was pleased that they had merely forgotten the rudiments of their craft. As he went from man to man, pointing out errors and giving reminders, he could see them become more proficient and confident.

The fighting moved on before Mengele and Hans realized that the field was empty of fragmented Germans. The captured Russians were left to care for their own by either dragging their friends and relatives with them as they were herded off into the west, or they left them to the mercy of the Germans.

These were the men, mostly young men, who laid out in the field with their lives oozing out of them while they prayed to Mother Russia.

It was best to keep an eye on them, but to keep away from them. They had been known to pull the pin of a grenade if any German got close to them, even medical men. So when you left a friend or a relative to the mercy of a German and you were what they considered <u>untermenchen</u>, then you were really choosing between letting him die now, or letting him die later. Because no German was coming within range of a live Russian who did not have his hands high into the air, but when your stomach is full of Swedish iron, your hands are on your stomach, and you pray to Mother Russia.

Mengele sat down on the passenger side running board of their ambulance, and he could still see the backs of the advancing Germans as they made as much distance as they possibly could before darkness and weariness shut them down. The ever-present infantrymen slugged by them, trying to make enough noise to wake the dead, but they never came close to making enough noise. A tank service company showed up, and the mechanics went over the burnt-out hulls of the wrecked vehicles, cannibalizing them for parts, but finding nothing of use.

Just off to the right were the trees from which the Russians had sprung gallant to their death earlier in the day. It was the first battle he and Horn had actually seen.

Horn broke out a tin containing crackers, sausage, and dried green peas, and handed Mengele a cup of water along with his share of the meal.

"You know, Herr Doctor," he said, "I hate this war with a passion. I hate the whole idea of this killing. But when I watched those men in battle this morning, I know I have never been so proud of being a German."

"I know what you mean, Horn." He took a sip of the warm water, tasting of tin. "What we witnessed was the result of thousands of years of proper genetics displaying itself in tenacity, ingenuity, and resolve. I would expect nothing less from German soldiers. It's in their genes."

Horn was resigned to the fact that Mengele was just about to deliver one of his lectures on genetics, and he hoped it wasn't the one about the 'clef in the chin.' He had heard that one twice before, and he didn't want to be bored so badly after being in this battle. He hoped it was the one on the fruit fly, which was interesting. He sat down in the dirt and leaned on the front wheel tire of the ambulance, his tin plate in his lap.

Mengele was just about to pick one to polish. He knew that you learned to lecture by lecturing. Since Horn had been his companion for the past few months, he had been the recipient of his rehearsal in delivering the "Summation of the Races" Lectures that would have students coming to him for knowledge and his colleagues coming to him for enlightenment. He decided on the "Man from Ice," one of his beginning lectures.

He quit talking immediately when a column of trucks pulled into view from the northwest, where the previous day's advance had bagged a town intact for a change. It was an opportunity to put a real roof over their heads, so a full Sonderkammando took up residency in a cluster of buildings around the village square. They found their accommodations both quaint and comfortable, and decided that they could find a lot of Jews in this area. SS-OberFührer Otto Ohlendorf, the Commander of Einsatzgruppe D, wanted numbers, not distance.

The trucks stopped at the edge of the woods, and SS men quickly dismounted, their weapons at the ready. The command car pulled to the front, and two SS officers got out. Mengele recognized Hobein even from this distance. Hobein snapped some orders, and the canvas was thrown back, revealing the other trucks to be full of people.

Mengele knew immediately what was going to happen. Horn just stared, more puzzled than anything else. He had heard the stories, who hadn't, but you couldn't believe them.

A squad of riflemen went on into the woods, and the rest positioned themselves to form a thin wall of defense. Horn watched as the first truck of civilians was unloaded and prodded into the woods. They seemed to be mostly women and children.

They could hear the wail of a baby who was angry, tired and hungry, or maybe just smelling the fear of her mother, a young pretty girl of twenty, who now secreted that special perspiration that is full of terror and despair and helplessness and makes the body smell of a stale stagnant stench that would make a baby wail in the arms of her mother.

Mengele sat quietly. A clock ticking inside his head. He was visualizing how long it would take once the Jews disappeared inside the curtain of trees.

He was thinking that it could be at any time now, when the fusillade of shots filled the air, followed by individual, spaced pistol shots.

Horn jumped to his feet, flinging his food onto the ground. "That sounded like a firing squad!" He looked back, expecting Mengele to be on his feet, but he saw that he just sat there.

"Horn! Do not interfere in something that you do not understand!" Mengele yelled, as Horn started in the direction of the shots.

Horn stopped, spun, and looked accusingly at Mengele.

"Why are they killing those people?!" Horn yelled at Mengele, as if a short shouted answer could make sense of why young mothers should die with their child in their arms, shot by men in uniform.

Horn quickened his pace towards the woods. He did not want to break into a run. He wished it was just a bad dream, and he could awaken and he would be back in Villingen and he would not be entering these woods where fellow countrymen had just murdered some people, and he would even be willing to give up the memory of Carola if he could just wake up, and these people would be alive.

Horn had spent very little time inside the major cities, where the killing squads took up residence, because that was where the Jews were. Assembled once again by Reinhard Heydrich, the

Einsatzgruppe, consisting of a little over three thousand men and a few women, was unleashed in the East with the orders to kill. When they found themselves in a position of not having any Jews to shoot, then many minority Slavic groups in the area were acceptable.

Today, Hobein was lucky. He had managed to seal off a section of a town, trapping over a thousand Jews inside it, making a mini-Ghetto. With Ukrainians willing to be the sentries keeping the Jews pinned in until they could all be disposed of, Hobein thought that if he played it right, he and his men could have a pleasant stay. It would be nice to live in a house for a couple of weeks.

He was scouting the areas to find suitable burying places when he had found this depression in the woods early yesterday morning. He was surprised to see that a battle had taken place here since then. He liked operating close to the forward units, where the civilian populations were still in a state of shock. You could just about have your pick of ethnic groups before they ran to ground. But damn, he did not want to be ahead of those units. He could see the Wehrmacht soldier approaching, amused that he was not carrying a gun, as he dashed headlong into the woods.

He really wasn't up to having to explain what he was doing to another pup of the army. He had hundreds of these conversations before, and he had long since quit arguing with their officers, and he was damned sure not going to argue with anymore of their privates. This is the way Der Führer wants it, and if you do not think this is so, then go to Berlin and ask him yourself.

Let RottenFührer Speeman handle him, Hobein thought. He had watched him handle an artillery Major who had gone to relieve himself and had wandered into them, forming a shooting line. He had been yelling and screaming at them, but Speeman had merely stood in his face, and continued to give the orders to kill. When the Major had reached for his pistol, Speeman had his out of his holster and jammed it into the Major's gut. He never knew what Speeman had told the Major, but he left in a hurry, and there were no complaints lodged.

That was just after the beginning of the invasion. The Wehrmacht was getting the message early from their Generals on down that they were not going to needle the Einsatzgruppe like they had in Poland. They were carrying out the policies of the National Socialist German Workers Party, and it was they who hired you, and it was they who fired you.

Hobein recognized Mengele as he came near. His eyes went to the Iron Cross on his chest, and he smiled.

"Mengele. Herr Doctor. So good to see you, and see that you have been a hero for the Fatherland. Heil Hitler!" He snapped a parade ground salute to Mengele.

Mengele returned the salute. "I think you are going to ruin the day of my driver."

"I hope he doesn't do anything foolish, Herr Doctor. My men are not in the best of moods."

Mengele laughed. "I did not realize that your men could get into foul moods. I would think a foul mood would stay with them."

They walked into the woods together and past the remnants of the camp the Russians had made the night before. They climbed a slight rise, and the trees thinned around an indentation in the ground. A sink hole, more than anything, wide, long, but not deep. Mengele thought the hole was not going to be large enough to accommodate the number of Jews that Hobein had herded into the woods.

Horn stood silently at the edge of the pit. The men, women and children that were intertwined at the bottom of it were now silent and unmoving. It seemed to Horn that he could actually see the color drain from their bodies. When he had first arrived at the edge of the ditch, he knew these people were not really dead because they had color to them. But now he watched the color fade from them, turning them all into the white flesh of skinned fish, and the flies descended on them, and the stink started to arise from them, and he knew that these people were really dead. And he had helped kill them.

He could not stop his eyes from searching for and finding the baby. She was not next to her mother. Her mother had been hit with a rifle shot and had involuntarily flung her child away when the bullet impacted. The baby had fallen alive and unhurt as she landed on the old couple who had been standing next to them. It was the RottenFührer's bullet that had finally blown off the back of her head and stopped her wailing.

The next line of Jews was ushered forward and positioned so that they could see into their crypt, a crypt made of the flesh and bones and blood of your own kind. Of your own people.

The men fired from five paces, and the people by the ditch fell. Mengele could see that many of them had been merely wounded. Speeman walked along the rim and pumped the death shots into those that had survived the initial firing.

"I thought that you were trying to get away from this type of firing squads," Mengele said, looking over to where Horn stood stone still.

"Orders," Hobein explained. "I think it's crazy to stand back and shoot. I have tried it. After a while, you start to see your sister and mother in your sights. You need to be able to stand up close where you can see what you are shooting."

"I don't understand."

"It's Ohlendorf. He is afraid that the men will be able to handle this duty only if it is carried out in the strictest sense of military decorum. What he means is that it is the only way he can handle his post. I am beginning to wonder about all of them."

"What do you mean?"

"Himmler went to a liquidation in Minsk the other day and about fainted when he saw the people fall shot. What did he expect to happen when you line twenty people up and you back away twenty paces with forty rifles and hope that the target in front of you does not remind you of a cousin or sister or daughter? I would just as soon train a dozen men in the shot you showed me, then have to wade in their withering bodies to shut them up."

They were interrupted as the third group of Jews was shot. Hobein broke off the conversation to walk over to the edge of the fast filling chasm of corpses, and taking his side arm from it's holster, pointed it down, and fired it into the final convulsions of an old man, ending the last dignity of the dance of death as a body twitched it's way into eternity.

"At least," Hobein continued, walking back with the smoking pistol held down to his side, "he refused the trailers."

"Trailers? What kind of trailers?" Mengele asked.

"You can't imagine what someone has thought up, Mengele. They took some big trucks and painted them with bright colors and flowers, equipped them with steel sides and an air-tight door with the exhaust fumes venting into the back. The idea that you just loaded them up and drove them to where you wanted to bury them."

Mengele could see no immediate drawbacks to such a device. Carbon monoxide was indeed a lethal gas.

Hobein watched Mengele get ready to agree with Berlin.

"Mengele, before you start to tell me that the truck seems to be a reasonable device, let me ask you. Have you ever tried to undress a dead person?

Seeing that Mengele was speechless, he continued, "Take my word for it," he said, gesturing with his pistol hand the third line of Jews already assembled, "it is much easier to tell them to undress and then kill them naked."

XIII

The war had gone so well for the Germans that their victories were wearing them down and wearing them out. The dwindling summer brought the German armies to within sight of Leningrad, Moscow, Stalingrad, and Rostov-on-the-Don. Soviet losses were staggering: the Uman pocket, 103,000 men, 300 tanks, and 800 guns. Minsk and Bialystok; 300,000 men, 2500 tanks. Smolensk, another 300,000 men and 3,000 tanks. In Kiev, the capital of Ukraine, the Soviets left an army of over 665,000 and then in Vyazma and Bryansk, another 663,000 men. In the first three months of the war, the Germans were able to kill or march off into oblivion over two million Russian soldiers, but their main objectives were a taste on their tongues. The cities stayed Soviet cities.

Along with her armies, the Soviets were losing huge expanses of territory, including more than half of their coal-producing areas, iron ore deposits, and industrial capacity.

Things did not look good for the Russians. Things did not look good for the English, who were counting on the Russians to bleed the Germans. Things looked better for the Japanese, who were now free to attack the round-eyes of the United States with Russia off her back and preoccupied with the Germans.

But things didn't look all that good to the Germans either.

In the second week of October, they were introduced to their first Rasputitsa, the time without roads. It started with a light snowfall that soon turned into a cold rain. The German generals and their officer corps were all subdued when they went about their morning routines. It was not like they had not been expecting it.

All of them had read and studied and argued into the night the highlights and finer points of Napoleon's invasion of Russia. They had all read the accounts of how hard it was to move an army over a sea of mud.

You build all your machines to accommodate the planet Earth as you see it as being either air, land or water. All of your war machines are designed for either air, land or water. There is no reason to spend engineering time and manufacturing resources to have vehicles of transportation or destruction that do not operate on either air, land or water. So when you encounter that deep admixture of two, land and water, you have mud, and none of your machines work.

So you are awash in a sea of mud that is unforgiving to the thread and the axle as the vehicles of the Reich sank to the depths of untrackability and you spin your threads or you spin your tracks but you just go deeper into the mud, flinging it into the faces of the men around you, and you sometimes inch forward. And the Russian winter is getting closer, but you were not issued winter gear because you are supposed to be victorious and wintering in the balmy regions of France, or at home in the company of family and friends around a burning fireplace, but right now the cold mud of Russia has you up to your knees.

As the infantry tried to find a spot to step where the mud would not suck you down sending a shock of cold up your spinal column until your legs became numb from the cold and from the exertion of lifting it from the earth turned quagmire that leadened your step so that soon the calves of your legs were burning, burning in the cold mud.

The only thing good about the mud was that you did not have to contend with the flies and the mosquitoes. They had tortured you for over three months but nature knew that the human psyche could not contend with flies, mosquitoes, men trying to kill you, and mud; or maybe it was just that the flies and mosquitoes had more sense than to try to contend with the mud, but either way, they left you alone to the mud, and men trying to kill you.

The mud made you miserable, but even worse, it made you immobile.

In both armies, to both countries, it was now a matter of willpower and a matter of reinforcements.

Germany had already committed the lion's share of her best. The men around Mengele's age, late twenties and thirties, who had grown up in the house of a <u>Strumableitung</u>, a storm trooper, a brown shirt, who would come home with teeth missing and knuckles bleeding and cussing the Communists and the Jews.

Younger men in their twenties and late teens who had first donned the brown shirt at the age of six and were capable of precise Nazi salutes to Der Führer, Adolf Hitler, and had nothing but wonderful memories of the Party rallies at Nurmenburg, Buckeburg, where they had camped out in tents and stood elbow to elbow with fathers, family and friends and felt a part of a divine mission of <u>Der Führer</u>, and the Fatherland.

The Fatherland, that portion of this whirling, swirling globe of Earth that forges the link through the eons, both past and present, to that common genetic birth that binds you to the survival of your species.

Which binds you to your race.

Young men who had sang together thousands of times at Nazi Rallies the song of Horst Wessel, a young German who wrote about raising "high the banner" and was soon shot to death by a young Communist who happened to love the beautiful young fraulein who had really inspired the lyrics. Men who fought as if in quest of the holy grail. Men who fought for the Fatherland.

But, in the first week of the war, the Soviets were able to call up an additional five million men. It would take time to form, train, and equip these men, but they were in the pipeline, and they were being outfitted and armed, and they would soon begin to show up in the face of the Germans.

A source that was immediate, effective and maybe even pivotal was the fully trained troops, numbering some seventy divisions, that were taken from the eastern frontier where they had been protecting Communist Asia from the Japanese.

Stalin knew from his master spy, Richard Sorge, that the Japanese were going to honor the Russian-Japanese Non-aggression Pact of April 1941. He remembered his conversation with their foreign minister, Matsuoka, right after toasting their Pact.

"Mr. Stalin," the wiry Japanese had said, "the treaty has been made. I do not lie. If I lie, my head will be yours. If you lie, be sure I will come for your head."

"Mr. Matsuoka," Stalin replied, "my head is important to my country. So is yours to your country. Let us use care to keep our heads on our shoulders."

He poured them another drink of the brownish red liquor. "You are an Asiatic. So am I."

"We are all Asiatics," Matsuoka agreed. Picking up his glass, he toasted, "Let us drink to the health of the Asiatics."

Stalin knew that the Japanese were going to attack the United States and stake their claim to the Asian-Pacific. They were, in a sense, soon to be somewhat allies in war with each other's allies. Russia could concentrate on Germany, and Japan could concentrate on the United States.

So for now, the German and Soviet armies fought the mud and prepared for the time when the temperatures would drop to freeze the ground to granite and the war would once again be mobile.

Now, time and distance were on the side of the Soviets.

As of the first of November, the Germans had lost 686,000 men killed or wounded. Of the one-half million motor vehicles they had in their invasion force, only about a third were still serviceable. If Winter and Mud were Generals, then their aide-de-camp was Colonel Dust, many of the vehicles of the Third Reich sitting idle because the grit of the steppes had eaten into the cylinders' walls, making it impossible to keep oil in them, or to keep their spark plugs from fouling. Oil and grease-caked mechanics worked twenty-four hours a day, but Panzer strength, the keystone of their attacks, was down to just thirty-five percent. Hitler finally went into wartime production in Germany. <u>Blitzkrieg</u> was now considered a stupid word by Hitler.

Before the winter was out, over one hundred eighty thousand horses lay dead in the field, or eaten by the troops. The German armies were at the end of long life lines, vital equipment and supplies just a trickle, as the rail gauges changed to the Russian narrow track, which meant rail replacement of an entire system. Only five hundred locomotives and 21,000 railcars were captured from the Russians, far short of what is required to keep over two-and-half million men fighting in the field. The Germans swallowed hard, realizing that they had only a month to accomplish their goal of ending the campaign in two seasons of battle, summer and fall.

The German generals met at Orsha on the first of November to reluctantly decide where they were going to end the first year's campaign, and settle down to an old-fashioned war where you kill enough of them that the rest give up. To the German Generals, there was still a chance to win, or at least time to entrench themselves in a position of definite conquest. They knew they had already added thousands of square miles of territory to the Reich, still inhabited by millions of people, and that could constitute years of settlement for a master race, or whatever it was that the National Socialists had in mind.

Hitler, however, ordered Von Rundstedt to take Rostov-on-the-Don, the key to the Caucasus. It was this region that Hitler had insisted was the most important part of the battle. The Generals' plea for the main thrust to be at Moscow was addressed and dismissed by Hitler, who explained to them the importance of taking over the means of production of your enemy. If the Germans could take Baku and the fields leading to it, then they would be shutting off over seventy percent of the Soviet oil capacity, adding it to their own. Hitler understood that if he could take control of the Soviet's basic raw materials: coal, iron and oil, then he could take control of all of the East.

13th Panzer and SS Liebstandarte Adolf Hitler were the spearhead of a stretched-thin 1st Panzer Group assault on the city of Rostov-on-the-Don. Attacking in subzero weather, they took the city intact, the Russians retreating in such a way as to not damage the city. They knew that they were coming back. The Germans were two divisions surrounded by the edges of three entire Soviet Armies, who decided that three days was long enough for the Germans to occupy the city and as they leaned heavily against the invaders, the Germans quickly collapsed in an orderly withdrawal, and the Germans retreated for the first time in the war. Hitler became enraged and started on his course of firing his generals.

Up until now, it had been Stalin firing his generals, and Hitler decorating his. Now it was time for Stalin to start to pass out the medals and for Hitler to bring out the sack. As the war dwindled down in the cold, von List, von Bock, and von Rundstedt would all be relieved of their commands, and von Brautisch would be fired and not replaced as Hitler assumed the status of Commander-in-Chief of the Armies of the East.

Mengele had waited until after dark before he gave up on finding Horn. He had searched in the nearby woods in the diminishing light, but to no avail. The last time he saw him was when he was standing there looking into the pit of those dead Jews. Knowing Horn, Mengele thought, he saw dead people instead of just dead Jews. He knew Horn had not arrived at the point of Nazi philosophy and understanding where you can look into a mass of dead, newly dead, and naked dead, and see them for just what they were, dead Jews.

The Einsatzgruppe were not the only people engaged in the killing of the Jews. The Ukraines, having their centuries-old hatred kept in check by the Communists who elevated the Jews to full citizenship, exploded onto the Jewish population with a zeal that even shocked the most experienced of the SS. In one incidence, after they had separated over two hundred men, women and children, the Ukrainian Police detachment begged a Sonderkommando of the Einsatzgruppen to allow them to shoot the women and children, a duty that the Germans were more than willing to give up.

Throughout the conquered territories, numbers came to Berlin like 2,000 Jews 'dealt with,' to date, there are only a few thousand Jews left out of thirty thousand, Einsatzkammando 4a happy to report twelve thousand shot, Einsatzgruppen 3 reports that 1,107 adult Jews were shot while the Ukrainian militia killed the 661 adolescents. The number of dead reaching Berlin was now in the hundreds of thousands, but their goals were in the millions.

Heydrich was happy to report to Himmler, Goering, and Hitler, having all three of them in his lines of upward communications, that the Soviet Jewry in the conquered territory was well on its way to becoming extinct. What they had not already killed, they had penned up in ghettos, forced into slave labor, or were still hunting them down like the vermin they were.

Of course, there were Jews behind the Soviet lines, fighting in their armies, digging their anti-tank ditches, working in their factories. If the Red Army is destroyed, then the Communists can no longer protect the Jews, even from most of the Russians, who hated the Jews as much as everyone else in Europe.

It did not surprise Hitler, Himmler and the other Nazis, that there were many people in the East who were more than willing to help them kill Jews. The Poles, Ukrainians, Hungarians, Romanians, Cossacks, Tartars, Slovaks, Lithuanians, Russians, Estonians,

Latvians, and forty other races were more than happy to help the Germans kill the Jews. There were also many people in the West of Europe who would help the Germans kill the Jews.

It was wartime.

It was a time for killing.

Everyone had their favorite person to kill. If you were a Ukrainian, then you liked to kill Poles, Russians, and Jews. If you were Polish, you liked to kill Germans, Ukrainians, Russians and Jews. If you were a Russian, then you loved to kill Germans, Cossacks, Poles, Ukrainians and, if you didn't think the Party would find you out, Jews. Everybody had somebody on their list of favorite people to kill, but they all had the Jews on their list, and the Jews didn't even have a list.

Himmler thought that the war against the Jews was going very well. The number of men devoted to this task was achieving excellent results. Sending in the Gestapo and other Police Units to the captured cities to dig out the urban Jews had freed the Einsatzgruppe for the countryside. He knew that the arm of the SS that reported to him through Heydrich; security service SD, with foreign and domestic intelligence duties; the Sipo, or security police including the Gestapo or secret state police, and the Kripo, the criminal police were all performing very well and did not hurt for manpower, suffering little causalities because the people across their sights were always unarmed.

His problem was with his Waffen-SS.

The Wehrmacht was still very much in control of the Waffen-SS simply by having first refusal on any recruit within Germany. That limited the amount of men available for Himmler to build his legions where he could, in fact, guarantee the safety of Der Führer and the Nazi Party. Hitler, however, still sided with the traditional army, but gave in to the argument that all of Aryan Europe could be armed against the Bolsheviks.

The recruitment posters in a half a dozen languages went up throughout the cities and towns of conquered Europe, and the first to heed the call were the young blond blue-eyed men of Norway. They were outfitted with SS gear; their uniforms, weapons, and nomenclature, and trained near Hanover in military tactics and recognizing racial characteristics. And when they were ready in mind and body, they dressed in their parade uniforms of dove gray with the SS lightning bolt runes on one collar and the dragon's head of a Viking ship on the other, and they stood in precise parade formation and raised their rifles in presentation.

"I swear to God this holy faith, that I shall always be ready to give my life in the fight against Bolshevism, like a brave and faithful soldier of Adolf Hitler." Then in salute of their Norwegian Nazi leader in Norway, they chorused out a "Heil Quisling!"

They joined other young men from Denmark to form the Nordland Regiment, the North Regiment. Together with the Oustland Regiment, the West Regiment, men from Belgium and the Netherlands, they traveled east to meet up with what was left of the 5th SS-Panzergrenadier.

The armoured troop carried the machines of the 5th, which were, for the most part, serviceable. Missing was most of the men who had jumped over the protective steel sides of the personnel transports in the fields outside Rudnia northeast of Smolesk the preceding summer, and when they advanced on open ground they were pierced to pieces by tiny bits of hot steel spewing from the exploding rockets that had been launched from the back of trucks in the distance.

The Katyrisha Rockets made their debut on the battlefield. 'Stalin's Pipe Organ' forced a change in tactics in attacking and left a political commissar with much more of a chance of not being shot on the spot than any crew member of these weapons.

The flying slivers of steel had been so effective that the machines needed more men, and the men of the North and the West were men without machines. The SS-Viking Division was formed. Himmler had tapped a new source of manpower for the Reich.

Josef Mengele received his promotion to OberstrumFührer, first lieutenant, on the eighth of January, 1942. That same day, he received orders to proceed west to join the SS-Viking Division. At long last, he was going to belong to a unit of the elite. He was going to be away from the obviously concealed distaste displayed by the Wehrmacht doctors who could not help but react to the killing of the civilians around them by the SS. But by now, they had learned to keep their mouths shut.

Mengele arrived by train in Kharkov a little past midnight, and took a billet in one of the run-down hotels that had a few rooms left, not destroyed by the fire and the shelling. The city was a major rail and road junction, and the Germans were using it as a supply depot. His new division was bivouacked in the south of the city, and it would be morning before he would be able to get a ride out to it.

He was exhausted from the trip and ignored the singing and laughing from a room off the tiny lobby as men from every part of

Germany sang songs and drank vodka captured from the Russians, twelve of whom died trying to keep it for themselves.

He went immediately to his room, so small that the twenty-watt bulb seemed bright, and undressed and climbed onto a lumpy, cold mattress and covered up with two thin blankets. The heat in the building went out in the night, and he awoke early the next morning in the shock of cold. He had taken his clothes off the night before so as to be somewhat fresh when he met his new commanding officer. Now, as he looked at them draped neatly over the chair next to his bed, he wished that he had gone ahead and slept in them.

As he coiled the blankets tighter around himself, he tried to recall those days in August when the heat had been oppressive and you longed for just a whiff of a cool breeze. He could have stayed in bed for another hour, but the cold drove him up and into his clothes.

It was still dark when he went outside and got directions from a sentry to a kitchen that was already serving breakfast: eggs, bread, ersatz coffee and horsemeat. He sat at a wobbly table that he had all to himself and looked out the window as a dismal rising sun seemed to struggle to turn on the day. The meal was cold, greasy, and chewy.

He reported in to III Corps Headquarters and was directed by a sleepy sergeant to a warehouse where someone from his Division was picking up supplies. He pulled his peaked cap down tighter on his head, and he turned into the wind and strode the streets with the walk that everyone had in this cold, and with that no-nonsense leaning forward quick pace, he soon covered the quarter mile.

The warehouse was served by a single rail track on one side and a wide courtyard on the other side of the long, narrow brick building.

Supplies were not actually stored, but for the most part, went directly to the waiting trucks from the rail cars.

A loadmaster directed him to a Sdkfz-251 being loaded by three soldiers in white winter outwear that made them the envy of the rest of the men who were dressed, wrapped or bundled in anything that could form a barrier against the cold.

Mengele walked over to white clad men.

"Viking?" he asked, admiring the thick padded mittens the men had on their hands.

One of the men stopped loading the straw containers of shells for their anti-tank guns. He saw the insignia on Mengele's shoulder.

"Heil Hitler," he snapped, his salute stiff in perfection.

A Wehrmacht private wrapped in two newspapers, bandaged with a tablecloth, working next to them, looked at his freezing comrades. "I'd salute like that if I had a pair of those pretty mittens."

"Heil Hitler," Mengele responded, ignoring the man. He had cut off too many men's hands just like his to rebuke him.

"I will need a ride," he said to the SS men. "I have been assigned to your Division."

"Happy to have your company, OberstrumFührer."

The vehicle, with tracks in the back and butyl tires in the front, was soon loaded, and Mengele climbed in and did like the other men and burrowed down around and into the straw. The driver pulled out slowly, and one of the young soldiers squirmed over to Mengele.

"Where are you coming from, Herr OberstrumFührer?" He asked in German with a Norwegian accent.

Mengele was relieved. At least some of them could speak German. "I have been with the Seventeenth for the most part," Mengele answered.

"There hasn't been any fighting down there?"

Mengele recognized youth wanting to combat. "No. Not a whole lot of fighting right now."

Mengele had spent most of his winter so far amputating a mountain of frozen fingers, hands, toes, feet, ears, and noses. Men who tried to keep their frozen limbs and did not report to the hospitals died of gangrene in the fields. The men of the Reich huddled in peasant huts and ditches, burned out and bombed out buildings, and sometimes even in the stomach of a freshly killed horse where you scrapped out the intestines and organs that would steam in the cold and stain the snow for a few seconds and as you pulled the skin flaps closed around you it was a glorious salty warmth that would at least keep you alive through the night.

General Winter was in command of the field. He had started by crystallizing the lubricants in the breeches of the weapons of the Reich just a few degrees above where the Soviets' weapons would freeze, which meant that in a lot of confrontations, the Russian guns worked and the Germans' guns didn't. Stretched to their limit and freezing to death, they were pushed back on all fronts. All the cities the Germans lusted for, Leningrad, Moscow, Stalingrad, and Rostov-on-the-Don, were still Russian cities.

After a grueling forty-minute ride, they reached the Viking Division that was occupying what was left of a factory that still had some usable space that could be kept warm. He found the medical center housed in a huge open room that once had been full of milling machines. The faint odor of sweet oil still lingered over the ether and the alcohol.

He found the office of the head doctor. OberstrumbannFührer Otto Becke was a pale, thin man in his fifties, but his voice was strong and his gaze firm.

11Glad to have you, Mengele. Heil Hitler.”

“Heil Hitler.”

Becke eyed the decoration on Mengele's chest. “You'll have to tell us at dinner how you got that. I'm sure that the General will be delighted when he finds out. The newness of this division leaves him shy of heavy medal wearers,” he explained, “and he believes that a general's worth is reflected on the chests of his men.”

“I'm afraid that it was not very heroic, and I think the medal was really for something else.”

“That makes it even more interesting.” Then the old doctor changed his tone. “You probably noticed that the place seems somewhat deserted. Since our men have winter gear and there is no fighting to talk about, most of our doctors are at First Panzer, treating frostbite, of course. Damnable condition. Damnable winter. Der Führer would have to pick the coldest year of the century to invade one of the coldest parts of the Earth.”

Mengele thought the remark was not worthy of an SS officer, but didn't say anything. He would be around this man for the foreseeable future, and decided he could be wrong about what seemed a criticism of Der Führer. He had come to expect such comments from Wehrmacht doctors, but was surprised to hear it from a member of the SS.

Becke misread the expression on Mengele's face. "Don't worry, Mengele. I won't be sending you over there. We need your help here." He picked up the phone and told his orderly to come in.

"Take OberstrumFührer Mengele over to supply and have him issued winter clothing, and then show him to his quarters," he ordered. "Mengele, dinner is at seven. Your workday will start tomorrow. Heil Hitler!"

Mengele followed the Dane up a set of steel steps bolted to the brick walls and emptied onto a metal meshed mezzanine that ran around half the building. His room used to be an office, but it was much nicer than the hole in the rubble he had at the Fourth. It looked like he was going to have to share it with just two others. The orderly put his new gear down by the door.

"Heil Hitler!"

"Heil Hitler!"

After the Dane had closed the door behind him, Mengele laid out each new piece of clothing on his cot. Wool-lined, waterproofed, and reversible to either camouflage or white, he tried on every warm piece of it.

XIV

Mengele slept the rest of the day. He had not realized the depth of his weariness. He remembered flopping onto his cot, pulling his new clothing up to his face and smelling Germany on them, and now he was awake, but not sure where. He was comfortable and warm, and that was unfamiliar.

Then it came back to him.

He was with an SS unit.

He was still in Russia.

He was about to meet one of the professional military men who had helped shape the Waffen-SS.

He finally found the showers. Fabricated from a steel kettle and copper pipes scavenged from somewhere else in the factory, it dribbled only lukewarm water, but he thoroughly enjoyed soaping and rinsing the grime of the winter from himself. He had been spit bathing, washing only one body part at a time for the past two months, and the skinny stream of water over his entire body felt delicious.

He shaved in the shower, toweled dry, put on his new insulated underwear, his old best uniform because his new one was suitable for the field, and his old hob-nailed boots that the orderly had polished. He then pinned on the Iron Cross Second Class and the Infantry Assault Badge on the left chest of his tunic, medals and insignia that most young men of the Reich would be proud to pin on, and unusual on the chest of an SS doctor.

He slid into his wool and rayon blend dove-gray great coat that Professor Verschurer had sent him at Christmas, and cinched it tight around the waist with the wide leather belt with the bright aluminum buckle with the German Eagle clutching the Swastika. He squared on his head the peak cap with the grinning skull and crossbones on the band.

Looking into his somewhat blurred image in the stainless steel panel that someone had polished and positioned for use as a mirror, he decided that he cut a dashing enough figure.

He wished Irene could see him now.

If only he were a little bit taller.

It had been dark for almost an hour before he managed to get out of the hospital. The factory complex was just a few buildings clustered around a courtyard with a frozen, solid, and useless water tower off to a corner by the rail sidings. The yard was full of fast walking men and slow-moving vehicles as the temperature was thirty-five degrees below zero and still dropping. The night was clear for a change, the moon out and beaming bright, but no one risked their face to the cold to look.

The dining hall was similar in size to the one that was serving as the hospital, and he could tell that at one time they had been used for the same purpose. Instead of beds, however, there were rows of tables, none of them the same size, most of them full. One wall was draped with a large Nazi flag and pictures of Adolf Hitler in different poses adorned the walls.

As Mengele made his way through the maze of tables, he could hear a lot of the languages of northern Europe being spoken, but the admonishment to 'speak German' everywhere.

The smell of cooking cabbages and potatoes was in the air.

The officers of the Waffen-SS were much more egalitarian than the traditional army, in many cases sharing the same mess facilities and menu as the men, but the commanding and senior officers still maintained a table of their own.

StandartenFührer Becke was already there with another colonel sitting beside him. At the far end of a table that would probably seat a dozen men, three unterstrumFührers sat intent on eating their meal. Becke motioned him over.

"Heil Hitler." Mengele greeted in the half held stiff arm Nazi salute suitable for use indoors.

"Heil Hitler," Becke responded, and then introduced the peppered-gray-haired man sitting beside him.

Gille was the Artillery Officer and a career military man who had quit the Wehrmacht at the highest rank he could ever possibly achieve, to join with Hausser and Steiner and other professional soldiers to help create a truly remarkable fighting force. His ability to gain the loyalty and high proficiency of his men led to rapid advancement based on military merits. It didn't hurt that he truly loved watching the flash of the muzzles, and listening to the blast from the breeches still sent a shaft of pleasure through his heart. He could recognize a gun with his eyes blindfolded and his ears plugged, simply by the smell of the gun after firing. All he cared about was his men, his guns, and his Germany. He was not too much into politics.

Mengele clicked his heels and bowed to the senior officer. "Good evening, StandartenFührer Gille."

Gille nodded at Mengele. "Hang your coat up and join us, ObersturmFührer. 'Viking' will be here anytime now."

"It is always easier," Becke chuckled, "to meet the General over bread than over business."

Mengele was surprised that the Becke had used the Wehrmacht rank for Steiner, and not BrigadeFührer, the SS ranking.

Gille laughed beside him. "Come now, StandartenFührer, he is not as bad as that. He can be quite cordial."

"He can be, but I don't think he is going to be," Becke nodded to the end of the table. "Those three are here on his request, and from the looks on their faces, they would rather be somewhere else. See how they are shoveling in that food. They know that what the General is going to say to them is going to take away their appetite."

"Anyway, it will be an interesting evening!" Gille boomed.

Mengele hung his coat on the pegs set into the wall behind the table and came back to sit in a rather comfortable leather chair across from Becke. He poured himself a glass of water from the decanter on the table and took a drink. It was ice cold. Everyone in Russia could have as much cold as ice water as they wanted.

The din of the dining room changed. Where it had been sporadic and spontaneous, and a rattle of plates and voices, it now became focused and intent. The Divisional Commander, SS-BrigadeFührer, or General, as he liked to be called, Felix Steiner, had entered the hall and had the attention of everyone as he made his way among the men at the tables offering greetings. He was not jovial and inquisitive, as he could be, but formal and serious, but he was welcomed at all the tables.

Felix Steiner had been in charge of a machine gun company in World War I. He saw how useless it was to fight out of trenches where you and your adversary just spread yourselves equally thin.

The First World War was fought for the most part ignoring the proven principles of manpower and firepower, or as the Confederate general in the American Civil War had phrased it, 'the firstest with the mostest.' Steiner had also read the accounts of how the Indians and buckskinned Frenchmen blended in with the scenery, and realized that if you had people shooting at you that being hard to see could be to your advantage.

He knew that waging a successful war was simply acquiring a series of advantages.

So he had resigned his commission in the Reichswehr at Himmler's enticement of being able to implement his idea of the soldier-forager-athlete as envisioned by B. Lindell Hart, out of the question in the traditional army as molded by von Sheetk.

Steiner had stressed athletics in training rather than drill and circumstance. He ran his men hard and trained them hard, and he was the first to dress them in camouflage so they would be hard to see, and armed them with machine guns instead of rifles so they could put out more bullets, and filled their belts with hand grenades to increase their firepower. He had helped mold the original SS fighting man of Germany while commander of the Germania Regiment of the SS-Verfugungstruppe. They all wore the skull and the crossbones.

He simply believed that an army should be hard to see, armed to the teeth, and dedicated to death.

He finally arrived at the table where all of the men had stood to attention. He stopped in front of Mengele.

"General. This is our newest surgeon, Josef Mengele," Becke introduced.

Mengele looked into the crisp, cool gaze of the crusty Prussian whose short-cropped gray hair crowned a stern, angular face still red from being outside. He had just come from the Sixth Army with new orders that pleased him.

"You have the look of a man who has been here from the beginning," Steiner said, acknowledging the decorations on Mengele's chest but actually reading his experienced expression. There is something in the eyes of men who have come close to freezing to death, a shallow shaft of nothingness that they all share that Steiner had learned to recognize.

He introduced the man standing beside him, a thick-chested, towering man who made Mengele feel uncomfortable, as Sturmbannführer Herbert Reichel, his chief-of-staff.

"I was with the Fourth in the Seventeenth Army in June, BrigradeFührer," Mengele responded, puzzled that no one rendered the Nazi salute to Hitler. The Wehrmacht was not yet required to render the political greeting, but it should be an honor for members of the SS. But here, like in the Wehrmacht mess, it was ignored.

"Splendid," Steiner said as he took his chair at the head of the table, "then you won't mind going back to the Seventeenth," he looked around the table and saw all of their heads were up and looking at him and announced, "because we all will be going to the Seventeenth, starting movement within the next two days."

"I knew this place was too good to be true," Gille said sadly, recognizing the fact that all the men he had seen come in from the southeast did nothing but try to get next to something warm. They would hover around electric light bulbs with their handsabsorbing the warmth and the light; they would stand four deep at a pot-bellied stove.

"I requested it," Steiner said, "we are winter-equipped and should give up the luxury and warmth of these facilities to other men who have only summer clothing."

"Can't we just give up the clothing?" came a voice from the end of the table. The man who said this immediately buried his head into his bowl of potatoes and cabbages and wished that he had kept his mouth shut.

Gille and Becke burst out laughing. Reichel just lowered and shook his head. Mengele thought it was something Horn would say, and hated the idea that he was going back into the cold.

"Leitner!" Steiner snapped, causing the other men at the table to stem their laughter, "You are already guilty of performance not acceptable to me, and now you are going to add buffoonery!"

"I am sorry, General," Leitner apologized. He was a redhead with freckles who had graduated last in his class from Bad Tolz, the SS officer corps military academy. Mengele thought him interesting genetically, and secretly wished for the war to be over so he could once again be the scientist. Scientists were always warm.

"All I thought I was doing was servicing an SS unit!" Leitner protested, already being informed in a loud voice by his HauptsturmFührer what had upset the General. All three of these young men were guilty in three separate instances of roughly the same transgression.

"They had a diamond on their sleeve with the SD imprint!" Reichel hissed, immediately losing his sense of humor because it was his responsibility to ensure that everyone in the division was exactly familiar with the insignia of all forces in the Wehrmacht, and especially of other SS units.

"We just changed out a generator and a battery from one of their cars, General," Leitner protested. "We just judged them on being in the German Army and being stranded."

Mengele realized that Steiner was upset over some help that a member of the Viking Division had rendered to the SD of the Einsatzgruppe. This seemed a peculiar conversation to be taking place at a table of men of the SS.

Steiner rapped on the table with the butt of his dinner knife. "You must understand that there will be no link between this division of fighting men and that firing squad!" His eyes narrowed and became mean as he glared at the three young men sitting at the end of the table from him.

"I sincerely hope you realize how strongly I feel about this. Der Führer himself has directed that while we are in a theater of war than we are under the command of the Wehrmacht. Our responsibility is only to the Wehrmacht, other Waffen-SS units, and our Romanian allies." He stared intently at the trio. "Do I make myself clear?"

"Jawohl!, General," they chorused.

"It is the Reichheinie's fault." Reichel exclaimed, referring to Himmler as the 'ass' of the Reich. "He should not have put us in the same command structure as those jackals."

Mengele expected every member of the officer corps present to explode in indignation and outrage at the chief of staff's reference to the ReichsFührer Himmler.

Nobody objected.

"The ReichsFührer is not in this conversation, Reichel," Steiner said softly, noticing Mengele's shocked expression. He wasn't worried about himself if this talk got back to Himmler, but he knew that the other officers at the table would go on a list and their loyalty would always be suspect, and promotions still came through signed by Himmler, and every soldier still loves a promotion.

Steiner began to eat. "Mengele, welcome to the Division. It is good to have experienced men."

Two days later, Mengele was in the vanguard of the Division's movement. They assembled their gear and equipment and loaded it on their trucks and joined the armored personnel carriers, and the command cars, and drove in convoy to the northern side of Kharkov where they waited until a lone lame locomotive valiantly pulling twenty empty cars of both flats and boxes finally appeared out of the freezing mist.

The first movement consisted of a regiment of Panzergrenadiers, a pioneer unit with their BMW 750cc motorcycles, signal and service companies, and one field hospital with Mengele in command. It took half the day to entrain. The pressure in the boiler was near the red line before the Russian-made locomotive gathered enough headway on the rails to begin the trip to the southeast.

As the train labored through the steppe and villages of Russia in the dwindling daylight, Mengele and the men from Scandinavia could see a uniform landscape dotted with makeshift pole gallows, that Himmler had designed, that were full of swinging frozen stiff peasants who had turned partisan, or suspected partisan, or had just pissed a German off.

Village after village shared their husbands, sons, daughters, and wives to the gallows. It was just one of the other things that everyone shared in Russia: death.

You had the cold.

You had ice water.

And you had death.

Most of the men on the train chose to ignore the landscape, and were actually relieved when the thick coating of ice formed on the inside of the window, making any viewing out impossible.

The men were not in any humor to sing and joke. They didn't feel like talking. For the most part, they just dug their faces deep into their field caps looking for warmth, and away from the sight of so much desolation, and they thought of home.

The train lost a lot of time detouring around the Izyum pocket where the Soviet winter offensive had created a bulge seventy miles wide and fifty-five miles deep in the German lines just forty miles southeast of Kharkov.

The train was in motion for just over nine hours, but with the delays it was the next morning before they arrived in Slavyansk, the city in the southeast corner of the pocket that the Germans had fought to keep in temperatures of minus fifty-eight degrees Fahrenheit below zero with a wind that was whipping in at thirty five miles an hour, and convinced the counter-attacking Russians that they were going to defend this city, or they were going to die trying.

The men of the Viking Division, even with their fine winter wear, were stiff, cold, and hungry when they finally arrived at their destination, but made rapid work of getting their equipment off the train. By lunch, they were huddling in a row of lice-infested peasant huts just vacated by frozen ghostly men who felt that they were delivered and rescued, and if they were told that the train they were boarding was actually heading into hell, they could not have loaded it any quicker.

The German soldiers who had just vacated these humble quarters had known that the lice-infested hovels of the peasants and the bombed and shelled destroyed buildings of the city were the only structures for miles. The only shelter. To retreat from this pile of rocks and sticks meant to spend the winter out on the steppe with summer uniforms, and if that was the case, then they were not retreating from this place even if Adolf ordered them personally.

They had taken a lot of months to get here to the cities of Balakleya in the north and Slavyansk in the south, the cities at the base of the bulge just about splitting the difference with Izyum in the center.

They were the old-fashioned foot soldier, the infantryman, been around since the first man got up on some kind of animal and left his fellow soldier on the ground. They had just walked, marched, crawled, and sometimes had to break into a run to cover the six hundred miles, all the way in those hob-nailed boots that they had once loved polishing to just the right luster and were fine for clicking against the cobblestones while goose-stepping down the Lindenstrasse in Berlin, feeling part of a nation; but now the hob-nails were nothing but a conduit for frostbite, a shaft of steel that sucked up the cold of the steppe and froze the feet that sometimes ended up under the surgeon's scalpel.

After you had lived through a few months of temperatures always in the twenties down through sometimes even the fifty degrees below zero mark, with the food literally freezing in your plate, and you had burnt everything you could burn for warmth, and you wrapped anything and everything around yourself that you could find just to get another layer between you and the cold, and you could not even empty your bladder all at one time because General Winter could turn your penis into a bluish rotted mass of flesh suitable not for a ladies lips, but for the surgeon's scalpel.

Mengele went back on loan to amputations, and, to his amazement, saber wounds, as the Soviet cavalry became the most mobile units on the field and were able to ride in close enough in the snow to swing their swords.

You prayed for spring, or you prayed for a glimpse of hell just so you might warm your hands on the heat from the doorway.

You dug your fingernails into your own flesh to scratch the tiny red welts that the lice left on you after they fed.

Everyone was waiting for Spring.

About the only thing you could hope for in this weather was moving your men around. There was an occasional artillery duel, and patrols getting careless would be caught out in the open and butchered.

But for the most part, General Winter was in command of the field.

Hitler was busy reinforcing his southern army for the coming spring. With Sixth Army attacking out of Kharcov from the north, and von Kliest attacking from the south with his First Panzer and Seventeenth Army, he would pinch off this salient as his opening gambit in his choice of going after the Caucasus and the oil instead of the objective that his generals had always favored, Moscow.

Germany was no longer capable of going after more than one prize at a time. By that March, German casualties would escalate to one million one hundred thousand men killed, wounded, or captured. General Winter would destroy another five hundred thousand men to disease and frostbite.

The Soviets were busy filling this pocket with five fresh armies with ideas of their own.

The Viking Division took up a north-facing position along the southern lines of the Soviet bulge.

Everyone was waiting for Spring.

And when spring came, the Soviets got off first for a change.

They launched a three-prong attack, two groups out of the Izyum pocket, with the pincers intent on picking off Kharkov and having

Sixth Army in the bag, and taking up where they left off in the onset of the winter, on the offensive.

Von Beck, now commanding Army Group A in the south, once again the heaviest fortified of the German armies, screamed for permission to help relieve Paulus as the Sixth suffered the devastation of an attack by three entire Soviet Armies that chewed through the forward units.

Hitler demanded that everyone stay in their station. Paulus was to hold in the North, and von Kleist was to stick to his schedule. Hitler promised and delivered the Eighth Air Corps from the battle in the Crimea at Sevastopol, and this added air power gave the advantage to the Sixth Army, which finally stopped the Soviet attack, leaving them spread out over a sixty-mile line.

Just hours before the Soviet attack had stalled, Von Kleist attacked with his First Panzer Army and the Seventeenth Army from the south, and within a few days, the German forces had trapped the Soviets in a ring of steel and began to systematically destroy them.

Mengele was assigned to a forward field hospital, and from his vantage point, he could see into the Bereka Valley. Here, some two hundred and forty thousand Russian soldiers were now surrounded and fighting for their lives.

The Russians tried some new tactics.

They launched packs of dogs, mostly Alsatians and German Shepherds, carrying explosives on their backs and trained to trigger it on the underside of a panzer.

The German infantry soon learned to shoot any dog they saw. Now the field became littered with the carcasses of large dogs that were a menace to foot and vehicular traffic, but the Germans continued to shrink the pocket.

That night, after a relatively easy day in the hospital tent, Mengele and other medical people stood on the hill and watched for the coming battle. The Russians, for the past two nights, had tried to break through the ring and flee to the east to rejoin their armies.

They came again that night, linked arm in arm, out of ammunition, but still swinging their rifles to slash with their bayonets flashing in the star shells as the German artillery kept the night bright for their machine gunners and mortarmen and riflemen who took aim on the Slavic men, some of them drunk on Volka and all of them high on fear and bravery as they came charging against the German line yelling 'Urra! Urra!'

Mengele watched thousands die that night. The way the Slavic men charged into certain death gave Mengele an uneasy feeling.

"I only hope our ability to kill them always exceeds their willingness to die," a blood-soaked surgeon said quietly to no one in particular when the battle finally faded off, and did not ask if anyone else could hear the moaning from the valley.

It was near the end of March, 1942 and the temperatures had already hit ninety at noon in the southern Ukraine, the United States had not been at war for three months yet, and the Soviet losses in the first month of the spring offensives in their attempt to take Kharkov back was seventy thousand men killed and another two hundred thousand to be marched off to the west, only a rare one returning.

The Germans also destroyed the Soviet forces in the Crimean and the Kerch peninsula, and Manstein and the Eleventh Army pounded the city fortress of Sevastopol with the huge guns named after members of the Krupp household and engineering staff.

Hitler and his armies were buoyant.

Surely the Soviets were getting to the end of it's capacity to lose half a million men with millions of pounds of material a month!

And the spring belonged to the Germans.

With the Izyum pocket eliminated, Hitler set about building Army Group A to just over a million men and concentrated his air power there as he laid plans to strike eastward to the Don, isolate and neturalize Stalingrad, re-take Rostov-on-the-Don, and come to control the wheat, iron, manufacturing facilities, and the oil of the Caucasus.

The Germans spent the next month preparing for their summer offensive. Stalin still thought the attack would be towards Moscow, but even after losing close to seven million men, he still had over six million men to confront a much weakened Germany and her allies of Romania, Hungary and Italy, that all supplied an army each to the eastern front. The Italians reached the epitome of their contribution by creating a buffer between the Romanians and the Hungarians, who would have preferred killing one another than their Russian adversary.

The battle line now extended from the Mius River on the Sea of Azov on a twisting snake of a two thousand mile front ending in the Gulf of Finland east of Leningrad. Almost twelve million men confronted one another.

The replacements in the German armies that hit the front that early summer were a lot older and a lot younger than their countrymen who had first stepped across the Bug just one year ago. From the time when they crossed the river, the rate of death in that part of the world was a million people a month in military and civilian casualties.

Mengele had convinced Becke that the medics and ambulance drivers needed direct supervision of a doctor in order to ensure that the procedures followed at the point of battle were the correct ones to get the men the best possible chance of survival.

Mengele was more than thankful to get out of the grueling grind of the operating room. He came to like the smell of the battlefield much more than the awful odor of men in the operating room; death and blood were not nearly as bad outdoors, where there was a breeze to carry away the stench. And he did not mind being a part of the battles.

Especially since he knew of many instances where hospitals were wiped out by the Soviet air force. As the summer offenses got underway in late June, the Vikings were attacking as part of the Seventeenth Army towards Rostov. But their attack was encountering only sporadic resistance, the same thing that the upper forces of the southern army were encountering. Retreating Russians were leaving everything intact. As the German pinchers clamped shut in hopes of netting hundreds of thousands, they acquired only thousands.

The Soviets had learned that holding fast too long, or advancing forward too far, would allow the Germans to surround you, and once they had you surrounded, they were the masters of killing you until you raised your hands in surrender.

Active defense seemed to give way to rapid retreat. The motorized infantry of the Viking Division seemed to be away from the main fighting as they closed on the outskirts of Rostov.

The advance units of the Seventeenth had arrived in the city along with units of First Panzer and this time the Germans came in sufficient strength to guarantee their strangle hold on the city that controlled the eastern part of the Don, that wide wandering river that was the soul of Russia, as the Volga was the heart.

And Ivan was not here to defend the city.

Since the spring had so decisively belonged to the Germans, it was their turn to strike first in the summer. After General Mud relinquished control of the fields after the spring rains, both countries shook up their supply lines and shipped everything they could to the fronts. The factories continued to turn out the necessities of life; the tanks, the anti-tank guns, artillery, ammunition, aircraft, armored personnel carriers, mobile guns, and thousands of other items suitable for use in killing millions of people piecemeal, or a whole lot of them all at once.

The German generals were still casting longing eyes at Moscow, the only place they could see Stalin amassing a decisive amount of his forces, where Clausewitz, the master tactician, could be satisfied with his teaching that only by destroying an enemy's army could one be victorious. Occupying his territories was not enough. The generals had quit bringing up the subject of Moscow because Hitler would just lecture them on their ignorance of economics.

With the weather turning ideal for massive movements of men and material, Hitler ordered the bulk of his army into the southern part of the battlefield, ordering Center and North to clean up the partisans in their area and hold their lines. The Einsatzgruppe was to continue to carry out its duty in the east. Thousands of square miles and about eighty million people in the eastern occupied territory came under the control of the Nazi Party. They came under the control of the SS and Himmler.

Von Bock, Commander of Army Group A, was given more than half of the available armed forces with orders to destroy the Soviet armies east of the Don, re-take Rostov-on-the-Don, destroy the Soviet armies between the Don and the Volga Rivers, neutralize Stalingrad and have Sixth Army and Fourth Army to secure Von Kleist's north flank as he turned Seventeenth Army and First Panzer south to the Causasus, at least to Maikop to get the oil so that Hitler would not have to, as he put it, pack this war up."

Foreign Armies East, a German military intelligence community, took into consideration that the Soviets had already lost close to seven million men. They calculated that the most the Soviets could throw into the coming summer battles was a little over three million. They arrived at that number by counting people in Russia like they would count them in Germany. Which would be fine if they were counting Germans, but they were counting Russians, and they missed the number of men in the opposing army by three million.

Their biggest mistake was in not counting the women.

The woman's place in Germany still centered around the kitchen, children, and church. Having been kept there because the Nazi Party had no room in the decision making process for women. The Russian woman had no church; it had been taken away by the Communists, the Germans were slaughtering her children, and they had little to cook in the kitchens. Which left her free to man the factories and the fronts.

Which meant that the Germans were preparing to attack three million men while the Russians were preparing to defend with six million men. When that happens, none of your planning will be good enough.

The Germans and the Russians had been at war for one year and one week and from the time the Germans had crossed the Bug River the preceding summer and the launching of Operation Blue, the German summer offensive, the rate of death in eastern Europe was clicking right along at a million people a month in military and civilian casualties, and was about to escalate.

The battle line in the east now extended from the Mius River as it emptied into the Sea of Azov at Taganrog, on a snaking two-thousand-mile front northward ending in the Gulf of Finland, just east of Leningrad. No matter what the intelligence people on both sides thought, there were actually close to twelve million men confronting one another.

Stalin thought like the German generals. To him, Moscow was the only logical target. He even ignored a portion of the Germans' plans that had fallen into his hands because a Wehrmacht officer had disobeyed orders and had them with him when his plane was shot down two miles inside Russian-controlled territory. The news of that sent Hitler into such a rage that he actually frothed in anger at the mouth for the first time in many years, to come over the next few years.

Stalin believed, however, that Germany was still strong enough to attack on more than one front, but told Churchill and Roosevelt that Hitler and fascism were all but finished, and if they did not open a second front soon, then only the Soviet Union would be dictating the terms of the German surrender.

He did have, however, enough forces so that he could give Timoshenko over a million men to defend the Caucasus and keep the oil from the Germans.

Oil that Germany needed more than ever.

And on June 28th, 1942, Hitler and his generals launched Operation Blue with Colonel-General Weichs' Second Army striking out from the most northern point of attack towards Voronezh, one hundred miles to the east, and two hundred miles south of Moscow. With Stukas and Panzers leading the way, they gobbled up the territory as they closed in on their first objective, actually on the Voronezh River, just a few miles west of the Don.

On their right flank, Herman Hoth's Fourth Panzer and the Hungarian Second Army blasted their way through the Soviet forward units, and they were a force not stopped by the defending Russians, and it was almost just like it was in the beginning. Churchill hoped that the Russians could hold out just long enough to get the Americans over here in force, because if the Russians folded, then Europe was going to be fascist for a lot of years to come.

And even their island could fall.

After inflicting the initial losses on the Soviets, the Germans pressed forward, expecting the counter-attacks and dying to the last inch of soil displayed by many of the Soviets, especially the Russians, but for the first time, the Soviets did not stand to be encircled and slaughtered. Nor did they launch counter-attacks to bleed their enemy and slow their advance–the active defense that Stalin had always ordered–nor did they launch a massive attack of their own. The last time they had done that, the Germans had destroyed them in embarrassing and frightful numbers.

Since they could not stand fast, or attack, or surrender, that left retreat. And to no one's surprise, it was the easiest maneuver to teach the troops. They left their forward units engaged, and they turned their armies to the east and they raced for the safety of the Don.

Two days later Sixth Army under Paulus launched their attack out of Kharkov south of Weichs, and only found the rear guard as the Soviets in their sector also raced for the east bank of the Don. The German armies were doing everything that had been asked of them. They were covering great distances in short periods of time and arriving fully equipped and loaded for Ivan. But Ivan wasn't there.

Mengele managed to convince Becke that he would be more useful to the division if he were placed in charge of the field medics and ambulance drivers. Becke had not wished to deploy his surgeons in such positions, and it was only after talking to a Major Reim on the telephone that he was convinced that it was worth trying.

Mengele was grateful to get out of the grueling grind of the operating room. He realized that he did not have the aptitude for performing surgery on men who had been acted upon by explosive external forces. He relished exactness and precision, and the thought of standing for hours, trying to piece people together, most of the time with pieces missing, made him dread the battle his unit was about to enter.

He hated hacksaw surgery.

He much preferred the battlefield, where he could see what was taking place and his work day was done when the wounded were all properly patched up and on their way to the field hospitals, and he knew he was not any safer in the hospitals because they were a favorite target of the Soviet Air Force.

It was stifling inside the cab of the ambulance that Mengele shared with Otto Lang. It was a condition both men had grown accustomed to: heavy, hot, unmoving air, the memory of the past winter already sweated from them.

The flies were back with the heat, and there were at least three of them buzzing against the windshield in an angry attempt to get out. There weren't, however, as many as there had been in the past summer. Mengele knew that the deep freeze of the winter had destroyed an unusual amount of larvae, and there were fewer horses around to contribute to their food chain. Information he probably would have shared with Horn.

Lang was a broad-shouldered, thick-chested man of twenty-five who had survived the first rocket attack of the war. He had been about to jump over the sides to follow men that he had joined the regiment with, rallied with, trained with, and now killed with, when they all heard something new. It was enough to make him hesitate and stay in the crouched position inside the vehicle.

The rockets hit and exploded just in front of the men who had already disembarked, sending them screaming dead to the ground full of glowing hot slivers of steel, their faces chewed red-raw and beyond recognition.

The 7.12mm steel sides of the armored personnel carrier had been thick enough to save his life. Only his exposed left arm was hit, and he could remember looking down at these men that meant so much to him and then looking at his own arm, pulling it, stinging and bleeding back inside the safety of the vehicle, and had sitting down heavily and vomited.

He had mended at the front and had been promoted to SS-UnterscharFührer, sergeant, and he knew he had earned his square tab of rank, that one solitary pip exhibited on his collar, by living long enough, and through enough, to get it.

With his injury, he was told, he could have made a case for going home.

Maybe not completely out of the army, but at least to a staff job in Berlin, or maybe even Paris.

Preferably Paris. It was not getting bombed like Berlin was being bombed, the British by night and the Americans by day.

But he knew that he was where he belonged.

He had been relieved and elated on his fourteenth birthday when the genealogical researcher had delivered his father's birthday present to him. It was the documentation proving the family of pure Aryan Blood to 1735, fifteen years longer than the actual requirement. He had wanted nothing in his life except to be the best, and be with the best, and everyone knew that only the very best became SS men. Only the purest of Germans could become SS.

He joined at the age of eighteen, passing the height requirement only after it had been dropped to 5'8." Himmler had all the voluntary six-footers he was going to get in his new SS, and he was still short of men.

Lang had always enjoyed perfect health. He had all of his teeth, pearly white and even, none of them with even the hint of a cavity. His complexion was clear, and his eyes were a very light gray that could seem to change depending on the light. When he was in uniform and with his fellow soldiers of the <u>Germania</u> Regiment of the <u>SS-</u>

<u>verfugungstruppe</u>, and they were in public and not in formation, the frauleins, and sometimes a frau, would become so bold as to leave no doubt of their intentions or desires.

Those women had seemed all bright and gay and full of life, and he soon learned that they expected an SS man to be demanding and pounding in lovemaking, and he was proud to be able to oblige them.

To put on that black uniform was to declare oneself one hundred percent Aryan. Guaranteed and certified free of Asian or Negroid blood, and especially free of any Jewish blood, the admixture of the two.

He hated Jews and Communists and free-masons and Gypsies and all the sub-humans that were infecting the landscape. He knew that the enemies of the Reich and of the Aryan Race were not in Berlin or Paris, but here in Russia.

He was an SS man. His duty was to be at the front and to kill the enemies of the Reich, to kill the enemies of the Aryan Race.

But he did not think it was noble to kill them from a firing squad position. He could see no honor in that.

He wore the Iron Cross First Class and the Bronze War Wound Badge, that oval with the profile of a helmet with the swastika and the swords crossed behind it, and he had been a panzergrendiar with the old 5th, the <u>Germania</u> Regiment when they had all been German and they had fought the Jewish inspired Communists together, but they were taken by surprise by the rockets that some Jew had designed that came sounding not like shells, but like a pleasant musical interlude of a play you were enjoying, until it impacted.

He had been at war since the invasion of Poland, and he knew that he could never let go of it. He could not go to Berlin and stand in polished splendor in front of some bureaucratic building housing a Nazi official.

He had probably, by now, personally killed over seventy people, most of them Russians, most of them men.

He ignored all the talk about the easy escapades with the sensuous French women brought back by men who had been stationed there.

He was in a part of the world where it did not matter if the woman was sensual or not, willing or not. If you wanted her, you threw her to the ground, or bent her over a table, or positioned her any way you wanted, and you took her. And if you wanted, you could shoot her afterward. Although he had never done that, he shot them afterwards, that is.

No. The war was here for him, and he knew in his heart that he was not ever going home from it. So he was going to do whatever he could do, and right now, with his arm injured, he was only capable of driving a truck, and the ambulance was one of the least vital of the vehicles of the division.

Lang pulled out right behind an armored personnel carrier as soon as it passed, joining the convoy heading east out of Slavansk. So far they could not hear any firing, only the whine and backfire of their engine, a four cylinder flat head, and the bang, clang, and squeak of the treads of the Sdkfz-251 in front of them churning up the fine sand and swirling it through their open windows filling the cab with particles that glistened in the sunlight filtering through the already filthy wind screen. It made Mengele sneeze, leaving the inside of his nostrils burning.

"ScharFührer! I would expect one of our Scandinavian troops to be foolish enough to get behind one of our tracked vehicles, but I thought you had better sense," Mengele fumed.

"I am sorry, ObersturmFührer, for the inconvenience of the dust and the noise, ' Lang apologized, "but I thought you wanted to stay close to the fighting. In order to do that, you must stay close to the fighters."

"Listen, Lang," Mengele said, holding on as the truck pitched in the potholes, "I want to be close to them in battle. Not in column! In the future, get behind only tired vehicles."

"This was supposed to be an attack, ObersturmFührer," Lang protested.

"Do you hear any guns?" Mengele asked.

Lang revved up the engine high enough to cram the gearbox into third so he could rest his left arm, tiring after the first few miles more from tension than the distance.

He had been on many advances and attacks, and he missed the sound of the guns.

"What do you think, ObersturmFührer, has Ivan given up?"

"Of course not," Mengele answered. "He is just pulling back to the other side of the Don. We will have to fight him for that river."

Lang looked out over the vast expanse through his side window. Nothing but distance, mile after mile of empty steppe.

He hated the time between battles, the time and distance between the rail and road junctions that Ivan would defend and counterattack.

Time between the rivers.

He hated the travel. The continuous march day after day across a boring land that did not seem worth conquering, and then all of a sudden, the Soviets decide to counter-attack, or they hit you with another weapon that you were not prepared for.

He had carried his gas mask as close as a second skin, but yet had to use it except in a false alarm, or maybe it was a drill, he never did find out which it really was.

Maybe Ivan was really dead. He died in the distance, and you were not going to have to contend with him ever again.

But Lang had watched the column of Russian prisoners marching out of the Izyum pocket. Men stripped of all insignia and rank and medal and weapon. Especially the weapon. If you were a soldier and another soldier had taken away your weapon, then you are a lamb to the coyote.

They were forty Slavic men abreast, most of them Russians, and they went trudging on for hours. There must have been miles of them. Miles of smashed men turned lambs, turning themselves over to the mercy of the coyote.

Another two hundred thousand men marching themselves into slavery and oblivion that the Germans had really begun to get organized.

Mengele sneezed again. "I do not want to breathe this for the rest of the day," he complained, but knowing that Colonel Dust was back on the battlefield, and he was going to be breathing it all summer.

The division took three days to cover the thirty-five miles to Kremennaya, not because of enemy resistance, but because their purpose was to push en masse and wait for Fourth Panzer to come down the east bank of the Don, and together these forces would smash the Soviet Armies defending the city.

It was late that evening before they had a chance to cross the Donerts River, made into a quick, muddy rolling stream by the early summer rains that had delayed their attack. The engineers who had wrestled the river for the right of passage were still wrestling the river to keep it as debris from the north washed up against the pontoon bridge's side.

Lang drove over the pitching and yawing plank and float span with an ease that made Mengele envious. When they reached the other side, they turned south, passing through a village, a cluster of burnt-out shells devoid of people who had decided to flee to the east.

There was just one hour of daylight left when they heard the roar of the 105s as the mobile artillery got close enough to fire on the rear guard of the enemy. An FW4 observation plane had spotted Soviet tanks, and there was hope that they could reach the rear of the retreating Russians by dark. They could give them a good shelling tonight and start shredding them tomorrow.

The next morning, Mengele took his ambulance company to form a line behind the attacking units of the Division. Mengele was thankful that all the men directly under his command were German, and not Scandinavian, but because of linguistics, not because of genetics. The division was full of tall, blond, gray or blue-eyed men. It was the first of many divisions to be formed with men outside of Germany, but the Army remained Aryan.

The 105s and the 150s opened up on the Soviet positions a few hours before daylight. They could have saved their ammunition as the Russians had continued to flee during the night, leaving only enough men to challenge the German patrols. As soon as it was light, the division surged forward in the wedge position for the first part of the day but encountered nothing.

This became a routine for the Viking Division over the next two weeks. Soviet resistance, thin at first, now thickened as the retreating Soviet armies funneled into the bridges in and near Rostov. To the Russians, the eastern side of the Don meant escape into the vastness of the steppe and eventually into the safety of the Caucasus or of the Volga River.

The Soviet Army knew that they would need time, or the Germans would overtake them. Rostov was fortified with the same NKVD troops, the elite unit of Stalin's secret police, that had forced Dietrich and Leibstandarte Adolf Hitler from the city the preceding November, with orders to delay the Germans.

They dug in and prepared to defend the city and all the bridges in villages up river against the German onslaught.

The Viking finally hit the fighting front just before the sun hit the high part of the day and really began to blister the dark soil of the steppe.

A Soviet tank brigade was fighting from the ruins of Novocherkassk. The Viking Division was trying to bypass to the east this leveled to rubble rather prosperous village, but it just gave the Russians the angle.

Mengele and Lang did not hear the crack of the Russian guns, but they watched as suddenly two of the personnel carriers in front of them exploded. Then the ground seemed to sputter all around them as missed rounds designed for hitting steel hit dirt.

Lang swung the steering wheel violently to the left and pulled in behind one of the still-burning carriers. They could see that all the men were dead. The smoke burned their eyes, and they could smell flesh burning.

"What are those!" Mengele yelled, looking around to his right as another PC came charging by, it's engine roaring as if it was in pain, the forward-mounted MG 34 blazing away in the hands of a Norseman directing a line of fire that raked the street in front of the concealed Russian weapon.

"Those are 50mm anti-tank guns, and that fool has just killed himself and eleven other men!" Lang yelled back.

Seconds later, his prophecy was only half fulfilled when a round hit the long, slanting hood of the vehicle and skipped into the face of the driver. The gunner, who had grown up in the same village, went up in the same conflagration.

Lang gunned the engine, down-shifted, popped the clutch and sped to cover behind the newly hit carrier, the ground erupting in angry dirt all around them. He pulled to a stop behind the still-burning armored car.

Mengele and Lang jumped from their ambulance and kept their heads down as they darted the remaining few yards to the half-track that offered their only cover.

Three of the men in the vehicle, dazed from the explosion, guessed wrong about the origin of the round, and when they swung themselves over the side they dropped into the direct line of fire of a heavy machine gun hidden in the rubble of what used to be the post office, and the 9mm high velocity bullets caught two of them standing and erupted their chests into an explosion of lung tissue, blood, and bone. The other one went down with a single gut shot, and as he lay grasping for breath, more rounds found him on the ground and finished him off.

Six others, their sergeant had been seated with his back to the driver's compartment and had not survived the initial blast, clamored over the leeward side where Lang and Mengele ushered them up against the nine-ton halftrack, now useless except for cover.

They were men from Norway, thousands of miles from home, sweltering in what seemed a desert to them, and they had just received their first real baptism of fire. Shooting, shouting, drunken charging men as they tried to break out of the pocket to live was not their baptism of fire. Shooting at a very distant retreating enemy was not their baptism of fire. Their baptism of fire was just now when their enemy put a 75mm round meant to cause havoc on steel and devastation on the flesh inside, dead on target.

And they did not kill you with it.

But they introduced you to the suddenly you are dead syndrome of the battlefield.

It was a few seconds before they began to come out of their shock. Then the anger swept over them, that bitter sour tasting anger that you feel when the enemy has taken a shot to kill you, and their shot should have killed you, but it did not kill you, and you were alive and now by God it should be your turn to try and kill them.

A private readied his weapon and peered out from behind the tracks to let loose a short burst from his MP-40 SMG machine-gun before the ground exploded in front of him as the heavy machine guns of the Russians answered his angry burst with an overpowering response.

"Everyone just stay down!" Lang ordered, knowing that something heavier was going to have to take notice of their predicament or the Russians would decide that there might be a lot of Germans yet alive on the other side of that smoldering scrap of steel, and decide to put another round on two into it just to make sure.

The Russians, an anti-tank company reinforced with a pontoon of heavy machine guns, were an ideal mix for stopping armored infantry.

Mengele set a broken arm and quickly wrapped a bandage securing it tightly against the chest of a young man of eighteen who was surprised at the prompt medical attention he was receiving, having had not such care when he had broken the same arm on the soccer field when he was eleven years old, where he had lain for hours before it was set by a doctor, and maybe for the first time really began to believe that Der Führer could actually look over you, as it was reported.

A shell exploded near them, and then another hit closer, showering them with dirt, and the young Norseman gave up any notion of anyone but God looking out over him.

Then the Russian gunners must have spotted the ambulance again when the dust and smoke abated, and the next round ignited it into a flash fireball sending a massive column of burning black smoke into the air.

They could hear the exchanges going on up and down the line, and they all realized that they were right smack dab in the middle of a battle and for right now, they were all at a disadvantage.

Mengele made sure that no one else was wounded.

He was an SS officer, but he was a doctor. In this situation, the experienced NCO took control.

"Let's sit tight for a second. Something will happen to take this pressure off of us!" Lang yelled.

Mengele watched as the closest 251 '5 turned to the north, recognizing that there did not need to be any more infantry in a can in that area. The Soviet 75mm's were just short as they made their shot on the evading Germans, who continued on in the direction of the river.

As they huddled against the steel treads that offered no spot of softness or comfort, they could see a company of panzers churning across the steppe, when two of them peeled off heading in their direction.

"Panzer on it's way!" yelled one of the Norwegians, excitedly.

"I wish it was a Stuka!" exclaimed Lang.

"What do you mean?" asked one of the other men, pale-faced and wanting a reason to think things were going to get better.

"That III has only a SOmm L40. That's a 75mm dug in over there. If they can shoot, and from what we have seen so far, they can shoot, then they have the distance. We need a Stuka to drop a thirty-five-pound bomb, or we need one of those 105s or 150s, I can see about a mile to the right over there." He looked at the young Norseman, who seemed very attentive.

"War is just good math," he explained, "learn how to add and subtract, and then watch out for all the things that you can not see coming. Then you can live through it."

"It might be the wrong maneuver for him, but I sure hope he makes it," Mengele said.

The German panzer started firing before it was within range, and its effect was only to stir the Russian gunners to take better aim, and their next round caught the Panzer high on the right side, stopping it and setting it afire.

The side hatch in the turret popped open, and Mengele could see the tanker put one arm through the opening and try to pull himself out, but the smoke was sapping the man's strength.

Mengele darted from his cover and closed the short distance to where the panzer was beginning to billow a silo size funnel of grayish-black smoke that made the announcement that the enemy guns had found them.

He heard the Russian machine guns open fire again.

Mengele grabbed the tanker by his shoulders and tugged, but could not budge him. He stepped up on one of the trains and swung one foot onto the treads. The Norwegian moaned. Mengele could feel the intense heat from the burning panzer as the fire spread deeper into the interior. He knew the tank was getting near the flash point. It could be the flash point of the ammo, or it could be the flash point of the fuel, but there was going to be an explosion of some kind any second.

He stood up completely on the treads and pulled the now nearly unconscious man from the death grip of the turret, and together they went backward to fall into the dirt, knocking the wind out of Mengele. He gasped, grabbed the tanker by his collar and started to drag him to safety. The Norwegian coughed and spit, but was getting some air into his lungs. He knew that the thing was going to explode, and he started to crawl on all fours. They had made twenty yards when it went off with enough force to separate the turret from the body of the tank, knocking Mengele off his feet face-first to add taste to his memories of the soil of the Steppe. The panzer now was just a hulk of smoldering steel.

The Russian machine gunners took notice of the two staggering and crawling Germans, and the last five feet was just ahead of a stitching line of fire that ended in ringing off steel as they scrambled behind their shield.

"All of you!" Lang yelled, "Get over here in the dirt." He judged the farthest point away from the disabled carrier and still out of sight of the machine guns. "They will put some more 75s into us!" He knew the machine gun fire by the private and the heroics of the lieutenant, would convince the gunners that there must be live Germans where there should be dead Germans.

The men hesitated, and the round hit just on the opposite side of the 251, the blast killing two outright, nearly decapitating them, and sent the rest of them sprawling. The one who had really wanted to understand the mathematics of war and battle wandered out dazed into the angle of the Russian line of sight, and the machine-gun got him, spinning and pirouetting him and then slamming him down hard, dead to the ground.

Then they heard an explosion from the enemy's position, and then another, and then another of high-impact bombs and Lang yelled, "Stuka's," and one flew over their position as he climbed out of his dive. The next two planes followed at precise intervals, all climbing in different directions. There was no more firing from the Russian position.

Lang went to tend to the dead, Mengele the living. Two had slight lacerations, and Mengele plucked some shrapnel from one man's shoulder, but their wounds were minor. They would not go too far west for recuperation. The third man had caught ricocheting steel with his eyes and was going to soon have a medal, a white-tipped cane, and a long, lonely train ride home along with the other maimed.

The tanker that Mengele had saved was now sitting with his head between his knees, his eyes tightly shut in an unsuccessful attempt to take out the stinging. Every once in a while, a corner of his eyelid would open, and a gush of tears would run down his black, sooted face. He had quickly learned that taking long, deep breaths would send him into a coughing spasm that left him feeling as if his ribs were split and digging into his lungs. He took slow, easy light pulls of the hot summer air still tainted with the smell of burnt machines and thought it was the most beautiful-tasting air that he had ever put into his lungs. It did not turn into tiny knives and razor blades once you put it into your lungs, like the fumes and smoke from a burning panzer did.

Olaf Mendenllson was twenty-two years old and had always been an achiever, but getting the air into his lungs he felt was the greatest achievement of his life. He was now certain that he was not going to suffocate. The sound of the battle was now to the east as the Germans pursued the retreating Russians.

"Here, tilt your head back," Mengele said, pulling Olaf's head back by the forehead, and began to pour a canteen of water slowly over the injured man's eyes.

"Open your eyes." Mengele gently ordered,

Olaf thought the man was pouring liquid fire into his eyes, and he clamped them tightly shut.

"It will sting a bit, but we are just going to help your tears that are trying to wash away the pain. So come now," Mengele coaxed, "let's help the tears."

He continued to pour steadily from the canteen and Olaf opened his eyes slightly, and then sensed that this was the same man who had pulled him from the panzer, and then he opened his eyes wide and took the initial pain and felt it abate in the stream of water pouring hot and thick over his eyes.

Then he began to shake and shudder. Mengele helped him to his feet and guided him to a spot in the shade of scrap steel. For the first time, Mengele offered him water to drink. It tasted hot and sandy. He longed for the cold water that he used to drink as a child, which seemed so many years ago. His lungs hurt.

Mengele cut off his boots, the leather steaming. "I think your feet are done enough, don't you?" Mengele asked, snipping off his socks. Olaf's feet were red, but Mengele knew that they were not burned. He poured water from the same canteen over them, and to Olaf, it felt like the cold water he knew as a boy in Kristlansand on the southeastern coast of Norway.

"I think just a couple of days of rest and you will be fit for duty, corporal."

"Thank you for getting me out. I would have died."

"Yes. You probably would have. But if you had not attacked when you did, that Russian gun crew would have had more time to shoot at us. So in this battle, maybe you saved us first." Mengele smiled, showing the wide gapped front teeth. "By the way, what made you do it. You were out-gunned, you know?"

"We thought we had a chance. Our first round was supposed to be smoke, and then we were going to change direction and come out of it within range and with the first shot."

"What happened?"

"I do not know. The gunner was a replacement just arrived. I did not know him that well. Maybe he just loaded the wrong shell."

"Stupid!" Lang spat as he walked up, hearing that explanation. He had just lined up eight dead men, pulling, carrying, and dragging them in the steaming hot steppe to neatly position them in a row, the sweat pouring off him in rivulets, and then he had taken their ponchos and shrouded their faces and as much of their torso as he could with it, but it still left plenty of exposed blood and meat for the flies, and he had looked into what he thought could be the drivers compartment and could not recognize anything that looked remotely human.

As he came close to the dead panzer, he could still feel the heat. He walked around it to make sure that none of the crew had escaped to the other side, knowing it was a lost cause but doing it anyway.

He did not even consider looking inside, knowing that all that would be left would be charcoal pieces of people. That would be up to the death detail.

That was war.

He was a sergeant who had seen a lot of war and had been shot at by Poles, French, English, Greeks, Cossacks, Ukrainians, and Russians, and he was still alive, and it disgusted him to think that with all the ways to get killed in the war, and there were thousands of ways to get killed, stupidity was the saddest.

"Stupid," he said again.

XV

Rostov-on-the-Don fell once again to the Germans on July 23, 1942, after a few days of heavy street fighting. Three days later the Germans had breached the Don and were rapidly pouring their armies across it. Hoth's Fourth, von Kleist's First Panzer, Ruoff's Seventeenth Infantry, and the Rumanian Third Army had all converged on the Don Basin, but Ivan was far to the east collapsing on Stalingrad and the Volga, and far to the south collapsing on the Caucasus. The summer battles had so far netted the Germans less than one hundred thousand men, and when the Russians did not defend the city that the preceding November had merited three entire Soviet armies deployed around it, it helped Hitler to erroneously conclude that "the Russian is dead." What had been left of him had died in their winter and spring attacks.

He then gave the orders that changed the outcome of the war. He decided to go after the whole cake and to go after it all at once, even if it meant splitting his forces inside enemy territory, and he did not care what von Clausewitz taught about that or what the quartermasters thought about supplying two armies from the same source in an already overloaded system as they diverged at right angles and began to open hundreds of miles between them.

Hitler decided to go after the city of Stalingrad itself, and not just occupy the territory west of it to protect von Kleist as he followed his new orders to take the entire Caucasus, all the way to Baku on the Caspian Sea. He turned Hoth from his southern attack to head once again to the Volga to help Paulus. Then he pulled nine divisions from the army in the south, including two crack SS units, Leibstandarte Adolf Hitler and Das Reich, and sent them back to France to equip them as panzer units to prepare for the anticipated invasion of the continent by the English and the Americans. After the fall of Sevastopol, Mannstein was originally to attack across the Kerch peninsula into the west coast of the trans-Caucasus, but Hitler broke this army up and redeployed its units in France and in the siege of Leningrad.

While he diminished his armies, he demanded more of them.

Operation Blue had been based on a series of attacks with limited objectives, culminating in the taking of oil for the Reich.

Oil.

The lifeblood of mechanized war. The black residue of millions of years of organic life compressed by millions of pounds of pressure over millions of years, the resource vital to a nation, especially a nation at war, and Germany did not have one drop of it under it's soil. It did not have as much oil as Pennsylvania, western Kentucky, or southern Illinois. The only oil they had access to was in the Romanian and Hungarian fields, which supplied just over thirty percent of their needs. The rest of their fuel came from coal.

They had plenty of coal, but it came in lumps and had to be dug out from under the ground by men willing to go down on a daily basis and wrestle it from the earth that could kill a couple hundred of them all at once by caving in on them, or blowing up on them, or catching on fire, or doing all three in a matter of a few minutes. Only then could it go into the processing that first had to turn it into a liquid before it began the refinery process that turned it into the fuels and lubricants for the internal combustion engines that carried their men and weapons into war. It was so much easier to pump oil from the ground, the liquid much closer to the refined products than lumps of coal. Coal gasification worked for them; it was just not as efficient.

Mengele, Lang and the rest of the Vikings crossed the Don River without incidence at Novocherkassk, twenty-five miles upriver from Rostov. At this time of the year, the river was running flat but rapid, was a mere six hundred yards across, and was right now full of naked, laughing, swimming German soldiers.

The Don rises out of Lake Ivan-Ozero near Tula in central Russia, sometimes glides ankle-deep in the dry summers and sometimes rages eighteen miles wide with heavy spring rains, drains thousands of square miles of territory as it winds thirteen hundred miles to empty into the Sea of Azov, touching the lives of millions of her people to become the very soul of Russia, and the Germans were crossing it as if they were out on a Sunday stroll and drive, and once across it, they were advancing uncontested southward on a hundred-mile front.

Which was beginning to get on Stalin's nerves. He was now convinced that retreating was becoming a way of life with the armies in the field, especially the ones trying to reach the east bank of the Volga, and he was sorry that his generals had convinced him that pulling back was more advantageous than being encircled and slaughtered. At least when they stood fast, they slowed the Germans down, made them work for their advancements, and made them pay for their advancements, but now the only shots being taken by the Soviets were over their shoulders.

Too late to help Rostov, on July 28th, the Iron Man ordered his armed forces to "Not take a step back" and gave the political commissars their old powers and their pistols back to ensure that the commanders and troops followed the direction of the Communist

Party, which was Stalin's direction, and it was simple and straightforward, kill Germans, and do not concede any more territory.

He impressed upon his field marshals and generals that the Soviet Union was not without limits, even if they had been losing it like it was.

The Germans had turned the corner at Rostov and were in a land whose people never had accepted neither the Tsarist's Russian domination nor the Communist's Russian domination, and now the oil of this region, which supplied the Soviets over seventy percent of their needs, was in danger of falling into the coffers of the Reich.

So far in the south, the Germans had taken control of the bread of the Ukraine, the coal of the Donert's Basin, the iron ore of Kiroy Rog, and almost seventy million people. Millions upon millions of people for the Nazis to turn into slaves to labor for the glory of the Reich. Millions of people infesting the land that should only belong to the Aryan Race.

A little over a week later, after crossing a steppe that seemed to grow in desolation as they preceded south, the Vikings were part of the III Armored Corps that reached their first objective of Maikop one hundred and eighty miles from Rostov, only to watch the night sky aflame as the retreating Russians set fire to the storage tanks and refineries which looked like a thousand panzers burning, and the next day the German oil engineers surveyed the damage and concluded that it was going to be a long time before these fields could be productive again.

They lingered here only briefly before their corps was transferred from Seventeenth Army to von Kleist's First Armor, which was stymied at the Terek River in their attempt to take the Grozny oil fields, the second most oil-productive area of the Caucasus and still three hundred and fifty miles from their final Hitler assigned objective, Baku, the Azerbaijani capital on the Caspian Sea. German daily advancements were beginning to slow and stop as the Russians started listening to the Communists with their pistols, and the people dug in, and they counter-attacked, and once again, they made it a battle.

It helped tremendously that the people of Russia were also getting pissed off at their armies, leaving so many people and places to the Germans who were now threatening their homes, which once had seemed so far from the front.

The Russian soldiers in the field were sick to death of being led to the slaughter and surrender by their generals, and they were sick to death of being slaughtered and enslaved by the Germans. They knew that the invaders were not any braver, or equipped with any superior weapons, but they seemed to always show up at the right time with the most ordinance which gave them the victories. The Versailles Treaty had limited the German Army to one hundred thousand men, which meant that von Sheek had the cream of the military crop to form the core of professional military who knew how to read a watch, which was Napoleon's strength, while most all the experienced timekeepers of the Soviet Army had been shot by Stalin in 1938 because they were mostly Jews trained by Trotsky.

But there was going to be a drastic change of attitude and a drastic change of tactics. The country was now convinced that they could perish in this struggle. The poets of Russia were told to tell it like it is, and they felt it in their souls, and the day that von Kleist took Voroshilovgrad, the Russians read in Pravada.

If your home is dear to you, where your
Russian mother nursed you;
If your mother is dear to you, and you can not
bear the thought of the German slapping her wrinkled face;
If you do not want the German to tear down
and trample on your father's picture,
with the Crosses he earned in the last war;
If you do not want your old teacher to be
hanged outside the old school-house;
If you do not want her, whom for so long you did not
dare even kiss, to be stretched out naked on the floor,
so that amid hatred, cries and tears, three German
curs should take what belongs to your manly love;
If you don't want to give away all that which you
call your Country,
Then kill a German, kill a German every time you see
one.

But the land was uncontested as III Armored Corps headed westward for a few days and then plunged south into the steppe to follow the Panzer Army. The men of Norway, so used to the sea and short, cool summers, were introduced to a land that only became harsher and hotter in the high overhead summer sun as they churned through a thick drapery of dust in a landscape devoid of color or feature.

Colonel Dust was once again contributing to the demise of the German war machine, filter design not having improved on the newly arrived gasoline engines that gulped in air laced with the grit of the steppe that robbed horsepower by lowering the compression of the cylinders of the motors that drove their machines.

It took them almost three weeks to cover the two hundred and fifty miles to their new command, where von Kleist sent them immediately into the attack, but the trek and the dust had worn them out. To the dismay of von Kleist, who felt that they should have been strong and equipped enough to take Ordzhonikidze, they bogged down, and the German attack stalled and died as they faced a resolute Soviet Army peering from fortified positions that over ninety thousand civilians had constructed to await the arrival of the now just dead dog tired men of the Reich who had breathed a ton of dust just to get there.

A week later, Mengele was summoned to Piatigorsk, one of all three of the watering holes in German control in the foothills of the Caucasus, where von Kleist had established First Panzer headquarters after it was evident that the bridgehead across the Terek was not going to be expanded, at least not in the next few days, which gave him time to hang some metals from the chests of his legions, an event that went on in armies no matter what the situation.

The two Norwegian Oberschutzen, private first classes, and the Belgium Unterscharfuhrern were all surprised when Mengele informed them that he wanted the wheel of the four-passenger utility vehicle with the spare tire riding on the long-sloping hood. They were all impressed by the doctor who wove their way through the crowded twenty kilometers of moving masses of men and material, and they all ignored the dust that coated their faces and clogged their nostrils. They told in turn their deeds of valor that had earned each of them that lump of black painted pot metal molded in the shape of the former cross that was going to be their badge of bravery forever, and this time, it was first-class for all of them. Mengele was getting his for pulling the tanker from the burning panzer.

When Mengele tried to turn into the main square, he was directed by a swearing and screaming sergeant to pull back out onto the steppe to park their vehicle.

They were early for the ceremonies and hungry, and they followed their noses to the smells of the field kitchens set up in the main street of the village. They knew it would be the same food, tasting different, but before he could enter the line to the cooked fowl and potatoes, he heard someone call out his name. It was Hobein, and he was hurrying across the dusty street. Mengele could see that he had been promoted to Hauptstrumfuhrer, captain. With him was a thin scarecrow of a man in a brown uniform devoid of rank except for party insignia.

Mengele's companions stopped with him. They did not like the looks of the two men who had hailed their doctor, but Mengele knew that any conversations he would have with Hobein would only confuse his companions. He ordered them to continue to the line forming at the entrance of the field kitchen.

"Heil Hitler!" both men greeted.

"Heil Hitler!" Mengele answered. "I must say that I am surprised to see you here, Hobein." The antipathy between the <u>Einsatzgruppen</u> and the staff of von Kleist had only become exasperated since Poland.

"We carry out the orders of the Reichsfuhrer, even if we have to encounter the snake in his pit!" the gaunt-looking Nazi with Hobein said.

Mengele was stunned. He did not like this conversation. He was under Wehrmacht command, and this man had just made a derogatory remark about his commander.

Hobein frowned, "Herr Homback, such talk will only complicate our mission." He held up the palm of his hand to stop Mengele from responding. "Herr Homback works for Reich Plenipotentiary for Labor Allocation, Mengele. Please excuse him, the pressures of his job sometimes rob him of any diplomacy.

"Do not make any excuses for me, Haupstrumfuhrer," the Nazi official spat.

Hobein ignored him. "Herr Doctor, we were told that you were going to be here today, and by the way, congratulations on your new Iron Cross. We have been looking for you since early this morning."

"What do you want of me, Hobein?" Mengele asked, hoping it was something he could refuse if it would irritate the idiot with him.

"We wish you to accompany us to First Panzer Headquarters. We need you to give expert testimony to the General."

"Testimony about what?"

"About the origins of these people," Hobein paused, "someone who can genetically sort them out." Hobein knew he had him.

Mengele was thoughtful for a few seconds. Meeting with the General would be something he would enjoy talking about long after the war was won. He was also elated to have the opportunity of taking the time to examine the people who seemed to become more numerous as they approached the foothills of the Caucasus.

"I will only participate as a scientist?"

"Of course. Herr Homback will be the voice of the Party, I assure you."

"I would be more than happy to render my professional opinions." Mengele turned to face Homback. "But he must show the proper respect for our military commanders. I am presently under their command, and I will do this only with the permission of the General."

Hobein looked at the tall, thin technocrat of the Party.

"Agreed." Homback reluctantly said.

The three men turned down the wide street full of men in German uniforms as they swarmed into the town to take their turns in luxuriating in the hot mineral waters that sprouted from the steppe. If your advance was going to be stopped by the enemy, then having it happen where you could occupy one of their spas, one of their places where their rich had traveled thousands of miles just to seek the cures offered by the waters, one of their places where comfortable hotels and numerous restaurants lined the streets leading to the pools of different tasting waters. An oasis after so much dust. Mengele vowed to use the waters before leaving.

They soon arrived at First Panzer Headquarters, housed in a two-story stick-and-stone hotel with a classical portico that more than one prince of Europe had stayed in. The flags of the Reich flew from the newly erected flag staffs.

The interior felt cool as they stepped into it from the glare of the noonday sun. Except for some tiny pictures of Hitler that the headquarters clerks carried with them and hung to pacify visiting Nazi officials, the once richly adorned walls were devoid of decorations, having been stripped and carried away by the retreating Russians. A grand staircase of polished stone dominated the huge foyer, guarded by two Wehrmacht corporals with rifles and bored expressions.

They stopped at the desk set to one side of the stairs with a Wehrmacht lieutenant in command of who should pass the sentries. His face fell to the floor when he saw Homback.

"We are here to see General von Kleist. Please announce us at once!" Homback demanded.

"But Herr Homback, we were not expecting you today," the young man answered regrettably, anxiously searching the log in front of him. He knew that no matter what happened over the next few moments, it was going to end with his ass being chewed out. If he was adamant, rude, and insulting, he might manage to turn this Nazi official away, but then Berlin would be on the phone, and they would have a conversation with some colonel for the shabby way an official of the Reich was treated by a lowly lieutenant of the Wehrmacht. Then, that Colonel would later summon the officer involved and tear him a new one. If he allowed Homback access to one of the officers present upstairs, they would immediately tear him a new one.

He decided that he might as well take it now. At least this way, he would not have to contend with this foul-mouthed, bad-breathed, ugly man who had already ruined more than a few of his days.

He excused himself and walked swiftly up the stairs and turned when he reached the top and disappeared from view. He walked slowly down the wide, rich, carpeted hallway, knocked loudly on the heavy, dark door, and entered when ordered.

Major-General Ernst Koestring, von Kleist's chief-of-staff, was staring at the maps on the table in front of him.

"General," the lieutenant said, "Herr Homback is downstairs with two SS officers demanding to see General von Kleist."

The young staff officer felt that the glaze of the senior officer as he looked up was just shy of constituting a full firing squad, and he could almost read his new orders, transferring him to lead some panzers into battle.

"Did you explain to the Reich official that the Commander of the First Panzer Army has a strict schedule?"

"Yawohl, General, I did," he lied, having delivered that excuse numerous times in the past, only to have it shoved down his throat. "The 1head slaver' of the Reich..."

"The who!" The older officer snapped. "He is an official of the German Government. You will only use correct titles for any and all officials of the Reich. Do I make myself clear?" He liked this young officer, and he did not want him to become loose with his talk that could get him in trouble with the Nazi Party.

"Yes, General!" Of course, General!" the aide sputtered, "Herr Homback of the Labor Ministries insists that he must see the General."

"Who are the SS men with him?"

"I do not know, General. One of them has the diamond of the SD on his sleeve so he must be with the Einsatzgruppen. The other one is a doctor from the Viking division."

Ernst Koestring had been in the army almost all his life, and he realized that this was one of those things that you had to deal with. He removed the monocle from his eye he needed to read with.

"Wait a few moments and then bring them to the office," he ordered.

Ewald von Kleist was a squared jaw, handsome man with light gray eyes with lids slightly hooded in the corner. He came from a long line of successful military men and had made the transition from General of the Calvary to Colonel-General of the Panzers. He was the first general entrusted with enough tanks to be considered a panzer army, and yet he was a Knight of Justice in the Knight of Honor of the Order of St. John Hospitaller of Jerusalem. The SS that had dealt with him in the past referred to him as 'General Fisheater,' but not in front of any of his officer corps. He viewed these wars in the East as part of history unfolding, following the course set thousands of years ago. While he did not like to march under the Nazi banner, he had, in 1934, along with the other officers of the Wehrmacht, given his allegiance to Adolf Hitler, and he was conquering lands for his country, the noble profession of a soldier.

He was just as annoyed as his subordinates about the arrival of the Nazi official demanding an interview. He had already had this argument with the politicians many times, but for once, he knew he was not going to lose it. Evidently, Sauckel, Homback's immediate superior, and his boss, Rosenberg, were out of touch with the thinking in Berlin. There was no reason to exploit these newly conquered people for labor in the Reich, especially when the Ukraine was still teeming with <u>untermenchen</u>.

Ever since crossing the Don, this Nazi was on his back demanding free reign over the people, but von Kleist had learned that you do not get the help of the indigenous populations by sending their young men away. In the Ukraine, he had watched people go from throwing flowers to throwing bombs. In the trans-Caucasus, he found people who did not miss the Russians, and if they did not alienate them like they had the Ukrainians, then they would make fitting allies of them, or at the least, they would not make partisans of them.

"The 'head slaver' also has two SS officers with him, one from the Einsatzgruppen and a doctor from the Viking."

Von Kleist picked up some papers from his desk and shuffled through them.

"Mengele. He is one of the Vikings to receive the Iron Cross today. I wonder why Homback has him in tow?"

"I do not know, General, but maybe we can settle some issues right now."

There was a knock on the door.

Von Kleist nodded at his trusted chief, who opened it wide for the delegation to enter.

"Heil Hitler." Homback almost yelled in his thin, shrill voice, reminding von Kleist of his one meeting with Heydrich.

"Gentlemen," von Kleist greeted, "what do I owe the honor?"

"Herr General, I have tried in the past to get your support in matters vital to the Reich, but all I get is resistance from your subordinates!" Homback whined.

"Why, Herr Homback, I do not see how anyone in my command could be impeding your duties."

"My duty is to supply the Reich with the necessary labor to make your munitions, to man the factories that make your weapons. Surely, you must know that the Reich is short of almost a million men, and yet you deny me access to these people who are now under our flag!"

"It seems to me that the Ukraine is still full of people, or at least it was when we left it just a few months ago. Surely you have not depleted it, have you?"

"Of course not."

"Does not Herr Hock, the Reichskommissioner for the territory, refer to the Ukrainians as 'niggers' ."

"Yes. That is what the Ukrainians are to us. What difference does that make?"

"Then send the niggers of the Ukraine into the factories, Herr Homback, and leave my people alone."

"Your people!" Homback exploded. "Your people are <u>untermenchen</u>. They are here to do nothing but our bidding!"

"That is the first thing that you have said that I can agree with. They are here to do as we tell them, and right now, we are telling them that they are liberated from the yolk of Communism, that they can go back to their old ways and be content to live in a land and worship their Allah and help us in keeping the hated Russians from the oil under their sands. The Karachoeris, Kabardines, Ossets, Azerbaijanis, Kalmucks, Uzbeks, Chechens, and even the Cossacks who live in this area all hate the Russians and can be made our allies. At least we will not make enemies of them by sending their young men away.

"And the Armenians?" Homback demanded.

"They you can have only because their debt to the Russians for stopping the Turks from slaughtering them will dictate that they remain in the enemy camp. That, along with the fact that we are close to getting Turkey to enter the war as our allies, and I am afraid that they will occupy themselves too much with taking up where they left off.”

“Herr General,” Hobein said, “I am here only to set one thing straight, and that is about the Krimchaks.”

“And what about them?”

“They are full of Jewish blood and must be treated accordingly.”

“Nonsense.” Kloestring commented, “Where did you get such an idea?”

“From our genealogical section in Berlin, of course. I assure the General that they were researched thoroughly, and I have with me Doctor Josef Mengele, a geneticist extremely learned in recognizing Jewish blood. I have arranged for him to study some specimens. I am sure he will confirm Berlin’s findings.”

Von Kleist knew that he would not be able to deter the Nazis if they were convinced that the Krimchaks were indeed considered Jewish. He, along with the rest of the officer corps of the Wehrmacht, had learned that the Reich’s policy, which was Hitler’s policy, could not be swayed in any form in regard to the Jews. He also knew that Mengele would find the physical evidence confirming Berlin’s verdict, whether it was true or not.

“That will not be necessary. I am sure Berlin would not err in such a critical area. So, Herr Homback, you may have the Armenians and Haupstrumfuhrer, you may have the Krimchaks. The rest of these people will be left alone. Do you understand my orders?”

“That is most generous of you, von Kleist!” Homback spat. “I will inform Minister Rosenberg of your decision. I am sure that he will pass along to Der Fuhrer himself your attitude about this matter," he threatened.

Koestring opened the door. "Gentlemen. If you please."

Homback stomped out of the room, Hobein and Mengele snapped their heels, sharply bowed their heads to the generals, and followed the red-faced, smoldering Nazi from the room. Koestring closed the door behind them.

"Why did you not just inform Homback that we were following Der Fuhrer's orders in this, Ewald?"

Von Kleist chuckled. "It will keep him occupied and out of our way for a while." He went over and looked out the window.

"These vast spaces depress me. And these vast hordes of people! We're lost if we don't win them over."

He came away from the window. "What else is happening?"

"I am sorry to report that nothing is happening. We are only inching our way forward, and we are killing men from new units that were not in the field yesterday."

"Ivan must be bringing reinforcements across the Caspian. They just keep coming up with new armies, and all of them well-armed. Any news from Stalingrad?"

"Just that heavy fighting is still occurring within the city itself. Paulus is losing a frightful amount of men."

"Such a pity. Hoth could have had that city in the first week of August if Hitler would have left him alone. I do not like it one bit what is going on there. If the Russians on the east bank of the Volga are like the Russians that made it to the safety of the fortifications in these damnable mountains, then I am afraid that Paulus is going to be in for even a rougher time. Has there been any response to my wire to Der Fuhrer?"

"No, Herr General."

Von Kleist went over to the wall where there was a European map covered with flags denoting unit deployments.

"Ernst, if the Second Hungarian stays deployed on Paulus's left flank, and the Third Romanian joins the Italian Eighth on his right flank, that will make Paulus dependent upon our allies. I am afraid that these people do not have the backbone of our German troops, and if we lose at Stalingrad, it will not matter if we can take Grozny and Baku. We also will be pinched off.

"If I was Ivan, I would attack the Hungarians there," he said, pointing to just where in the next few weeks the attack would actually take place, leading to the encirclement of an entire German army, the first time that the Soviets had managed to do that.

"I am afraid that Der Fuhrer is still thinking that Ivan is already defeated."

"Our casualty reports will eventually convince him otherwise," von Kleist answered ruefully. There was a cold chill in his stomach.

"But come, Ernst, let us decorate our brave fighting men."

XVI

The Caucasus is a raw, rugged mountain chain running for seven hundred and fifty miles north to south in an easterly direction from the Black Sea to the Caspian Sea. It is one of the dividing lines between Europe and Asia, and on the south, it would even be assessable to a rare migrating black man out of Africa.

In parts, the chain is a cluster of perpetually snow-capped cold eruptions that stretch into the heavens. Mt. Elbruz, where Zeus bound Prometheus to punish him for giving fire to man, reaches 18,784 feet to become the highest point in Europe, if you concede that it is in Europe, and it shares these lofty heights with eleven other peaks that are higher than Mt. Blanc, the highest peak of the Alps.

It receives more snow than the Alps.

It is colder.

All along the foothills of this backbone of extinct volcanoes is a variation of terrain. There are long swooping valleys laced with streams and rivers teeming with trout, rocky expanses of short green growing grasses for the grazing of horses and sheep, conifer and deciduous forests, with birch trees reaching thirty-five feet in diameter, long rolling valleys and deep gorges cut by raging rivers. It is a diamond jubilee of diversity with one thing in common. The cold.

It is home to more distinct sub-species of man, more languages, and more religions than any other part of the earth. It is a polyglot of peoples, an ancient blender of the Aryan and the Oriental in varying degrees spiced with an occasional African.

When the Romans reached it, they conducted their dialogue with the people with the aid of one hundred and thirty interpreters. The mountains, in their vastness and pockets of isolation, set the conditions for many tribes of people to remain intact over many centuries, each fiercely guarding their customs, their languages, and their blood. There are people with blond hair and blue eyes, people with dark eyes peering out from slanted eyelids, there are fair-skinned people with blazing brown eyes, and people with the high cheekbones of the Asian with the pigmentation of the African. There are more genetically different people in this part of the world than any other, from tribes of hawk-nosed Jews too ancient to have a Talmud, to relatively recently arrived blond giants carrying on the bloodlines and weaponry of the crusaders.

For centuries, it was called the 'end of all the earth.'

For centuries, it was called the 'lost world.'

The Caucasus Mountains are, in fact, a true stone Tower of Babel.

It was the first time since Mengele had been in Russia that the army he was serving with was stationary in good fighting weather. Like the rest of the army, he was used to moving forward between the rain and the cold and found spending the fading September in place distasteful. The front was now just about static all along its twenty-five hundred mile snake from the Terek River in the Caucasus to the Barents Sea in the north.

Giving the commissars back their old authority to countermand the orders of the military men in the field had worked as a stop-gap effort and helped stem the eastwardly flight of the soldiers, but now the concept of dual command was once again causing confusion, dissension, and death. What Stalin finally realized was he had to award his commands on military ability, and not political reliability, and give them the responsibility of reading the watches and coordinating the attacks.

The Institute of the Supreme Council of the Soviets, fifteen men who shook their heads up and down for yes and sideways for no depending upon which way Stalin directed them, issued a <u>ukase</u> on October 9th, 1942, abolishing the post of the Political Commissars in the Red Army forever. From now on the military men would be in control of the battles. And they were in command of a more resolute force made up of many battle-hardened and experienced men to train, teach and lead the hordes of Russians; and the multitudes of Ukrainians, Belorussians, Jews, Tartars, Mordvinians, Kazakhs, Georgians, Armenians, Latvians, Uzbeks, Bashkirs, Karelians, Ossetins, Azerbaijanis, Chuvashs; not to mention the Gypsies, Assyrians, Poles, Greeks, Bulgars, Czechs and even a sprinkling of Spaniards who wished to do nothing more than to kill the German "parasite." To finish off Fritz.

To kill him here in your own country and then shove his ass back into his country where you can burn his cities, destroy or steal his culture, eat his crops, piss in his streams, and fuck his wives and daughters for a change.

Mengele had to spend his time on duty in surgery and contend with the steady flow of men that was not overwhelmed by their numbers like a major offensive could produce. The wounds would be as severe, but you could take more time digging out the pieces from them, sewing up huge gaps and slices on them, or cutting limbs off of them, and to some of them, you had to do all three. You could work the whole morning on one man because he needed it, and you had time to do it, and just before noon, just when you were making your final stitches, he would die on you.

But it did not matter. They would have another for you after lunch.

He dreamt of the university, of the sounds of the empty lecture hall and the smell of the laboratory, of the faculty parties where people of education and merit, intelligence and wit gathered over fifty-year-old brandy after scrumptious meals, all steaming and hot, and talked of the pathways, evolutions, and fallacies of man. He longed for the tradition of having the smartest young men of Germany dressed in tails appear at midnight at his residence, asking for permission to attend his lectures.

Letters from Irene were bright and full of hope. She wrote of where he could teach, and they could live after the war. She told him to stay safe and that her father had given his customary teas, and the young men who were entering the university now were all just one year shy of reaching the mandatory draft age of twenty and could talk of nothing but the war news, a dull lot to say the least for such tall, handsome young men.

He hated it.

He really didn't care if the men lived or died. He found that if he cared that the man lived or died, then he had to face the fact that so many of them died. It was better that none of them mattered to you. There were days when he felt that he was not going to display his surgical skills on a man who comes to you literally in three or four pieces and he is still alive because his heart wants him to be alive, but it had not quite prepared itself for the shell exploding so near, or the lone rifle bullet to be so accurate, or the saber slash to be so violent, or the machine gun bullets to be so heavy.

There were days when the only reason he did not let them all die was it would look bad on his records.

In late October he was happy to be ordered once again to the vanguard of the fighting. The fall rains had been extremely cold, but the rapustisa was much milder and shorter in this part of the world. Von Kleist went for one more stab at Grozny, for the oil, before General Winter took command.

He had been at the Terek for over a month and felt a nagging rage at himself for not moving forward. His inner discomfort did not show as he was always in command of himself and usually everyone else in the room. He took no consolation from the fact that on this same spot, the Russians themselves were held at bay for over one hundred and sixty years, before they finally managed to subdue the Chechens and claim the territory for Mother Russia. The Tsar's Cossacks had camped along this river for generations to hold this fertile valley with the breathtaking view of the mountains and mineral springs percolating up from the desert, but von Kleist had seen enough of it to last him a lifetime.

He was worried not so much at what was in front of him as what lay three hundred and fifty miles due north of him at Stalingrad. That thin ribbon of dirt and polluting industry strung out for thirty miles along the west bank of the Volga, that was transformed on the first day of the assault by the bombing of German VIII Air Corps, from concrete and steel buildings into concrete and steel bunkers. Stalingrad was changing the German yardstick of conquest from countries to kilometers, to streets, to buildings, and sometimes even to floors, and men were now dying over rooms in the rubble.

And this German army that was fiercely engaged had Italians, Hungarians, and Romanians protecting it's flanks. Von Kleist could see the vigor of the people that he was up against grow stronger and knew that if Stalin could reinforce this army so far to the south, then he was surely doing the same along the line north and south of Stalingrad.

He finally realized that the Fuhrer was not going to heed his warnings about risking so much on the backbone of their allies, and decided that it was in the hands of God and turned his full attention back to the only way he knew he could secure his own position. Gain control of the oil at Grozny, capture the passes over the Caucasus, and cross them in the spring, which should bring Turkey into the war as their ally. If Rommel could be successful in taking Egypt then the two armies could link up, and all the wealth of Asia Minor could be in their control.

He launched his final winter offensive by dispatching III Armored Corps, which was the 14th Panzer Division and the Panzergrendiars Viking Division, almost thirty thousand men, on a flanking movement that sent them due west and then arcing back to the east with orders to take Ordzhonikidze, the capital of the North Ossetian Autonomous Republic, and the intersection of the Georgian Military Highway, gateway to one of the passes over the mountains. Then, drive into the oil fields at Grozny from the southwest in the rolling plain running between the Terek and the mountains.

Mengele, with Lang, behind the wheel of a utility vehicle, was in the column of supply and support trucks that made up the third line of deployment. On their right raced the armored personnel carriers and self-propelled artillery, and then, closest to the mountains, the panzers with their turrets trained south. They traveled west the entire morning, always going uphill or downhill, the engines racing and clutches and gears shifting, searching for the right ratio to power this hill or to descend this grade as the mechanized army moved forward.

Mengele held one hand on top of the windscreen and the other clutching the seat frame by the door as they bounced across terrain that wore men out in just holding on. Mengele and everyone else who had the luxury, kept their eyes on the hillsides that seemed to offer thousands of places for the Soviets to hide a long list of things that could kill you.

There were stone fences put up thousands of years ago and huge boulders forming outcrops of ambush, and even the dumbest private understood that looking up meant that the enemy already had the high ground. They crossed the Ardon without being challenged and raced for the wells at Nalchik.

Mengele saw an occasional horseman gallop along a ridge for a few hundred yards and then disappear. Finally, one of them had the misfortune of getting too close and staying too long, and one of the panzers pumped a 45mm that struck just a few yards away and sent rider and horse into pieces onto the ground. The word went down the line in an angry order. Do not ever waste one shell on one rider and one horse at any time.

Twenty minutes later, their column halted. Piss call was taken, and the men up and down the line emptied their bladders as rapidly as they could, gallons of urine, steaming yellow in the cold steppe. When they started back up, they had not gone more than a mile when they spun south and entered a wide scoop between the hills and rumbled into the Fiagdon Valley, a wide rocky arena of brown autumn grasses stretching for miles under a canopy of gray cloud cover anchored to the lower mountain tops, blanking out the sight of the majestic peaks that loomed over these foothills.

Neither Mengele nor Lang heard the shots over the noise, but they both saw the telltale column of spiraling smoke at the same time. The gun that took the first two successful shots protesting their entry into the valley was a 76.2mm that the same seven-man Russian crew had hauled for over three hundred miles, either manually or with the aid of horses, sitting on it to eat, laying next to it to sleep, living with it for over three months, and by now they really knew how to shoot it, and they put those first two shots dead on target. The German gunners in the panzers could also read the crosshairs, and the shell of the fourth panzer caught the gun just back of the breech, shattering it and its entire crew.

Then, the whole hillside lit up as the crack of the Russian guns echoed across the mouth of the valley, and the Corps came under serious fire. Lang swerved the wheel hard to the left which nearly threw Mengele from the bouncing car as the earth exploded in missed shots. There were now more burning panzers, but the rest poured into the valley as they sought to put distance between them, and the guns dug into the hillside.

The last thing that Mackensen, the commander of the Corps, wanted to do was to get into a gun battle with Russian anti-tank guns holding the high ground, but he was forced to wheel an entire company of panzers to the foot of this hill to engage and destroy, or just keep them busy while the rest of the Corps slipped into the valley and sped out of range. Everyone missed the Stuka's, who could have made short work of these emplacements and cover, but there were few of them deployed this far south, and the low ceilings of the valley precluded their participation anyway. Mengele looked back and could see the burning hulks of quite a few panzers at the base of the hill, but no fire coming from it.

As soon as the valley widened enough, the Corps formed the standard 'mott puk,' a wedge of panzers spearheading the advance and the rest deployed down both sides of the advancing Corps with the supply vehicles, artillery, and panzergrendiars tucked to the inside positions. Then, the trucks in front of them began to explode as artillery hiding in the scrub of the land had them bracketed and began to pound them. Personnel carriers were hit, and men were now dropping from the burning hulks of steel. The odor of burning grease and steel and flesh soon hovered in the air. The self-propelled guns spun on an axis and pointed their guns to return fire. Panzers surged forward, their guns blazing. The Germans, Norwegians, Danes, Belgians and the Dutch closed on the withering fire, and after an eternity, they silenced the Russian guns.

They took Nalchik in the late afternoon and secured their place for water. The next morning, they resumed their attack and closed on the Red River, named after the color it had flowed one day seven hundred years earlier when the Mongols had encountered the Ossentians guarding their valley. Heavy Russian fire stopped them just a mile shy of the stream, and the fire intensified, and then they heard explosions behind them. Mengele looked, and at first, he did not see anything but smoke pouring from a dozen burning trucks, and then a horse and rider came charging out into the clear followed by other screaming men.

"Calvary!" Lang shouted, reaching for his weapon. The next rider through, his saber down in his belt, carried a fragmentation grenade, and with his horse racing alongside a personnel carrier, he deftly tossed it over the side where it went off, but the explosion did not get the gunner, and when the horse and rider crossed over in front of him he sawed the man off at the waist, the horse galloping on. There was the sound of small arms fire all around them. They realized that they had been breached by enemy cavalry.

Lang drove to the burning carrier and they both jumped out and up on the tracks. The gunner had since gotten down from his spot and was already helping the men from the now-smoldering can. It looked like there were only a few men dead, but all the others had taken some of the steel splinters, and they were all dazed by the concussion.

They took out the live ones first and laid them in a row on the ground. Lang took a position behind the ambulance with his machine pistol and joined other men who had gotten out of their vehicles to take defensive positions against the charging Ossentians, who seemed to ride out of nowhere to dart between the panzers, ignoring them to get into the more vulnerable center. They could hear trucks exploding and the rattle of small arms fire all around them. Mengele stayed crouched over as he made his way from man to man, tying off arteries and stuffing bandages into seeping wounds. Their parked ambulance was a flag, and other wounded soon began to stumble in on them or were carried there by comrades who had just barely set up, supported by a mortar company, when the panzers pulled forward, making the enemy cavalry think they would have a free ride into the thin guts of the Germans.

They broke from cover and began the dash across the few hundred meters of open ground, but they were soon shredded by the fusillade of bullets and smack of the mortars. Their charge broke early, and the survivors scrambled for the safety of the rocks. There were still hundreds left inside the ring of armor, however, and they went to their death fighting and, if they had the chance, escaping to fight another day. Escaping just to be free to come back tomorrow and be able to charge into this mass of stinking steel brought here by fish-eyed Germans and throw grenades into their laps.

The day was now a gray, gloomy shade of early night. All around them was a reminder of the battle they had just fought. Everywhere you looked, you saw dead men, dead horses, and wrecked vehicles. The wounds came to Mengele in a wide variety to the field hospital they fashioned by draping a tarp from the top of the burnt-out Sdkfz. There were a lot of burns, and burns were like frostbite in one sense. The limb was usually destroyed and had to come off. But he was not going to start in on that for just now. He kept himself busy doing other doctoring so he would not have to face the amputations.

He stepped outside for a breath of air and found Lang, who was staked out with his weapon at the ready.

"Lang. The battle is over. I am going to need your help inside."

Lang turned and looked at Mengele and shook his head softly.

"If it is over then I would not be hearing an occasional shot, Herr Doctor. Something is happening, and I am not sure what, so until I know what it is, I will wait right here," he whispered.

The answer irked Mengele, but not enough for him to make an issue of it. He had sensed the state of rapture that Lang had exuded all day as he had the opportunity to empty his gun numerous times, killing both horses and men that came charging through the maze of a battlefield just to be in his sights. Mengele left the soldier alone.

He stepped back under the canopy and went a few meters before he focused on the Ossentian that had slipped in from the other side. He was short and slight, with an immense black mustache. He had just killed two Norwegians by slashing their throats with well-aimed strokes, and he now had one foot on the chest of a third man to help wrench his blood-stained sword free of the still-squirming soldier.

Mengele realized that the man was going to kill him next, but he was frozen in place. The Ossentian looked up from his grisly work, his soldier's duty, and gave out a yell and leaped with a bloody boot across the distance between them, taking a long arcing swipe at Mengele, the saber opening Mengele's winter parka, and he felt the blade slide through his skin leaving a fiery line behind it.

He clutched at his guts and backed away from the swinging saber that passed so close to his face on the second swing that he could smell the blood on the steel. The next swing caught him on his side, and he went down hard and watched the man step up and raise the sword over his head; Mengele pissed in his pants, but the sword did not reach him as the chest of the Ossentian exploded as Lang caught him with a burst from his machine gun, sending him sprawling backward into the tent, where he fell landing face to face with a young terrified Belgium who watched him die with his eyes wide open full of hate and fight.

Mengele looked down and saw that he was covered with blood, which wasn't unusual, but this time it was his own blood, which made all the difference in the world. After seeing so many similar wounds, he was now introduced to the feeling of having your body violated by a blade, a sharp, heavy piece of steel designed to maim and kill, and as he pulled himself to a sitting position, he could taste the cold metal in his mouth as if particles of the saber were lodged under his tongue. He fought off a wave of nausea, knowing that vomiting would be a painful price to pay to get the bitterness from his mouth.

Lang circled their position, encountering no one but Vikings searching for any more of the mountain men who must have hidden in the carnage to spring alive and deadly as soon as the enemy thought it was safe. He soon returned, slinging his already fully loaded machine pistol over his shoulder by the strap, grabbed the dead man by his boots and pulled him out into the night away from the tent site. He came back and helped Mengele to his feet and moved him under the tarp where a few heaters were just barely taking the chill out of the air, and the battery-powered lights cast dancing shadows that made Mengele see racing men on horseback swinging their sabers.

He passed out.

Two days later, a surprised fellow SS doctor informed him that he was ordered back to Germany for convalescence. It was the same doctor who performed the surgery on him and told him the next day that his wounds were not bad enough to get him out of Russia. They might be severe enough to get him to Rostov, but no farther. But he should cheer up because Rostov could be a charming city if one liked to visit the cathedrals and the churches.

Mengele thought after the man had left, after giving him the news that he was going home, going back to Germany, he thought the man could take the sights of Rostov and the cathedrals and shove them up his ass.

The machine gun companies were ordered to the flanks as the panzers were needed in the front to help deal with the entrenched Russian artillery and anti-tank guns.

XVII

Dr. Josef Mengele received his notice of promotion to SS-Hauptsturmfuhrer, captain, the same day he was ordered to use his own medical judgment as to the earliest possible date that he could terminate the convalescence leave he was taking in Gungsburg and report to Amt IV of the Genealogical Section of the Reich Central Race and Resettlement Office, in Berlin.

He had cabled back that he would be on the earliest possible train.

Irene sewed on his new collar insignia, three pips and a bar, under the watchful approving eye of Wallaburga, who was thankful to Mary, the mother of Jesus, that this Lutheran wife of her oldest could at least stitch.

Josef sat slouched in a huge, overstuffed dark maroon chair that he once had taken naps in curled up as a child and thought of his own wound, now a serious itch along the healing edges of the saber slash. He knew that the surgeon who had placed the stitches had ensured him a scar that ascended the wound, and to him, he would always be grateful. It was a wound of honor, a rendering of his own flesh and a testimony to his duty to the Reich, to the Aryan people.

He tried to focus on his mother and on his wife getting along comfortably together on the divan and could almost remember when that would have made him feel good, but now they would not quite come into focus. It was usually at this time of day, right after dinner, when Russia would come back rushing with the memories.

The quiet and security of Gungsburg had been a blessing. He had breathed in the sight and smell of the countryside as it turned from late fall to early winter, and he had his beautiful blond bride with him to bicycle through the town that he had grown up in, recalling all the good things that he had experienced as a boy, visiting places where important things occurred in his life, and he mended in both body and spirit as everyone fawned and doted on him and treated him like a hero and he did not tell anyone that he pissed in his pants when he thought he was going to die.

A fire just stoked by Maria was roaring in the stone hearth of an already warm room, but she had heard talk about how the men had suffered in that first winter in Russia, and she somehow knew by looking at Josef that he would enjoy the heat. All the small glass panes of the massive windows of the large room were half-crescent circles of sweat as the heat tried to drive the moisture from the air. The fire wheezed, crackled, and blew bombs of escaping gases.

His father sat across from him and angrily folded the <u>Volkischer Beobachter</u> he had been reading and slapped it to the floor, interrupting Josef's attention dancing in the flames.

"Once again, there is no mention of Stalingrad," Karl complained, "don't they know that to cut us off from the news will cause more harm than good. Everyone is beginning to think the worse. Goebbels should realize that we Germans can take the bad news along with the good news." He reached up and switched off the floor lamp that hovered over his chair, light bulbs already becoming more difficult to get.

Karl saw that the women were going to ignore him, refusing to be drawn into yet another conversation about the war, and Josef had always talked like a doctor ever since he had come back from the eastern front. He had never been so proud of any of his sons as he had been the day it seemed like the whole town had turned out to greet the train, and he had watched with the others as Josef had walked doubled over in pain but holding his head up and smiling, his chest teeming with ribbons and decorations. His son had accorded himself well in battle.

But the senior Mengele, along with many others in the Reich, were beginning to see the clouds forming over the battleground in the East, and Der Fuhrer had Germany in a two front war. If you were naive enough to consider engaging the enemy from the edges of the Artic Circle south through the cities of Leningrad, Moscow, and Stalingrad in the thickest part of Europe, to the edges of Asia Minor along the Caucasus Mountains, to the northeast of Africa in Egypt and Libya to the southern Mediterranean and the island of Malta, and Sicily and then along the western coast of France all the way north of Norway back into the Artic Circle, as two fronts. Karl, Sr. was not naive.

"What do you think is happening, Josef?"

Josef looked at his father in the dim light of the room and, for a second, thought about telling him the truth. That there were millions upon millions of people in the East, and they bred like flies, and he was beginning to wonder if they would ever be able to kill enough of them to take away their ability to bring new legions armed to the teeth into the field against you.

"I have no way of knowing any more than you, Father." He finally answered.

"I keep hearing that the Russians have the Sixth Army surrounded at Stalingrad. Could this be true.?"

"I guess it could be possible." Josef hesitated, thinking back to the sentiment in the army, and decided to share it with his father. "I know von Kleist did not like the fact that we had Italians, Hungarians, and Romanians guarding the flanks of the Sixth Army."

"And I thought we were all but finished with our campaign in North Africa, but now we hear about this great British offensive there." Karl Jr. chimed in as he entered the room, causing his father to frown, not because of his son's arrival but because of the topic of conversation he had discovered them in. The old man felt that he could talk with his oldest and not have to worry about being misconstrued. Karl Jr., on the other hand, could take such talk to the extreme and even border on endangering the name of Mengele within the Nazi party, and if the Germans were to lose at Stalingrad, the Party, along with the military, will have to come up with some answers. The old man ran a factory, and he knew how short some of the essentials were becoming far in advance of the public.

The tall blond Karl, a slim copy of his father, crossed the room and hugged Irene around the shoulders. He beamed and kissed his mother on the cheek, who ignored him and walked back to the other side of the room where his father and older brother sat in a conspiracy in front of the fire. Feeling somewhat chilled from the late evening air, he stopped in front of the hearth, his hands behind his back to take the sting of the flames, but moved immediately away from it when he noticed the pained expression on his brother's face, having learned along with the rest of the nation that one should not come between the fire and men who had spent that first winter in Russia.

"Ulrich Schneider was arrested today." Karl Jr. announced, taking the matching chair next to his older brother. "You remember Ulrich, don't you, Josef? He used to come with his father and family to all the company picnics. He has that really pretty sister, Helga, who used to flirt with you. Herr Schneider is one of your foremen at the factory, Father. There are three more sons with Paulus at Stalingrad."

"Yes, I am well familiar with the problems of Herr Schneider," the senior Karl snapped. "It is a shame that one of his sons is stupid enough to say treasonous things in public!"

"All he was saying was what everyone else can plainly see, Father. That there are a lot of young men hobbling around Germany these days. That and the fact that Poland is as far east as the gauleiters' sons are posted, if they are not made to suffer their duties in France."

He acknowledged his brother for the first time. "I am sorry, Josef, I was not going to talk politics, but Ulrich is a friend of mine.

"I remember Ulrich," Josef said quietly, whispering into the flames. "I know what he is talking about because I see them on the street everywhere, and when I do, I wonder if I was the one who had to cut their feet or hands off."

Josef's voice grew stronger. "But I also know I have amputated the foot of a close relative of a gauleiter, including a son, which means his jokes fall on bloodied ears of men maimed for the Reich. There is a war in Russia, and now is not the time to be spreading defeatist attitudes when we are far from defeated!"

"It seems we are also just as far from being victorious," his brother argued, "and I know, Josef, that we are at war in Russia. Do you know that we are at war with the world?"

"Enough!" Karl Sr. snapped. "We are sorry about young Schneider, Karl, but he should know that he could not disparage the Party and Der Fuhrer."

"I can agree with you on that, Father," his lawyer son replied. "There is talk of them introducing the guillotine to deal with people found guilty of treason or of sabotaging the war effort. It seems Ulrich is lucky to keep his head after risking it on the eastern front. The legal system is frozen in fear of the Nazis. The judges do what the gauleiters tell them to do, or they are forced into retirement or into disappearance. There is no voice raised in opposition!"

"It is better that the Party take control and not allow the army to be stabbed in the back like the Jews inspired in the last war!" Josef growled.

"I said enough of this!" The old man pronounced, squashing their arguing. "You two can not solve the problems of the world. Besides, Karl, now is not the time to fight with your family. Josef has received another promotion and has been ordered to Berlin. So let us have some peace in this house tonight."

Congratulations, Beppo," Karl Jr. said, reaching over and squeezing his brother on the arm. "In the direction I'm going, I will probably need friends and family in high places."

"You are not going in that direction any longer, Karl," his father informed him, "the times have become too dangerous for that. But that is another time and another discussion, and it will take place between just you and me."

"But for now, we must not talk of the war, and we must not talk of politics. We must talk, family." Both of his sons sat silent and attentive.

"I do not know which way this war is going to go, but I know which way my sons must go, and that is to look out for each other."

He leaned over to get closer to them.

"You are both fortunate that your younger brother, Aloxis, has the desire and the ability to run the factory. Which means that you, Josef, can become a schoolboy doctor, and you, Karl, can afford to be a bad lawyer."

The two brothers grinned at one another. Their old man had not lost his anger at them for not following him into the factory. It was a relief to the three of them to have familiar family frictions. The two sons looked at their father and silently agreed that he was no longer the massive stern statue they had always known. He was softened by the war and the years.

The truth was, however, that their father had not changed much at all. It was just that they were living in a world full of stern, dominating, grim-faced, determined men, and along with their own reflections, their standard of severity had risen substantially.

Irene finished with the final uniform, held it up in front for her own satisfied critical inspection, and then showed off her handiwork to her mother-in-law. Both women knew that Josef would accept them only if they were perfect.

"Hauptstrumfuhrer Mengele," she sang, up and spinning across the room to lay the dress tunic across his shoulder. "What do you think, Papa Mengele? Can your son be proud in Berlin?"

"He looks fine enough, I guess." The old man acknowledged.

"My Josef will do very well in Berlin," Wallaburga said, coming up to stand beside her oldest, the one who favored her the most, the one that had taken her dark Swabian looks. Her good catholic boy who had become a doctor and had fought against the stupid

Communists who wanted to do away with her private property! What more could a mother ask for in a son, except, of course, for him to have married a Catholic.

"My Josef does everything well," she pronounced proudly.

"When do you leave?" Karl Jr. asked.

"Tomorrow morning." Irene complained."

"As soon as that?"

"Some people have important things to do tomorrow, Karl," the old man said. "Josef has to be off to Berlin and back to service to the Reich. Aloxis and I have to go to the factory tomorrow to labor for the Reich and the family. And you, Karl, being a lawyer, can sleep until noon."

Irene did not wish to be in the middle of the animosity of this family, having been reared by even-tempered, affectionate professional people, and could never get used to how this family ridiculed each other. She picked the tunic back up and folded it carefully over her arm.

Josef, I must start to pack for you." She turned to her in-laws, "Good night, Mama Mengele. Good night, Father Mengele." She kissed Karl Jr. lightly on the cheek. "Please do not be long, Josef," she whispered in her husband's ear as she left the room.

Josef followed soon afterward, leaving his brother to their parents who were just warming to the task of convincing him that he needed to take a much lower profile with his feelings. He would have liked to have stayed and reinforced them, but Irene had never packed his bags before and he knew that she would not do it correctly. He hurried after her in order to take an active part, only to discover that she had merely placed his cases on the bed while laying out his articles next to them. She then retired into the sitting room, where she sat down at her vanity and began to unwind her hair, finger combed the major tangles out of it, and then brushed it.

She could hear Josef in the bedroom whistling Wagner while he meticulously and quickly packed his belongings. Her fair complexion and blond hair gave her a pale and ghostly look in the mirror. Sighing, she picked up a glass container and, with her long, slim finger, dug into the last bit of makeup that she had. The fat shortages of the year before had devastated the cosmetic supply, and she hoped that she might have enough left to apply a touch-up in the morning when she would need it to see Josef off in the light of day.

His whistling stopped, and she could hear him lift the bags from the bed and place them on the floor. When she finally came out he was already in bed with her covers thrown back for her.

The next morning, her goodbye kiss was warm, tender and loving, and he had enjoyed the way that she had clung to his left arm even as he shook hands with his father and only grudgingly let him go long enough for him to give his mother a quick hug.

The train was running just a few minutes late, but there were only a dozen passengers getting on here at Gunzburg, and they were quickly hustled aboard by the conductor. Josef had just time to wave from the steps before the train pulled in lurches from the station, the crew intent on making up for time so they would arrive in Augsburg on time.

Josef had no trouble finding his compartment. He stowed his gear on the upper rack in a well-practiced maneuver and took an inboard seat, his eyes ignoring the other men but out the window, watching his home, watching his town, watching his boyhood country slide by as if the window was a movie screen and it was showing his memories.

After a while, the view through the window blended into the bleak countryside, and he then took notice of his traveling companions. There were two young Nazi technocrats uniformed in the brown of the Party, both sitting straight-backed with solemn expressions and refraining from shop talk involving statistics because the other passenger, a Kreigsmarine, whose bearded fierce face was now hunkered down under his peaked cap and brown leather jacket, had earlier, calmly but deadly told them both to shut up.

Now they were both thinking that this was just what they needed, a short SS Hauptamt with his chest full of badges and medals and reeking of Russia. They wondered why they could not have been fortunate enough to have that gauleiter with his daughter for a company like the last time they had traveled by train. She was only slightly plump and only slightly homely, but she had managed to get her father out of the compartment long enough on one pretext or another with one and then the other, leaving her alone with one at a time whom she overwhelmed with blatant aggressive sexuality where her opening gambit was to unbutton their flys, which made it a memorial trip. Now, they were between Captain Nemo and the SS, and the trip to Berlin stretched even longer before them.

The door opened and they all thought it would be the conductor, but were surprised to see another SS officer.

"Heil Hitler! Doctor Mengele," Hobein greeted from the aisle. "I thought that was you on the platform. I must say Frau Mengele is indeed looking well."

"Heil Hitler," Mengele responded. "I am truly surprised, Hobein, to meet you once again on a train. Especially on a train going to Berlin."

"No more surprising than you being ordered there." Hobein replied." He looked at the two minor Party officials.

"Why don't you two young men find yourself somewhere else to sit. The doctor and I are old friends and I am sure that you would not deny us an opportunity for some private conversations. My compartment is 45A; there are two empty seats there. I am sure you will enjoy the gauleiter and his fat ugly daughter. They seem a world of fun. You will not even have to take your luggage. Just come back here just before we arrive.

They looked at each other and decided that there was indeed a God in heaven, and they quickly nodded assent and crowded past Hobein in the doorway, only to linger in the passageway to see how the SS officer with empty eyes was going to handle the submariner with the empty eyes. Just then, the conductor came and chided them for being congealed in the way of people who were about their duty for the Reich and for the Fuhrer because you indeed have to trust your trains to get you there on time.

He took Mengele's ticket and went off muttering under his breath, the two technocrats trailing in his wake.

Hobein slid the door shut and sat across from Mengele. He looked sideways at the kreigsmarine, who had not budged and decided to ignore his presence.

"I see that you have been wounded, Herr Mengele."

"Nothing serious," Mengele replied.

"Don't be modest, Doctor. I was in Russia for a long time myself. There was no such thing."

"Hauptsturmfuhrer Hobein," Mengele said behind a half smile, "you are forgetting that I am a doctor."

Hobein thought a moment. "You well might be right, after all, Herr Doctor. In your line of work, I guess you could see a lot of non-serious wounds, but in my line of work," he laughed, "all the wounds I saw were fatal."

Hobein followed Mengele's eyes to the submariner, who still had not stirred. There were things they both knew that should not be discussed in front of some of their countrymen, but this one seemed dead to the world.

"Are you just coming from the Caucasus, Hobein?" Mengele asked.

"Absolutely not. I left right after I saw you at First Panzer. I really was just delivering a message to his eminence, Pope von Kleist. There were not enough Jews in the area for me to stay there."

"Then where have you been?"

"Rostov, of course. It is a beautiful city, and I even had time to visit the cathedrals. I think I enjoyed it even more than Krakow. But maybe that was because there were a couple of hundred thousand Jews within a day's drive of Rostov. I slept in a bed for over six straight months because we could turn in numbers that kept the Reichsfuhrer happy. At least after a while, he stopped pressing one of those damnable gas vans on us.

"Hobein," Mengele whispered, leaning forward, the train putting him into a rocking motion, "why do you think you are being called to Berlin?"

"What do you mean, Mengele?"

Mengele frowned. "I mean, Berlin would be a waste of your particular talents. It would be like posting an admiral to the Desert Command."

Hobein chuckled. "I do not think I will be a beached whale in Berlin, Herr Doctor. But I know what you mean. I have wondered about that myself. Olendorf even asked for verification twice about the orders. He thought that I had requested it, but when I told him I had not, he thought it was a mistake. Berlin confirmed it twice."

"Could it be that there are a lot of Jews left in Berlin?"

"Mengele, there are a lot of Jews left all over Germany. I am amazed at the ones I have seen in the streets of our own cities. At least the ones in the east have learned to keep their heads down until we dig them out and march them to their graves." He thought for a second. "Maybe <u>Der</u> <u>Fuhrer</u> has decided that he needs some men with a backbone in Berlin. They surely miss Heydrich."

Mengele laughed. "Hobein, it would not be your backbone that they would be interested in, but your pistol finger."

"Well," Hobein smiled, "isn't identifying Jews one of your many specialized talents, Herr Doctor?"

"Of course."

"Then maybe we will be working together. With your nose for the Jew and my trigger finger, I am sure we will make short work of the lingering parasites in our capitol city."

"That will be taken care of with or without us, Hobein. And I can not believe they would exist in any number that would cause you any excitement."

Hobein turned solemn. "I would hate to think that." He sat back and crossed his arms as if even refusing to consider it. "No. I would not be ordered to anyplace that was Judenfrei, Mengele. Killing Jews is what I do best."

Lieutenant-Commander Paul Lehmann was used to sleeping in noise and confusion. Aboard a submarine, there is no quiet even as it glides along under the surface. The pulsating air-sucking of the pumps, the snap of switches, motors whining, and valves opening and closing were a constant reminder that you are living inside the bowels of a machine. The other noises of voices, grunts, coughs, sneezes and farts remind you that you share this machine with a lot of other men.

You learn after a time to stop trying not to hear the din around you. You learn to fall to sleep listening to the noises, picking out the ones that come on a regular basis, and you blend them into a lullaby, and you ride that rhythm to sleep.

On his last cruise, he had taken his u-234 from Wilhelmshaven and circled north until he lay in the lanes of the way to Archangel, were the Allies were shipping supplies to the Russians. He had sunk three ships, adding up to twenty-five thousand tons. He had sent them to their death by fire, concussion, drowning, or freezing to death in the unforgiving waters at least one hundred men.

Then they had sat terrified as an American destroyer had dropped death charges on them for over six hours when it only takes the first few seconds to realize that the only thing between you and icy death is a thin shroud of steel.

He knew that the Allies were getting much better at their anti-submarine warfare techniques, and the Americans seemed to be able to build ships as fast as some countries used to build cars, and he knew that they had lost the battle of shutting off the supply lines to either Britain or Russia.

And it came to him in an icy realization as he was rocked over the rails that he would die in a stinking boat with a handful of other terrified screeching, yelling, praying, and sometimes cursing young Germans. And he would go to his watery grave knowing that he had not really died for his country, for his Fatherland. That the last thing he would do in life was try to breathe sea water, and maybe it was all because men like these wanted to kill the Jews.

He wished he could vomit on demand.

Because if he could, he would throw up on these two Nazis.

XVIII

A military taxi shuttling from the Charlottenburger Strasse railway station took Mengele east through the center of the Tiergarten, then crossing the Hindenburg Platz; they took the Brandenburg Gate using the center, the widest of the lanes and the six concrete pillars capped on each end with massive Doric columns caverned by.

The driver loved passing under the <u>Tor</u>, even in the dark.

He could remember years ago, that day in May, when his father brought him and his brothers here and told them of that other day in 1871, when his father was twelve, and he had climbed to the top of the Tor to claim a spot near the flaring hoof of one of the outside horses. He was the youngest man to reach such heights in the entire parade route, as the youth of Berlin scrabbled for positions of viewpoint, clinging to monuments, flag staffs, lamp posts, and rooftops, while men in cutaways, and ladies in bright hooped dresses and fancy hats, climbed out windows to walk down newly constructed wooden catwalks to take up positions in grandstands built out over the gabled roofs of the flanking buildings, while two dozen maidens dressed in white, in a special ground level place of honor, joined one hundred thousand people amassed in the square. Another million people lined along and above the one-mile parade route to the Palace of the Hohenzollerns.

From his viewpoint, his father had first seen the plummed tops of the helmets of Chancellor Prince von Bismarck, von Molkte, the Chief of Staff, and von Roon, the Minister of War. Then, the newly crowned king of all of Germany, the Ceasar of the Germans, Kaiser

Wilhelm I, rode into view. Riding beside him was the Crown Prince Friedrich Wilhelm and his grandson Wilhelm proclaimed in the Hall of Mirrors in the French Emperor Napoleon III's captured palace six months earlier, the new monarch led his victorious army in parade.

The city and all of the newly united Germany had five months to plan the celebration. And what a grand parade it was, as the Calvary, Infantry, Canons and Cassions, dispersed with smartly clad military Bands, paraded into his father's view from the highest point on this earth that his father had ever attained, and his father spoke of how proud the soldiers were, and how proud and joyous the people were, to welcome and pay homage to their warriors and their generals, and especially to their Kaiser.

He had grown to yearn for the day when he too could march in triumph under the Tor, and he had even been sent to war by the boy grown to manhood that his father had seen that June day, and against those same Frenchmen who had been the cause of the whole event forty years earlier. But a Frenchman's bullet had shattered his ankle, ending early his military endeavors, and since he would never be able to march in lockstep with a returning victorious army, he loved to listen to his echo as he drove under the Tor.

He loved the goddess that drove the quadriga, the four-driven charging horse chariot that crowned this massive monument. She was the goddess of Victory. Originally carved as a beautiful well, endowed nude, curvaceous stature whose stone nipples and exposed derriere had so offended some of the Berliners, whose statutes usually were in uniform, she was soon clad in copper armor. She had been whisked away by the French under Napoleon when he had occupied the city in 1806, but the Prussian troops had recovered her in 1814, the coppersmiths had reclad her, and she was put back on her pedestal sixty-five feet high.

Immediately on the other side of this monument, built in 1788 to commemorate the victories of Kaiser Frederick Wilhelm, was the Pariser Platz.

The Paris Plaza.

On their left was the old glorious French Embassy, now occupied by the Vichy French, while DeGaulle and the Free French were busy fighting against the Germans, and the Occupied French were exchanging three skilled French craftsmen willing to travel to and work in the Reich, for top wages of course, for every French prisoner-of-war held by the Germans. After all, the French were blood cousins. The only real thing wrong with them was they exhibited just too much of their Mediterranean influence. Too much of the Roman had rubbed off on them. But maybe they had not been 'verjudenunged' or 'verniggerunged' beyond redemption.

The Pariser Platz does not narrow as it becomes Unter den Linden. Mostly lime, interspersed with chestnut trees, lined the boulevard that stretches for a mile to end at the Palace of Kaiser Wilhelm I of Germany, the first Kaiser of a united Germany as orchestrated by the great chancellor, Otto von Bismarck. Before they reached the first intersecting street, Wilhelmstrasse, the black Opel sedan, pulled to a stop in front of the Aldon Hotel.

Centrally located between the French and British embassies, it was built to be both lavish and luxurious and reflect the wealth and might of a great nation as host to visiting dignitaries. It was where the royalty and the wealthy of Europe who were visiting Berlin stayed. The stone and concrete balconies on the second story and the stone and wrought iron railings of the fifth floor, afforded some of the best views of the returning victorious armies as they entered Under den Linden to march down the wide three-lane boulevard.

It was the showplace of a capital city that was home to four and a half million people, the third largest city in the world. The city was full of parks, gardens, courtyards, canals, and green spaces spread out to take advantage of the two rivers, the Spree and the Havel, in the wide expanse of the German Plain.

Mengele was amused when a porter appeared to take charge of his gear, and he suppressed a smile remembering reporting to Viking just over a year ago, riding that half-truck, half-track armored personnel carrier that was to become so familiar to him. They passed through black-out dyed canvas curtains made from German-grown hemp to emerge into a lobby with the sparkle and splendor of a museum.

It was after three in the morning, and there was little activity. Mengele noticed a man in a long black leather coat standing near the lift with a newspaper tucked under his arm, leaning against the wall. Everyone knew that he was Gestapo, but he did not care if you knew he was Gestapo. Everyone also knew that there was another one close by, even if you could not see him. There were enemies of the state and spies everywhere.

The Gestapo was everywhere.

Heinrich Himmler knew everything.

Mengele was soon checked in by a man who seemed to be asleep on his feet but was immediately ushered away by a burly baldheaded man who set off at a rapid pace and stormed the steps to the second floor with Prussian efficiency. They turned right at the head of the stairs and followed the hall all the way to the back side of the hotel, going halfway down this long corridor lined with oil paintings and statues before the porter stopped and opened a door for him.

The room was not one of the suites but must have been created to lodge secretaries, mistresses, traveling companions, or other entourage of the elite. These rooms overlooked beautifully well-kept gardens that were a blaze of color and fragrance in the spring and summer but were right now under a blanket of snow.

Over by tall casement windows was a heavy wooden bed with a bright quilted bedspread. There was a small desk with a gooseneck lamp and a straight-back chair. An armoire sat catty in the corner. There was a small chest of drawers. A picture of Der Fuhrer, the one showing his face, his political face, was the only wall adornment.

"I hope that the Herr Captain will enjoy his stay here at the Aldon," the porter said, checking to see that the room was in order. Even in these rooms, let out in a block and at reduced rates for the Reichsfuhrer, the service was to be impeccable.

"In case of an air raid," he continued, "I am pleased to inform you that we have one of the best shelters in the city. It is yards of concrete and it is thirty feet down. It is why Herr Foreign Minister Ciano likes to stay here when he is in Berlin," he said, referring to Mussolini's son-in-law. He held open a door and showed Mengele a semi-private bath, sharing it with just the person occupying the room next to him. The porter checked to see if there were fresh towels, then he was on his way.

Mengele stripped and submerged himself in a steaming hot bath to wash the trip away. He soaped himself slowly, scrubbed his hair and splashed water in cascades over his head with his cupped hands.

The water ran down over his fingers as he held them over his eyes. The room was somewhat chilly, and he had goosebumps.

If Hobein was a serious witness, and he had no reason to doubt him, then the <u>Einsatzgruppen</u>, operating in the captured territories, had already killed well over two million Jews. That was not counting the Poles, Gypsies, and Communists they had also killed. Of course, he had known what the duty of the <u>Einsatzgruppe</u> was, but he had not truly realized how extensive or how seriously committed the Nazis were to the destruction of the Jews.

A couple of million of them already dead.

Just like Der Fuhrer had promised.

He thought about how the submariner had finally come to life at a stop in the middle of the night and had surfaced from out of his coat to look furiously and accusingly at the two SS men. There had been no exchanged greetings as he wrestled his gear down and brushed past them and out the sliding door.

Hobein had smiled. The SS was bound to secrecy on the matter of making death the 'final solution' for the Jew. The knowledge of it to be kept from the general public, of course, but Hobein seemed to relish talking about his job. Of course, in the East, he was killing only saboteurs and spies, and it was common knowledge in the East that all the Jews acted as saboteurs or spies. Even Jewish children were spies. He did not mind telling other Germans what it actually was that he did for the Reich, but he kept from boasting about his work simply because it was much easier to continue the charade of rounding Jews up to send them to 'relocation' and 'work' camps, then it would be to round up Jews to send them to 'death camps.'

Mengele was beginning to believe that Hobein might be right.

His job was going to be to track down Jews.

He still wondered, as he sat on the edge of the bed pulling on his long underwear, why he was taken from an arena where his services as a surgeon ministering to the wounded legions of the Reich, would seem to be of the utmost importance. His medical file noted that his injury was too severe to allow him to be returned to the front.

He knew that it was not.

He wondered if von Verschurer had anything to do with his posting. He was sure he had something to do with getting him this room. He instinctively knew that this hotel would be full of men much senior in rank and position. He did not know where he fit in, but he was beginning to believe that there was indeed going to be a place for him in the hierarchy of the SS.

He was not to report until late in the afternoon, having taken into consideration his arrival time, and he took the opportunity to lay back and look out over the courtyard to the back of the British Embassy building, its form taking shape in the gloom of an early misty winter morning. He could see steam rise from the tiles of its roof, and he pulled the thick quilt up to his chin. He was so happy to be in Berlin.

He was awakened by the activity of men moving in the hall and exchanging noonday 'Heil Hitlers.' He felt refreshed and energetic as he donned his uniform, and with a final check to see that his medals and badges were in the correct form, he left his room to enter a crowded hallway. Most of the men he passed were wearing the runes of the SS, and most of them were senior to him. He exchanged 'heils' all down the hallway.

In the dining room, the waiter ignored the food coupon he offered but showed him to a small table by the windows looking out onto the wide boulevard alive with vehicular traffic, but buses, automobiles and light trucks, and not panzers and armored personnel carriers.

He might be junior in rank to many of the men that filled the dining room, being only the equivalent of a captain in a minority arm of military service, the Waffen-SS, but he had fought in Russia from the very first day, and he had the medals, ribbons, and the look in his eye to prove it.

A waiter in a white apron brought him roast pork, potatoes, and pumpernickel bread, which was filling and tasty, and he washed it down with a delicious white wine. There was more food in Germany this winter than last year, but then the Aldon always had food.

The dining room was full of men in various uniforms of the Reich and her allies. Mengele saw at least a dozen high-ranking SS, a few Wehrmacht officers, a whole table of Luftwaffe generals, men in business suits and a few women. At the table closest to him were two Italian colonels, or they could have been majors, having lunch with two lovely young German women who managed to find enough cosmetics to radiate. By the far wall, he could see a Romanian brigadier-general in whispered conversation with a well-dressed countryman, probably attached to the Romanian Embassy. He wondered if they were talking about Stalingrad, where, for the second time in the war, the Romanian army had been mauled by attacking Russians. He wondered if the two Gestapo agents eating lunch a few tables from them were wondering the same thing. He finished his wine, breathed in the splendor of the room, and ate a delicious lunch. He could not wait to have dinner here.

He collected his overcoat from the check room where he had left it and put it on, and placing his peaked cap squarely on his head, he headed out the door held open for him by a uniformed civilian doorman.

The early afternoon winter air was cool and crisp, a low cloud cover just barely able to hold out a weak winter sun, but to him it seemed only like a fun kind of cold. A toy cold. He knew that warmth was just a door away. Not at all like the cold of last winter when you could freeze to death inside while you were sawing off frozen pieces of people.

He walked down Unter den Linden and crossed over Wilhemstrasse before turning south. The street was full of people, most of them scurrying back to work in the bureaucracy that issued the directions to the German people throughout the nation.

Of the Third Reich.

He had plenty of time before he was to report in. He looked across the street to the slim side of his hotel, and then next to it, the used to be British Embassy, now flying other flags. From the other side of the street, he passed this majestic gray stone seat of British representation in prewar Berlin, so close to the government of the German people. He understood what his father had meant in his concern of not having the English on their side. Because if you did not have the English on your side then you did not have the Americans on your side. Having both of them against you while you were locked in a struggle with the Slavic hordes of the east made no sense, especially when you are a Nazi.

The Germanic tribes of the Anglo, Saxon, Jutes, and later the Normans blended for centuries with the earlier arriving Celts into the

English, and the Picts disappeared, and what remained in that isle became the British, and they were the vanguard of the Northern Europeans that established the great countries of Canada and the United States, wrenching it away from the Asiastic Indians.

But these Aryan people were again the enemy. These tall, handsome men of the English and the Americans were their enemy, and the swarthy Italians and slant-eyed yellow-pigmented Japanese were their allies. Some things took a lot of trust in der Fuhrer.

He crossed over Behrenstrasse, and once past the Justice Ministry, he was at the Nazi Party Headquarters, where Hitler, Goring, Goebbels, and Bormann all maintained offices. The rest of the block was controlled by Dr. Josef Goebbels. The club-footed dark-hair dark-eyed slim face Dinaric ghoulish-looking Nazi, who always blamed his deformity on a blotched childhood operation and nothing genetic. A born orator that even Der Fuhrer could listen to, and Der Fuhrer could not listen to very many people. A man Der Fuhrer could also count on to carry out his whims and wishes with just comments.

His dominion was directly across the street from the new Chancellery, and the entrance to his Chamber of Culture was on Wilhelm Platz. He was the gauleiter of Berlin, making him the head of the political party in the city, and his function as Minister of Propaganda meant he controlled everything the citizens of Germany heard or read.

Except the letters from their sons and husbands fighting at the fronts. Here, the Reich Security Main Office had the final say, and they were reading every letter from the men at Stalingrad and not delivering any of them since ninety-five percent of them said something negative about the Party, or the War, and even of Der

Fuhrer. Himmler had the feelings of men dying in a cold hell of concrete and starvation, of fighting an enemy who had bullets in his gun, and you had only one bullet in your gun, and you were seriously considering using it on yourself; he had their last words destroyed.

The hard pavement felt good under his boot. Fresh snow was ridged up along the recently shoveled walk. The shops were open but Mengele was not interested in even seeing what was available. He would have time for that later.

After viewing the panorama of the steppes, that flat uninterrupted ocean of land where the sun sank in the horizon as if into the sea, and then the magnificence of the Caucasus, that snowy finger to god, the confines of the city made him feel as if he was in a canyon of man-made shallow mountains.

The tallest of the buildings were just a towering five stories, and the one thing they all shared was their limestone exteriors, except for one plaster one that turned out ugly. The variations in the architecture are done more by using stone from different quarries, different depths and different colors that ran from a brown through the light beige and even into the grays. Elaborate mantels angled and curved and arched over tall wide windows set in arches and rectangles.

A double set of trolley tracks divided the middle of the street, with cars stopping to dislodge the afternoon shoppers, fraus and frauleins of the more wealthier class of Berlin who could afford to shop for items that found their way to places where members of the Nazi Party were concentrated.

The streets were full of men, mostly uniformed, epilated, medalioned, decorated, and braided with silver and gold. No different than in all the other capitals of the countries engaged in world war;

London, Washington, Tokyo, Rome, Paris, among dozens of others. The most sedate being Moscow. In Moscow, the military was still dressing as true Communists, simple in cut and style, maximizing material usage.

But Stalin liked what he saw at Stalingrad. He told his quartermasters to dress up his officers and his soldiers. Their allies, the English and the Americans, pondered over a request to furnish them with thousands of yards of gold braid.

Stalin's reason for optimism, Stalingrad, was the reason that the people of Berlin, like the people all over Germany and Austria, were somber and grim-faced, moving about their business with an ear cocked ready to hear news about their sons and husbands surrounded at Stalingrad. They tried not to appear worried, but they could not help but pray for their men at Stalingrad. It seemed as if everyone had someone at Stalingrad. And they had not heard from them in so long.

Nothing was being said about Stalingrad.

Mengele passed a smaller office building on the next block that was the private office of der Fuhrer. It was a thin, tall, sandwiched building, and Mengele wondered why der Fuhrer would ever need a private office so close to his gigantic office in the new Chancellery, but he had one, and the guards posted were SS. They looked cold as they stood there at attention, which would be a hysterical sight to any of the other sons of Germany left alive and fighting from the frozen rubble of Stalingrad.

Railroads and Transportation shared the next block. They had gotten used to supplying the Reichsfuhrer with trains for 'special movements,' along with the rest of the priorities of the Reich, like supplying ammo and food to the men at the front and raw materials to the factories.

Mengele reached the corner of Voss Strasse where he could see down the long edge of the Chancellery, the two-story stone palace built by Albert Speer in just a little over a year using forty-five hundred German craftsmen working day and night, using many stones cut at the quarries owned and operated by the Reichsfuhrer, under the SS owned German Stone and Earth Works.

A building fit for a Fuhrer.

Mengele was at the center of the Third Reich.

He felt a shiver of pride and felt like he was on the verge of greatness.

He could see Hermann Goring's Air Ministry and then his Prussian State Ministry, running together, giving the Grandfield marshall of the Luftwaffe one whole block for his dominions. It was said that Goring was out of the city making up new titles and uniforms to go with them for himself, trying to keep away from der Fuhrer, who was holding him responsible for Stalingrad. It had been Goring who stupidly promised Hitler that his Air Force could fly in all the supplies the encircled Sixth Army would need, with Wetzel, the new Wehrmacht chief-of-staff, calling him a liar or an idiot, right in front of Der Fuhrer. The short, pugnacious army chief had turned out to be right in both assessments.

He was here in Berlin with Hitler, Himmler, Goring, and Goebells. All within a few minutes of fast walking were the offices of men who held sway over millions and millions of people. The original Nazis. And they controlled a big hunk of Europe.

Next to the Chancellery was the Foreign Office, with an idle Ribbentrop not having anyone of importance left to be diplomatic with, 'war being failed diplomacy,' but it seemed to him that he was spending all his time talking to his allies about their Jews.

He crossed Wilhelmstasse and looked down to No. 8 Prinz-Albrecht Strasse, to the building that housed the Gestapo, the most famous and most feared address in all of Germany. This is where Goring had also attempted early on to establish a national police force but had to trade it to Himmler for his cooperation in getting rid of that faggot Rohm. Now, the Geheime Staatspolizei, or Secret State Police, used the basement for terror, torture, imprisonment, and death. The building's use had not really changed with the arrival of the Nazis to power. Every civilized capital of the world had such a building close to the heart of its government. Himmler had an office on the third floor but stayed out of the building as much as possible. It seemed that when he was in his office here he had only unpleasant tasks to perform.

For some reason, Mengele did not want to be seen looking at this building with more than a passing glance.

The first important address taken over by the SS in Berlin was at No. 74 Under den Linden, which now housed the Fuhrungshauptant, the Operational Department, which was the staff headquarters of both the Waffen-SS, the Allgemeine SS, and the members of the concentration camp guard units. The Reichsfuhrer was silently thankful that none of his units were at Stalingrad, although he had raised these legions to die for the Fuhrer if necessary, but he preferred that they die in victory.

As Mengele went just a few hundred feet along the street, he came to the old palace of Price Albrecht, 102 Wilhelmstrasse, Himmler's favorite Berlin address, sharing a courtyard with the Gestapo building.

Mengele 'heiled' his way through the door held open by a white-gloved SS Rottenfuhrer while another one looked at his identification and orders and instructed him up the wide stairs to the second floor, where he was met by a tall blond Unterscharfuhrer who looked like a recruitment poster and after glancing at his orders motioned for Mengele to follow. They marched down the hall, their heels clicking off the polished parquet floors, and they had not gone a few steps before Mengele's foot slipped out from under him, and he almost went down.

"Do not worry, Herr Hauptstrumfuhrer, you will learn how not to break your neck on these floors," his escort grinned.

They stopped in front of massive sliding pocket doors, which rolled easily open, and they stepped into a bright room crowded with a dozen desks. Mengele could see that he was outranked by a few of the men sitting and working at these stations, and he had a sinking feeling that his position within the SS was not going to be that exalted after all.

He followed the sergeant through the narrow aisle, where they paused briefly while his escort rapped loudly on the door, and they were ordered to enter.

Obergruppenfuhrer Richard Hildebrandt, in command of the Reich Race and Resettlement Main Office, was a tall, handsome man who had taken over when Walter Darre was finally dismissed from the position by Himmler as being only a theorist who could not get into motion the immense tasks set before the SS. Hildebrandt had waded in, and immediately, the department, created initially only for the verification of good blood for its own membership, was now responsible for verifying the blood of millions upon millions of people to ensure they had enough good blood in them to help re-populate the vast lands that were now becoming available as the Reich sought to establish Germanic peoples in the conquered lands.

They had the duty of protecting the blood of the Volk, for finding the blood of the Volk, and, like all SS everywhere, for perpetuating the blood of the Volk.

They exchanged heil Hitlers.

Mengele stood at attention.

Hildebrandt flipped through the folder on the desk in front of him that contained Mengele's records.

"I have read your records with keen interest, Hauptstrumfuhrer. I must say that I have not seen such praises from a more diverse and respected group of commanding officers."

He closed the folder, leaned back in his chair, crossed his arms and fixed Mengele with a stare from shallow blue eyes. "Your accomplishments to date reflect well on you, Herr Doktor. You are well-trained and experienced in field surgery. You are a racial examiner trained in both genealogical documentation and genetic characteristics, a rare commodity in these times. In battle, you must have the heart of a true SS man."

"Thank you, Herr Obergruppenfuhrer."

"I also see that you jeopardized your career in the SS by marrying a woman who could not pass the requirements as set down by the Reichsfuhrer and enforced by this very office," Hildebrandt continued in a voice growing icy, "and you may be the only man in my command here in Berlin who has married since 1935 whose off-springs can not be registered in the <u>Sippenbuch!</u>" Mengele stood stunned, his face reddening, his lips drew into a tight, thin line. He hated being talked to in such a manner. He hated most of all that the Gruppenfuhrer was right.

"I am sorry that we could not prove my wife's lineage, Herr Obergruppenfuhrer, but I can assure you that I did not marry a woman with any taint of Jewish blood," Mengele responded, hearing the weakness in his own voice.

"How can you assure me of that!" Hildebrandt angrily responded. "I do not have a degree in medicine. I am not a geneticist. But I do know that your wife just might have a Jew for a Grandfather!" he hissed.

Mengele stood silent. There were seven levels of rank separating him from Hildebrandt, the equivalent of a captain standing in front of a lieutenant-general in the army or a lieutenant to a vice-admiral in the navy. Too much rank for even the Iron Crosses and the Wound Badge and the time on the Eastern Front for Mengele to overcome the burning chastisement that was raging inside of him.

"I am glad that you do not try and insult my intelligence by actually giving me reasons why you know your wife has no Jewish blood," Hildebrandt continued, some of the edge leaving his voice. He put both forearms down on the desk and leaned forward.

"I admire many of the things you have accomplished, Herr Doktor, but if it wasn't for entreaties by some people whom I respect very much, I would not have you in my command here in Berlin, to be a continuing embarrassment to me with the Reichsfuhrer."

He pressed a button under his desk, and his aide stepped into the room.

"Show Hauptstrumfuhrer to Herr Standartenfuhrer Milwien," he ordered.

Milwien, his new immediate superior, turned out to be a wiry little man lost in his uniform and whose face was continually darting about as if looking for the fine print. He was shorter than Mengele, bald except for a band of thin gray hair, and he smelled of muscle ointment. He was a long-term member of the Allgemeine SS and a professor of ancient literature and manuscripts until the Reichsfuhrer attended one of his lectures on forgeries and the importance of keeping records. The next day, he was ordered to 102 Wilhelmstrasse and offered the post of head of the Genealogical Section of the RuSHA. He could tell by Mengele's expression that the Obergruppenfuhrer had not given his new aide a rousing welcome.

"Do not be too upset over anything the Herr Obergruppenfuhrer might have said to you, Herr Doktor." He did not want his new aide to get off on the wrong note. "It is just that right now, doctors and professors are not his favorite people."

"And why is that, Herr Standartenfuhrer?"

The older man felt briefly that he might not be acting in loyalty to his commanding officer but decided to go ahead and tell his new officer anyway.

"It started out with routine marriage requests. Two brothers. We found a Jew born in 1663 in their lineage and forwarded the information to Professor Schultz, the head of <u>Race</u>. He wrote on the file that the Jewish chromosomes would have dissipated in three generations, and he could certify the brothers as being free of Jewish blood."

Mengele was surprised that someone could arrive at such an important post as head of <u>Race</u> and be so ignorant of the mere basics of genetics.

"It gets worse," Milwein lowered his voice, "the Obergruppenfuhrer is not a man of science. He was HSSPF from Vistula-Danzig. He offers an opinion to the Reichsfuhrer that in view of this information, the genealogical section should limit their searches to just six generations'"

Mengele laughed out loud, the sting from his meeting with the Obergruppenfuhrer fading rapidly.

Milwein grinned. "I assure you, Her Doktor, the Reichs-fuhrer found nothing amusing in all this. He had Schulz escorted from the building. There was a joke going around that he was going to have the Herr Obergruppenfuhrer shot! So you can see he is still not going to be thinking too highly of the academia."

"Then I will work to gain his confidence." Mengele asserted, but there was something else bothering him. "I thought the <u>Sippenbuch</u> requirements were just to the year 1750, Herr Standartenfuhrer. When did that change?"

Milwein thought for a moment, scratching his bald head.

"I don't know if it was ever formally changed. The Reichsfuhrer instructed me to search all applications for marriage by the SS all the way to where we lose them to a tribe," he smiled, showing a set of perfect false teeth that glowed in his parchment skin and colorless lips.

Mengele still did not have all of the answers he wanted. "How did the Reichsfuhrer rule on the applicants?"

"Oh, them. They were allowed to marry. But their children are not to be listed in the <u>Sippenbuch.</u>"

Mengele realized that the old man knew that any children by his own present wife would also be denied entry but was not going to make an issue of it. It was curious that the overall criteria for joining the Waffen-SS were continually relaxed while the requirements for entry into the kinship book were becoming more strict. It was no doubt because the cream of the Waffen-SS, those tall, young, handsome men, those true warriors of the Reich, went to their deaths in disproportionate numbers serving their <u>Fuhrer</u> and their <u>Volk</u>. Yet their ranks swelled as Obergruppenfuhrer Berger recruited from the <u>Volkstrum</u>, genetic Germans living in other countries, especially from the Baltics and Romanian. The Wehrmacht still had first refusal of the men born in Germany.

"Come with me and I will show you to your duties, Herr Doktor, and introduce you to the men."

Mengele followed the stooped-shouldered old man out the door and down the grand hallway lined with tall oil paintings to where a sentry opened wide one of the highly polished wood double doors of what once was the ballroom. Mengele could hear the activity and stir of men before he stepped into the spacious room. Most of the men were Allgemeine SS, still in the black. Some were busy pulling three-by-five meter cards on a thin wood backing from racks that lined the wall underneath the windows that ran around three sides as the grand room stretched the width of the palace.

As they walked to the center aisle, Mengele could see that the back wall was lined with shelves and drawing easels. The cards were being added to by men using thin tipped quills. At the far end of the room, he could see some officers carefully handling and examining a potpourri of documents.

"The Reichsfuhrer himself chose these rooms for <u>Genealogy</u> when he first moved into this beautiful drafty old palace that used to belong to Price Albrecht," Milwein said as if conducting a tour. "It is perfect for us. It is on the south side of the building, the side that catches the most light. And in the work that we do, as you well know, light is an important part of our profession."

Mengele knew he was referring to identifying forgeries of birth, marriage, and sometimes even death certificates. The art of printing had originated in Germany, so there was no shortage of very talented men capable of putting out high-class documents and if needed, making them look a couple of hundred years old.

"Many Jews have already slipped behind the identity of a German," Milwein complained. "Jews are even still fooling many of the regional offices of RuSHA. Plus, the workload has caused us to contract out much of the work to <u>sippenforscher</u>, who are either not trained sufficiently in recognizing duplicity, or they are not motivated to vigorously pursue the laws protecting the blood of the Volk."

The task had become a gigantic bureaucracy with overlapping authority and responsibility. Himmler had consolidated many of the upper offices into the SS and created a new position for himself, <u>Reichskommisar</u> <u>for</u> <u>the</u> <u>Strengthening</u> <u>of</u> <u>German</u> <u>Blood</u>. Now, all applications for marriage within the Reich filtered through the Office of <u>Race</u> <u>and</u> <u>Resettlement</u>, and it was going to be one of their duties to spot-check the findings of the various scattered race examiners to ensure their competence, and their loyalty.

Mengele looked closer at one of the cards. In five-millimeter-high letters were the names of Germans, as their family trees gave the card the appearance of a finely cracked egg.

"Most cases of SS applications are a matter of mechanics," the old man explained, "the hardest part is staying on the correct limb of the family where it branches and to follow it true. We start with checking previous petitions to see if there is a cousin or brother who has just been researched. Sometimes, we pick up a family three hundred years ago and start from there. We have the complete verified genealogy of hundreds of thousands of German families, and we are adding to it daily."

The old man rubbed his thin chin, and a gleeful glaze filmed over his shallow gray eyes. He took Mengele by the arm and walked him away from the other men out into the center of the room.

"Along with your regular duties, Herr Doktor, I am placing you in charge of dealing with the petitions of the <u>Mischlingen</u>," Milwein said, just coming to that inspired decision.

"What type of duty will this be, Herr Standartenfuhrer?"

"It is the German mother of a <u>Mischlingen</u> that can give you headaches," Milwein explained, reading with satisfaction the question on his new man's face.

"You will be surprised, Herr Doktor, of how many German fraus will petition this office declaring that while, yes, they are married to a Jew, they are also willing to swear on a stack of bibles that their husband is not the father of the children. She keeps a kosher kitchen, but the butcher gave her some good German pork, and the butcher is really the father of Abraham, you see!" he burst into a high crackle but quickly covered it up with a thin, almost transparent hand, looking about as if expecting to see the Reichsfuhrer standing in the doorway, and the Reichsfuhrer would hate his joke.

"You do a physical examination of the children in question do you not, Herr Standardtenfuhrer."

"Of course we do. And, of course, you will. I will put you in charge of a new desk. I think I will call it the Genetic Desk of Genealogy, and I will refer all of the petitioners to you. And once you have given them a thorough examination, what do you think you will find?"

"That even the ones with outward Nordic appearance will have slight Jewish characteristics," Mengele responded.

The old man smiled again. He was really going to like this young man.

"The Mischlinge are also a thorn in our side. There are about one-hundred-sixty-thousand of these half-and quarter-breeds, but we know where they all are," he proclaimed proudly. "One day, we will deal with them just like we did the Rhineland bastards so many years ago." He had a wistful look on his face, and Mengele wondered if the old man had anything to do with the first positive move of the Nazis to protect their bloodstock from being 'verniggerunged.'

"There are the ones, however," Milwein continued, with a note of sadness, "who have a German father by name but are a Jew by sperm. Those I am afraid we will never detect. It will take hundreds of generations to bleach them out. "Or, he sounded more hopeful, "it will take men of science to come up with the solution."

Mengele thought Milwein had a strange expression.

"But here I go rattling off like an old man tying up your afternoon. Let me introduce you to your section and then you can be on your way for today."

They walked through the maze of tables, the men stepping out of the way and nodding respectfully. They reached a simple desk with three drawers. The desk faced a long table with partitions built to afford privacy as eight men with their backs to them were intent on the work they were performing in their cubicles.

"Heil Hitler," Milwein greeted.

"Heil Hitler," the men responded, turning and standing to attention. The rest of the room ignored them. Mengele saw that most of the men were at least in their forties, except for one young unterstrumfuhrer dressed in the gray of the Waffen SS.

"Gentlemen." Milwein spoke, "Let me introduce you to your new immediate superior, Herr Doktor Hauptstrumfuhrer Josef Mengele. He comes to us direct from the Russian front where he was a hero many times over. I am sure that you will find him just as diligent on the matter of accuracy as he was heroic. I am sure that he will continue to insist that all applications are checked and double-checked and verified and passed only with the assurance of this entire office our findings verifying the good blood of our people."

Mengele could see that the men's faces were friendly but serious. They seemed to be dedicated professionals, and he knew that the men would be diligent and correct in their tasks.

Then he looked down at one of the forms the men had been working on and saw that it was just verification of citizenship of the Volk, which meant one had only to prove three German grandparents to be considered legally German and issued the all-important abstrammungs bescheid, or certificate of Aryan descent. It was going to be an extremely boring assignment.

"The Hauptstrumfuhrer will be here in the morning to start his duties. I am sure we will find many ways to use his unique talents here in Genealogy."

Milwein then led Mengele out of the room. "I do look forward to having your assistance, Herr Doktor," the old man said as he paused at his door, indicating that Mengele was free for the rest of the day. "I do suggest that you go on back to your billet, Herr Doktor. There is an invitation awaiting you there for dinner at Herr Professor Verschurer. I will pick you up at six. I hear that you are at the Aldon?"

"Yes I am, Herr Standartenfuhrer." Mengele was elated. He had been going to telephone the professor when he had gotten back to the hotel.

"I had lunch there one time with the Reichsfuhrer." Milwein reminisced, "splendid hotel. Absolutely splendid," he muttered as he closed his office door, leaving Mengele alone in the hall, putting an end to his working day with plenty of time to prepare for this evening.

XIX

Newly promoted Field Marshall Friedrich von Paulus, once described as looking like a born martyr, shunned blowing his own brains out and surrendered himself and his staff of the German Sixth Army on January 31, 1943, to the commander of the Sixty-fourth Soviet Army at Stalingrad. Over the next two days, the remaining starving, weakened, frozen men of the Reich, no longer capable of carrying on the fight, followed his example and raised their hands in surrender like a dog rolling over and baring his throat after a long ferocious fight with the mercy of the enemy the least of his consideration.

The mighty German Sixth Army, some three hundred thousand men, fully armed and equipped, had marched into the city of Stalingrad at the end of August at the height of the might of the Third Reich. They came with the air support of the streaking Messerschmitts and the screaming of the Stukas, ground support of one hundred panzers, and allied armies advancing or attacking to the north and south of them. Their victories were legendary. Their dependability as sure as the iron born into the guts of the men who carried its' banners.

But now, over two hundred twenty-five thousand of them were already dead and buried or frozen in the rubble of a dirty, stinking city on the Volga, and the remaining seventy-five thousand Germans, raised their frost-bitten hands and were marched off into oblivion.

Goring had lived up to Zeitzler's accusation that he was both an idiot and a liar, and the Luftwaffe failed miserably in supplying the surrounded army, and the Reich lost one-fourth of their war machine as the Hungarians, Rumanians, and Italians all chipped in with at least one hundred thousand men apiece.

It took almost nine hundred thousand Russian casualties to win at Stalingrad, but they achieved their first great victory of the war, and their colonels and generals were wrapped in silver and gold epaulets as a reward.

The people of Germany were informed on February 3rd that their sons and husbands, privates and generals, had gone to their deaths shoulder to shoulder, defending the Fatherland from the Jewish Bolsheviks.

The Nation was in shock.

Goebbels worked overtime, stirring the populations to swallow hard and prepare for a 'total war' effort. Now was not the time for weeping but for forging the weapons that would avenge the death of their loved ones. It was going to take a renewed commitment to continue the fight against the Bolsheviks. Albert Speer was finally given permission by Der Fuhrer to convert all of industry to war material, and if the lack of consumer goods was going to cause the population to revolt, then let them. Guillotines were rather easy to produce, and it was not going to take too many of them to keep the population in line.

Now, Germany was becoming a country besieged. There were so many things outside of their control, and only faith in Der Fuhrer sustained the people of Germany. They believed he would find a way to eventually triumph over their enemies.

The taste of the defeat was still in the mouths of the Nazi hierarchy when Goebbels promised Der Fuhrer that at least one thing would be accomplished immediately, and that was to rid Berlin of the forty-thousand Jews still living and working in the city. Earlier attempts to deal with them had led to an outcry by the industrialists who convinced the Nazi leadership that these Jews were skilled laborers and were not replaceable. Their loss would deal war production a severe setback, along with the argument from the industrialists in charge of the factories that so and so was a good Jew and he should not be transported to the East.

The Jews' continual existence, however, was beginning to sicken Der Fuhrer, and his Minister of Propaganda and Gauleiter of Berlin, Joseph Goebbels, ordered that the capital city of the Reich was to be made <u>Judenfrei</u>. This order fell to the Reich Central Security Office of the SS for implementation, code-named <u>Factory Operation</u>.

Hobein was ordered to cover the western part of the city. He was pleased to see that his old friend Mengele was to be involved. He summoned him to his office on the northeast corner of the same building that housed the department where Mengele worked.

The men exchanged "Heils."

"It will be a pleasure."

Hobein smiled. "I am afraid that all the real pleasure will be denied us. It is a shame that we can not just shoot them, but our orders are to proceed with the minimum of brutality. Goebbels is still afraid of offending the citizens."

As Mengele worked closely with the police officials and the SD, who were supplying the manpower for the round-up, the English were laying plans for their first real heavy bombing of their enemies' capital. The Russians had been the first to drop bombs on Berlin, sending overflights of PC-8s on August 11th and 12th, 1941, which were far more symbolic than destructive, much like Doolittle's first raid on Tokyo. The first thing the English had dropped on the Germans was five and a half million pieces of paper warning the German people that they were doomed if they followed their present leadership into this war. This was two days after Germany had invaded Poland, on September 3, 1939.

Since that time, the English had become rather proficient in dropping things that were far more effective in getting the attention of the German population. When the war first started, the effort, of course, was to bomb only targets of military value, but the difficulty of pinpointing them, along with the fact that the enemy could concentrate their defenses of anti-aircraft fire and fighter protection in these areas, lead to very high mortality rates for the crews of the bombers. In the East, their Russian allies were pressed to the wall by the invading forces of the Axis, and unrestricted bombing of Germany was decided by Churchill and placed in the hands of Sir Arthur Harris, who took to his duties with such fervor that he soon earned the nickname of 'Bomber Harris.'

Goebbels called it 'terror bombings.' To the British and now the Americans, it was the only way to penetrate 'Fortress Europe' and bring the war home to the German people. It also helped Churchill and Roosevelt to wave photographs of bombed German cities at Stalin to show that they indeed had opened a 'Second Front,' and they were more than contributing to the defeat of the Hitlerites.

When they first started, the heaviest of bombs were about nine hundred kilograms. By now, the British and Americans were delivering bombs up to 3600 kilograms and were developing heavier ones. They had learned that dropping just explosive bombs was not the most effective way of reducing the German cities. They still dropped the big bangers; they were excellent for blowing out windows and door frames and creating ventilation, but then following them immediately with more numerous and smaller ordinances filled with benzene, gasoline, liquid asphalt and other flammables, made fire a far more destructive device. Then, they learned to drop delayed anti-personnel fragmentation bombs, to discourage arriving firefighters.

It was in May of 1942 when the city of Cologne had been introduced to the first one thousand-plane raid. In an hour and a half, one million five hundred thousand pounds of explosive bombs, phosphorus bombs, mines, and incendiary canisters were dropped. It was just a harbinger of things to come, and it taught the Germans to take their air raids seriously. Now, the Americans had shown up on the scene in broad daylight with their 'flying fortresses,' a term that Goebbels refused to use in his releases to the papers. Their first attack was at Wilhelmshaven on the U-Boat pens, the source of America's first casualties, and Lt. Commander Paul Lehmann barely got his boat into the protection of the pen as the bombs exploded harmlessly on top of the thick steel reinforced concrete overhead.

Now the cities of the Reich were not safe in either the day or the night. Factories began to go underground, and cellars and bomb shelters became familiar places to the people.

In the East, the armies that Mengele had served with, had just barely managed to make it up back north as the advancing Russian armies threatened to cut them off in the Caucasus, a disaster avoided by the cunning of von Kleist and von Manstein. They held off the attacking armies from the north and south as they led their armies to safety. For once, Hitler was not screaming that the generals of his retreating armies were cowards and idiots. In fact, he promoted von Kleist to Field Marshall, to honor him in the brilliant way he had saved his army.

Cities that once were in German hands, Voronezh, Kursk, Rostov-on-the-Don, and Kharkiv, now passed back to the Russians.

There was no panic in the Reich. There was concern, however, that there could be a time limit on dealing with the Jews. The destruction of European Jewry was the second avowed goal of the Regime, second only to winning the war against the Bolsheviks. Everyone involved was told to step up their efforts.

Mengele met with a unit of SD men in front of the old palace. He climbed in the back seat of a Madras sedan where Hobein was already seated. The car was cold, and their breaths were smoke in the interior of the cramped car.

"Cold enough to remind you of Russia, isn't it?" Hobein seemed to be in good humor. The administrative duties that he had been assigned since coming to the city had all but killed him with inertia, and he was pleased to be doing something active. Mengele had filled his time by teaching courses at the University and renewing his studies under the direction of Verschuer.

"There is no cold after Russia," Mengele replied, wiping cold water from the window in order to see out. They were the lead vehicle in a convoy of trucks, the first one full of armed men and the next dozen empties. It had been dark for a couple of hours.

They headed west from the center of the city, out past the Olympic Stadium. Built to house the 1936 sporting event that saw a black-skinned Jesse Owens outrun everyone in the field, including the best of the Reich. Eight miles later, they entered the industrial suburb of Siemerstadt, where a lot of the Jews were employed in an electrical equipment factory. The Jews all lived nearby.

To Mengele, who stood in the street by the car, it did not seem to take but a few minutes before the Jews, men, women and children were being herded down into the streets and into the empty trucks. He could hear young children crying and their parents trying to quiet them. A teenage Jew pulled away from the policeman who had a hold. The convoy pulled to a stop in front of a row of workers' tenements. The troops jumped down from their trucks and formed a line along the sidewalks. They were pointed to their assigned buildings by their NCOs, and the sound of hob-nailed boots soon filled the hallways. Pistol and rifle butts were pounded on the doors. Of his coat and tried to run down the street. Mengele watched him approach and was wondering what he was supposed to do when a SS man stepped out of a doorway and landed a rifle butt. Mengele could see the teeth and blood explode from the running Jew's mouth before he sat down hard on his ass on the pavement, a dazed and bewildered look on his face. The SS man then grabbed him by the collar and pulled him to the back of a truck, where two other policemen picked him up and threw him inside.

The SS man had not said anything to the Jew. As he walked by, he looked Mengele in the eye. Mengele knew this man had been with the Einsartzgruppe in Russia. He was just one of the dependables who went about his duties day after day without ever really earning the respect of his countrymen, nor ever considering the need for their approval.

The canvas-topped Opel trucks were fast filling when the air raid sirens went off in the distance.

The SS men went about their duties. The trucks were soon full, and an unterstrumbannfuhrer, somewhat elderly for his rank, made a head count and consulted a clipboard he carried. He came up to Hobein.

"We have all of them on our list but fourteen of them, Strumbannfuhrer."

Hobein looked blankly at the man who seemed to pale under his graze. "How can you have them all if you have missed fourteen of them?"

The older man swallowed hard. He had not been outside Berlin in years, but he had heard talk about this major, and failing him was something he had not cared to do.

"Leave four men to search further," Hobein ordered.

The men watched as the searchlights went on for the flak units, and they could hear the drone of the Royal Air Forces's Lancasters high overhead. The first bombs seemed to fall way to the east of the city, and they watched as the blackness of the night sky was interrupted by the flashes of explosions. The street around them came alive as German citizens fled their apartments and headed for the bomb shelters. They looked at the trucks full of Jews and the policemen guarding them but knew to ignore them as they made their way to the safety of the underground.

The eastern sky was now alive with the flashes of the explosions and they could see some major fires now lighting the horizon.

"What do we do, Strumbannfuhrer?" The older man asked, looking nervously at the sky where they could still hear the drone of high overhead aircraft. The city seemed to be exploding in all directions from them.

Hobein stood unconcerned. He had seen too much death to think that you could actually run from it when it was falling from the skies. Mengele stood to his right and did not trust his own voice to make any type of comment. He would, of course, do whatever Hobein ordered.

"We might as well just wait here until it is over. We sure are not going to take these Jews into the bomb shelters with us, nor are we going to allow them to go while we put some concrete over our own heads for protection. Have your men posted and ensure that no one escapes." Hobein ordered.

For thirty minutes, the city was under attack. They thought that it was going to take place all around them in the distance when they all heard the screaming whistle of bombs falling close. They huddled next to the sides of the buildings as the street exploded. They were just across a canal of the Havel when the locomotive works was hit, the fire lighting up the immediate night sky. Incendiaries began to hit all around them, but the buildings were still intact, and they did not catch on fire like the ones that had been made drafty by preceding explosives. The volunteer fire brigades appeared on the scene, and water was soon extinguishing the small fires.

The bombing stopped, and they heard the all-clear siren.

Mengele followed Hobein into the back seat. The driver did not wait for an order but immediately pulled off with the trucks following. They drove straight to the rail yards where the Jews were ordered to get down and form in groups by the rail sidings. There were probably a couple of thousand Jews already assembled here, and they were already being loaded onto the rail cars.

Hobein had spoken with an officer by the main loading ramps, and he came back to Mengele, who had stood silently watching the proceedings.

"Come with me, Mengele. We have been ordered to where they have your Jews assembled."

"My Jews?"

"Yes. Your Jews. For some reason, they were ordered not to be brought here."

They drove back through the center of the city. They could see that some of the bombs had hit close to the governmental buildings on Wilhemstrasse, just barely missing and hitting on the street over from them. Their offices were still intact.

"How do you think they came so close in the dark?" Mengele mused, as he watched the professional firefighters tackle the burning public buildings.

"They have a new bomb sight that allows them to see in the dark," Hobein grinned.

Mengele thought that, at times, Hobein could be quite mad.

"Do not even jest about such things," Mengele whispered.

The car pulled up in front of an old warehouse on Rosenstrasse, just around the corner from the Gestapo headquarters. The two men got out of the car and 'heiled' past the sentries standing by the door.

Inside was a large room not much warmer than outside, just barely lighted by overhead bulbs in huge green reflectors. There were about two hundred Jews assembled here. They were made to sit still on the floor, leaving room for the police who walked among them. The Jews had concern on their faces, but Mengele could not see any real fear.

"So these are our 'special Jews,'" Hobein said, walking down the narrow aisles between the men sitting on the floor. Off against one wall were three Jewesses who were married to German men. Mengele knew their names and wondered why women of good blood were so overwhelmingly willing to marry the Jew while men showed the proper attitude towards marrying outside of their race. He could see that all three women were beautiful, especially one with blond hair and blue eyes. She reminded him of that beautiful German girl, one he had seen which seemed so many years ago, that he had stopped from marrying the Jew who tried to pass for white.

A very tall and extremely skinny Gestapo agent came up to him. "Are you Dr. Mengele?"

"Yes." Mengele acknowledged.

"Herr Doktor. All medical personnel in the immediate area have been directed to the hospital to deal with the casualties from the bombs. There is a car outside waiting to take you to the hospital."

"Very well," Mengele replied, waving at Hobein as he made his way out of the building.

Outside, he could see a few German women gathering by the doorway but kept from entering by the guards. As he brushed past them, he could hear them demanding to know why their husbands were being held. After all, these people had married before the laws on miscegenation had been passed, and the laws were not made retroactive.

The street was full of vehicles from the professional fire brigades and the volunteer firefighters. Mengele could see that the fires were not raging from building to building. His car turned out to be an ambulance, and he climbed into the back. Burns were something he was familiar with, and the first of his patients was a woman who had phosphorus on her hands and arms.

She had tried to scrap the chemical from her six-year-old daughter, who sizzled to death right in front of her eyes, and Mengele could not tell if the woman was wailing in pain or in grief. He pulled her down, threw a blanket over her burning parts and poured water over it. He knew it was the only thing he could do for now.

The back of the ambulance was full of the odor of burning flesh, a smell that he could go without for the rest of his life. A boy in his early teens was the next one that he turned to, but the youngster was already dead before Mengele could do anything for him. The other three victims in the ambulance were unconscious but seemed to be stable.

There was something hauntingly familiar in the scene as he entered the double doors of the hospital. Patients were lining the hall. He could hear doctors barking orders and could see nurses and orderlies bustling through the narrow corridors. He found the doctor in charge and reported it to him.

The fat, nearly bald old man, dressed in a bloodied gown, looked more like a butcher than a doctor and barely acknowledged him. "Do you have any specialties!" the old man demanded, not really looking at him.

"I have just returned from Russia," Mengele responded, wanting to walk back out of the hospital.

"Good. Then help Dr. Schneider in sorting them out when they come through the door." He ordered and then began yelling at a nurse who seemed to be spending too much time with just one patient. They were going to be pressed to the wall that night, and the idea was to keep enough of the people alive until no new casualties arrived. Time and supplies dictated the quality of the medical care.

Mengele worked through the night near the front door of the hospital. He saw broken bones and burns, lacerations and burns, people in shock with burns, and listened while one of the drivers told of finding at least two dozen people who had their lungs actually pulled through their mouths from the vacuum caused by exploding bombs.

The hospital treated over four hundred people that night, and he felt a familiar weariness when the sun came out the next morning. The old doctor thanked him for his efforts in an accusative tone of voice that seemed to imply that anyone in the SS was the reason for the devastation in the first place and did not really deserve thanks but blame.

Mengele walked the few blocks from the hospital to the hotel, and after bathing and putting on a fresh uniform, he made his way down Wilhelmstrasse to work. The smell of smoke was still in the air, and he saw that the Reichstag and the Chancellery had both taken hits, the damage negligible.

The firemen were just now coiling up their hoses. A Catholic Cathedral was the only structure actually totally destroyed in the raid, and there were muted jokes that Goebbels had actually paid the British for the bomb that had hit it dead center.

When he reached the palace, it was full of men filtering in, reporting on the results of their activities of the night. Hobein was in his office. He looked grave, unshaven, and disgusted, his normally resolute and determined face anxious and dour. Something had happened, something that he had not encountered, even in the East.

"You will not believe it," he said, motioning Mengele to take a chair. "You are lucky that you were called away when you were, Herr Doctor."

"What happened, Hobein?" Mengele asked, "Was there a delayed bomb that went off after I left?"

"I wish it was that simple. Did you see any women out front of the warehouse when you left?"

"Yes, I did. There were a couple of women asking about their Jewish husbands. So?"

"I wish I had known they were out there. I would have arrested them and sent them to Gestapo Headquarters. By the time someone bothered to inform me that there were irate women outside, there were fifty or sixty of them. Within an hour, every Jew we had in custody had their wives yelling for their release. That wasn't bad enough. They were soon joined by Berliners on their way to work, who took their side. By nine o'clock, we had a real mob in front of the place, demanding that we let those Jews go!"

"I can't believe it. What did you do?"

"I called Kaltenbrunner. He called the Reichsfuhrer. The Reichsfuhrer told us to get our instructions from Goebbels and let him decide what was to be done. After all, he was the one who ordered that we should include these Jews in our arrests and deportations.

"Goebbels drove by in his car but didn't stop. We thought about loading the Jews onto a truck and taking them to the rail yards where they should have gone to in the first place, but every time we opened the front doors, we had to fight those screaming, yelling hags who tried to make their way inside."

He rubbed his eyes. "I'm telling you, Herr Doctor, I have been in some unusual positions, but I have never felt in fear of my life. But those women had me convinced that they were capable of tearing me, and my entire force, to pieces with their bare hands!"

"All of your limbs are still attached, so what happened?"

"The Doctor of Propaganda gave in, of course. We were ordered to let the goddamned Jews go!" Hobein snarled, pounding his fist on the desk.

Mengele knew that this man had spent many hours in the East, killing Jews without so much of a look back, and now, in his own country, he had not been able to deal with just two hundred of them, and all he had wanted to do was load them onto a rail car.

Mengele could not help it; he burst out laughing.

Hobein stared angrily at him. After a few seconds, the absurdity of the events crystallized in front of his eyes, and he began laughing along with Mengele.

Wiping tears from his eyes, Hobein said, "I don't know why I'm laughing. I have probably reached the top of my career with the SS. After all the good work I have turned in, I'll probably be remembered as the SS man who had to give in to a bunch of Jew-loving bitches."

"I do not think that will be true," Mengele consoled, "you were following orders through the whole thing. It will be the Propaganda Ministry that will be remembered as giving in. How did the rest of the operation turn out?" Hobein consulted a paper on his desk. "We have about thirty-six thousand Jews on trains or in the pens at the rail yards for shipment. There are a few stragglers being apprehended, but it looks like there are a least four thousand Jews left somewhere in the city. They are all underground by now. We will have to come up with other ways of smoking them out. Goebbels is calling for all members of the police, citizens, and the army to help locate them. To find them is going to take pure police work."

"Well, policemen are something we seem to have enough of. Don't worry about these Jews. Shit floats, and the Jew will surface, and we will be able to skim off this scum. Our bloodlines will be made pure; I assure you of that, Standartenfuhrer."

Hobein searched Mengele's face. "You talk like you know something that is not common knowledge, Herr Doktor. Can you enlighten me?"

Mengele gave him a ghost of a smile. "I wish I could, but I have not been told myself. It is just some things that Doktor Verschurer says every once in a while that leads me to believe that there is a solution, even beyond the physical means that you have been pursuing. When I ask him point blank, then he becomes evasive. This is not new. It started when I was a student of his in Frankfort."

"Mengele. You have some idea, don't try and tell me that you don't. We have been friends for many years; at least tell me what you think is going on."

Mengele thought a moment. If he was not convinced that Hobein was the epitome of a Nazi, then the Aryan Race was not the dominant race on Earth. "I am not going to take wild guesses about what is going on. I will tell you that Verschurer is one of the most eminent medical scientists alive today in the world, and he spent many years studying the genetic specificity of diseases."

"Mengele. Talk to me like I am a layman," Hobein demanded, "just what in the hell does all that mean?"

"I think he is working on refining a disease that only kills Jews," Mengele whispered.

XX

It was the first time that Mengele had ever been on an airplane. He climbed clumsily aboard the Junker-88 right behind the Professor, who had scaled the metal ladder with ease to disappear inside the corrugated skin of the tn-motor converted bomber. He followed him as they squeezed down the narrow aisle to take upright and uncomfortable seats. They buckled in.

The noise inside the craft surprised Mengele as the three engines, one at a time, coughed themselves into starting but quickly settled down to a low growl that vibrated through the floor and up through his feet. It was cold, and he pulled the seat belt tight around himself and looked out the small window just in front of his seat, where he could see the starboard engine and wing tip.

The plane began to pick up speed, and Mengele could see the ground rushing by, and when the lumbering giant finally lifted clear of the ground his heart was in his mouth. He could not help but wonder if the wings were supposed to shake so much as the plane fought for altitude.

They had taken off from the military airport not too far from where he had accompanied Hobein on the Factory Operation, but because they flew west, he was denied the sight of the heart of the city from the air but was enraptured by the quilt patch of browns, tans, and an occasional blanket of white lingering snow as it passed underneath. He watched as the roadways became nothing but tiny lines on the landscape, with insect-sized vehicles moving slowly along. The plane leveled off at seven thousand feet. Feeling the cold, he wrapped his collar tighter around his neck.

It was too noisy to have any type of conversation unless you wanted to yell, and yelling was something that neither he nor the professor was very good at. Verschuer had his notebook out and was busy transcribing his thoughts as the plane bucked slightly in the thin early spring air. The professor looked up, gave him a weak smile, and then went back to work. Mengele settled in, content to watch the German countryside slide by.

He had become very bored with Berlin. Milwein had turned out to be an exemplary technocrat who had established a procedure within his department that required very little, if any, improvisations on the part of his people. The only satisfaction that Mengele had enjoyed was once again being at a university. But even here, his duties were not any different than what he had done before the war and after Russia, lecturing on defining and cultivating the correct racial groups had lost some of its appeal. It was a necessity, but he felt he could make far more substantial contributions to the Reich than lecturing on the fundamentals.

Two nights ago, when he had reached Dahlem to teach his evening class at the University, he found a note in his box telling him to see the Professor before leaving that evening, which was strange because he always saw the Professor. It was then that he had been invited to accompany Verschuer to Wewelsburg.

He had been in a state of excitement ever since, even before he had been told that they would be flying there. He had felt important when he had boarded the plane, and now the excitement was still growing inside him. He had confided to Hobein about his upcoming trip, and after a long discussion, they agreed that it was neither Mengele's rank nor his past accomplishments, that had caused the invitation but some future duty that merited the plane ride to Westphalia when fuel was in short supply all over the Reich.

It took them just over two hours to reach the small field that was now familiar to the pilot, and the plane descended and landed with the violent braking necessary to stop before they would be off the runway. Verschuer had become accustomed to the wild landing, or at least expected it. He could see the fear in his protege's face but had not warned him. It gave him an opportunity to appear fearless. The pilot cut the engines immediately upon coming to a stop.

Mengele felt exhilarated as he followed the professor from the plane. The concrete runway gave way to crushed rock that crunched under their feet as they made their way to the Mercedes waiting for them. The air was crisp, its cold bite made thin by the sweet smells and visual displays of coming spring. It felt good on the face. He knew that there would not be much activity in Russia. In Germany, everything was in full swing. Mud now ruled supreme in the East.

Thankfully, Manstein, one of the few Wehrmacht generals who still had the respect of Der Fuhrer, had prevailed upon Hitler not to fire SS-General Hausser for abandoning Kharkiv in February. Instead, they gave him command of a corps of Waffen-SS. In late winter, the first time a corps of Waffen-SS, under SS leadership, struck in battle, they retook the city after savage fighting, inflicting heavy damage on the advancing Russians and stabilizing the front before the mud. Everything was still up in the air in the East.

They rode in a contented silence, Verschuer always enjoying the short car ride to the castle. He looked forward to his visits, especially when the Reichsfuhrer was away. When he was there, he would work in some ceremony which interfered with the time spent with Richard, but over the past year Himmler was busy overseeing his machinery of manufacturing and of death.

Vershuer was surprised to see only slaves working on the grounds and stone walls. The critical need of craftsmen of all trades had precluded the Reichsfuhrer from employing them further here in his private domain. There had been too many inquiries by Party Officials to visit the site where such resources of the Reich were being employed. Himmler had forbidden their visits and adopted slave labor to remove the wedge that the Party had for their inquiries. By now, it did not matter. The castle was completely restored to a grandeur that it had not ever known before, even when it had first been constructed by the Saxons.

Mengele was impressed. He felt the history of the German people flowing through his veins as he came into the entry hall lit with tapers and light streaming through the windows. The first thing that caught his eye was a tapestry of a beautiful, tall, shapely nude Nordic woman with long golden hair flowing over round, upturned breasts. She had the look of virginal innocence on her face, but her body was a promise of bearing many children and giving a man a good time while she did it. She gazed with Nordic blue eyes across the richly carpeted stone floor to where her Nordic man hung on the far wall. Muscular, with a chiseled, handsome face, he stood, armed with a bloodied broad sword, victorious over his enemies that lay slain at his feet.

Mengele surveyed the rest of the room. Swords and rapiers with Toledo and Solinger steel blades encased in ornate hilts made with silver, gold, or translucent ultramarine enamel embellished the stone walls. Wheel lock pistols, muskets, pikes, oil paintings depicting scenes of the Thirty-Years War, and coats-of-arms embellished with all the symbols of the tribes of Germany; the wolf, key, crown, snake, dragon, and lion added to the wall adornments. A stone fireplace roared with the conflagration of eight-foot timbers. Above it stood a four-meter-tall painting of Der Fuhrer clad in silver armor and riding a black steed, its nostrils flaring. In his hands was a battle lance flying the red pennant with the black Swastika. Suits of armor were set to each side of the fireplace, and two more stood steel sentry to the steps leading to the second floor.

"It is rather impressive, is it not?" Verschuer asked, still feeling the impact, even after all his previous visits.

"I hear so many different stories about the Reichsfuhrer, Herr Professor. After seeing what he has surrounded himself with, I am surprised that he concerns himself with any science."

Verschuer smiled. "You will find that the Reichsfuhrer is on our side."

An unterstrumfuhrer with a gold braid wrapped around one shoulder, indicating that he was staff, came up to them. He welcomed the professor like an old friend and was introduced to Mengele.

Verschuer knew the way to his room, and. Mengele followed his escort down a dim hallway. His room, however, was bright with daylight. He put his overnight bag on the four-poster bed with a goose-down mattress. He walked over to the shutters and opened them. He could see over the Alme River to an orchard of apple trees just beginning to bud. Farther on, the forest was stark trees standing strong, awaiting the spring rains. It was good to be out of the city.

There was a knock at the door. The Reichsfuhrer and the Professor were waiting for him. He followed the messenger down the hall and up the grand staircase to the second floor where Himmler kept his office guarded by two SS armed with halberds, with the coat of arms of the Electorate of Saxony engraved on the ax part of the three hundred-year-old weapons.

Mengele entered the large room. Verschuer and the Reichsfuhrer were sitting facing one another on leather couches over by the window. He stood still for a moment as the two men were dcep in conversation and had yet to acknowledge his arrival.

Finally, after what seemed an eternity to Mengele, HimmlerHimmler looked up at him. He had seen the Reichsfuhrer on more than one occasion, having been handed his SS ceremonial sword personally by the Reichsfuhrer just four years ago. The Reichsfuhrer had the look of a man rapidly aging under his burdens. His face was calm and composed but struggling to mask an inner pain. He gave Mengele a tired smile. Mengele hoped that he would not remember that he had, in a sense, defied him by marrying Irene.

"Heil Hitler!" Mengele greeted.

"Heil Hitler. Welcome to Wewelsburg, Hauptsturmfuhrer Doktor Mengele," Himmler's voice was low and soft, barely audible.

"Thank you, Reichsfuhrer. It is an honor."

"Please, come join us," Himmler invited, indicating that Mengele was to take a seat next to his mentor.

Mengele clicked his heels, nodded his head and followed the Reichsfuhrer's instructions. He could never imagine that he would have an audience with whom he thought to be the second most powerful man of the Third Reich. The honor to him was second only to having an audience with Der Fuhrer himself.

"Your career has been quite an interest to many of us in the SS, Herr Doktor. I have reports from many of my most trusted men that your heart is true with the aims of our Fuhrer," the Reichsfuhrer said, picking up a decanter of water and pouring a glass for Josef and handing it to him.

"It is to young men such as Josef that we must trust the future of our race, Reichsfuhrer." Verschuer interjected.

"You have done very well in the Eastern battles against the Russian Bolsheviks, Herr Doktor. It is not hard to see that they are the enemy of our people when they come at us with tanks and guns, and they wish nothing more than to subjugate the people of Europe under the guise of an economic system concocted by that Jew Marx.

"But now I want to talk to you about the other enemy of the people. The ones that do not come at us with weapons of war, but with guile and deception, but whose aim is the same as the Russians. The destruction of our <u>Volk</u>. That there is a World Jewish Empire, and it seeks nothing but the defilement of our blood. They seek nothing less than the domination of all the Aryan peoples of the world, and they laid out the blueprint for accomplishing this in their <u>Protocols of the Elders of Zion</u>. But they could not foresee that the German people would be blessed with a man who only comes along every two thousand years with the wisdom of seeing the Jew for what he is, the arch-enemy of the Volk, and with the will to stop them!"

He sipped at his water. "In the beginning," he continued in his pedantic voice, "I was guilty of thinking we could solve our Jewish problem by simply removing them from the Reich. We were even heavily involved with the Mossad in trying to facilitate their immigration to Palestine, and when the English cut this channel, we considered the island of Madagascar, just like the Poles had considered for their Jews. But the French refused to cooperate. Then Der Fuhrer pointed out that we must not allow the Jews the benefit of acquiring a homeland from which to direct their heinous deeds. That as long as a Jew exists in the world, he will be out to destroy the blood of the Aryan peoples and to hold dominion over them as the beasts of the field, just as promised to them in their Talmund, or the Old Testament of the Christian bible.

"The power of the Jew was exhibited once again when he led the English into declaring war on us when we invaded Poland to take the land we needed to secure our eastern borders from the hordes of the east. That was proven when England did not declare war on Russia, which also invaded Poland just two weeks after we crossed the borders. However, the Jews were also in control of Russia, and the Western Jews would not declare war on the Eastern Jews. Now, the Jews of America have led that once-white nation into a war with her own kind.

"Der Fuhrer promised that if the Jews brought the world to war once again, he would make sure that the biological basis of the Jews in Europe would be destroyed. We are well on our way to accomplishing this, Herr Doktor. Of course, the details are top secret; the common German, in his simplistic soul, could never come to the understanding that we must destroy them–every man, woman, and child of them."

"From what I can piece together, Reichsfuhrer, I think we have managed to kill about two million of them," Mengele said, hoping to surprise his two superiors with his knowledge and already including himself in the collective that had picked up the endeavor of fulfilling Der Fuhrer's will.

Himmler stared at him through the thick lens of his prinz-nez. "We believe it to be over three million, but we have so much more to do. That is why I have called you here."

He picked up his near-empty glass and walked over to the window to look east out over the river. "We have established camps here in the Reich and in the Government General, to take care of the physical extermination of the Jews. Even as we speak, the trains are rolling to these camps from all over the Reich, from the ghettos within the Government General, and from our allies.

"We are close to finishing the expansion of one of these camps. It is equipped with the most modern and proven methods to deal with this vermin. We want you to be the head doctor of this camp. Make no mistake about it, Herr Doktor, it is a 'Death Camp.'"

Mengele was surprised, but knew that there had to be more to it than his just serving as a doctor. He was sure that the Professor was involved in a line of scientific inquiry that had been of monumental importance.

"Josef," Himmler said, coming back and sitting down and fixing Mengele with the shallow gray eyes. "I know that you are a true Nazi. But before I tell you what your other task will be while you are at this camp, I must have your pledge and answer, to join us. If you do not want to, tell me now. You will be flown back to Berlin. I would just ask you not to even mention that you were here."

"Reichsfuhrer," Mengele did not hesitate, elated that he had been correct, "does Der Fuhrer know of this project?"

"Of course. Der Fuhrer has ordered it."

"Then I want to be a part of it, Reichsfuhrer," Mengele stated emphatically.

Himmler looked at Verschuer and gave him a slight nod and then turned back to Mengele. "It is well known that I do not have much respect for many of the men in your profession, Herr Doktor, but you men in research can render a service to the Reich and to the Aryan Race, that far exceeds any of the accomplishments of any of it's generals. You will be helping us to perfect a weapon so fierce and so exact, that it will let us destroy the Jew no matter where he is. If he is hiding behind the identity of a German he will not be safe. If he is even as far away as America he will not be safe.

"Now, if you will excuse me, Gentlemen, I have other work that I must attend to. Herr Professor, please show Doktor Mengele our laboratory here at Wewelsburg. Introduce him to Professor Richard. Acquaint him with his new duties."

He reached out and Mengele shook his hand, surprised to find his handshake cold and limp, his hand feeling small, like a child's hand.

"Welcome to Project Twin Research, Herr Doktor."

Mengele and Verschuer 'heiled' their way out the door, and then the Professor turned and smiled at Mengele. "I knew that you would not refuse the assignment, Josef."

"Somehow, I have known ever since I was wounded that you had some unusual opportunity for me, Herr Professor. I only hope that I will be able to carry out the duties assigned to me

"You will be surprised, Josef, that what is expected of you is well within your qualifications and your training. Come along. I think Professor Richard is better at explaining the details. He is also a brilliant young man. Herr Professor Rudin introduced me to him years ago and I must say that I continue to be impressed by him. The whole thing is really his project."

Verschuer guided Mengele on the walk from the castle proper through the massive inner courtyard, where crocus and tulips were already pushing up through the ground.

They reached their destination, and Verschuer led them through a door. Mengele was surprised. After so much antiquity of the castle, stepping into the most modern medical laboratory that he had ever seen was completely unexpected. The walls were painted white, and the room was made bright by electric bulbs. He looked around the lab. He could see four very modern microscopes on one table. There were bottled gas-fired ammonia coolers with copper heat exchange coils rattling on top of the units. There were numerous labeled ovens used for growing cultures.

Professor Richard had been expecting them. His hair was totally gray, long and unkept, and quite the contrast to his still youthful face without the trace of a wrinkle, not even a laugh line around light blue eyes. His complexion had the ghostly pallor of a man who had not seen the sun in many years, but his skin was firm. He had long fingers, the nails clean and manicured.

"Professor Verschuer," he greeted. Then he gave a slight bow of the head. "You must be Doktor Mengele. I have heard much about you."

Mengele could not tell how old this man really was, but for some reason, he felt older. He had never heard of this man until now, but he knew he was in the presence of a remarkable intellect. He felt it an honor to meet him. The man radiated an aura that made Mengele immediately his assistant, his student.

"Doktor Mengele is one of the most promising geneticists within the Reich today." Verschuer introduced.

"I know, Professor. When I read his exacting study on the lower jaw portion of four racial groups, and he held that previous studies failed to note differences even when they occurred, I knew that he was someone who could contribute to my research and experiments."

"And what work is that, Doktor Richard," Mengele asked.

Richard looked at Verschuer for permission.

"I am happy to say that Doktor Mengele is joining us," Verschuer said. "The Reichsfuhrer is arranging it, so he will be in a position to supply us with information that will help us tremendously. He will have access to dozens of the races of Europe. In fact, the amount of medical information a diligent medical man will be able to extract will probably make him one of the premier scientists of the century." He looked proudly at Mengele. "Josef is one of the most exacting scientists that I have had the pleasure of being associated with!"

Mengele beamed.

"Splendid!" Richard cried, slapping his hands together. "There is so much to do. I am relieved that, at last, I will have someone that I can count on. Someone who can give me accurate information. Someone in a position to supply the body fluids we need."

"Please, Doktor Richard. I haven't been instructed about any aspect of the project, and I have not been informed about what is expected of me," Mengele said.

"We have two avenues of research that we hope will one day converge," Richard explained. "One of the things that we must accomplish is the construction of the genetic map of man."

Mengele thought for a moment. "You are talking as if you have identified the actual agent for genetics. Have you proven what the genes are?"

Richard smiled. "It is in the chromosomes. It is the chemical compound called <u>nuclein</u>.

"I was sure that it could not be in the blood!" Mengele beamed. He grew somber. "I still do not understand how I can contribute."

Verschuer spoke up. "We need to compare physical manifestations of an individual with their chromosomes. You will not be alone in compiling the data, Josef. I will be able to place samples throughout the universities of the Reich. What we need from you is the exact measurements, physical descriptions, pathological findings, and all data that can be physically determined on a subject. From that, we can start to look for similarities and differences."

"I see the importance of twins in this research, Herr Doktors!" Mengele said excitedly.

"Exactly. If identical twins can have slight physical differences or react to external stimuli in different manners, then we can compare their <u>nuclei</u> and zero in on specific gene functions. Can you see how valuable a set of identical twins would be that showed up with one having brown eyes and one having blue eyes?" Verschuer said.

"Or someone that has one arm shorter than the other or other abnormalities. Dwarfs and midgets. The possibilities are endless."

Mengele finished. He now knew what was expected of him. He thought about the other line of research.

"I can see what monumental task I will be involved in, Herr Doktor," he said to Richard. "You will be using the results, but just what is the line of research that you are doing?"

"Come here and take a look." Richard invited, gesturing to the closet microscope.

Mengele stepped up to it and peered into the lens. He had only to adjust it slightly when a simple bacteria came into focus. It looked familiar. He could see nothing extraordinary about it. With the proper references he would be able to identify it easily. He looked up with a slight frown. He was not afraid to admit that he did not see anything of significance.

"Please. Now look at this one." Richard said, indicating the next microscope.

Mengele hoped for something obvious to leap into his eye, but the next slide was also of a simple bacteria. He looked up with a puzzled expression. Surely, the professor had not been duped by some pseudo-scientist. So far, all he could see were two simple bacteria. One probably from the mold of cheese and one from the mold of bread. Nothing of significance.

"One more," Richard said, indicating the riddle would be soon solved.

Mengele glanced at Verschuer and then put his eye to the lens. He focused and, at first, thought that he was going to have to look up admitting defeat. He looked at the cellular shapes of the microscopic creatures swimming in the manmade soup under the magnification.

They also appeared normal, but if this slide was the key, then they could not be normal. He spun the fine-tuned dial to make sure he was in optimum focus. As he looked closer, he had the impression of seeing parts of each cell somewhere else.

He must be looking at a combination of the first two bacteria! He looked up, startled.

"Doktor Richard has learned to splice pieces of bacteria together, Josef. And then it will replicate. He is the first man to create a species of life!" Verschuer announced to a stunned Mengele.

"Please, Doktor," Richard said, "only in culture, and I am extremely far away from achieving any success in multicellular organisms.

Mengele was thunderstruck. Richard was the first man to create life in a dish. It was just a mutant of very basic bacteria, but it had replicated itself, and it could at least survive long enough to be viewed and studied.

It was all beginning to make sense to him. He knew that Richard was working in a world far different from any other known scientist. Everyone else would have rushed to publish. Science is a series of discoveries just waiting for the next man to find it. If you are working on it, then someone else is working on it, and if he puts out the information about the discovery just one day before you, then it is his discovery. It will have his name, and you can, at best, be a collaborator.

Mengele was awed by the scope of the project. He was smug that they had recruited, maybe even groomed him for the project. He had not a clue about how this man had recombined these genes.

"How do you accomplish this miracle?" Mengele asked.

"I use a body chemical to cut the <u>nuclein</u> apart. When I mix them, they will recombine, sometimes trading pieces with each other and forming a new identity," Richard explained, "it is really quite simple."

Mengele was silent. His mind raced past hundreds of possibilities. "What body chemicals?"

"Enzymes. I require much and have access to so little," Richard complained.

"Which is why you will be so important to the project, Josef," Verschuer spoke. "You will be in a position that will allow unrestricted gathering of a particular body part that is full of both <u>nuclein</u> and enzymes. They are easily shipped and handled."

"What body part, Herr Professor?" Mengele asked.

"Why, eyeballs, of course," Richard answered.

Mengele nodded in understanding. So far, everything was straightforward enough, but he still did not see how this line of research was going to become a weapon aimed at the Jews.

"Herr Doctors," he asked, "how is knowing the genetic map of man and having the ability to make new cellular creatures going to rid us of the Jew?"

"Do you remember the disease that I identified as being only found in Jews?" Verschuer asked.

"Of course. It is that skin cancer that attacks only older Jewish males." Mengele had recalled it easily because it was one of the ways to identify a Jew hiding behind a German name. Then, it suddenly all became clear to him.

"I see. At least, I think I do. We splice the genes that cause the skin cancer onto a bacteria and feed it to them?"

"No. We splice the genes onto a virus. Then we let the virus distribute it among the Jews," Verschuer explained.

"Virus. That makes sense. But which virus. All the ones that we know of will attack anyone not vaccinated against it."

Richard looked at Mengele. He did not see the need to let him on everything. Wonder if he was captured, he was going east. But Verschuer had not seemed interested in keeping anything from his protege.

"We have a man in Africa who is searching for a suitable virus," Richard reluctantly announced.

XXI

If it could be tabulated, Auschwitz had a prison population of one-hundred-thirty-six-thousand two hundred and eighty-five inmates when Mengele got off the regularly scheduled train bringing supplies, replacements, and men returning from leave. It was the beautiful spring day of May 30, 1943. Mengele was thirty-two years old. He was two hours and ten minutes behind the last arriving Jew train, but before he reached the Commandant's office to report in, sixteen hundred thirty-three people had been poisoned in the chambers and were now being loaded into the crematoriums, and another thirty-seven had died in the compound proper by accident, disease, or as for an example.

As if the inmates needed to be taught another example.

The roadway was concrete, with whitewashed stones lining the right of way. There were stop signs on the main road leading to the administrative building, a two-story stone with a thatched roof. The grounds were well kept. In front was a flagpole flying the red, white and black Nazi flag.

As Mengele stepped out of the car that had picked him up at the station, his nose curled in the air. Like all animals that can sniff out dead animals, especially one of their own kind, he knew instinctively what he was smelling that was barely a whiff in the wind. It had an arid sweetness in it, a component of men and greasy machines burning to death together. Or the fumes of a chemical that burned the flesh with an unquenchable fire like phosphorus. He knew that if he was closer, he would be able to smell meat sizzling without the acidity of hair, the heavy murkiness of machines, or the heat of chemicals. He walked out into the middle of the street in order to see more clearly the two black plumes of smoke spewing from the chimneys in the distance.

Smoke.

You could never escape it in war. He had seen tanks burning, airplanes burning, fields burning, armored personnel carriers burning, villages burning, and buildings burning. They all wickered smoke.

Smoke is the visual destruction and release of carbon material. Everything that produces smoke when it burns contains carbon. Human life is made up of a lot of carbon and carbon compounds, and when they talk of life, they talk of 'carbon-based' life. So what Mengele first saw at a distance of just over a mile was the black greasy smoke released when fourteen ovens feeding two chimneys utilized to the maximum, when one normal adult, one emancipated adult, and one child were put in a retort together in order to minimize the need of coke, an important commodity, and utilize fat, a very combustible material, to help feed the fire, as the fat Jew helped vaporize other thinner Jews. The principle being the same that Eichmann had first introduced into Austria after the Anchuss, where the rich Jews were made to help subsidize the immigration of the poor Jews.

Out of the country.

Up in smoke.

The Jews stuck together.

Mengele did not dwell on the sight and smell but marched smartly into the office, where he was greeted with the Nazi salute by the sentry.

Oberstrumbannfuhrer Rudolf Hoess was expecting him.

Hoess had been just fifteen when he entered the army in the First World War, becoming its youngest non-commissioned officer. He came home after the war to join the Freikorps, killed a Communist Jew, and had to spend five years in prison. He joined the Nazi Party in 1931 and was recruited early by the Reichsfuhrer, having met him previously in the Artamen Society, a group that worshipped the bucolic life but really did everything else but live it. He had traveled to Hadamar in 1938 to watch the gassing of twenty-eight feebleminded or incurably insane Germans in the chamber at this hospital for the mentally ill. Carbon monoxide contained in a cylinder was the lethal propellant.

He had trained at Dachau and Sachsenhausen under Theodore Eicke. Eicke, who had personally dispatched that homosexual Roehm with a pistol shot, and later set the stern procedures and rules that became in-bred into all the concentration camp SS men. This was when most of the men on the 'other side of the wire' were countrymen, although Communists, criminals, or homosexuals. Eicke took his original camp guards into the Waffen-SS as the Totenkopf Brigade, where they helped contribute to their own legend as being both brave and brutal, and whose Wehrmacht commander made sure they always had plenty of opportunity to die for Der Fuhrer. Eicke himself was killed by Russian artillery fire.

Himmler had sent Hoess to Auschwitz in early 1940 to establish the camp that was on the rail line just forty miles west of Krakow. It had once belonged to the Polish Tobacco Industry who abandoned the place as surrounding marshes caused the tobacco to mildew and rot instead of age and cure. Later, a Polish cavalry unit set up there, building stone barracks and stables, but the marshes kept both man and beast just not quit well, and they abandoned the area as not good for anything but fishing.

The Germans first used the stone barracks and stables in 1940 to house Polish prisoners-of-war and political civilians who had escaped the initial firing squads. After Barbarossa, the camp began to fill with captured Russian soldiers who were used to expand the camp, while the SS guard units deported the people from the nearby villages.

By 1941, the camp was struggling to maintain twelve thousand people, now mostly Russians, when it was visited by Otto Ambros, a schoolhood friend of the Reichsfuhrer and an officer of I.G. Farben. The giant chemical consortium had sent him out to the conquered territories to find such a juxtaposition of prison labor and natural resources.

It was out of the range of the Anglo-American bombers, served by a main rail line, situated between the confluence of the Sola and Vistula rivers, and had timber and deposits of coal, lime and salt. Ambros reported to the Reichsfuhrer that the place was ideal for the manufacturing of synthetic rubber known as Buna and synthetic fuels, both vital to the war effort.

Himmler visited the camp soon afterward and instructed Hoess to expand both the living quarters and the killing capacity.

Operation Reinhardt was to be fully implemented—the biological destruction of the Jews in Europe was to be carried out. They would be soon arriving in massive numbers to furnish labor for the factories, and fodder for the gas chamber, which at this time consisted of one small chamber still fired by carbon monoxide.

In less than a year, thirty thousand skilled laborers from all over Europe built facilities for I.G. Farben, Siemens, and Krupp. Chemicals, steel, explosives, and electrical devices were soon being manufactured by ten thousand inmates whose labor value was paid for by business into the coffers of the Reichsfuhrer. This part of the camp came to be designated Auschwitz III.

Hoess did not have to worry about the management of the factories. All he was required to do was deliver the workforce. He was also responsible for carrying out Operation <u>Reinhardt</u> and quickly realized that the actual killing center should not be inside the main camp where the factory workers were housed. It would be bad for worker's morale.

He opted for the expansion of this, the initial primary function of the camp, to take place in a stand of birch trees situated west of the main camp.

Birkenau, or Auschwitz II, was constructed by ten thousand Russian prisoners-of-war who had been marched from Lamsdorf, Stalag VIIIb, a prisoner-of-war camp run by the Wehrmacht that was nothing but open ground where two-hundred thousand Russians lived in holes dug into the dirt with their own hands, and were provided with nothing but a bullet if they got past the few strands of barbed wire that enclosed them. Men, who were so starved that they continued their cannibalism when they reached their new destination, even though there was at least enough food provided for them to sustain life. They were available to help refine the killing process. A mere handful of these men survived.

Hoess always had reservations about carbon monoxide. It was too slow, and the machinery was unreliable. He had attended the demonstration by SS Strumbannfuhrer Christian Wirth, known in higher SS circles as the Chief Executioner of the Reich, at Chelmno, when it took two hours to get the 250-horsepower diesel engine started. The people inside waiting began to raise a ruckus when they finally figured out that the pipes leading into them were not carrying water for showers.

Showers.

All the killing centers, Chelmno, Treblinka, Majdanek, Sobibor, Belzec, and Auschwitz, all had one thing in common.

Showers.

When you were crammed into a foul-smelling rail car with other people for days, and your sanitary facilities were a bucket, where grandmothers had to squat over a pail on a moving rocking and rolling train in front of their grandchildren. When fathers and mothers were forced to defecate in front of their children and their parents, when young men and women had to grunt in front of their sweethearts and their parents, when no one could wipe or wash their hands. When people, who had taken great pains to scrub their children's faces clean, even with spit if that was the only moisture available, and everyone felt soiled and gritty and stinking when they arrived at these places where the train stopped and the doors were slide open for the first time in days, and the Germans were yelling at you to 'Schnell, schnell,' then going to the showers sounded like a welcome relief. They just hoped that the water would be a little warm and they would not mind so much sharing a spray of water with their grandchildren and their neighbors whom they had known all of their lives but had never been naked with.

Hoess was not ready to put his faith in the internal combustion engine. He wanted something that would react far more quickly than carbon monoxide.

They found it when Hauptstrumfhrer Karl Fritsch watched Tesch and Stabenow, pesticide contractors, carrying out the fumigation of one of the existing wood huts that were crawling with lice and fleas. He watched them as they proceeded to rope off the area, don gas masks and enter the buildings, only to emerge seconds later with efficient haste. He quizzed the technicians about what they were using and learned how lethal the pesticide Zyklon B actually was. He quickly rounded up a dozen Russians and had them confined in a nearby cellar jail. He put on a gas mask and entered, slinging the powdered pesticide at the feet of the terrified Russians and watching them just fall dead.

As soon as Hoess had returned to the camp, Fritsch burst excitedly into his office and told him of his discovery. Hoess soon tried it out on seventy more Russians, and as the yellow chemical sublimed, going from the solid state directly to the gaseous state, he knew he had found a gas he could count on.

Hydrogen Cyanide.

Deutsche Gesellschaft zur Schadlingsbekampfung, the German Pest Control Company, assured Hoess that they could supply the SS camp with an unlimited amount of the chemical, and BASF, part of I.G. Farben, could indeed stop putting in the tell-tale almond odorant in order to warn of its presence so that people could take deep fatal breaths of it without fear.

They did not make the product.

They just made it better.

"Heil Hitler!" Mengele clicked his heels together.

"Heil Hitler!" Hoess greeted his new Chief Doctor for Birkenau. He stood and came out from behind the massive mahogany desk with brass inlaid legs, "Welcome to Auschwitz, Herr Doctor."

He was not much taller than Mengele but thinner through the shoulders. His dark hair was cropped, and the widow's peak pronounced as his hair receded in an avalanche. He had not personally killed anyone since he had helped kill that Communist Jew. Now, he was the Commanding Officer of the largest of the killing camps.

"Thank you, Herr Standartenfuhrer," Mengele answered.

"The Reichsfuhrer himself informed me of your posting, Herr Doctor. I must say that he went out of his way to impress upon me the cooperation you must receive."

Mengele stood silent but smug. He could detect no resentment in Hoess. He was at least among the purest of the Nazis, those charged with carrying out the physical extermination of a race of people dispersed over the entire continent of Europe.

"There are many other doctors assigned here in research activity, Herr Doctor," Hoess said. "Some of them even manage to avoid the selections at the ramps. Herr Doctor Clauberg has convinced the Reichsfuhrer that he can carry out the sterilization of one thousand Jewish women a day. That will doom their race to the remainder of their generation and allow us to have their labor for so long as we decide to keep them alive. He is a civilian, so the good doctor does not have to take time out from poking into the genitals of young Jewish women in order not to make the selections at the ramps. You will find the twenty-two SS doktors equally reluctant to perform their duties at the ramp."

Mengele understood the concern of the Commandant. "I will be able to fulfill all the duties assigned to a medical doctor. My research will not interfere with the needs of the camp."

Hoess looked his new man over. The importance of the post made him silently hope that the Reischfuhrer had indeed sent him a man who could do the job. He was tired of hearing about how the doctors were showing up at the ramp drunk to do their duty. One thing that was always available to the men and the few women who were carrying out a directive of their government to commit organized mass murder, was all the alcohol they wished to consume. Now one of the doctors had started referring to the camp as the 'anus mundi,' the 'asshole of the world,' and it was catching on. Nicknames like that were not good for the morale of the troops that supervised and guarded the camp.

Hoess had long been dissatisfied with the caliber of SS supervisors serving under him. All the really good men must have followed Eicke into the Waffen-SS. What was left, and the replacements, were either sadistic, incompetent or just uncaring, not to mention sharing a high degree of stupidity. The commandant of Sauchenhausen had first refusal on the men, and the commandant of Ravensbrook had first refusal on the women. Auschwitz was the end of the line for a lot of people, career-wise.

It took intelligence to know your function in a killing factory.

Or it took true devotion and undying belief in der Fuhrer.

Hoess looked at the medals on Mengele's chest and realized that he might be the most decorated soldier in the entire garrison, and he was not even a military man but a doctor in military service. He would soon see if Mengele would measure up to the job.

"Your special equipment arrived two weeks ago and I am told that it has been installed. Come, let us inspect it together," Hoess invited, putting on his peaked cap and leading them outside, where they climbed into the back seat of a utility car with the blackened polish-hemp canvas top down. After listening to his instructions, the driver started the car and drove slowly down the main road where he turned left and pulled up to a gate with 'Work Brings Freedom' spelled out in big bold letters cut from iron plates, painted yellow and bolted across the barbed wire fence. The guards spun the tall, wired gate open.

The prisoners who first read this message displayed near or on all the gates, quickly learned that work would not set you free, but it would keep you alive until you could no longer work or you got sick beyond a few days' stay in the hospital, or you made a German mad at you, or a train was delayed, and the machinery of death was sitting idle, and the compounds were canvassed for the raw material to utilize the death making equipment to capacity.

They drove down a row of two-story stone barracks that served as the living quarters for most of the skilled workers. These buildings looked like worker's tenants and, along with the birch trees lining the road, made it a neighborhood suitable for raising a family, but there were no women, and there were no children here. Only men and none of them were in sight as they would all be in the factories at this time of day. On the average they would only be spending five hours a day here.

The car turned left on a crushed limestone road and jarred over a rough railroad crossing that was being worked on by a detail of men dressed in trousers and jackets of yellowed dingy white with faded blue stripes. Shaven-headed Jews doffed their caps and bowed as the Germans drove by.

They sped along the road in the open field between the two camps. Mengele could see various work parties scattered about. He had no idea what they were doing unless it had something to do with irrigation or sanitation. He could see just a few SS men scattered about the fields with leashed dogs.

When Hoess pleaded for more men to guard the ever-swelling prison population and, at the same time, was being berated because of the amount of escapes, he pointed out that the camp was now over twenty square miles, and he had only one regiment to contain it.

They told him to put up more electric fences, and they would supply the high voltage to run them. This worked to keep the inmates in, especially at night. The dogs were to keep them in line everywhere, especially out in the fields, especially with the women, who somehow found being lunged at by a snarling frothing at the mouth over one hundred pound animal of <u>cannus domesticus</u> that had nothing but hate and ferocity snapping in inch long fangs, and you had watched as they bit others inflicting severe wounds as the beasts were capable of ripping out huge chunks of flesh and muscle, which if it did not kill you then and there, then it sent you to the hospital so badly mauled that the lack of an antiseptic lead to an inflammation where your numbers were eventually written down and they sent you to the chambers in a camp selection.

They passed under the tower guarding the main entrance of Birkenau. To their right, on the other side of electrified wire, they began to pass barracks, each twelve yards wide and forty yards deep, ten rows of fifteen deep, ugly flat wood buildings, with a wash house and a shit house capping off each row. They were built as stables with celestial windows and wide swinging doors located at the end of the wood building. Across three tracks stood other buildings enclosed behind another row of electrified wire.

Mengele could glimpse movement behind the wire and the buildings, as if rats were scurrying in the sudden light.

"Over there is the women's camps," Hoess pointed out to Mengele. "The poor conditions you will find I can contribute in part to misguided selectivity at the ramps by the doctors who think they are being chivalrous. Many of them have a tendency to save more than they should, especially the females, so the barracks fill up with many undesirables. We simply can not keep expanding to hold the trains that the Reichsfuhrer is sending us."

The car came to a stop at an intersection of Lagerstrasse, the main thoroughfare of the camps and one of the connecting roads between BI and BII. Mengele saw carts riding on narrow rails being pushed by women dressed in grab-gray dresses with dull scarves, and they looked to him to be a part of the earth and nothing more.

"We were originally instructed that all Jews arriving at the camp were to be exterminated upon arrival," Hoess explained, "but before that first group could reach us from Upper Silesia, we received instructions from the Economic and Administrative Head Office that all able body people, including the Jews, were to be put to work. This, of course, an order of the Reichsfuhrer. Those barracks were just thrown together by some dying Russians when we realized that we were going to have to house women.”

“So you continue to cram them into the existing space and feed all of them less, and the overall health of the camp declines,” Mengele said.

“Exactly, Herr Doctor.” Hoess was impressed. At least the Reichsfuhrer had not sent him a stupid man. He decided to trust this doctor.

“So you can clearly understand my position, Herr Doctor, let me explain it in simple language. Eichman and Muller of the Reich Central Security Office want them all dead now. Pohl and Mauer of Economics and Administration want to keep them alive, fed, and in a condition that they can perform a good day’s work, and your SS doctors are hounded by both.”

“So what does the Richsfuhrer say, Herr Standartefuhrer?” Mengele asked.

“Of course, I am charged with carrying out both orders,” Hoess ruefully replied.

“I think I understand.”

“If you do, then that makes only two of us. Although I suspect the Reichsfuhrer understands completely the situation.” He let his newest officer think about that for a moment.

“On your right is the Gypsy Camp,” Hoess pointed out.

Mengele could see, just on the other side of the wire, people milling about, including children.

"Berlin made us clear a lot of them out. They make very poor labor, but we still feed them better than the Jews. It is the only place in the camp where you will find children."

"These are Aryan peoples, Herr Standartefuhrer," Mengele explained, "or at least two families of them are pure Aryan." He decided to establish his position. "I am afraid that I will be requiring that some more children remain alive. All twins, no matter what their age, must be assigned to me. That also means I will need a barracks in all three of the camps. Women's, men's and Gypsy's."

Hoess smiled. He had just explained that there was a critical shortage of space in the camp, and the new doctor had understood it but was still demanding space that was presently housing close to two thousand people.

"I will leave that to your own devices, Herr Doctor," he said, silently happy that the incompetent witch in charge of the women's camp was going to be caused some grief by this new physician.

They turned left and crossed the tracks but turned right instead of entering the women's camp and proceeded down the road that ran parallel to the tracks. After a quarter of a mile, they came to a stop in front of the crematoria, an innocent-looking brick building with one huge chimney dominating the roof line. On the other side of the tracks that they had crossed earlier was a similar building. The smell of raw meat was not as noticeable here closer to the fire.

The two men got out, and Hoess led the way around to the back of the building and up an outside wooden staircase and entered the building through a second floor door.

Mengele was impressed. Here, he had a pathology room with the most modern equipment. There was a green marble dissecting table and three wash basins, all with nickel taps. There was a long workbench with four microscopes still in their factory covers. There were two counterbalances and many beam scales. The spacious room off of the laboratory was his office. Shelves lined the wall and were full of medical journals and needed references.

"This will do splendid," Mengele said, delighted. Verschurer had promised that he would see to it that he would have the tools to accomplish his tasks. The German Research Council had indeed been generous.

They both heard the whistle at the same time. Hoess consulted his watch.

"Come with me, Herr Hauptstrumfuhrer. This is the last train arriving today. We can acquaint you with the procedures before we take you to your quarters."

They went back to ground level and climbed into the back seat of the car. The driver crossed the tracks, turned right at the other bunker and drove down a service road, passing four rows of the barracks and stopping just shy of Lagerstrasse.

They watched as the yard locomotive began to shove the cars into the camp, but before the lead car had crossed under the tower, a truck pulled passed them, and Mengele watched as prisoners jumped down. SS men by car, trucks, motorcycles and bicycles soon arrived and dispersed along the ramp.

The yard engineer put the leading car at the rail stops. The SS men immediately took their stations at the foot of the doors, unlocked them, and on signal, all the doors of the train, consisting of some twenty-two cars, were slid open, and the SS men began their bellowing for the occupants to get down from the car!

At first, it was a trickle, with those closest to the doors, the only ones whose eyes did not burn with the light because they had the benefit of thin shafts of light that came through the slats of the door. It was soon made obvious to all the Jews that no one else was going to help them, but they had better get off the train and better damn well get off the train now! The Jews unloaded themselves and were instructed to stay in the area in front of their car doors.

They looked strangely at the stripped men of their own race that stood silently among the Germans. These were the Sonderkommando. They were all Jews. To the newly arriving Jews, they at least looked fed, and they seemed healthy enough. If having to wear those pajamas like uniforms with the rakishly worn matching caps was going to be the punishment for being Jewish, then maybe this place was going to be bearable.

Even before the cars were completely empty, the SS men were demanding that they form two rows of five with men next to the cars and the women to the outside of the ramp near the center rail. The SS men had holstered side arms and carried thin canes, and Mengele watched as one of them swatted an old man on the back who wanted to stay in line next to his wife. Nothing really vicious in the swipe, but enough to get the message across that the Germans were not going to take anything but obedience.

"With your permission," Mengele asked, indicating that he wanted to get closer.

Hoess looked at him. "Only the able body, Herr Doctor. But women, no matter how healthy, must go to the chambers with their children. All children under fifteen. Pregnant women go to the chambers. No one past working age or anyone else not fit to put in a day of hard labor. Of course, any diseased or distressed persons must go to the chambers."

"I understand my orders, Herr Standartefuhrer. But now, all twins, dwarfs, midgets, and deformed persons must be saved from every transport. Plus, I need to personally inspect all old male Jews."

"As you wish, Herr Doctor. Hoess invited him to precede while he sat back into the brown leather of the car. Whenever he made a physical appearance on the ramp, the doctors always seemed to insist that the commandant should himself look through the shuttle of the chamber and see the dead intertwined bodies, as if to confirm that people in authority knew that this was going on. In the nine years that he had spent in the concentration camps, he had seen enough deaths. He really did not like being at selections. Maybe he now had someone else in his command who knew how to balance the tightrope of his duties.

Mengele walked to the head of the column, where there were two SS doctors and a half dozen cane-equipped NCOs. The doctors were turned away from the forming columns, so they watched him approach. They could see the ribbons and medals donned on the immaculate uniform with the highly polished boots. He outranked everyone on the ramp, and from the looks of him, he was going to make it apparent. He stopped within a few feet of them and, at first, peered over their shoulders at the people forming into their ranks.

"My name is Mengele, Herr Doktors. I am your new commander." He introduced himself nonchalantly, seeking someone out in the crowd behind them.

The two men in gray overcoats and soft caps looked at one another. They both realized that showing up on the ramp as his first official duty at the camp, even before formally introducing himself at dinner or at morning quarters, indicated that their new leader was here by choice, and a man like that would have a way of changing things. He was here now, obviously, to change the way selections were made.

"Welcome to <u>anus</u> <u>mundi</u>, Herr Hauptstrumfuhrer." Ernst Bethune greeted. So let him do that. Anything to the present orders would be a welcome change.

Bethune staggered somewhat on his feet and felt mad at himself when he wished that the new man had not seen it, but Mengele seemed like a cat who took it all in. He really had only a few glasses of schnapps all day, and this was, after all, the second train today. When it was over, he could go on about his duties doctoring no one and doing nothing and then his turn would roll around for selection duty again, and he would have to be here, and now it was even his turn to be in front of the women and children's line, having to sort the men on the earlier train.

After a while, he stopped thinking of it as selections. He thought of it only as sorting.

Sorting.

They stopped in front of you. Sometimes, it would be five strong, healthy young women, and they would distinctly look him in the eyes because there was a pride within them that refused to make them bow their heads. They had done no wrong that they were aware of, and this was a civilized world. There was no shame. He knew that he would soon be beaten out of them.

You sorted them to the right in twos and threes, and then they were grouped in the twenties and marched in different directions around the camp until they ended up at the delousing stations where other women prisoners shaved the hair off of their heads and pubic areas. They then quickly showered and were sprayed with chemicals to kill any vermin, and they gave you a worn gray dress still stained with the filth of the last inmate who had worn it until they went up in smoke.

The ones below eye level, the children, you did not even look at. You never looked down. You did not want to look down and see three and four-year-olds standing there waiting with their mother or their grandmother, and you had to tell them to go to the left; they just looked at you with big eyes, but they knew to follow their elders, and they did it quietly. You just automatically pointed to the left when you had to sort them. Old women sometimes even leaned in that direction because they had been watching, and they followed automatically the women they had sometimes known since childhood, and they sometimes took their grandchildren with them. And after you sorted them, you never turned to watch them trudge across the tracks and turn right for the quarter-mile walk to the underground chambers where they gassed you, and members of your own race shaved your heads and pulled the gold teeth from your mouths, and then hauled your body by leather straps thrown around your wrist and you were hauled to elevators that whisked your remains to the first floor where members of your people loaded you into the fire, and it was your own people that beat into dust with a wooden mallet any clumps of bone left over from the raging fire.

"Starting with this transport, Herr Doctors," Mengele ordered, "all twins, no matter what their age, will be culled out and handed over to me. Along with dwarfs, anyone obviously deformed from births, and anyone displaying physical peculiarities. I also want to see all the oldest men before they are sent into the chambers."

Bethune looked at him with a shocked expression. Now, he was going to have to start to look down!

XXII

Lagerfuhrein SS-Strumbannfuhrer Gertrude Langefeldt was furious. She had just effectively fought off the encroachment of her authority by the Commandant, who had the gall to appoint the Rapportfuhrer of the men's camp, another male of the same rank she held, to be her superior. Thankfully, the Reichsfuhrer himself restored the proper chain of command, having the wisdom to know that a woman must be in charge of a camp built by starving-to-death Russians to house some twelve thousand women, but crammed with over fifty thousand of essentially child-bearing age, and feeding them an average of four hundred calories a day.

Now, just when she was beginning to feel safe in her position, this Doctor Mengele shows up, and she could not believe her eyes. He made life miserable for her a few years ago in Krakow, but now he has a chest full of medals, which was like giving fire to a dragon. When she decides to immediately exert her authority over him, he insults her and gives her a list of things he would be requiring, including an entire block!

When she complained to the Commandant in person about his demands and demeanor, he told her that whatever the Doctor wanted, he could have. When she went over his head by telephone to complain to Pohl, who was always ready to kiss her ass in the past, he told her that whatever the Doctor wanted, he could have. And, when she complained by telex to the Reichsfuhrer himself, he himself telephoned to tell her that he would come down there personally and have her shot if she did not quit crying and let the Doctor have what he wanted.

So she had sat tight-lipped, as only a thinned-lip person can do, while he preceded to take over a block, leaving her to deal with where to house the eight hundred women now occupying the block. Block 25, the 'Himmnel' station for women found in a camp selection, was, as usual, already full. She could have had the women assigned among the other blocks but knew scattering them among her controllers and supervisors on such short notice would devastate their already disastrous roll calls, which made her look like an idiot in charge of fools. She had been forced to ask Hauptscharfuhrer Koeing for a special favor, and he stayed later than he was planning and they emptied four hundred women from block 25 because that was why they were there, to top off the chamber, so Hoess would not be chewing their asses for inefficiencies, and the NCO had solved her immediate problem. She now owed this fat pig with the atrocious breath a favor, and just the thought of owing a man a favor on account of another man made her furious.

She had even set Irma Gresse, one of her supervisors, onto Mengele to distract him from his endeavors. Irma was a beautiful young sexy blond bombshell who had been the nurse of Der Fuhrer's physician, who thought it best that she get out of Berlin before she fucked the brains out of the bigwigs of the party, especially himself. Since she was fourteen, she thought her pussy was the center of the universe and had many others helping her come to the same conclusion. Langefeldt had watched as many men and many women lost all sense of themselves when Irma poured her sexuality on them. When she had strutted her stuff encased in the tight black pants, jack boots, black tight blouse, braless, stained with the heat and with stretching nipples and wearing her black holster with the 9mm pistol and carrying her black whip and she had focused all that sexuality onto Mengele, he leered at her, which was the usual response Irma elicited in males, but then the leer quickly faded into what Langefeldt thought to be a silly buck-toothed grin, and the doctor had went on about his business.

Mengele had Block 15 in camp B2F fumigated with gas and painted on the inside. He had fresh bedding installed and was now meeting every train, and even before the selections started, he was striding up and down the ramp yelling "zweilings," "zweilings," and when he found a set of twins, he would be as elated as a proud parent on hearing news of their newborn, and if they were identical twins he could even evoke a smile from old Jewish women who loved to see men dote over children and to see an SS man go exuberant over Jewish children was a heart-warming sight indeed.

Sometimes, he sent their mother along with them, and sometimes, he even sent a father along with them. They did not go through the 'sauna' where all body hair was shaved. They even had a tattooed at the beginning of their numbers, and everyone in the camp learned within days that you did not fuck with these kids who seemed to run amok about the entire camp, but if you put a swipe on them, then you had Mengele to contend with, and if you damaged one of his twins and you were a Capo you could become smoke, and if you were SS you were lucky if you did not end up on a transport to the east to take a position in front of the Russians who by now had a terrible reputation of killing German soldiers.

The son of a bitch had not been in the camp a month before he was in control of it!

Mengele did not feel in control of anything. He had set a hectic pace for himself, trying to establish some routine and procedures for his research, and Berlin and Wewelsburg were already clamoring for samples and specimens. It seemed like every time he had some moments that he could spend on establishing a system, another train would arrive, and he just could not trust any of the other doctors to follow his directives.

Doctors everywhere have the tendency to ignore authority, and Auschwitz was no exception. They seemed to be either dedicated men who were pursuing their own line of research, like the Luftwaffe doctors who were freezing Jewish men in vats of frigid water and having a naked Jewish woman see if she could rub life into them with their own body warmth, and then they tried to see if two naked women could do it twice as fast. Or boring holes through the skull into the brains of homosexuals to see if they could straighten them out. Clausberg, of course, was working on the vaginas of the Jewish race, while the pharmaceuticals of IG Fargen were paying for the experimentation of their experimental drugs on any of the diseases it was possible to inflect, including typhus, spotted typhus, and gas gangrene. And if the doctors were not engaged in their own research, then they were here to stay off of the front, eat good, stay drunk, and, for the most part, refuse to look down to save the twins, dwarfs, or the deformed for him.

So he was forced to recruit his research staff off of the transports and issued orders that all doctors, dentists, nurses, and other scientists of any discipline were to be separated and spared.

His first find was Miklos Nyiszli, a Polish Jew pathologist who, after a short interview, was immediately installed in the laboratory in the wing of the Crematorium I overlooking the railroad tracks and who soon learned that everybody handed over to him required a very painstaking autopsy. It became a matter of his life and death, evident to him. Which did not make him shun his work but made him do his work more carefully. He could also walk out in the corridor and down a hall to where he could watch the bodies being loaded into the oven if he needed any more encouragement about doing his duties with an extremely high degree of accuracy. Mengele wanted the organs weighed and re-weighed until there was no mistake. His findings were, to be exact.

Then Mengele found Martina Puzyna, who had studied under the Polish Jew anthropologist Jan Czekenouski, who had established the measuring techniques that Mengele had so long admired, adopting them while still a graduate student in Munich. He installed her in her own private quarters in one of the women's hospital blocks. She was given a set of precision stainless steel Swiss-made sliding, hinged, and coordinate calipers in a stainless steel velvet lined case, osteometric boards of hard rock maple from Massachusetts, a bean bag and donut ring for head support, and a Western Reserve Model Head Spanner. She knew it would be the exact equipment that Mengele would be using in his own studies.

Her first set of twins were twelve-year-old Gypsy girls with huge brown eyes and a carefree, loving nature about them that Mengele had also measured and after twenty-four hundred and thirty-five distinct measurements, which took her over a week to complete, when you added them all up there were only five millimeters separating her findings from his, and he told her that she must do better.

And she promised him that she would.

He now had thirty-three sets of twins established in the men's camps, fourteen in the Gypsy camp, seventeen in the women's, and a total of eleven sets of identical twins. They were all too valuable at this point to be squandered, and they were kept on a healthy diet.

Mengele began to extract as much blood from them as he possibly could, and specimens, samples, and measurements were sent to Verschurer in Berlin.

It had taken him a while, but he had started to fulfill his part of the project, supplying Richard with the information he would need to construct the genetic map of man.

To find the Jew genes.

He was also sending huge quantities of eyeballs for the extraction of the enzymes.

He did not miss Berlin, where he was just another minor official in a sea of officials, and his only real joy had been at the university and even there, they had him teaching the basic, now boring lectures of racial identification. The move from the center of the Reich to the largest laboratory in the world had charged him with a new feeling of life that he thought impossible, and he only dreamed of men on horseback swinging sharpened swords every once in a while.

His quarters were on the top floor of the south corner of one of the two storied SS barracks built with tall attics and in the traditional H block and located just outside the wire on the northeast corner of Birkenau. He had a large room with a clear view of the rail track and the entrance tower. The windows were wide open, and a large oscillating big blade fan moved the hot air across his naked body as he lay across the wide bed in the stifling room.

It was Sunday, and there were going to be no trains for the rest of the day because saboteurs had blown a bridge. He thought that he might be able to write Irene and his parents a letter, but his mind was racing too much and he put down some drivel and ended both letters with a promise to do better in the future.

The Jewish symphony assembled by Hoess began playing Wagner's The Flying Dutchman in the courtyard behind the SS kitchen, and he began to whistle along. On days when the ramp was full of newly arriving Jews, Mengele had often watched panic leave the faces of many people when the sounds of the orchestra drifted down the rails and onto the ramps. Men of the Sonderkommando also whispered assurances to the more nervous of the newcomers right into the chambers, and any recalcitrant people were quickly separated and taken behind the nearest building and given the neck shot with a small caliber pistol.

He got up from the bed, walked over to a mirror hanging on the wall, and stared at his naked form. His face was still smooth, just some laugh lines at the eyes. He could detect no fat as he turned to study his profile. He was still lean and muscular, and he had once heard two women prisoners whispering that they thought of him as an Adonis. They did not have the opportunity of seeing very many men, and when they did see a man of their own race they could not keep the accusations from their eyes.

Their men; their husbands, fathers, uncles and cousins had allowed them to be taken from their homes, loaded into box cars and shipped to this hell on earth where their mothers, sisters, cousins, and nieces were debased, degraded, worked under the whip, and gassed. Their grandfathers, grandmothers, and young nieces and nephews usually went directly up in smoke. They had followed their men, and their men did not defend them, and they had let this happen, and now they were at the mercy of some of the most brutal women on earth.

In the women's camp, the Capos were called Controllers and were, like Capos, privileged prisoners in direct charge. Mostly prostitutes, murderers, thieves, and Communists from all countries under the Swastika, they held their positions as long as they could convince the SS Supervisor that they could inflict enough punishment and terror to keep the women one hundred percent under control. Most of the time they did it right, except at roll call.

It was hard to count and account for over fifty thousand women. Some could be simply sitting in the latrine thinking of the good old days of home, or they could be pissing a German off, and some of them would knock you to the ground and kick the life out of you, and you bypassed the gas and went directly to the smoke. He did not tell anyone, and they could not find you for over fifty minutes, which meant everyone else in the camp had to stand in front of their blocks and be counted and counted and counted, and you so much wanted to break and fall to the ground but if you did that you would look weak and looking weak was not a good thing to do. One of the things you learned in the camps very quickly is that you did not piss a German off.

And you did not look weak.

Other women prisoners, Czechs, Poles, Ukrainians, Estonians, Latvians, and Russia all had someone to look down on and to torment. Sometimes, a Jewish woman could reach Capo status. When they did, they also proved their capacity to write down your numbers in a little book in a camp selection, and they came for you and took you to Block 25.

The Jew was at the bottom of the scale in Auschwitz.

The Jewish woman was below the bottom of the scale in Birkenau.

To them, any man who could walk around immaculate and smell good in all this squalor, torment, and death, that was capable of whistling and smiling when he sent you off to the chambers and with the same whistle and smile sent you off to life, he could be seen as an Adonis.

Mengele gave up trying to stay in the room, knowing it would only become bearable long after the sun went down, if even then. He decided to eat and go to his lab. He liked the sound of it. His lab. There was work that he could be doing.

He sponged himself off as well he could in the beautiful porcelain wash basin with hand-painted delicate roses brought miraculously some four hundred miles in a crowded swaying boxcar by a seventy-two-year-old woman who worried about it sitting in all the other goods and belongings now looking like a stack of trash on the side of the rail car while she was marched to the bunker. It was full of fresh water brought to him by one of the Seventh-Day Adventist women who were in demand for their trustworthiness and attention to detail, but they would not do any laundering. They would go to the gas before touching anything remotely military, like a uniform, which was the reason they were in the camps to begin with. Try being a pacifist in a country at war. Try that in any country, and you will find yourself in the same position. You will be somebody's prisoner.

He tried to towel dry, but the sweat was winning out. He sprinkled scented talc on himself, dressed quickly but carefully, left his room and walked down the steps and into the compound. The hot summer air was heavy with the moisture of the marshlands making his clothes stick to him. He joined other men on their way to the dining hall. Four other doctors greeted him as soon as he came in the door, and they made room for him at their oval table. He had really exerted little pressure on them. A few of them had even found some twins for him.

"Hauptstrumfuhrer, the trench is excellent," Bethune said, putting a fork full of the fresh fish into his mouth.

"You have a way of making anything to eat look good, Doctor." He smiled wide showing the gapped front teeth. "I think the fish will do just fine." The prison waiter went off to get his order.

Thilo Mundy, a round red-faced man with thick, bushy eyebrows, poured white wine into Mengele's crystal glass procured from a Polish prince. "They should make this happen every Sunday. Stop the trains. It's good to settle back after a hard week's work and break bread with one's colleagues and not have to worry about dashing off to do something."

"I totally agree, Herr Doctor," Bethune seconded. He addressed Mengele. "Doctor Mengele, maybe you can intercede with Berlin and impress upon them how good for morale it would be if the doctors of Auschwitz were given every Sunday off."

"Very well." Mengele went along with it. "I'll call the Reichsfuhrer and turn in a list of all doctors requesting every Sunday off. How is that?"

"No way! You can leave me off of that list." Bethune said, in fringed fear.

"Me too," Doctor Erich Reicher chipped in, thinking that they were just joking but not wanting to take any chances. He wanted no complaining reaching the Reichsfuhrer with his name on it.

The waiter brought Mengele his fish, baked to a golden brown and served on top of some fresh greens with whole boiled potatoes swimming in butter sauce, Brussels sprouts, cauliflower, and little round onions. A loaf of fresh bread was placed on the table by his side.

It was delicious.

The wine was excellent.

Paddle fans created the semblance of a breeze. The dining room was full of SS men. There were at least three pictures in various poses of Der Fuhrer on each wall. The sound of Wagner came through all the opened windows. The doctors at the table were mellowed out by the heat, the food and the wine, which was the only true way of beating the heat and the humidity in Auschwitz.

"Doctor Mengele, may I ask the nature of your twin study?" Erich Reicher asked as the meal came to a close, and the doctor stopped off their wine crystals. Reicher had found one of his identical sets of twins, beautiful black eyed girls of fifteen. Mengele had wondered if he would have found them if they had not been so striking.

"Herr Professor Verschuer has always stressed the importance of studying twins to unlock many genetic and anthropological secrets," Mengele explained. "One of the things that I hope to discover is the secret of multiple births. One of the prime objectives of the Reichsfuhrer is, of course, to increase the population with good Germanic blood."

"I see," Hans Eissler said, "we make our women have our children two at a time. That makes sense." He was third-generation medical man, having been tutored by both his father and his grandfather in the homes and clinics of rural Germany and from the University at Munster. Joining the SS had made sense to him and his father, and his grandfather had agreed. None of them had actually read <u>Mein Kampf</u>.

"I still do not understand how studying twins," Eissler continued, "will tell you anything but that they occur as a statistic and are spread throughout the populations. And it seems to me that if you wanted to find out how twins were made, then you should be studying the twin-makers? Why are you not studying their mothers and their fathers?"

"It has long been proven that twins are prevalent in certain families. The secret of multiple births is held in every twin."

"I'll have to take your word for that, Doctor. But what about the other ones you want? The deformed ones. The hunchbacks. I'm sure you do not want to unlock the secret of their birth so you and the Reichsfuhrer can have them come into the world two at a time," Eissler sarcastically said.

Mengele and the rest of the men laughed.

"You remind me of a rotten fuhrer who drove for me in Russia," Mengele said, ignoring the question. "He looked at things a lot like you do, Herr Doctor. He disappeared one day."

"He was killed?" Reichert asked, always worrying about being sent to the Russia front.

"No. He just disappeared. One moment he was standing there watching a special operation, where some Jews were shot in a pit, and the next minute he was gone. I did miss him. He was humorous."

"There is also something else you can tell me, Doctor Eissler refused to back down. Where could they send him from here? He had arrived on the first of January, but it was after Valentine's Day before he stopped acting like all new doctors to the camp who had to ask all the other doctors continuously how they could do what was being asked of them to do, and the only really answer he ever got was that somebody had to do it, and after you had done it a dozen times you just began to do it. You just began to sort them. He had watched Mengele on the ramp and saw that he did not mind doing it from the very beginning.

"Weren't you somewhat surprised when you first found out what you had to do? I mean, on the Ramp?"

The other doctors at the table groaned. They hated this conversation. A pleasant afternoon was going up in smoke.

"I wish you would just shut up, Doctor," Bethune said, pointing his fork at his comrade.

"Please, Doctors," Mundy pleaded, "let us have a professional discussion. Let us talk of something pleasant."

"Like the war news?" Richter asked, also wanting to help turn the conversation.

"He said something pleasant." Bethune corrected. "Let us talk of women."

"A delightful subject." Mundy agreed.

Mengele just smiled across the table where Eissler was ignoring the displeasure of the other men and was waiting for his answer.

"I do it because Der Fuhrer wills it, Herr Doctor." Mengele finally said quietly.

That took the vocal argument out of Eissler. The last thing he wanted to do was to say something derogatory about Der Fuhrer in an SS mess. He was not a stupid man.

"Herr Doctor," Mengele said to make sure Eissler and the rest of them understood how he felt about it, "Der Fuhrer wills it because he knows that the Jew is intent on taking our country away from us. They will not succeed. Instead, they will be loaded onto rail cars, and they will be brought to us, and until we find another way to deal with them, we will use the present methods, as barbarous as they seem to you. There will soon be over a half million Jews heading our way in the next year. We surely can not house, let alone try to feed that many people."

"Then leave them where they are," Eissler argued.

"My God!" Mengele exploded, "There is a war on! Our enemy, the Jew is pushed into ghettos in the cities, and there is not enough food to feed them there. Nor is there enough space to bury them all there. No matter what you and I or the Commandant feels, they are going to be loaded onto the trains, and they are going to be brought to us here. We can not change that fact. We are here to deal with it!"

Eissler sat stunned. No one had ever explained it to him in such a clear manner, and now, for the first time, he really understood it all and that the trains were never going to stop, and he could feel his soul grow cold. He looked across the table at Mengele, whose face was still calm but was now not showing any trace of a smile, Mengele was looking back at him with the dead eyes of a man who has seen many deaths, and he realized that his only chance for survival in this place was not to think like a doctor but to think like a Nazi. When you put on the Swastika, you put it over the Hippocratic oath in Auschwitz.

These other doctors that he had been serving with now seemed almost innocent in their beliefs but not in their activity, or they were clearly just plain nuts.

"Doctors, please," Mundy said once again, trying to ease the tension on the table between the other two men. He liked Eissler enough except when he was in one of his pious moods like he was now, but Mengele did not seem to be the type that would take too much of the young man's impertinence.

"Have you not listened to Der Fuhrer's speeches on the reasons why we must rid ourselves of the Jew, Herr Doctor?" Mengele asked, ignoring Mundy. "Where you never at any of the party rallies? I know they have radios where you come from. Surely, you have listened to Der Fuhrer on the radio. Have you not read <u>Mein</u> <u>Kampf</u>? Do you think Der Fuhrer has idle words? He says that Germany is for the Germans and not for the Jews. That he saw them for what they are, a parasite in the body of the Volk and he would rid our country of this virus that has lived as a minority for thousands of years among the peoples of Europe. Now, we ask that you function like a doctor of the German people. It is your duty to help destroy this virus."

All of the men sat silently at the table. The heat suddenly descended on all of them. Eissler was crushed in his chair. He was not going to argue with Mengele any longer.

"Gentlemen," Bethune said, breaking the silence, "I, for one, am not going to let this gorgeous afternoon go by without enjoying some of it." He stood up and grabbed one of the wine bottles and pushed the cork into it. "I am going to the swimming pool."

"That sounds like an excellent idea, Herr Doctor," Mundy agreed. He would have gone just about anywhere in the camp to get away from this table. He hated it when his comrades fought each other.

"A swim does seem to be enticing," Reichert said, thankful to get away from Mengele, the ardent Nazi and Eissler, the crybaby. "Maybe Irma will be there. Maybe she will prance around the apron, diving into the pool from all angles like she does. I love watching her in a bathing suit."

The three doctors stood, leaving Mengele and Eissler to stare at each other across the table.

Mengele was in command here.

Eissler decided that a swim was the best thing that he could do. He stood to attention, clicked his heels together and bowed slightly to Mengele.

"Would you care to join us, Herr Doctor," Eissler invited Mengele. "Maybe Irma will indeed be there."

"No, thank you. I have work to do," Mengele answered, smiling enough to show his gapped teeth. "Besides. Irma has the face of a pig."

"It is not her face that we look at, Herr Doktor," Bethune replied, as the rest of the doctors left the mess.

Mengele sat alone at the table, thinking through the rest of the day. He decided that he had time to fillet some saroma from the elderly male Jews he had isolated for such an event. The retorts were empty, so the bodies could be thrown inside them and be the first to the fire in the morning.

After he left the table, a stripped figure gathered the plates and scrapped the scraps into a metal trash can that he would haul over to the women's kitchen, where it was dumped into the vat already cooking the evening meal for the women of Auschwitz.

XXIII

They were the Sinti, Lalleri, Rom, Litautikker, Kelderari, Lovari, Drisari, and Medvashi. They once had their own country under their own king on their own piece of land in Northern India, and it had a small yet dependable river running through it. They spoke Romani and worshipped the same gods in the same way their ancestors had worshipped them. Then an angry army of sword-swinging horsemen came yelling and screaming about their God Allah, and their land was taken away from them, and they were forced to always wander another man's land.

They started out with very dark skins, black eyes and black hair, but as they lived passing over the centuries through the other races of Europe and northern Africa, they seduced many a man's daughter with their music and sincere sexuality and raised many a stolen blond child, so that now their skins were much lighter in color, but their hair was still mostly black and wavy and their eyes a very dark brown, sometimes even black, at least as black as the eyes of some of the Celts, and the men wore rings in their pierced ears and sometimes wrapped their heads in colorful scarves.

It seemed like every troupe of them would have a beautiful young girl with luxurious black hair, radiant blue eyes and olive skin, who would dress in shiny fabrics and dance in such a manner, showing a lithe and rhythmical female form swaying to an ancient rhythm born of the soil as she had rode over the lands of the earth. Her entire life on the wood and iron wheels her great-grandfather had forged and hammered out, and the music and movement were part of her soul, and she could purse her thick sensual lips and look at a man from half-hooded eyes that made many a local lord's son to be driven to distraction.

They lived off of the land and by their wits, and they could look into your palms and tell you your future, and after they were gone, you discovered that they took something of yours with them.

The Gypsy.

They played their music and tended their horses and tinkered for money and saw no immorality in thievery from the people who owned the land. They were a traveling breed of mixed-bloods who, early in their trekking, managed to enrage the church, the state and the guilds. Only by smiling, laughing and singing songs, doing somersaults, walking the wire, throwing knives at each other another tied to a spinning board, did they manage to both frighten and entertain the people. It was their diversionary skills of providing amusement that had let them survive, even just continually traveling across another man's land.

Now most of the lands they roamed were controlled by the Nazis, who did not like the fact that a band of mixed-blood people should exist in their midst. The <u>Ordnungspolizei</u>, the municipal police, were charged with their round-up and deportation to the camps. The Gypsy Menace was at last going to be addressed.

If you had only one grandparent who was even half Gypsy then you were Gypsy, and you went to the camps. Gypsy blood being stronger than Jewish blood. No matter what the law said, if you were Gypsy and you were married to the blondest woman in Germany, it did not protect you like a Jew married to a German. If you were a Gypsy they sent you to the camp and tattooed you with a 'Z' to start your numbers, and they would tattoo her with a 'ZM' to show that despite her Nordic appearance, she was indeed a Gypsy.

Over the centuries, many Gypsies had settled in one area and began the slow, painful assimilation into their host population throughout Europe. There were men serving with the Wehrmacht who had a Gypsy grandparent, and they were being dismissed from their duties because of their blood, and the civil police did not care that the men sometimes had awards of bravery for their fighting. They were even taken from the front lines and shipped to staging areas where they were loaded onto the trains and sent to the camps, the medals still warm from the award ceremonies. It did not matter what you did for the Reich. You could have killed a hundred Russians with your bare hands, and it would not matter. It only mattered what your blood contained, and if it contained Gypsy blood, you were bound for the camps.

Or they just killed you where you were.

Those already in the East were shot, clubbed, and strangled to death by the Bohemians, Croats, Estonians, Hungarians, Latvians, Lithuanians, Poles, Romanians, Serbs, and Slovaks. Those in the West were happily loaded onto the rail cars by the Germans, Austrians, Belgians, Dutch, and French and sent to the camps in the East where the war always seemed just a little more vicious, if such a thing was possible, and the war gave all of the people no matter which side they were on an opportunity of dealing once and for all with these traveling bands of mixed-blood riff-raff that kept crossing your lands.

Himmler had initially instructed that two tribes, the Rom and the Litautikker, be allowed to roam the Reich within prescribed limits because they were a walking monument, one of the original Indo-

Germanic people and were worthy of study in their natural habitat. They spoke an Aryan language and could be kept under close supervision and, on occasion, even be used for military operations.

And Martin Bormann told him that was bullshit. The police could not be expected to distinguish between one Gypsy and another. And anything Martin Bormann put out over his position in the party was definitely the wishes of Der Fuhrer.

And Himmler quickly sang another song, and all the Gypsies were rounded up and sent to the camps along with all the other Gypsy, half-Gypsy, and might-be Gypsy.

No one to protest their imprisonment.

No one to raise an outcry throughout the world because

It did not take long for the camp built by the first arriving Gypsies to house ten thousand, to become stuffed with over sixteen thousand men, women and children. When Himmler visited the camp in 1942, he saw sick and starving people with black hair, dark eyes, swarthy skin, and reddish tongues; he told Hoess to destroy them.

Hoess had pointed out to him that a lot of the interned were to be exempted under the law, only arriving here because of the police running amok. Himmler thought of the shriveled man he had just seen in the filthy defrocked uniform, the Iron Cross pinned to his chest, and he reduced his order to the elimination of the camp. He then cabled Nebe to get the Kripo off their No one to raise an outcry throughout the world because who would listen to a Gypsy who did not have any land of his own? Asses and review certain cases, and if the interned fell outside the law, they should be released immediately.

The remainder were to be treated like the Jews.

It had taken over two years, but now the order was close to being carried out. The fit for work had been transferred to the main camp, other camps, and to the farms, factories, fisheries, or mines of the Reichsfuhrer's SS. A few, a very damn few, were actually released because they should not have been there in the first place. Many quarter and eight-castes were given the opportunity of rejoining the Wehrmacht on the increasingly treacherous eastern front, which many accepted, and of course King Typhus and other diseases finished them off in droves.

What was left in the camp were the old shrunken, and frail brown whiffs of old womanhood, old manhood, and children who were slowly rotting away from the outside-in as 'water cancer,' a severe noma of the skin caused by bone chaffing the underside of the dermis, kills the children with raging sores, and the parents and grandparents know that their children and grandchildren are as good as dead as soon as the sores start to form, they start to eat their children and grandchildren's food to hasten that death where the body decays before it dies, and you are eight years old and your last weeks on the earth were spent with the ever-present buzzing of flies as they swarmed on your open sores in the late July early August sun in the flat marshy lands of a place that your father by choice would not shit in let alone pass through.

Through it all, they remained a simple people, and as long as they were allowed to keep their violins, guitars, tambourines and trumpets, their souls were soothed if they could dance and play their music. They could play their music and dance and watch their children and grandchildren rot and could even smile at the SS man, and the rotting children would even dance for the SS man because the SS man was not killing you like he was killing the Jew, and the SS man let you have your wife and children with you even though the SS man had sent your healthy young men and women away from you, but the SS man sends you food daily and puts you in a position where you can even steal some of the Jew's food, and the SS man would come into the camp and not beat you with those canes like he would beat the Jew, and the SS man was not letting his dogs bite you like he would let them bite the Jew, and the SS man was not marching you to the bunkers and sending you up in smoke like he was the Jew. And the war would one day be over, and you would be released from this place where a man could keep no horses, and they expected a man to take a shit in the same place as another man, even another man of another tribe, and shitting in the same place another man had shit was a sting into the soul of the Gypsy.

Commander of the SS Guard Regiment Strumbannfuhrer Friedrich Hartjenstein was worried as he stood on the unusually empty ramp and looked south across the three sets of unusually vacant tracks to the Gypsy camp. His brother had served with the Einsatzgruppen in Russia and had told him what soon became common knowledge, that the Gypsy did not line up very well to a firing squad. Nor would he march into the trees, take off his clothes and lay down on top of dead friends and family and let you shoot him in the back of the head. The Gypsy would give you nothing but a moving target, call you a tremendous amount of names, call curses down on you and your children, attack you with his bare hands and spit on you with as much mucous as he could clear out of his throat.

He now had four thousand of them left in Birkenau and orders to destroy them immediately.

After consulting with Schwarzhuber, the First Commander of the protective Camp Birkenau, and Hauptscharfuhrer Koeing, in charge of the bunkers, it was decided that they had better take out the entire camp in one action. If they did not take them all at once it was going to be extremely difficult to come back and get the rest. And they sure as hell were not going to try to get them to undress first. When they got close to the bunkers, they were to be forced in.

He called out his entire regiment for the operation. Guards were doubled in all the towers, the Jews were buttoned up tight, and the dog units were stationed along the routes as the Gypsy were to be herded to their destinations where the story to them was that they were to be deloused and then transferred to where there were kinsmen. The plan was to move them out in four groups, take them along different routes and use all four bunkers.

After the gas, they could leave them in the bunkers, and they would be first into the ovens and onto the pits as soon as it turned light. Anglo-American bombers could now reach Auschwitz and anywhere else along the Vistula, and the military commanders in the area would be screaming about the open pit fires now necessary behind III and IV. The arriving Jews from Hungary were healthy people with a lot of fat content–grease makes a hot fire–and III and IV were built of inferior construction deep into the war when Germany was on the defensive, and IV was completely burnt out beyond repair, and III was going to take extensive work to put back on line, so in the meantime open pit burning was necessary.

It was agreed that they could cram all of them into bunkers designed to hold a little over three thousand; after all, none of them that was left took up much room. The Gypsy had a lifetime of crowded conditions; he would not mind a crowded chamber. The problem was to get them there without having it turn into a shoot.

A two-hour action could turn into an all-night ordeal, and no doubt he could even lose a few of his own men. He could see them shooting each other in the dark and in the confusion. Hell, he could see them shooting each other in the bright of a calm day, and while his troops weren't much, Schwarzhuber men were even bigger idiots, and they were the ones who were actually responsible for herding the Gypsy. This whole affair could get out of hand and dissolve into chaos, and of course, his name would be recorded as the officer in direct charge.

Hoess had conveniently been called away on more pressing matters; besides, putting four thousand people to the gas was no big deal. They had just that day put over five thousand newly arriving Jews to the gas, and the last of them was now the thin tendrils of smoke from the visible stacks of I and II, and a low haze from the open pits behind the distant and out of sight bunkers III and IV. The hot, humid summer early evening air was not moving, and it was full of the smell of roasting humans. And grease burns with the same smell, no matter what the animal.

He lit another cigarette and looked at his watch. It would not be long now. He strolled along the ramp, a rather tall, thin, angular man tapping his cane lightly on his leg, until he came to the intersection of the ramp and Lagerstrasse. He looked down the wide avenue with barbed and electrified fences lining the way. Two of the handlers deployed across the tracks to funnel the Gypsies straight ahead were wrestling with their animals, a Saint Bernard and a Doberman, who were trying to get at each other's throats.

"Get those damn dogs under control!" he finally bellowed louder than the snarling and scuffling dogs after seeing that the men were allowing them to square off. They needed to save all their energy for the Gypsy.

The Rottenfuhrers surely did not wish to get on the wrong side of the Strumbannfuhrer, and they quickly got enough leverage on the choke collars to wrench the beasts into obedience. Haldjestat stood there long enough to glare at the men to get his point across. He had been in the prison camp system from the very beginning and he had no tolerance for buffoonery of any sort, especially during any action, and the glare had become sufficient enough for him to control his men. It was just when they were out of his sight they were dangerous.

He wished Mengele were here instead of on his high horse. Mengele was a man who knew how to get along with the Gypsy. The Gypsy always trusted Mengele. When he visited their camp, he would have candy in his pocket for the children and would rub a salve on their open sores that would not bring any relief but helped to keep the flies off, and they called him 'Uncle Pepe' to his hand-clapping delight.

With his skin not unlike the color of many of the Gypsy, and his hair the texture and color not unlike many of the Gypsy, it was no wonder he would travel by train to Krakow and then by plane to Berlin where he pleaded his case to save the Gypsy but came back denied. The remaining Gypsies in the original Gypsy camp were still to be eliminated immediately.

There were enough of them left in other camps throughout the Reich, and there were plenty left at Auschwitz to satisfy any scientific line of inquiry. Mengele had a total of twenty-three pairs of identical Gypsy twins, and he was going to have to complete his scientific research with what was left to him. The remaining Gypsies at Birkenau were not capable of taking up productive employment of any kind, and the Reich was definitely at the point where if you could not contribute to the war effort, then you would not exist.

Haldjestat heard the first group of the Gypsies and then watched as they came into view as they turned right out of their wire. He could see that the people had put on their finest clothing. The men wore their pin-stripped suits with their fedoras and wide-brimmed leather hats that was mere tatters of their once splendor, and the women had on their brightest dresses stained by captivity, and they were now just filthy people in filthy clothes crawling with vermin. They came out of the wire onto the rail crossing, and they trudged slowly towards him. They looked at the dogs with fear, and they squeezed themselves into a thinner line to get as far away as possible from the beasts that were really now getting themselves worked up and all the handlers were on the choke collars.

"Herr SS-Man Haldjestat," an old man with parchment for skin stopped in front of him. He took his hat off and held it in front of himself in nobly worn hands to show respect. "Why do you have your dogs out for us? You know we never cause you no trouble."

"We are afraid that you would run like rabbits, and you know my men are old and slow, and we would never be able to catch you, Djemajl Malijoku," Haldjestat answered, surprised to realize that he knew this man well and many of these people by their names. The column had stopped behind the old man, and he knew that this was a critical time.

"I am sorry about the dogs. Those were my orders. Move along now. We must have all of you ready by in the morning if we are to keep our rail time."

"Why can we not just stay here in our camp until the trains get here, Herr SS-Man?" Maljoku persisted.

"Because you are crawling with lice and fleas, old man," Haldjestat explained.

"We are Gypsies, Herr SS Man. We are used to the lice and fleas. They are our lice and fleas. If you kill all of our lice and fleas and send us somewhere else we will just pick up new ones. We would just as soon keep our own lice and fleas. I am too old to get used to new bugs."

"We would not think of sending you to your nice new camp crawling with pests. What would the SS men in your new camp think of us to send you to them so infested? Why they will complain to the Reichsfuhrer, and we will hear about how we sent our Gypsies to another camp without delousing them. Now go on to the sauna and get clean for the first time in years, old man."

Haldjestat knew that he had said enough, and if the old Gypsy did not start to move soon, he might have to physically move him, and they were still over a half-mile to the doorway of the bunker for which this group was headed, and the rest had not even started.

The old man looked at the SS man in front of him and could hear the dogs going wild as the people had to stand stationary in front of them, just out of range of the snapping jaws, and the old man decided to take a chance that they really were just going to be deloused. He had been in the camp for over two and a half years, and he knew that the buildings on each side of the tracks were where the Jews were killed, and he knew that the Jews who were not going to be killed right away were marched down this road between these other camps; Maybe there was no reason to jump on this SS man and quickly tear his eyes out. He turned and started walking again; the rest of his tribe began to follow.

Haldjestat watched them all finally pass, many of them barefoot in the hot earth even though Canada, the storehouse of looted goods, was teeming with shoes. The last of them reached the turn where they cut out of view. He could no longer hear them, not even the shuffling of their feet.

He signaled for the second group that quickly came into view and followed the route of the first ones. He recognized many of them also.

When the third group was taken on the route straight through the women's camp to Number 1, the peaceful movement of people stopped. He could hear their voices begin to rise in a panic, and they stopped dead in their tracks, and they began to wail and moan and cuss, and Haldjestat clenched his fists and ordered his men to apply force.

He heard the cries from the other side of the camp as the others had reached their bunkers. They had never seen the buildings before, but they could recognize a gas chamber when they saw one. They tried to turn, and the SS men stepped in with their canes, and they whipped the people hard over their heads and their backs, and the dogs strained at their leashes, and the people were slowly forced into the cool interior of the concrete-walled room. Maljoku tried to break free and go and find the SS-Man so he could strangle him, but another SS-Man shot him in the face and kicked his body to the side. The old women were wailing and crying, and the children were screeching, and the old men were calling down curses, and they were all forced into the bunkers and the doors were screwed shut, and the pellets were thrown in, and the Gypsy joined the Jew in the gas and in a few hours they would join them in the smoke.

The action had gone rather smoothly.

Mengele had stayed in his lab above Bunker I while it was going on, not wanting to take part in something that he was totally against. He had, however, ordered that certain Gypsies be brought to him from the bunker when it was unloaded in the morning. They were all fathers or mothers of some of the four sets of twins he now had sitting under guard in the storeroom. Although he deplored what had happened to his Gypsies, it was too good a research opportunity to pass up. There was only so much blood he could take from his twins and send to Berlin, where it was dispensed throughout the universities and laboratories to any facility with an electronic microscope. All of them studying the chromosomes, looking for the gene that caused the eyes, and then they would focus on finding the gene that determined eye color.

Doktor Robert Ritter headed up the Racial Hygiene and Population Biology Research Unit and maintained his offices just down the hall from Verschurer at the Kaiser Wilhelm University at Berlin-Dahlem. He had control of the genealogical Gypsy family tree in one-millimeter-high letters on precisely drawn branches all the way back to where they first started staying within the confines of Germany over five hundred years earlier. The charting had started in 1933 and was now nearly complete.

They had the genealogy in Berlin, and they had Mengele in Auschwitz.

The Gypsy were a geneticist's delight.

They were an Anthropologist's dream.

They were ideal research material.

"It is a sad day," Mengele said to Nyiszli, his Jew from Poland pathologist, "when we treat the Gypsies like the Jews."

He was angry that the Reichsfuhrer should order such an event. He refused to participate in sending to the gas an Aryan people he had befriended. He had listened to their brief uproar as the people had neared the doorway of the bunkers, but the camp was now quiet. He could not even hear any dogs.

He went over to a white cabinet hanging on the wall, opened the door and removed two large vials. He took a metal tray, laid out a towel on it and broke open a new box of syringes. He took the paper casing off of the needles and put five cc of phenol into eight of them. He lined them in a row. He then filled eight more with two CCs of chloroform and aligned them right under the sedative. He carried the tray over and sat it down next to the dissecting table.

"Bring me Lodi." He ordered.

Nyiszle went to the door of the storeroom and told the SS-Man which child he wanted first.

A young, beautiful girl with an oval face, thick dark hair and a radiant smile came naked through the door, unashamed but fearful. She had spent many hours without clothes in front of this Doctor who had measured and re-measured and weighed her and drew so much blood from her she wondered what they could be doing with all of it, and he had watched her sister give as much, but he had never really hurt her, and she knew living like a twin had been very good for them. There was no chance that they would get the 'noma.'

"Lodi," Mengele said, "please lay down over here." He motioned for her to come across the room and get up on the table.

The tile floor was cold to her feet, and she shuttered as her buttocks sat on the cold marble table. Mengele took her by the shoulders and laid her gently down.

"I promise you that you will not have to be cold long," he said softly, soothing the young woman.

She was used to the needles being poked into her by Uncle Pepe, so she was not alarmed but even smiled at him as he injected her with the phenol that immediately put her to sleep. He then picked up the other syringe and feeling around her healthy female breast, the nipple engorged from the cold, he injected the chloroform directly into her heart, and the young woman who had only dreamed of having her own man to dance for gave just a slight twitch, a mere tremor, and she was dead.

He picked up a thick-bladed scalpel, cut her along the edge of the eye and pried the skin apart, exposing the skull. With a thin saw, he cut a whole large hole enough to get in a spoon-bladed pry that let him pop the eye undamaged from the skull. He stretched the eyeball out, exposing as much of the optic nerve as he could and then severed the connection of the sense of vision to the brain with a set of heavy shears and put the specimens into a glass jar already labeled with her name and her number. He turned her mutilated face over to get at the other eye.

Nyiszli was busy removing the other organs. The long slit was made, and the heart, liver, lungs, kidneys, gall bladder, liver and finally the brain were removed, weighed, labeled and bottled. Mengele reminded him to get the ovaries.

The once beautiful young woman was now an unrecognizable heap of blood and bones and viscera. Three Sonderkommando came in when Mengele opened the door to the outer catwalk that led to the ovens. They snatched up the remains and carted her to where she was thrown into one of the retorts. The Doctor had strict orders that anything coming from his lab was to go immediately to the ovens, even if they weren't being fired.

The other two worked quickly in washing down the table and the blood and the offal soon disappeared into wide drainage pipes. Nyiszli carried the jars full of the organs and he could not help but think of the Pharaohs as he placed them in the wicker and straw crate set up in the office and already addressed to Berlin.

It had taken only twenty minutes total to deal with Lodi, the beautiful young Gypsy girl with the extremely rare eyes.

When everything was clean, Mengele nodded at the SS guard on the door, who opened it and pointed inside, and Lodi's identical twin Modi stepped naked into the laboratory, somewhat fearful but not ashamed.

And the marble was wet and cold to her.

XXIV

Josef Stalin was jubilant.

The Hitlerites were retreating. His armies were killing them by the thousands, capturing them in the hundreds of thousands and marching them off to camps in the east. The Anglo-Americans were finally ashore in Europe, killing and capturing a lot of Germans and surviving what the Boss thought was a 'toy' counter-attack by the Germans in the Ardennes. A weak German offensive doomed to failure that the Allies were calling the 'The Battle of the Bulge,' a condition well familiar in the East. He had to admit, however, that the aerial photos of the bombed-out cities of the Reich that Churchill and Roosevelt had shown him back in late '43, took a lot out of his argument that Russia was fighting the Fascists by itself.

A part of his own army, a behemoth of mechanized death, ten million strong and equipped with the most modern weapons on the battlefields, had reached the German jugular, the Oder River. They were forty miles from Berlin and could steamroll forward on his orders, while the allies were still recovering from the only serious attempt Germany had made to take the initiative in the West.

Soviet factories were still working day and night, turning out even more tanks, airplanes, artillery, and trucks, and all the ammo the breeches of their weapons desired. Shot and shells of all caliber and all purpose from lighting the night sky to boring in milliseconds through the armor of the Panzers, or the Shermans and Centurians if it came to it. And young strong men to man all the weapons the factories could produce, to form new divisions and corps and armies to be deployed in the west. He was preparing for when his armies were across the lines drawn on a map, across the rivers, forests and fields, and even across the street from the English and the Americans.

The Boss was also very pleased with himself for making his two Allies, Churchill and Roosevelt, travel all the way to Soviet soil for their second conference. It gave him great pleasure that Roosevelt, whom he knew to have an enlarged heart and high blood pressure, had made the exhausting trip by airplane and ship almost eight thousand miles to reach Yalta in the Russian Crimean, and the American came ill-prepared to deal with the final disposition of a post-war Europe.

After the Man of Steel met with the Giants of Western Democracy for the first time at this summit held beginning on February 2, 1945, at a reception given by the wheel-chaired American, he was no longer concerned that they could be enticed to switch sides and join the Fascists. They were licking their chops over this 'United Nations' organization and desperately sought his participation. He telephoned Marshall Koniev and told him to stay in place. The fall of Berlin would be the end of the war, and he was not quite ready to let it end. He directed his armies to attack to the south and north to occupy as much territory as they could before the cease-fire. All land under the feet of his soldiers, when the shooting stopped, was land added to the hegemony of the Soviet Union and Communism.

He even chuckled when he thought of the way things were turning out. Not in his wildest dreams could he have imagined the conquest of so much land and so many peoples, without the aid of his allies, Britain and America. The thought of Britain and France going to war over Poland in the first place was hysterical. The war had destroyed their Empires, ending their abilities to sustain their colonialism in Asia. Japan was losing their war with the Americans, but beginning the struggle of making 'Asia for the Asiatics.' Before the war,

England and France were world powers. Now, they were merely the lap dogs of the Americans, who had the biggest stick in the west, and right now, it was carried by a sick old man of sixty-two who could not even walk.

The Americans did have an Army of sixteen million spread throughout the world. But the Americans were not really tried in <u>Blood</u>. Not like the Russian was tried in <u>Blood</u>. He had read the report of the interrogation of a captured German soldier, who fought on the western front for six months and could not even remember seeing an American but was steadily pounded by their overwhelming artillery and airplanes.

Soviet military losses, mostly Russians, were approaching twenty million killed or missing.

The Americans, on all of their fronts, including their war with Japan, had lost not yet three hundred thousand men. Just about what the Germans had lost at the battle for Stalingrad, but merely one-third the number of men that it took for the Russians to win there. He was confident that in a war with the West, when the American losses reached a few million, something his own military juggernaut was capable of inflecting, the American public would demand the return home of their sons from those damnable killing fields in Europe.

Most of the two continents would be his. Indeed, the Soviet Empire would stretch from the Pacific Ocean across all of Asia through Europe to the Atlantic, and everything south of the North Pole to the Mediterranean, which would become a Soviet Sea, and the Island Nation of Great Britain, all would be under the fold of the Kremlin.

Joseph Stalin did not know or care, if his Empire would last a thousand years or twenty minutes after his death. He just knew it would far surpass anything that Alexander, Napoleon, or Hitler had achieved. The Man of Steel felt that he had the world by the balls. He had outfoxed and outfought them all.

Even the Jew.

When he had sat on the Supreme Council of the Soviet Union as one of twenty-four chairs presided over by Lenin, he shared the table with six Jews and one half-Jew. The Jews of Russia were two-percent of the population, but they controlled more than a quarter of the seats of the ruling membership council. He even heard Jews laughingly refer to the <u>All Russian Central Committee, Vserosiiskii Tsentral myi Komitet</u>, as 'Vu tsen idn Komandeven,' or, 'Where ten Jews give the Orders.' They were dispersed throughout the Party in places of power, and they all thought that the Jew Trotsky would take over when Lenin died, and the Jews, those Kazars who refused to give up their Race under the guise of not giving up their Religion, would at last, be in complete control of the Soviet Union.

They had not counted on the cunning and ruthlessness of Stalin, who took power from under their very noses when Lenin became ill. Stalin eventually saw to it that the Jew Trotsky got a pick ax in the back of his neck in faraway Mexico, where he had tried to hide. Trotsky had built the Red Army back during the war with the Whites, and allegiances ran deep. Only with Trotsky and his cronies dead, accomplished with the blood purge of the officer corps in 1937, did Stalin at last feel that the army was truly his.

He pondered his position of carrying off actual world conquest. He could go into history as the greatest conqueror of all times. World revolution did indeed occur. The Spectre was real, just as the Jew Marx had predicted, but Communism was not being driven by the Jew, as they all had envisioned, but by a Georgian. A Man of Steel who could export grain and let seven million Ukrainian peasants who grew it starve to death. A man with the blood of millions on his hands.

A man who hated the Jew as much as Hitler.

So the Jews gave the atomic bomb to the Americans first, who would drop it on the Japanese, to show Stalin that the West would indeed prevail if he continued the war.

Mengele stood in his office above the crematorium and looked out over the railroad tracks covered in a fresh blanket of snow. There were just a few gaunt ghost-like creatures moving in slow motion as they shoveled the roadways clear. He could see the guards in the watch tower jumping about to stay warm. The electrified fences hummed like large bumblebees, angry for being in the cold. Food was becoming very short in the camp, even for the Germans. There were no supply trains coming in. The Russians were less than a hundred miles away and there was really nothing between them and the camp but distance.

All of the other chambers and ovens had been destroyed by order of the Reichsfuhrer. This was the last one left, and the charges were already placed that would blow it down. He wondered how close they had come to winning the war on the Jews. Near the end, the trains were arriving throughout the day, and the Jews were crammed tighter than usual as the ones from Hungary began to arrive. It was their misfortune to reach the camp when their value as slave labor was far outshadowed by the will of Der Fuhrer, who had given the SS the responsibility of 'destroying the biological basis of the Jew in Europe' and since things did not look good for Germany, they were to press on in haste. Most of the Jews from Hungry went directly into the chambers.

All that was over by order of the Reichfuhrer. Even the most ardent Nazi was finally reaching the conclusion that the war was lost. Even the war against the Jew. Mengele knew that they had not eliminated all the Jews of Europe, that millions of them had escaped the chambers, and now, with the victorious Russians and their dupes, the English and Americans, the Jews would once again be loosed to profligate among the peoples of Europe.

No matter how much they had tried to reach their goal of the physical extermination of this vermin, of surgically removing this cancer from the Volk, there were enough of them left alive to laugh at Hitler's attempt to rid Europe of these peoples who continually debased the people they lived among.

He watched the two trucks that he had been waiting for turn through the tall rail gates, crawl their way through the snow, and come to a stop at the rear steps. A phone call from Verschurer had alerted him to pack his papers and experimental results in crates of a specified dimension and wait for transportation that would be coming from Munich. The professor himself had shipped from Berlin seven truckloads of material back to Frankfort-on-Main, that looked like it would fall to the Americans. An action normally judged as being defeatist that would get you shot in present-day Germany, but the Reichsfuhrer himself had given the order. It was to include the laboratory here at the camp, and for security measures, Josef was to destroy all correspondence between the camp and the University.

The two SS men who had driven up from Munich carried a special crate that Verschuer had alerted him was coming. It was made of steel and approximately four feet long and a foot high and deep. Mengele directed them where to set it down. He opened the top of it, revealing the insulation that lined the interior, kept frozen by the dry ice that took up most of the space. He opened the door to the freezer in his office, extracted two sealed and frozen aluminum boxes, and placed them in the niches that had already been prepared to accept them. He fastened the lid and hoped that his specimens would remain frozen; he sure had put enough work and time into acquiring the contents, now a murky reddish fluid. The two SS men carried the container out of the lab, and it was the first to be loaded onto one of the trucks.

Mengele walked out onto the second-story platform and nodded at the Rottenfuhrer, who stood at the front of a work detail, a half dozen emancipated Jews in tattered prison garb. The Jews were put to work loading the rest of the wooden crates. In their weakened condition, it took them over two hours to complete it. When they were done, the Rottenfuhrer took the work party out to the pits and shot each of them in the back of the neck, and as these Jews slid dead to the bottom of the pit, through the clean white snow, they stained it red with their blood and gray with their gore.

Mengele opened the truck door and ordered the surprised driver to move over. He started the engine, slipped the truck into gear and drove out of the camp, if camp could be the apt description of a place where over one million people were gassed and cremated.

He stopped a few hundred yards away, climbed out of the truck and raised his arm in signal. The crematorium, chambers, and pathological station crumbled in a cloud of concrete, steel, dust and snow, and while it was still a swirling cold haze, he pulled out of the camp and turned onto the highway to Munich. He had the orders of the Reichsfuhrer tucked into the inside pocket of his tunic, so he had no fear that he would be pulled from the cab of the truck by the roving bands of SS firing squads and lined against the wall and shot for moving west when the orders from Der Fuhrer was to hold in the East. The trucks were also mined with explosives just in case they were about to be overtaken by the enemy.

They stayed on the western bank of the Oder as they traveled northwest, passing through countryside that was defended by the remnants of the once almost invincible Wehrmacht. The trains were impossible to take by this time because of the uncontested control of the skies by the Soviets and Allies. They had to take cover under trees many a time throughout the trip. The villages they passed through were for the most part intact, but full of people with dead expressions on their faces, fear in their eyes.

Mengele pushed them onward, stopping only to get fuel and meager rations and at the numerous roadblocks manned by unsmiling SS, who starred long and hard at the signature on the bottom of his orders. Since there were three of them and two trucks, Mengele insisted that they continue to travel at every opportunity, taking turns sleeping.

They covered a little over four hundred miles, reaching Wesermunde on the North Sea on the afternoon of the fifth day of the trip. They pulled their trucks right down to what was left of the harbor after a half dozen raids by the Allies left the docks as splintered debris of timbers and concrete. The harbor was full of half-sunken merchant ships as their captains had sought to take their crippled ships to shallow water to keep the channel open, their superstructures keeping score in rusting hulks of twisted and burnt steel. The military base of

Bremerhaven, just a few miles up the coast, was hit even harder, but the bay was still navigable.

Mengele had been surprised at how much damage had been done to the Reich in just the past nine months since he had been home. During the same time period, he had been to Berlin once to meet with Verschuer, and their meeting had been intense and encouraging as the professor brought Mengele up on the progress of the project. It was the only thing they had to look forward to and become excited about. Mengele knew that the Jews left alive would hound him to his grave, but he was consoled by the fact that he was going to be able to continue the fight, even after Auschwitz.

Mengele was directed to the new office of the Harbor Master, which was now in a bombed out warehouse valuable because the building still had part of its roof intact.

Otto Balack had lived in the city all of his life and could remember being on the pier when he was just a child, and to him the smell of the ships in the harbor, a mixture of coal, diesel fuel, burlap, and wood crates mixed with the taste of the salt air was ambrosia to him. He hated what he saw now when he looked out over the destroyed basin. It saddened him that he was too old to see it all ever rebuilt. He sometimes hoped that one of the Allied bombs would find him so he could die with his harbor.

He had been expecting the SS man. He turned on the transmitter's finals and allowed them to warm a few moments before he hit the send switch and spoke briefly into the microphone. Mengele could hear a voice come through the static on the speaker, could not make out what was said, but Balack had ears of experience and understood perfectly the response. He gave Mengele directions to where he was to be met.

An hour later a motor whale boat with three Kriegsmarines pulled to a stop alongside the quay and the crates were loaded over the side and stowed and lashed secure. Mengele heiled the two SS men whom he had traveled with and climbed gingerly down to join the cargo.

The coxswain started the diesel engine of the forty-foot craft and backed slowly away from land until he had enough room to go forward, turn in a tight circle, and head out towards the sea. He opened the throttle, and the wind whipped in over the gunwales and gave Mengele a chill that he had not felt since Russia, but he managed to keep his expression calm and not panic as cold sometimes brought back so many fearful memories that glazed his face over.

The wide beamed boat bounced and swayed its way out into the bay and the coxswain cut the engine to idle and then they really began to bob in the choppy frigid waters. They rode in circles for almost an hour, and Mengele was beginning to stiffen from the icy salt spray that soaked him. Mengele was just about to order the boat back to the dock before he froze to death, when one of the sailors shouted and pointed. The diesel revved and the boat began to move through the water again and Mengele could make out the periscope that was closing the distance between them.

The submarine broke through the surface of the water enough to expose the long, narrow deck. Mengele could see the number of U=XXX painted on the conning tower as an officer and three other lookouts took their position with binoculars to their eyes searching the sky for enemy planes. A hatch in the rear of the sub opened, and a group of sailors scrambled out on deck. The coxswain maneuvered the boat to come alongside the steep black sides of the sub. Lines were thrown to the men on board the wooden craft, and they hooked them to the crates that were pulled quickly aboard and man-handled down into the after-torpedo room. Mengele now understood the reason for the limits on the size of his containers. One of the sailors tied a line around Mengele and his feet hit only once or twice on the hull as he was jerked aboard and then hustled down through the hatch. The steel rungs of the ladder were cold to his ungloved hands.

He found himself in the aft torpedo room, but the explosive fish had been removed to make room for the crates that were being stowed along with other crates already lashed securely. Mengele was surprised to see two helmeted SS men draped with SP-40 machine guns in the crowded compartment.

"Heil Hitler!" The SS men greeted.

Mengele returned the salute.

"Hauptsturmfuhrer, welcome aboard," said a lieutenant wearing a tired, worn face and a gray leather oil-stained jacket. Mengele did not realize the man was still a teenager.

"If you will follow me, please," the submariner requested. Mengele expected the lack of room as he squeezed himself down the narrow passageway and he followed the seaman forward. War machines, whether tank or sub, left very little room for the men to live in while they carried their weapons to war in order to kill other men crammed in their own machines of war. It was full of pipes, valves, cables and gauges. On a VII-C class submarine, there was no special compartment for food, so from the overhead, dangled sausages and smoked hams, and huge loaves of round dark grain breads were nestled in wire racks.

As Mengele, following the example of his escort, slung himself through the round hatch leading into the control room, Kapitanleutnant Paul Lehmann looked up and immediately recognized the SS man who had shared a railcar compartment with him one time so long ago, so many patrols ago, so many dead ago, but he had never forgotten the conversation he had listened to on that train ride. He bent his head down to hide the disgust that he felt crossing his face. This mission was becoming more and more strange. He had been ordered to strip his boat of as much as he could and make it available to the commands of the Reichsfuhrer. He had to plead with the Admiral to keep two torpedoes for use in defense. He had been given his orders verbally of the rendezvous points and had seethed in anger yesterday when his boat was boarded by four armed SS men along with the strange white-headed man with the wild eyes and the soft immaculate hands, hands that were so clean and so out of place for the men of the submarine service that the crew were still joking about them.

Lehmann finally looked up when Mengele came up to him.

"Heil Hitler!" His new passenger said in a low voice, respecting the new and unfamiliar environment. He noticed the questioning look on the faces of his men who had not used the Nazi greeting even when it was made mandatory after the Wehrmacht officers had blotched their attempt to blow Der Fuhrer up in the bunker on the eastern front, an iron-clad order that only U-Boat men could safely ignore, but not with an SS man.

"Heil Hitler." He responded regretfully. He saw his men turn their eyes away.

He could see the puzzlement in the eyes of Mengele. He knew he was trying to work out where he had seen or met this Kriegsmarine. Lehmann decided not to enlighten the Nazis. Nothing good could come of it.

He had no feeling of triumph anymore when he was able to put a torpedo into the side of an enemy ship, the opportunities becoming far less available and the consequences becoming just about guaranteed fatal as the Allies had worked out the sonar and weaponry and tactics that just about ensured a shooting subs demise. His crews seemed to be getting younger and younger, and they had started out at the beginning of the war as the youngest enlisted men on the average of any of the other services, and he had decided that getting them through the rest of war alive his last true mission. At first, he was relieved that what could be his last cruise of the war was going to be nothing but freighter duty, but transporting this SS doctor as part of the assignment did nothing but fill him with dread. He did not know what these men were about, but he knew in his heart that he, and probably none of his men, would agree with whatever these SS men were setting out to do.

But he had his orders.

"Your comrades are forward," Lehmann told Mengele, "they are expecting you. Lieutenant Diehls will show you the way." He motioned for his officer to take Mengele out of the control room, and as he watched the retreating back of the SS man, he tore open the envelope that contained his orders that he had been instructed to open as soon as all of his charges were on board. He read the single sheet of typed instructions.

His executive officer, Lieutenant Max Treuhand, a veteran of as many cruises as his captain, but the first time he had served under Lehmann, came over to receive his navigational instructions from his captain.

"Max.

"Jawhol, Captain."

"It seems as if we are going to Africa."

Mengele was surprised when the young seaman rapped on the water-tight door with the toe of his boot, giving Menqele a sheepish grin as the noise generated by his efforts was barely audible. The seaman pulled the lever up that loosened the iron dogs of the door and swung it open as soon as it was free. He indicated that Mengele should proceed on. Mengele stepped into the aft torpedo room and the sailor secured it closed behind him.

"Doktor Mengele!" Richard greeted warmly, climbing out of the hassock with much effort. The men shook hands.

"Professor Richard," Mengele responded, delighted to be once again in the company of the genius. It had been over a year since they had met. Richard had came once to Auschwitz in total secrecy, and even Commandant Hoess had not been informed of his identity. Mengele and Richard had conferred on exactly what Josef should concentrate on.

Richard was dressed in a blue civilian suit and a white shirt with an open collar. He looked somewhat frail, timid and frightened as he was in elements completely alien to him; the one day of being aboard had not in the least acclimated the scientist to his new surroundings. He was dependent upon others and placed in a position of not having his work to occupy his hands and his mind, and the close confines of the sub had already rasped his nerves. He was happy to see Mengele.

"Herr Doktor, it is good of you to join us. Did you bring the samples that we will need?"

"Of course, Herr Doktor." Mengele answered, "Everything is stowed forward."

"Excellent. I am afraid that where we are going, we will not have access to the necessary biological agents that are crucial to bringing our research to its successful conclusion. I am sorry that we ran out of time to finish while still in the Reich. But no matter," he continued wistfully, "all that is really important is for us to have a laboratory to finish our work."

"That is true. How close are we to achieving our goals, Herr Doktor?"

Richard beamed. "You will be amazed at how much I have progressed over the past few months. In my last interview with the Reichsfuhrer, he shook my hand over and over and told me that he was traveling straight to Berlin to inform Der Fuhrer."

"Our we that close, Herr Doktor?"

Mengele watched a veil drop over Richard's face. He had been reprimanded before for talking too much in front of people who did not need to know. He indicated that with the presence of the two other SS men in the compartment that now was not the time to talk shop.

"We have plenty of time to confer, Herr Mengele." He stood aside. "Let me introduce our traveling companions. They are our protectors."

The two SS men stood up and came forward. They were both tall, muscular, squared jaw men with blue eyes and blond hair.

"These troopers are Englehard and Baer. Gentlemen, I want you to meet a colleague of mine, Doktor Mengele," Richard introduced.

"Heil Hitler!" The two enlisted men snapped simultaneously.

"Heil Hitler!" Mengele returned the salute. "Norwegian?" He asked Baer.

"Jawhol, Herr Doktor Sturmbannfuhrer." Baer answered.

"I was with the Viking Division in Russia." Mengele informed them. "You can be proud of the way your countrymen fought the Bolsheviks, Hauptscharfuhrer Baer."

"My brother was in that division," Baer replied. "He was killed while they were breaking out of the Cherkasy Pocket."

"Gentlemen," Richard interrupted, "I have been instructed that you should spend this traveling time in becoming less military."

The other men nodded in understanding, and Mengele raised an eyebrow.

"You should learn to address each other as if you had no military experience. That is what I was told to impress upon you. And you and I, Herr Doktor, must learn to speak English, a language in which the rest of our party is already fluent."

"How many are in our party?"

"There are just the two men on guard beside us," Baer answered.

"How long is it that we will be traveling, Herr Doktor?"

"I have no idea."

"Do you know where we are bound?"

"Yes. That is no longer a secret since you are aboard, and it appears that we are underway. We are going to Africa."

"Africa?" Mengele said, surprised. He had heard the rumors that South America was the intended sanctuary for SS escaping vengeful Jews.

Vengeance.

The code name of the Russian army as they burst upon the German people in East Prussia. To ensure that their troops got the message, whole units were gathered to listen to the testimony of battle-hardened veterans who had experienced the ruthlessness and butchery of the Germans firsthand in the initial invasion of Mother Russia. Now they had Fritz right where they wanted him. In his own country where it was the German's turn to watch their wives and daughters have their legs spread as groups of men took their turns fucking them and then even nailing them to the barnyard door when they were finished with them. There was no mercy in the heart of the Russians as they had fought through the scorched earth of their own country, and now the fires and devastation were to be wrecked upon the defeated Hitlerites. News of their ferocity spread rapidly throughout the Reich, and the Germans fought on, now not for Der Fuhrer and his ideals, but to hold the lines open long enough for the people to stream to the west where the Allies were administering a conquest not based on complete destruction and death.

The war in the West was to end much like it had been fought. White people settling political differences. In the East it was the Slavic man taking retribution on the Aryan man.

XXV

Hugging the coast of Denmark, their diesels took them north, and they made it without incident across the white-capped Skagerrak Bay. They were soon slouching in the relatively safe waters of the North Sea where it laps along the rough edges of Norway, still securely in German hands, as the fjords provided good cover from the Allied Air Forces simply because there was plenty of war to the south. And besides, going down in these waters was going down forever.

It was much safer to fly over any kind of land because if your machine was shot out from under you had a chance to ride a parachute or your plane down to the ground. Sometimes you got lucky. If you were an American, Englishman, or a Canadian captured by the German, they fed you and treated you somewhat like a human being and they gave you your Red Cross parcels and not one of you died by dog bite. And if you were German and you were captured by the Americans, then sometimes you had to go to Indiana and work on a farm where you could flirt with a farmer's daughter and live in dormitories with hot showers and hot meals and be paid a wage to do this. You could go down in the warm Pacific and float around for a few days and if you could keep the sharks from eating you then you had a pretty good chance of being picked up by a friendly group who would give you water, feed you, and take you home to your side.

But if you went down in the North Atlantic in these frigid waters, then you had maybe six minutes before the cold, choppy waters took you down to Neptune, so you would much rather fly south, over the land, and that made it relatively safe for a submarine to diesel north.

But they then steered due west into the North Atlantic, right into the middle of a February storm of the North Atlantic Drift, that massive movement of water always getting its way called a current, and now it was in a very angry mood.

Lehmann was thankful for the storm for a lot of reasons. He clad himself in his rubber Northeastern and joined the watch topside. His beard immediately drew tight as it began to freeze from the frigid ocean spray and his own breath. The lookouts and the officers on the bridge were lashed to the railings in their safety tethers; they grabbed him until he secured his own line.

The waves towered over them, sending them crashing downwards and then wrenching them upwards. Some of the waves broke on the bridge, hitting the men with a cold, salty, dark grayish fist to first punch you to knock you off of your sub and failing that, it would drop down to your knees and sweep all around you like twisting limbs of some god awful creature called the sea trying to pull you from your machine.

As they bounced around at normal cruising depth, with the bow submerged and the waves braking against the bridge, the boat wallowed on the verge of corkscrewing as they went into fifty-degree lists, because that is where the waves were taking them, and at times, the sea would shake the vessel like it was a stick in a waterfall, and all you could do was hold on, try to enjoy the ride as the sky at noon was an ugly gray and black swirling mass of cold clouds whipping up angry icy water.

The conning hatch was closed to keep the water from pouring into the boat. Lehmann knew that the watch's eyes were on the seas and not in the air. Anything out in this storm is too busy fighting for its own life to engage in trying to sink an enemy machine.

Of course, all of the crewmen aboard the sub knew that the iron bars it carried for ballast would right the boat; heavy seas could not sink a sub. No one bothered to tell the SS men and the civilian with the dainty hands this well-known fact, leaving it for them to worry through their nausea whether or not they were going to spiral to the bottom out of control, and sometimes when the gags came in like a battle-ax swung by a muscular giant, they wished maybe it would be better to go ahead and drown if that was the only cure, if that was the only way to get relief for this sickness.

Leifson, the true Norseman, had been to sea all of his life, been in a few storms such as this one. He had rode them out hale and hearty and found them exhilarating, but this was the first one he was sailing through inside a twisting steel tube, with the smell of vomit heavy in the air and the physical particles hanging and swinging from seemingly everything, and even if he was immune from sea sickness he was not immune from watching other men throw up, and having to smell their sickness he too succumbed to emptying the contents of his stomach until nothing was left but the sickness.

When Lehmann felt the crew on the edge of exhaustion and complete paralysis, he decided to take her down to where the water was calm, and they could go on one-third battery power for a few hours and give everyone some respite. He knew for sure when you are being tossed about you can not sleep, and they would be entering treacherous waters when the storm lifted. He needed his crew alert, and most of them were experiencing the same dilemma as the SS men, except they knew the sub was not going to sink.

Mengele listened to the horn going off and he did not care what it meant, he was not going to let go of the rails on his rack, and he was not getting up. If he was going to drown then he was going to drown right here, right in this position. He had pressed himself tight against the thin mattress and felt the immediate cessation of the violent rocking motion. He could feel the slight pressure in his ears as the boat submerged to thirty meters, and they were away from any turbulence as the sub now glided smoothly through the water. It was an immediate cure for the entire crew.

They surveyed the shape of their compartment, narrow two-tier bunks across a thin aisle with a table that also served as a bed. They had room to spare, however, as there were always at least two of the SS men on watch forward.

A seaman opened their door and handed them some buckets of salt water along with some oily rags, and Mengele started cleaning the compartment, swirling up the organic debris and wringing it into the salty buckets. The physician performed this disgusting task much better then Leifson and Urbright.

"Why did we not submerge hours ago!" Richard accused, feeling hollow and sapped of his strength.

"They don't like to run on their batteries unless they are escaping detection or running an attack," Leifson explained, having learned much about the boat.

"Well, I will tell you one thing, if they try to surface in this, they are going to be under attack!" Richard threatened.

It took many buckets of the vile fluids throughout the ship to reach the two heads, the commodes, for the complicated shutting and opening of valves that sent it to the wastewater tanks where it took air pressure to spill it into the sea. After a few hours of effort by the crew, the air was losing some of the smell of sickness, once again taking on the smell of the machine, of steel, oil, and grease, and with the charged new batteries not far away, the smell of churning acids.

Mengele was toting the last bucket forward, and as he was crossing the control room, he came face to face with Lehmann, climbing down the ladder from the conning tower.

"I hope you are feeling better, Herr Doktor," Lehmann said, noticing the contents of the buckets and the splattered remains on Mengele's tunic. He had gotten his wish after all. Too bad the other one on the train was not here.

"We are just wondering, Kapitan, why we did not submerge sooner," Mengele said in good humor.

"We have a long way to go, Herr Doktor. We have only one opportunity for refueling. It would not be wise to go empty before we reach it, now would it?"

"I could not agree with you more, Kapitan. At least now, that is how I feel. If you would have asked me a couple of hours ago, I might have had a different answer." Mengele smiled.

Lehmann kept the ship down for the next ten hours, coming back to the surface just after midnight. The seas were still rough, but the fury much abated, and they made their way west towards Iceland. They submerged just before dawn and stayed clear of the many convoys they sighted. At night, he doubled the watch on the bridge and kept the crew on alert; these skies were the domain of enemy planes.

Twelve days later, they were four hundred miles east of Bermuda, and the weather was getting better daily as they traveled towards the equator. A week more and Lehmann allowed the hatches to be opened and the SS men were the first to crowd around the galley hatch. The sky had never been bluer. Light and fresh air streamed in a column from the round hatch and felt delicious on their sun-starved skin.

They had steamed close to eight thousand miles and time became a concrete schedule of boredom as the crew settled into the daily routine of living in a boat with fifty other men. The menu never varied. It was sausage, bread, potatoes, cheese, and ham, water and coffee the only drinks. Cheese was good, it bound your stool and limited bowel movement; and when there are only two heads to service fifty men, then constipation was indeed a blessing for everyone. They took their vitamin C in capsule form to keep the scurvy away.

It was extremely rare for German submarines to be in these waters so late in the war, and Lehmann allowed the men to come out on deck in shifts of three to hover around the open hatches. He posted two extra men to the bridge as the climate turned hot and humid as they neared the center of the earth and the men shed their clothing and came out on deck to bask in the sun. Inside their boat, sweat became part of their daily lives, their racks sodden with the salty moisture squeezed from their bodies as they steamed through the South Atlantic on the first of March. The summer sun turned the steel decks hot, and the only relief was looking into the sunset on a clear night. That seemed to make the heat less severe.

Then, one day, there was a lot of commotion as the boat dived to just where the bridge was out of the water and after traveling that way for a few miles, they came back to cruising depth. Word was passed to form topside to take on fuel and stores from a rusting tanker operating out of Montevideo, Uruguay, a country technically at war with Germany, having declared belligerency within the last month along with Paraguay, Peru, Turkey, Venezuela, Egypt, Syria, Lebanon, and Saudi Arabia, and was paid an exorbitant sum of money for running the risk of refueling a belligerent.

Monkey fists with trailing thin lead lines were tossed across, and the sub's crew secured them. They began to haul the four-inch hoses that were wrestled over to the external fuel inlet valves, connected, and with a curt signal, the fuel was started to transfer to the almost now empty submarine. Other lines were cast forward and soon food stores were sent across to be shoved through the galley hatch, the crew more than happy to help in catching the crates and boxes and spreading it rapidly fore and aft. It was the food they were taking aboard, and the electricians, pipe-fitters, quartermasters, torpedo men, and enginemen performed as surgeons, or maybe as priests passing sanctified bread as the new food and fresh fruit and vegetables was relayed aboard and stowed away.

Replenished, they made good time and rounded the Cape of Good Hope on the southern tip of the continent of Africa. They were now in the Indian Ocean and passed a few hundred miles off the east coast of Madagascar, the island studied by Germans and Poles as a possible dumping ground for the Jews of Europe.

Lehmann knew he was going to reach his destination right on time. Then he could unload these SS men who seemed to pass their time learning to speak English, which probably wasn't such a bad idea the way things were turning out. The two doctors could put their heads together in whispered conversations for hours, and a lot of the crew believed that Der Fuhrer's secret weapon was aboard their boat, kept in a frozen locker forward, and these strange men were the only men who knew how to work it. This meant that the crew treated the SS men with respect, although wondering among themselves if this was the secret weapon and why they were carrying it away from the battlefields. Their radio, of course, was tuned to the optimistic Allies who did nothing but brag about their victories.

Lehmann knew that Germany had lost the war. He did not know what he was going to do with his boat and crew once he completed his mission. With only two torpedoes abroad he knew he was really no longer an offensive force. He decided that he would just try and stay in safe waters until the war was over. He would listen for instructions from the Admiralty. In war or loss they would have to issue some final orders for the ships and boats at sea, except now Germany had nothing afloat except a few stray subs, and they were like the turkeys at the shoot.

It was a beautiful day with a bright, warm sun, and the sea was a gently rolling blue; visibility was at least ten miles, and his forward watch picked out the freighter on the horizon. They went into alert, and he took her down further into the sea at surface attack depth until they got close enough to verify that it was the target ship because she was flying Echo Charlie and the Union Jack. She was a twenty-ton sleek single stacker built for speed with a painted black hull and gray superstructure, a wrap-around bridge and exposed flying bridges, giving the ship a military look, which in these waters could not hurt a thing.

He brought his boat back out of the water, and the two vessels closed rapidly.

The SS men were in a state of euphoria. Their journey was at an end. They were getting off this boat, and they could never see any reason that they would ever have to climb back inside a submarine, and they were like kids let out of school when they were told to come out on deck.

The entire contents of the forward room were emptied of the cargo brought aboard by Richard and Mengele, who were both present to watch as Leifson opened the freezer door and removed the elongated trunk containing the still-frozen samples. He passed the front end to Hemment, and the two SS men carried it up to the ladder where two seamen took over and, with expert ease, squeezed it out on deck and passed it over the side to the ship riding just fenders away in the calm water, and the sailors aboard the ship hurried it to their reefer.

Richard waved at someone, and Mengele looked up to see a tall, thin man who stood with an air of authority as he watched the transfers take place. The cargo was quickly transferred to the Orion. Mengele followed Richard up the few wood steps hung with rope risers laid out over the side and stepped aboard the ship. They went forward and climbed the steel steps to the flying bridge where Whittle was waiting.

"Gentlemen. I am happy that you made it." Whittle greeted with a crisp British accent. He was dressed in khaki shorts, a shirt, and canvas shoes and was wearing a white pith helmet.

"Mr. Whittle?" Mengele asked, clicking his heels and nodding his head.

"It is good to finally meet you, Herr Doctor," Whittle said. "I must say that we can not thank you enough for your contributions. But if you will excuse me for a moment, I have an item of business to tend to."

With just his hands on the rail, he slid down the ladder with a practiced motion to the main deck and walked over to the railings. He swung over the side of the ship and dropped a few feet to the deck of the submarine, where he walked over to the bridge and spoke up to Lehmann, and Mengele saw the Kriegsmarine nod in response. Mengele watched as another container was brought out of the hold of the ship and was swung on a davit down to the sub, whose crew took it aboard and wrestled it through the forward torpedo hatch, where it disappeared from view.

Whittle saluted the Kapitan of the U-Boat and quickly climbed back aboard his own ship. The lines fore and aft were cast off, and the vessels began to drift away from each other, and then their screws began to turn over, and in just moments, they had opened up almost a mile between them.

Whittle regained his position on the flying bridge and all three of them stood there watching the U-boat diminish in size. Then there was one huge muffled explosion sending up a geyser of water, and Mengele watched as the sub's bridge was ripped from the boat and tossed into the air with bodies flying like broken rag dolls from its railings and the brow of the boat shot out of the water at an upright angle as if it was going to climb out of the sea, and it even hung poised there for a second and then she slipped silently backward beneath the waters. Richard and Mengele looked at Whittle, whose face was resigned and calm.

"It seems that you got off of that boat just in time, Gentlemen," Whittle remarked innocently. '10h well, at least no one knows, or will ever find out that you came here. Please, join me for dinner in an hour."

All that was left of the sub was a spot marked by the ever-widening, ever-diluting oil slick. Whittle entered the bridge proper to confer with the captain, leaving the two doctors alone. There was no attempt to search for survivors. Richard was white. Mengele had seen too much death to be moved by it. Obviously, all traces of their voyage were erased with the drowning of the crew that brought them here.

"How come you have not mentioned Herr Whittle to me before now?" Mengele demanded, really irked that he had not been informed of Whittle's position within the organization.

Richard looked at him with a blank expression. "Because Whittle told me not to," he explained simply, as if why would anyone try to cross someone who is capable of killing fifty of his countrymen and extending invitations to dinner at the same time.

Leifson broke out on deck and rushed to the side and searched the sea, shielding his eyes with the palm of his hand. "I thought I heard an explosion."

"It was nothing," Mengele hollered. "Go on about your duties!" He ordered, afraid that any concern showed the crew of the sub would lead to possible reprisals.

Mengele was shown his quarters by a diminutive black man dressed in white shorts, showing off bony legs and broad, flat, bare feet. He wore a red vest over a dirty white shirt and had on a red fez with a dangling gold braided cord.

His cabin was a small rectangular cubicle that seemed spacious, especially since he had it all to himself. It even had its own porthole. There was clothing laid out for him on his bunk. His escort had told him where the showers were located, and it was requested that he avail himself to their soothing waters before he joined the others for dinner. He stood under the spray, wetting himself thoroughly and then soaped himself, and then stepped back into the miserly stream to finally rinse all of the soap and filth from himself. He felt clean and renewed as he put on the white cotton shorts and white shirt. He laced the tennis shoes up, and they felt incredibly light on his feet.

He worried about Germany. He worried about his parents, and he worried about his wife and his new baby boy that he had sired when his wife had visited him in Poland, but he decided that he could not help them, so he had better look to take care of himself and to complete his mission.

He stepped out into the passageway when he was ready and a sailor directed him to the dining room located amidships used for passengers when they booked passage on cargo ships. The room was paneled in a light oak. There were padded seats sitting around the perimeter, and an unattended bar was at one end of the room with the liquor bottles stored in wire baskets screwed to the bulkheads.

Richard and Whittle were already seated at the table draped in white linen and taking up most of the room. They were talking to a third man dressed in a sweat-stained white tropical suit, who had a handkerchief in constant mopping motion on his bald head, and that was with the open portholes and a paddle fan rotating at high speed actually making the room comfortable, or as close to comfortable as possible this close to the equator. He used the same cloth to polish his glasses. His nose, large, was made red by years of alcohol.

"Josef," Whittle said, beckoning Mengele to take a chair beside Richard, "allow me to introduce Doctor Horace Franklin."

The name was indeed familiar to Josef. He remembered reading his text on viruses, a very thin volume, nevertheless, but it was through Franklin that he had come to somewhat understand these mysterious beings, which up until recently had been considered not living organisms. They failed to replicate on their own, therefore not passing all the qualifications of being classified as a living entity.

"Doctor Mengele," Franklin said, standing up and nodding to Josef across the table, "it is good to meet you at last and to thank you in person. The scientific information you have provided us over the past year will keep many eyes and minds busy for decades."

"Thank you, Doctor," Mengele recalled the university that Franklin had taught at. "Are you still not at Cambridge?"

"Dr. Franklin has taken a leave of absence, Doctor," Whittle answered. "In fact, he joined us just before you. While you were serving in Auschwitz under the most extreme duress, the good doctor has been living somewhat like a king here in Africa."

Franklin read the expression on Mengele's face. "Not all Englishmen share our Prime Minister's politics, Doctor Mengele. Nor are they under the influence of the Zionist." He laughed and raised his glass of rye whiskey in toast, "I assure you that Africa is no place for a man to feel like a king. It is always hot, dry, or raining so hard that you eventually just have to ignore it. The wine helps."

"Come now, Doctor," said Whittle, "the white man has been living in Africa for years, and not all of them rely on alcohol in order to tolerate it. I think you just look for an excuse."

"You may be right, Sir Whittle," he answered, "but I do not know very many sober people living in these climes. I traveled to Kenya, and what was true twenty years ago is true today, and that is if you are white, you only do two things to occupy your time–commit adultery and drink with the other whites.

Whittle laughed. Richard sat silent, picking at his food. Mengele could tell that he was adrift in his mind, seeking possible solutions for the many unknown questions besetting them. From the extent of the frown on the man's face Mengele could tell he was wrestling with some new piece of information coming to his attention.

"Please do not discourage our colleagues, Doctor," Whittle said, "I believe we are very close to bringing everything to a successful conclusion. I do not want them thinking that the environment they are going to be working under will cause them to be unproductive. I will just have to point out to them what you have managed to accomplish in the past two years working in this dreadful continent."

The little black man who showed Mengele his cabin entered the room, followed by two other black men, tall gangly men feeling out of place in their European clothing, and directed them to serve the meal to the white men seated around the table.

It was a leg of lamb covered with some vegetables that Mengele was unfamiliar with, but after a few bites, he thought at least he could learn to like African cooking. The black men left the room on orders of Whittle as soon as the food was served. They ate in relative silence, the ship barely swaying in the calm seas as they made for port just a couple of hundred miles away.

When they were alone again, Mengele wanted to hear more about Franklin's discoveries. He knew they were the reason for Richard's churning mind.

"Sir Whittle?" Mengele asked.

"During war, titles are sometimes handed out like medals in England," he explained. "I was fortunate of rendering countless services to the United Kingdom and felt the touch of the blade from our King George just a few months ago. Along with a half dozen other men, I might add. But all that pales in comparison to what you three men of science have achieved."

"I have seen the genius of Doctor Richard under the microscope. I do not think my contributions have been anything more than precise mechanics up to this point," Mengele said, "what, may I ask, has Doctor Franklin discovered?"

"Tell him," Whittle ordered.

"It's very simple," Franklin responded, putting down his fork but picking up his glass. "When I discussed the project with your mentor, a man I have immense respect for, by the way, von Verschuer, we both decided that the only way to deliver this new disease that you were to create was by enlisting the aid of a virus. Much like that Frenchman d'Herelle envisioned, bacteriophages as eradicating diseases caused by bacteria, it occurred to all of us that a suitable virus would work just as well in delivering a disease. After we agreed on that, Africa was the one true place to find such a virus. The continent is literally crawling with them, you know. In fact, I dare say that without the many diseases rampant in these climates and carried by their damnable bugs, especially the tsetse fly and the mosquito, then we Europeans would be a long way in killing off the native populations and replacing them with white people from Europe, like we did in the Americas. But here in Africa, the microbes are on the side of the black man. Anyway, Africa seemed the ideal place to come to search for the virus that would suit our needs."

"And you found it?" Mengele asked excitedly. "We will be able to see the results."

"Not exactly, Herr Doctor," Richard complained, "our first step is in another part of Africa that we will not be seeing."

"When I first came to Africa, there was really only two places where I could set up shop, so to speak," Franklin explained, "around people who would respect my privacy and allow me the latitude to carry out my work. I spent the first few years in one of them."

"Herr Doctor," Whittle continued the explanation. "I do not know how familiar you are with the colonies that Germany had to give up at the end of the last war, but one of them is the country called Cameron. Fortunately, there were a few German settlers deep in the countryside that the English failed to root out. There, our Doctor Franklin got well acquainted with the bottle and a particular species of monkey, Cercopithecus aethiops, more commonly known as the green monkey."

"Actually, I believe the virus came out of a sooty mangabey," Franklin corrected.

"He found a zoonone," Richard interjected, referring to a virus that infected animals but was not capable of causing any distress among humans, simply because the microbe lacked the key to unlocking the outer membrane of any human cells.

"And thanks to techniques developed by Doctor Richard," continued Franklin, "I managed to alter them enough where they could cause infections in humans."

"Splendid. Are your samples frozen like ours?" Mengele asked.

Franklin smiled. "Not exactly. The samples I brought have just served us dinner."

XXVI

The Savior, Jesus Christ, had been nailed to the cross seven hundred years earlier, but the Prophet, Muhammad, had not yet been gone a hundred years when Arabs sailed south in their bland but beautiful lateen-sailed dhows flying the green flags out of the Red Sea that Moses, the Lawgiver, had parted almost two thousand years before. They skipped around the Sahara Desert and hooked back over the Horn of Africa, and they brought with them the word of Islam and trade goods. Further south, they found a lush green coastal plane with plenty of deep water harbors lived in by men of from a deep black color to a high bronze color, all of them with human flesh on their breath, but who were willing to trade ivory and gold for colorful glass beads, and all the ingredients of establishing successful trading posts were present for the Arab.

The Arabs moved in with their superiority in organization and weaponry and their Allah, and the first outside confluence of peoples in this part of the world in recorded history, led to the blending of the Arabic man with Bantu-speaking black women, and the Swahili-Civilization was born along the east coast of Africa. The skin of the people began to lighten while they constructed majestic city-states in deep water ports at Lamu, Mombasa, Dar es Salaam, Kuwa Kisiwani, Lindi, and Miwara, along with establishing the island kingdoms of Mafia, Pemba, and Zanzibar, all of them built with minarets that let a man climb high up above his city and his harbors and his sea, and thank his Allah for making it all possible.

In the immediate interior, there were a couple of hundred tribes, who had managed to settle in certain areas and remain tribes for thousands of years, and they would war on one another and feast on one another's flesh but would never think of intermarrying. The chiefs of the more powerful tribes found that shackling the vanquished members of weaker tribes and marching them to the coast to trade them into slavery was as profitable and a lot easier, than gathering up and carrying the heavy elephant tusks to the coast. You had to wait for one of the big beasts to die of natural causes because going after them with hand-tossed spears was not a very good idea.

So enslaving the weaker black man was a well-established practice before the first Europeans, the Portuguese, sailed around Cape Horn searching for a passage to India, bringing with them their Christ and their trade goods. They found this civilization which seemingly had everything, except heavy cannon and the cities of the Swahili were devastated by the Europeans just eight years after they had discovered that their glass beads did not purchase much from the Sultans, the rulers of these coastal lands, who had built a thriving trade with India and even China, before the Chinese decided that they did not want to have any dealings with the Occidental and the Negro.

To counter the Portuguese, who did nothing but kill and maim, the Swahili invited even more Arabs, the Omani, into their waters, trading a coyote for a wolf. In 1840 the slave trade really began in earnest as ship after ship of black men, women, and children were efficiently stacked aboard vessels destined for the new world to satisfy the need for cotton pickers, as the southern portion of the nearly new nation of the United States of America rushed to import the cheapest labor in the world, because they thought it was a good idea, ignoring people in the North who knew that it was going to be impossible to keep these Negroes as slaves forever, and all the South was really doing in all its glory and bull-shit, was importing huge amounts of Negroes onto their continent where they were going to be among your people forever.

Up until the boom in cotton in the Americas, most of the black men from Eastern Africa entered the lands ruled over by the Indian or the Arab. Who, for the most part, made them leave their cock and balls at the border, as these societies introduced a whole new sex of people, Eunuchs, who neither entice the women in your harem nor put their genes into your people's blood.

The British flag was first raised here in Mombasa in 1823, when an impetuous naval captain, acting without orders but on Christian principles, aligned his country with the ruling Swahili sultan to stop an Omani fleet that was closing in to fill its ships once again with human cargo. His action was disallowed by the Admiralty, but the precedent was set. By 1850, the presence of the Englishman was well established under the guise of stopping the slave trade–it made far more sense to enslave the people right where they were. They were joined by the Germans, newly united but desirous to get a start on building their own empire, following a version of Mark Twain's advice 'to buy land, they are not making any more of it,' rushed in to carve out a huge expanse of a territory full of people they could cultivate and dominate.

German and English explorers mapped the hinterland, found the source of the Nile, marveled over the snow atop Mount Kilimanjaro and were called liars in London by men of science, who knew snow could not exist that close to the equator; and they discovered two huge lakes, naming one Victoria after the British queen. It was the land in which Stanley went in search of the long-lost Livingstone, who was not lost at all but himself still searching. It was the land in which, a few short years later, in the Olduvai Gorge, the Leaky's would dig up what they say are some two million-year-old bones of creatures that could have become man.

In a large part of the land, the insects rule supreme, like the tsetse, which gave you a virus where you sleep your way to death; tick, which carried a hodgepodge of sicknesses; mosquito, which brought you sporozoan parasites that could put you in a ranting coma and was with you forever, and the boring beetle that would enter a man's brain through his ear. A beautifully diverse piece of land.

With the Treaty of Helgoland in 1890, England got Kenya and Uganda, and Germany got the territory south of the line that went on the maps of the time as German East Africa. The boundary ran basically on a straight line in a northern direction from the coast, except for a jog around Mount Kilimanjaro, so Queen Victoria of England could give her grandson, Kaiser Wilhelm of Germany, a gift befitting their royalty. When it reached Lake Victoria, it shifted to an east-west line dividing the lake just about in half and continued until it reached the lands of King Leopold of Belgium, who had claim to the vast Congo regions.

By 1890, Africa had been carved up by the British, French, German, Italians, Portuguese, and the King of Belgium. The Blackman was no longer king of his own home, his home for a couple of million years.

The Germans were first challenged by the Africans in the Maji-Maji uprising in 1905, and over the next two years, members of nine tribes finally discovered a reason to unite but found out after seventy thousand of them lay dead, that they could not run the white devil from their country with spears and stones. Then World War I broke out in Europe. England and Germany had much earlier agreed in 1885 that any European conflict did not have to spill over into Africa; white men warring on white men was not a good example to set for the indigent populations, who outnumbered them by the millions. The English, however, fired on the Germans at Dar es Salaam, and for the next four years, English officers with Indian and black troops, fought a bloody, indecisive campaign against a handful of Germans commanding their African troops.

When the war was over, part of the Treaty of Versailles stripped Germany of all her overseas possessions, and German East Africa became Tanganyika to be administered as a British protectorate mandated by the League of Nations. The German settlers were dispelled for a few short years but were then invited back by the British to their farms and plantations of tea, coffee, and cotton. So, except for a few years, the Germans were settlers in Tanganyika for one half a century.

Mengele was already awake when Ibn knocked on his stateroom door to bid him in his high-pitched, rapid-fire English to come for early breakfast. It was still dark, and Mengele dressed quickly, liking the feel of the light cotton and the seeming weightlessness of the canvas shoes and feeling himself already attuned to and liking the tropics. The air could be heavy with heat, but so far, the winds of the Indian Ocean had kept it comfortable. He thought it was a lot better than breathing the dust of the Ukraine in August.

He stepped out on a slippery deck made wet by the drizzling rains as they had arrived on the east coast of Africa at the same time as the rainy season. He was soaked before he reached the dining room. Richard and Franklin were already there.

"Welcome to the tropics," Franklin said, smelling of garlic and alcohol.

"I think our journey ends today," Richard informed him as he joined them at the table.

Ibn shuffled into the room and served them from a platter holding both eggs and rice, poured them lukewarm tea from a polished metal decanter, and silently withdrew.

Mengele hesitated, picking up his eating utensils. These blacks were carrying a virus that previously had only caused sickness in monkeys.

Franklin noticed Mengele's reluctance. "Do not be alarmed, Doctor. The virus is not very easily transmittable. Ibn was the first one that I was able to even get the virus to grow in, and the only way I have been able to spread it to others is by direct transfusions of his blood. I am hoping his women are also infected from his semen, but I was not given an opportunity of determining it for a fact. Since all the early serum I formulated were based on his Negroid cells, we still do not know if it is even capable of even infecting Europeans."

"Do you have any idea what the symptoms are going to be?"

"Not really. The monkeys lose appetite, become lethargic, go through periods of nausea, but for the most part, live almost a normal life. So far in Ibn, and the other two blacks, there is not a sign of any illness. It is a slow-growing virus in monkeys, and that seems to remain the same in man. I am not even sure that is a negative thing. It would be advantageous if it took a long time to blossom into a killer disease. It would give it time to spread in their populations before the alarms went off. But, my dear Doctors, we have plenty of work yet to accomplish, and in the meantime, it is safe to be served food by them."

"Why are we not going to Cameroon?" Mengele asked.

"One doctor could work in that isolated place without causing too many questions. A team of doctors would surely bring an investigation from the authorities."

"We are going to a populated area?" Mengele asked, surprised.

"Somewhat. I think you will see that Sir Whittle has taken many things into consideration when he selected our new facility. As a matter of fact, two doctors and a lab technician are normal staff for an operating clinic."

They all felt the engines shut down through their feet, and then the thud rattle splash of the anchor dropped into the sea as they had reached their destination. Mengele did not ever remember volunteering to doctor niggers in Africa.

"I believe that we must hurry," Franklin said, and the men stood up from the table. "In more ways than one. You probably are not aware of it, Dr. Mengele, but the Americans have announced that deoxyribonucleic acid, which they term DNA1, is the genetic engine, the genetic map behind all duplication of the cell. They are only a few years behind us now, Gentlemen, but with a lot more resources."

"All the more reason for me to be in the lab," Mengele stated. "You had better mend your staffing to one doctor and two technicians, Herr Doctor."

Franklin smiled, delighted and not surprised at the German's stance. He did not like doctoring either. He should have realized that this young German, who had seen more death than Dante in his dreams, was not about to be anyone's puppet.

"We will call it a research clinic. We will all take turns giving injections to the niggers," Franklin said, with a dour mischievous grin.

Mengele nodded. He was satisfied that he was not going to be expected to heal any Africans.

They went out on deck as the crates they had brought from Germany were carried out and stowed over the side into one of the lifeboats that the crew had put into the water while they were having breakfast. The only one missing was the one that required freezing, and it was not to be seen. A tarp was pulled over the rest to keep them from the rain that was now really beginning to pour down in dime-sized droplets.

A large four-prop airplane with a thick fuselage circled them like some gray ghostly bird soloing through the misty drizzle and then skidded into the ocean, its pontoons and powerful engines throwing a spray of misty white salt as the aircraft landed on the calm but rain-peppered waters, and then taxied to a stop close to the ship.

"It is time, Gentlemen," Whittle announced, stepping up behind the trio of doctors standing under the tarp that had been stretched from the superstructure to provide them shelter from the rain.

Mengele and Richard had no trouble making the transition to the smaller boat, but the rotund Franklin found it difficult to maintain his balance, and if it wasn't for the two crewmen who reached out to support him, he would never have made it into the boat without taking a dip in the ocean. They all sat down on the wet bench.

Olaf Liefson, Baer, Ibn, and the other two blacks came out on deck and deftly stepped into the boat with the frozen locker, securing it to the bottom of the boat. Whittle stayed aboard the freighter.

"Good luck, Doktors," Whittle addressed them in German, "I am sorry that I will not be able to accompany you to your final destination, but I have been away far too long from England. I must return immediately. I am sure that you will find everything that you will need where you are going."

"What about the other men?" Mengele asked, noting that the other two SS men were not present.

"Do not be concerned, Doctor," Whittle answered, "they will be going with me. I assure you that you will have adequate security. We do not need to flood the place where you are going with too many obviously pure Aryans." He ordered the coxswain to shove off.

The boat backed away from the ship and, within minutes, was at the open door of the plane, where the men were taken aboard. They were hustled forward to buckle into their seats by men in the blue uniforms of the airlines, but who were obviously in the employ of Whittle. Who else would land out here, out of sight of land in the Indian Ocean?

"Just what does Sir Whittle do in England?" Mengele whispered to Richard sitting next to him on the plane.

"Why, he owns the largest pharmaceutical factory in Kent," Richard whispered, his eyes on the back of the bald head of Franklin, who seemed content to brace himself in his seat with a white-knuckled grip.

The four large Rolls-Royce engines came to life, and the plane rocked across the water for what seemed an extremely long time before it was able to shake both pontoons free of the water, and they were finally airborne. It took forever for the heavy craft to gain altitude, and they were still climbing as they crossed over the Island of Zanzibar, which quickly faded from view. They could not see any land at all as they were above the cloud cover by the time they reached the mainland some thirty miles away.

The men were silent as they all found a window to look out of for the next few hours as they flew into the interior of Africa. The clouds thinned, dissipating to white tendrils, revealing the wild green of the plains merging into the highlands of forests and mountains. Kilimanjaro towered off to their right, the snow-capped mountains catching the rising sun and glowing strong enough to be a beckon even in the daylight hours. It was after they had chewed some semblance of a meal for lunch that the land seemed to jump up, diminishing their altitude as they crossed the mountains into the Serengeti Plains. They could see but not distinguish between the endless herds of wildebeest, antelope, giraffe, and elephants crawling about as ants.

They flew over the eastern edge of the second largest lake in the world, twenty-seven thousand square miles of fresh blue water that was the source of fish and amazement for the people who lived around it. For the Zinza, Sukumo, Kuria, Kisii, Luo, Luyia, Ganda, Ankole, and to where their plane was headed, the Haya, who lived on the western shore just south of the equator, but the entire lake was at a relief giving altitude and was blessed with a lot of cooling rains. Through breaks in the rocks, the lake spilled over, becoming one of the headwaters of the Nile, the longest river in the world.

The plane began a lumbering descent and covered the last twenty miles just off the top of the water. The passengers could see the shoreline when the plane suddenly dipped and hit the waters with a resounding thud, momentarily scaring them. All three Africans were praying to whatever god they had, but the plane skidded and stayed in the water and splashed into a boat ride. They could feel the water on the other side of the sheet metal slide beneath them, and they taxied for the last few hundred yards to a moss-covered wood pier jutting out into the water. The shoreline was covered in green papyrus. On shore, fishermen wove the plant into nets. The beach was full of scantily clad black people who stopped their work of living out of the water to stare at the arriving airplane.

The heat hit them as they climbed from the plane out onto the pier. Mengele could swear he could hear the insects buzzing along the water's edge, as if warning him that this was their territory, but they were welcome because they were diners.

Ibn took command, and the boat was unloaded. Slow-moving porters, dressed in shorts and sandals, loaded the heavy crates onto dollies and pulled them down the pier to the dirt street where an open vintage rusted-out truck awaited them. The container from Auschwitz went into the trunk of a long black Rover sedan. Mengele and Richard piled into the back seat, while Franklin lumbered into the front. The driver smiled at them through large yellow teeth, finally got the car started, and with a grinding of gear teeth, they were off, the dust a familiar sight and smell to Mengele.

They drove through a village made up of square waddle and daub huts on dusty streets full of people of a skin color not unlike the blackness of a gorilla. The women were draped in brightly colored blue, yellow and red silk, their hair cut short into tiny kinky curls where they carried baskets on top of their heads. There was a lean, muscular man pedaling a bicycle with a perch large enough that he had to strap it to his back to get it to an interior village where he would sell it.

There was one motorbike in the entire city, but it usually stayed broken down, and that was all well and good because no one liked the high whining sound it made.

"What is this garden of Eden?" Mengele asked.

"Bukoba," Franklin answered, finding it difficult to turn around in the seat. "I assure you, it is civilization compared to where I have spent most of my time here in Africa. The people speak only Bantu, but they are a fairly friendly lot once they get to know you. The women here are always more than willing to give you anything you want but be careful that their husbands do not catch you at it. They have a severe way of dealing with adultery. All the tribes in this region practice circumcision on their females. They try to cut out the parts that makes the woman feel good during copulation." He laughed, "They just can not cut out the parts that make a woman think it feels good. We are still in Tanganyika, but a few miles to the north lies Uganda, where the people are not quite so friendly to anything European. They still practice cannibalism, so if you are prone to travel, I suggest that you go south. Even here, please remember that you are English. They are not fond of anything German," and after a few moments of silence as they drove through the town, the narrow streets full of cattle, goats and sheep, he added, "but they are not that fond of the English, either.

They came to the town center, a few white washed buildings with rusting corrugated metal roofs. The largest was the hotel, with open porches on the second floor and the bar through the swinging doors off of the lobby, which was one of the few places within three hundred miles where you could get something cold to drink. Just down the dirt street sprayed with oil, they passed the police station manned by khaki-clad black men with a British military jeep parked out front. Shops owned by Indians brought here to build the railroad from the coast to the lake, lined the dusty street. The flies were everywhere.

They passed a row of concrete buildings with shining metal roofs, sitting idle now but would soon come ablaze in the next few months as the coffee bean ripened and the women brought it out of fields.

Leaving the city, they climbed the low ridge of hills that lined the east side of the lake. They passed through a few miles of broadleaf forest growth that opened onto a cleared huge field, planted with cotton.

Cotton.

There was still only one way to get the cotton off of the plant, and that was to pick it. White men owned it, and the black man picked it, and things had not really changed that much through distance or time. It did not matter if it was in America or Africa; the white man owned cotton and the black man picked cotton.

They dropped over a rise to see a whitewashed, rambling two-story house sitting in the middle of palm trees. They drove up the side door and stopped. Black servants dressed in white shorts and gold silky vests and wearing red fezes piled off of the veranda to help unload the truck under the watchful eye of Ibn. The crates were taken to the right side of the house, which had its own entryway through fragile wood folding doors leading off of the veranda that ran around the entire perimeter of the house.

All of the equipment came in through these doors and was stacked neatly in the center of the room. The special container was brought in and Mengele opened it and inspected the contents. Satisfied that it had made the trip from Auschwitz intact, he stored the aluminum vials in the gas-fired ammonia freezer.

Their new lab was a large rectangular room with two walls almost open to the outside, and Mengele and Richard sat down on the crates of wet wood and looked out over the wide porch to the expanse of green that was their lawn. The low overhang of the porch roof limited their vision. They were both silently wondering how long this was to be their view.

Baer and Liefson came into the room carrying wrecking bars, and they all pitched in and stripped open the crates with the sound of protesting nails and splintering wood. Mengele had long guessed that some of the crates made up an electronic microscope, and he was not disappointed. He was surprised when Liefson and Baer went right to work assembling the complicated, fragile instrument, not waiting for any directions from anyone.

Mengele and Richard unloaded and arranged a row of incubators along one table and plugged them into the outlets that jacked out of the conduit that ran along the midpoint of the wall and was supplied electricity from the generators tucked away in a small outbuilding not far from the main house. Mengele pulled the crate containing his notes over to the far wall and began to stack the books along a shelf over top of a long table. He pulled two conventional and very heavy microscopes out of their packing, placed them on the table, unwrapped them from the wax paper, and then pulled off the soft cotton shroud. He sent his anthropological measuring devices to his room with his personal belongings. He would have no function here as an anthropologist.

Richard took the center table to arrange a series of blenders, condensers, and Chamberlain filters, those precision-fired ceramics with such a tight molecular structure that only a virus could pass through them. There was a double stainless steel sink on the wall leading back to the main house. The paddle ceiling fans were comforting in their motion but not seemingly healthful.

The wing of the house they were in was a recent addition but of the same construction as the whitewashed mud and wood frame main house with tall well screened casement windows, new looking with a fresh coat of green paint. It had been built by a German family that oversaw the running of a huge piece of land for the cultivation of coffee and cotton.

They had possession of the entire complex, and they were to live in the fully staffed main house with no other chore than to come into the new addition and do nothing but their research, while they were being waited on hand and foot by black men. Franklin was to be the nominal head of the household, with Ibn in charge of the servants.

The men worked late into the evening. There was no one demanding that they do this; they had been in constant motion for a month, and it takes the body a few days to stop after such a trip, but they were anxious to get back to their research.

Franklin stepped through the door from the main house for the first time after it was almost dark, and they were working by the electric lights that were a call to dinner for the tiny winged predators that beat at the screens in the windows.

"You have made wonderful progress, Doctors," Franklin complimented, looking around as Liefson was gathering up the last of the packing to be taken out into the yard. "It is really beginning to look like a laboratory."

The men, stopping at the immediate tasks in their hands to listen, were suddenly overcome by their weariness. They had all noticed that they were having to struggle to accomplish the simple things, and they realized that they had reached the point where the law of diminishing returns would perhaps cause them to start making errors.

"Come, Gentlemen," Franklin bid, also realizing that their driving pace could lead them to a disastrous mistake, and it was a long way for replacement parts to travel if they broke something. "Ibn has seen to preparing you a light snack before you go to your rooms. You have achieved much in the past few hours, and I do not want you to burn yourselves out."

The men did not protest but followed Franklin from the laboratory to the dining room, where they chewed half-hearted on some unrecognizable meat and a stringy vegetable, and they all silently hoped that the food would improve. They were too tired to talk, and Mengele finally gathered enough strength to get up and follow a house-boy who showed him to his room on the second floor. When the door closed behind the man, Mengele sat down on the bed with a large bamboo headboard and a lumpy mattress and realized that it was the first time that he had been alone for the past month.

He kicked off his shoes, laid back, and closed his eyes. The room was still in motion as being at sea was still with him. He wondered how long it was going to take to get his land legs back. He wondered what in the hell he was doing in Africa when his country was being laid to waste by its enemies. He knew that no matter how successful they would be, it was going to be too late for the Third Reich. The wireless reported that the Russian was at the gates of Berlin. He hoped his wife and baby were safe.

He hoped that the samples that he had so carefully obtained were actually viable. He was still not convinced that Richard was right, that rapid freezing of tissues could keep the cells alive indefinitely, but he hoped that the hours that he had spent in Auschwitz, with his scalpel filleting the skin cancers from the screaming old Jews, would indeed become part of the bullet that killed all of the Jews.

XXVII

The virus is the most simplest of creatures. It is merely a strip, or at most a few strips, of deoxyribonucleic acid or ribonucleic acid, DNA or RNA, wrapped in a coat of protective protein. It is the smallest entity capable of sustaining itself generation after generation, surviving through the millennium like every other surviving species– by reproduction, adaptation and mutation. It has evolved, sometimes even thriving, living on the bare edge of existence, and it accomplishes this task while not carrying its own genetic ability to make copies of itself.

It must first fight through the fact that it carries with it a genetic key that fits only a few of the billions upon billions of different locks representing the tough outer membranes of cells that make up all living organisms. Unless the virus can find this one in a billion cells that it has the key for, that will allow it in, it will decay naturally, or it will be destroyed by immune systems that have ways of recognizing its alien outer coat. If it does find that one in a billion cell that allows it anchorage, that allows it to lock on, it will find a way to penetrate the outer membrane of the host, and shedding its protective outer coats it frees its nucleic acid so it can swim through the cytoplasm of the attacked cell, dodging and slithering and floating around the Golgi Apparatus, Lysosomes, Filamentous Cytoskeletons, Peroxisome, Mitochondrion, and numerous other functioning cellular devices, to then squirm its way through the maze of the Smooth turning to Rough Endoplasmic Reticulum, and finally penetrating the outer membrane of the Nucleus to find what it had been looking for, the exposed DNA organic molecules of the host.

It is in the control room of all life. Just what it needs in order for it to survive.

When the strip of viral DNA now encapsulates itself within a sequence of host nucleotides, it has ensured the survival of its species for at least one more generation. It stays inside at the controls of reproduction and copies itself as much as it wants. It is in the cell until that cell is dead, and it dies with the cell, but in the meantime, it could have produced thousands of tiny strips of DNA or RNA, and they are let loose with one key and billions of locks to try them in, but the mere fact that they were created meant that there were cells nearby carrying the genetic locks that their genetic key would fit, and the chances of reproduction are good for them.

They come in a lot of varieties in a half dozen or so shapes, from brick-shaped to icosahedral hexagonal orbs to elongated helical rods to the Bacteriophages that look like spaceships and live only on bacteria. In 1921, the Frenchman d'Herelle wrote about how this particular virus could be genetically engineered to kill all the bacteria harmful to man, but penicillin was discovered, and funding for 'vector virus therapy' was abandoned in lieu of manufactured antibiotic medications.

Unfortunately, the worlds of animals and plants are inhabited by viruses. Fortunately, they do not frequently share their viruses. The tobacco mosaic virus cannot find a cell inside of man that it can latch on to, so it dies or is killed by immune-generated cells before it can cause any harm. The polio virus could be dumped by the billions on a growing tobacco stalk without any effect, but one single virus could enter the human body in fluids or airborne up their nostrils, and the attack on the nervous system would leave the people incapable of breathing unassisted, or causing them to be pushed around in wheelchairs the rest of their lives. Smallpox viruses killed millions upon millions of people and scarred and disfigured millions upon millions more over a two thousand year period, even achieved total genocide of the Amerindians, those people that once inhabited all the islands of the Caribbean, but never caused a moment's discomfort to any other living creature or plant life.

Some viruses can make the jump. The virus that caused the Spanish Flu that killed close to twenty-one million people worldwide in 1918 and infected close to a billion people worldwide even managed to make a few dogs and cats sick. Rabies can just about attack any animal that suckles its young. But most viruses stay in their known environments. It is rare for a virus to be able to jump from infecting one species to another species. It can happen. It is just rare. Usually, when they try their keys in unfamiliar host cells, they find no locks their key can fit, and they die or cease to exist if a virus is to be considered non-living.

Ibn did not find it unusual that three days after their arrival, the doctors wanted more of his blood. He stretched out his arm as he had hundreds of times for the fat old doctor to tie it off just above the elbow with a rubber band, and he felt the sting of the needle penetrate his engorged blood vessel. He understood now that his duties were going to remain the same as they had been for the past three years while he worked for the fat old doctor in Cameroon. There he had run the household for the fat old doctor and gave him blood whenever he wanted it. He was even allowed to recruit two of his nephews to help care for the rows upon rows of cages full of the monkeys that lined most of the clinic. He did not think it unusual when the fat old doctor began taking their blood also, and he was thankful because it gave his arm a chance to heal somewhat. He did wonder what the fat old doctor did with the circumcise foreskins of their tribal ceremonies that initiated their young men to manhood.

He had jumped, however, at the chance of coming with the fat old doctor to this strange country because, with what they were paying him, he would soon be a wealthy man, and he would be able to go back home and buy a herd of cattle and have at least ten fat young women who would be there for any way it decided to have his manly way with them, and what more could any man want then plenty of good meat to eat, milk to drink, and a variety of women living in a community with his children dedicated to serving him. only problem he could see was that he did not have the energy he once had, and his nose seemed to be always itchy and running. He had no idea that since he had volunteered to accompany the fat old doctor, he had avoided making the journey in frozen pieces.

The vial of blood filled rapidly. The needle was withdrawn, and the puncture was swabbed by a cotton ball soaked in alcohol.

"That will be all, Ibn," Franklin dismissed him.

All three of the doctors were wearing rubber surgical gloves, and Ibn, a skinny knob kneed black man, could not help but think how cowardly and carefully they handled his blood, as if it could kill them by merely touching them. He padded barefoot quietly out of the room.

"Doctors," Richard said as soon as the men of science were alone in their laboratory, "shall we get to work."

Mengele got out the Chamberlain filters and placed them on the tile-topped counter. Franklin took the fresh blood and poured it into the neck of the filters that would trap everything larger than the virus they were seeking. He opened the door of one of the incubators and pulled out a white porcelain bowl full of a black, pinkish tissue that left a rusty ring of blood on the inside surface. Richard looked into the bowl and had no idea what it was, but Mengele knew exactly what it was.

"These are the circumcised parts of the females I was telling you about, doctors," Franklin explained, "the clitoris and a generous slice of the labia of a couple of ten-year-olds. Just the right culture to grow a striving community of our virus."

"What makes you think so?" Mengele asked.

"I used the circumcised foreskins of the males in Cameroon as a medium," he explained, "and if I added new material frequently, I found I could keep the new virus alive. At least, that is what I think was happening."

He dumped the contents into the blender and turned it on, gently rotating the dial, causing the rotors to whirl with a whine, coating the outer surface of the glass in a bloody ooze as flesh turned into a reddish-brown puree. He poured it out into a petri dish and placed it under the discharge end of the filter.

"What just exactly is our virus, Doctor?" Mengele asked.

"To be specific, Doctor," Franklin answered, "I am not sure. I know that it is fragile as hell, and so far seems to not cause any harm. But where there is experimentation, there is hope, is it not?"

The two other scientists waited.

"I only managed to get a few glimpses of them on the electron microscope. I never did manage to get a decent picture. These new gadgets do not always perform at their best around me," he complained, "and all I can tell you about them for sure is that they are orbital in shape."

He turned to stare into the petri dish as if he could see the virus falling onto his newly blended culture.

"In chemical tests, Dr. Richard, I ascertained that they are not made of your nuclein," he announced.

"What?" Richard gasped, "That can not be true!"

"I am sorry to say, Doctor," Franklin answered, turning around with a smile, "that they are not composed of deoxyribonucleic acid."

Richard was undaunted. "If these viruses are not based on Nuclein," he argued, "then they do not pass the criteria of being alive."

Franklin smiled again, his thin lips sinking deep in his thick jowls now beaded in sweat. He was a very fat man and all of his fat made it worse for him in the stifling heat as they had shut all of the windows that surrounded the walls of the lab for this part of their work, blocking the breeze that would normally be drafting this room to comfort.

"Do not be upset," Franklin said, "whether or not they are alive is still unresolved, Doctor. However, I must confess to you that they are made up of a very similar compound."

"How similar?" Richard asked.

"They seem to be composed of just a few different compounds. I do not begin to understand the difference," he mused. "I did test the original virus in the monkey and found that this quirk of nature was not something we caused."

"So what do we have, Doctor?" Mengele persisted.

"Please, Doctors," Richard said, "we will not have much time. You must begin, Doctor Mengele. We want everything to have a chance to grow together."

Mengele walked over to where he had earlier placed some of the samples of the sarcoma in a saline solution. He could see that the thawed strips of blackened flesh appeared not to have changed that much in color since his knife had sliced it from the screaming old Jews. He deftly snipped off a minute piece, sandwiched it with slides, put it under the microscope, and took just a few seconds to get it into focus.

"Freezing has been successful, Doctors." he whispered in relief, "we have live cells!"

"Excellent," said Franklin, "please continue."

Mengele went to another blender on the same counter, slid the thawed strips of sarcoma cells from the tray into its beaker and added sterile water. He had to turn the machine to a higher speed and it took longer to break up the harder pieces to turn them into a mush.

"It is ready," Mengele announced, stepping back away from the counter to make room.

Franklin picked up the petri dish from under the filters and poured it on top of Mengele's mixture.

"This glass container, Doctor Mengele," Franklin explained, "now has the virus of a monkey, spliced with genetic information from human cells which influences the outer shell, where it can now at least survive and reproduce within Africans. We have our virus. It is floating around mixed in with the cells from a growing skin cancer we have every reason to believe can infect nothing but Jews. Nothing but good can come of this. If we are successful, we will have our vector."

The fat old doctor winked at Mengele. "Doctor Richard, we are ready for your magic potion."

"Nothing magic about it, Doctor," Richard answered, "just a mixture of bodily fluids, mostly enzymes extracted from the eyeballs supplied by Doktor Mengele."

He poured the clear solution into the beaker and took the controls with his long white fingers and the stainless steel blades swirled and blended it all together. He switched it off and then poured the genetic soup into a clear glass beaker and sat it on the counter.

"Please continue, Doctor Richard," Franklin asked, "the rest of this is your expertise."

All three men stood and stared into the jar at the soup that looked like dirty cream of wheat.

"The enzymes will have dissolved the outer membranes, cutting strips of Nuclein into thousands of pieces. I think it cuts it into actual genes. It evidently does the same for the core of the virus, whatever it is made up of," he said, shooting Franklin a look of finality about the subject.

"The enzyme action is only short-lived. It seems to be absorbed and somehow neutralized, and then the real miracle begins. The fragmented parts of <u>nuclein</u> will begin to reassemble, putting itself back together in exactly the way it was before it was shattered. But, if there are shattered genes from some other organism in the same culture, then sometimes they will mix genes as they reassemble. Right now, we have the free genes from the virus, floating with genes from the genitals of the Africans and the genes of sarcoma of a diseased Jew.''

''Hopefully,'' Franklin whispered 'our virus will put itself back together relatively intact, except for one important strip of genetic material. Let us hope that enough of the genes that cause the disease in the Jew is now part of our virus. If it is, then Doctors, we have achieved our goal. Of course, there are probably thousands of different combinations taking place. We can just hope that one with the traits we desire will thrive.''

"Doctors," Mengele asked, "how do we know that this virus is not going to be able to infect Aryans? How do we know that the virus will not spread among the Volk?"

There was a pause, a heavy stillness came into the room and began to ride on top of the already humid, unmoving air scented with the smell of flesh and blood.

"We do not know. We will have to test it, of course," Franklin said.

Mengele looked at Richard, who returned his gaze with dull, vacant eyes, much like the same expression he had when the sub blew up.

Mengele already knew the answer but asked anyway. "How are we going to test it, Herr Doktor?"

"That is why we have our Norwegian friend with us, Doctors," Franklin answered.

The fat old doctor picked up the beaker and placed it in one of the incubators. "Let us get some air in here, Doctors."

Mengele immediately went to open the windows, swinging them out on their hinges. He did not feel the breeze until he was working on the last wall, and when he opened them, the cross breeze caught him in the face. He stood in front of the last window he had to open and looked out over the green expanse that rolled away into the distance. He could not, but for some reason, he really wanted to be able to see the lake.

Instead, he watched as a car, pulling a funnel of dust with it, came speeding down the road. When it got close enough, he could see Olaf behind the wheel. The car had not come to a complete stop before the big, handsome Norseman jumped out and came running to where he thought he would find the Germans.

"Something has happened," Mengele alerted the other two doctors.

He stepped out onto the porch with the other two men following. He went all the way to the edge of the steps to stop the tall Norseman in the yard; he did not want him in the lab.

"Herr Doktors!" Olaf cried excitedly, forgetting all of his English-only training. He gulped hard, "Der Fuhrer is dead!"

"What!" Mengele snapped.

"It was on the radio," Olaf explained, "they are saying that he shot himself in his bunker. Admiral Donitz is now the new leader of the Reich."

"And the war?" Richard asked.

"It goes on, but it is just a matter of hours. The Russians have all but taken Berlin. They are bragging on the radio that they have the city surrounded with seven thousand guns!"

"I must sit down," Franklin said, making his way around the younger men to take the big, wide, wicker rocking chair painted in heavy coats of white paint with a green cushion with split sides that protested violently in a gasp of air as his weight came crashing down on it. He did not give a twit's ass about that fool Hitler.

He was thankful to him for putting into motion the events that allowed everything to happen so he could be here on an avenue of science that would reward him immensely, and he could get out of this godforsaken hell hole and go to Europe to dine in the finest of restaurants. He was confident that the brew cultivating in the warm chamber inside would put together some sort of a viral missile capable of making a large number of people very sick, maybe even killing some of them. And, as they learned how to design these diseases, Sir Whittle in England would learn to create the cures, and they would both grow immensely rich–designing diseases, designing cures.

And he could live out his days eating in the finest restaurants of Europe.

Richard sat down in the glider. He consulted his watch. He wanted to record the exact time that he was told of the death of Der Fuhrer. It was a shame that Germany had lost the war. It was a shame that Adolf Hitler was dead. He worried only about how this would affect his arrangements where he was provided the best of everything as far as equipment and funding, and a decent place to live, with the promise of retiring whenever he wished to immense wealth and scientific acclaim. There would come that day, he had been promised, when he was going to be presented to the German people as the man who made it happen, who had found a way to kill the Jew no matter where in the world he lived. That was surely not going to take place.

The adulation of his peers was not going to take place either. From the medical journals he could see where the medical scientists in America were rapidly catching up with what he had already discovered or surmised. It would be just a few years and all of the things he had pioneered would go to print under someone else's name. No doubt, Nobel Prizes will be awarded to men who will be doing nothing but echo his work. He decided that he would press Whittle into providing him a place in England. If science was all that he was ever going to have, then he was at least going to live in a civilized land to do it. He did not trust these Africans. He did not want to live among people who practiced cannibalism.

Mengele had known when he had fled Poland in front of the advancing Russian Armies that it was just a matter of time before the Reich was going to collapse. Now that it had done so, the pain in his stomach was from the last dying pieces of hope. The struggle and the dying in Russia had been in vain. The German people were in peril. All of the people behind the Russian lines could perish. Thank God his family were behind American lines. That was one thing he would not have to worry 'about. The surviving Jew would, of course, raise a cry to find him and punish him. The talk of war crimes was already going on.

He thought about the last conversation he had with Verschuer, who had told him that the end of the project was in sight, and the Reichsfuhrer had been so informed, and he had immediately passed the word to Der Fuhrer who was elated to hear that as his armies crumbled against the Russians and the Anglos, the war against the

Jew was as good as won. The biological machinery was in motion that would seek them out and destroy them, no matter where they lived in the world. Just as Der Fuhrer had ordered, Mengele knew that Der Fuhrer committed suicide, knowing that the war against the Jew would continue. And maybe had even been already won.

But he knew that Der Fuhrer would not approve of letting loose a virus that was a threat to the Volk. They would indeed have to test it.

He looked at Olaf, and he was reminded of Hobein. He wondered if his old friend was still alive. With Hobein's luck, the only Jews who could testify against him would be the ones in Berlin who were detained overnight under his command, and the worst thing that they could say about him was that he made them all go to the toilet at the same time. Hobein would probably not see the humor in it.

Mengele thought of the Jew. He thought of the countless faces that he sent directly to their deaths. Of the countless others that he sent to their death, even after knowing them for months. He thought of Der Fuhrer promising that if world Jewry would once again plunge the war into the world, that the Jewish race would cease to exist in Europe. He had, of course, changed his orders to include the Jews of the entire world as soon as he was informed of this scientific possibility.

But Germany was defeated, and the Jews all over the world would rejoice and think that they had won. He knew that the number of people killed would be tabulated, including the number of Jews, and of course, the way they were killed would come into question. They will probably blame him for single-handedly killing millions. The Jews would come hunting him with a vengeance, that was for sure.

They would soon be looking all over Germany for him, but for now, he felt safe here in Africa. He did not think that their work was close to completion. There was plenty yet to be done. He still had a laboratory and he was working with two of the greatest minds of biomolecular science in all the world. He was actually very fortunate with the way things turned out. He would not give himself much of a chance if he was still in Europe. The closest Jews to him, he was told, were in South Africa because there was gold there. But there were none around this Lake region. This area was <u>Judenfrei</u>. Hobein would like it here.

He knew that there was much work yet to be done. They had all made Der Fuhrer a promise. In fact, they had reported it to him as an order carried out, as an assignment accomplished. It had not been an outright lie. The goal was in sight. There were just a few things standing in the way.

"Olaf," Mengele said, looking down at the young man standing at the foot of the steps, at the tall, square-jawed, long, handsome face, the white glistening, even spaced teeth, the clear glacial blue eyes, and the bright blond hair. As good a specimen of Aryan man that existed

"Yes, Doctor." The Norseman answered.

"Have you been vaccinated?"

"Vaccinated?" Olaf answered, puzzled. He thought the Nazi doctors would be stunned into silence and despair. Instead, they were worried about giving him a vaccination shot.

"No, Herr Doktor."

"Then see me right after dinner, Olaf. We do not want you coming down to one of these African diseases."

536

www.ingramcontent.com/pod-product-compliance
Lightning Source LLC
Chambersburg PA
CBHW051129300726
48978CB00011B/207